Mayfair Rebel

MAYFAIR REBEL

Beverley Hughesdon

C

CENTURY PUBLISHING
LONDON

First published in Great Britain in 1985 by
Century Publishing Co. Ltd
Portland House, 12–13 Greek Street, London W1V 5LE

ISBN 0 7126 0836 2

Photoset and printed in Great Britain by
Photobooks (Bristol) Ltd

To Adrian

Prologue – April, 1905

'*Dearly beloved, we are gathered together here in the sight of God, and in the face of this congregation, to join together this Man and this Woman . . .*'

A wide shaft of sunlight slanted through the high glass window and illuminated the bowed head of the bride. Her mass of shining dark hair gleamed through her tulle veil. Her slender form, draped in soft white satin, looked too frail for the heavy, ivory velvet train which fell from her shoulders in smooth folds as she stood beside her tall, broad-shouldered bridegroom. Close behind her was the first of her bridesmaids, tall and supple, her golden hair shimmering under its wreath of moss roses, her lovely face serious and attentive.

The Dowager Marchioness of Andover, elegant in subtle shades of silver-grey and the palest lavender, her fine features enhanced by one of Paquin's most exquisite confections of velvet and ostrich plumes, looked on approvingly.

A very pleasing wedding; the bridegroom not, of course, as well-endowed with worldly goods as one might have hoped – but still, Emily was a practical girl, and only one's step-granddaughter, after all. A classical beauty; Lady Clarence had, it was well known, hoped for an elder son for her, but Emily had shown surprising determination in one so well-behaved and otherwise so biddable. It was ironic, reflected the Dowager, that it should be Lady Clarence's own daughter who had, despite all her mother's care, formed an attachment so young, not even out of the schoolroom; and then remained so amazingly faithful. Still, the Fortescues had always been a rather boring family . . .

The Dowager pulled herself up sharply; really, one should be delighted at the thought of a lifetime of fidelity in front of a

1

bride on her wedding day! And dear Emily, so upright, she would never know what she had missed . . .

The Dowager's eyesight, keen as ever, detected a faint ripple of movement in the satin-clad shoulders of the chief bridesmaid. Darling May, now, there was a difference! May reminded her of herself as a young girl, so impulsive, even headstrong – a little too much of her mother in her, perhaps. Still, as a younger son Clarence had had to make a choice: breeding, beauty and wealth were so seldom allied in this unfair world, and he had certainly secured two of the three in young Mary Frears. And then, after her early death, having lost the beauty but still in possession of a considerable portion of the wealth, he had married breeding. There had been no doubt of that with the widowed Lady Julia Fortescue – and so much propriety. The Dowager cast a covert glance through her eyelashes at her daughter-in-law in the front pew . . .

'*But reverently, discreetly, advisedly, soberly, and in the fear of God* . . .'

Lady Clarence Winton's face expressed her accustomed unruffled composure, her gaze steady on the couple at the chancel steps as she ticked off in her mind all the arrangements for the wedding breakfast. Haines and Mrs Jameson were models of efficiency: she would not have retained their services long had they not been, but one needed a firm hand on the reins. Nothing must go awry on a day like this.

Dear Emily! William Target was a worthy young man with a promising career ahead of him, but who would have believed her gentle daughter would prove so stubborn? And have formed such a lasting preference at so early an age? Such a success as she had been in her first Season, Lord Caistor so interested, his family one of the oldest in the country, his estates totally unencumbered. Lady Clarence could still remember her astonishment at Emily's firm reply: 'I cannot accept his proposals, Mamma, my affections are otherwise engaged.' So unlike her docile Emily, one did wonder – May's influence? 'There has been no concealment, Mamma. I have had no communication with Lieutenant Target since he left England, but my own feelings remain unchanged.' Not

2

that she had ever had any fears of that nature with regard to Emily, always so upright and correct, though no doubt May had preached rebellion.

At this point Lady Clarence's sense of justice reasserted itself. She must not be unfair, there was nothing underhand in May's nature either; whatever her other faults her step-daughter was always open. Too much so sometimes: direct defiance would have been her response in a similar situation. Yet she had so many good qualities too . . . but if only it had been May standing before the altar now; if ever a young woman needed the firm, guiding hand of a husband, surely it was May!

'*Who giveth this Woman to be married to this Man?*'

Lady Clarence's attention turned to her husband. He would, of course, perform his task impeccably, she had given him full instructions, but a wife's responsibilities never lapsed . . .

Lord Clarence Winton stepped forward and placed his step-daughter's hand in that of her future husband. Then, with the distinguished bearing which characterised all his movements, he strode back to the place reserved for him.

A good girl, Emily, one of the best. Should have been given away by old Chippenham, but she'd insisted he was to be the one to escort her down the aisle; had explained so prettily to her uncle, no one had been offended. Tactful girl, she deserved a good husband, and William was a fine youngster, he'd make his way.

A very pleasant occasion, everything going off like clockwork; but then, what event organized by Julia ever dared to be less than perfect? Perfection like that was not always comfortable around the house, but she knew what was due to a husband, no question of that. His autumn shooting and winter hunting, never a word of interference, unlike some wives he could mention; Old Squiffy Wortham, for instance; and Maud Wortham, she'd been a goer in her day, too – never a hint of that with Julia, by God no!

His duties in the ceremony safely over, Lord Clarence turned his gaze to his own daughter.

3

The very image of her mother, though May stood up straighter; that was Julia's doing. Mary had tended to stoop a little: she'd bent over his arm as they'd walked down the aisle together, twenty-three years ago next month! Dammit, it seemed like another lifetime. They'd all believed he'd been after her money; thought he'd pulled off a clever coup; but it hadn't been like that, he'd been head over heels the minute he'd clapped eyes on her, over at old Benson's place in Wiltshire – a lovely girl, and so young.

She'd not looked a day older when they'd carried her in from the fields on a hurdle, that bitter winter of '84, with May just a babe in the nursery. He'd never borne to see her hunt, she knew why; that was one decision she'd never argued with, though she was her mother's daughter, full of life and spirit.

Terrible time, that, just couldn't take it in for years. Lucky he'd met Julia. Young May had been left to the servants: his mother had her own social life. Dora had offered, of course, but he'd not wanted to lose her like that, swallowed up in the Stemhalton nursery. Both of them out of control, really; he'd been drinking too much and May had been giving her governesses the slip and running wild. Julia had soon seen to that – strong sense of duty, Julia, knew what was right and what was wrong. Poor little May, it hadn't been an easy time for her: a clash of wills there, but you could back a woman in her thirties against a ten year-old any day, especially a woman like Julia.

May had learnt the wisdom of submission, well, most of the time; and Julia was fair, no doubt about that. Bent over backwards to treat the two girls alike, though there'd never been any doubt which one cost her the most trouble. Emily had never caused a moment's anxiety until the business with young Target here, and even then she'd behaved so correctly – she wasn't her mother's daughter for nothing. Always been a nice little girl, though, and she and May so close; pity about India, Emily had been the peacemaker: could be a collision course ahead.

If only May would make up her mind to take young Yoxford, nice enough youngster, could have sworn she had

4

an eye for him. Come to that, she could do worse than think of her cousins. Not Bertie, perhaps, bit of a stuffed shirt, but surely Archie was lively enough for her; a younger son, of course, but May would have more than enough for both . . .

'*Lord have mercy upon us . . .*'

His mind already dwelling on the rest of the day's festivities, Lord Archibald Winton twitched the faultless creases of his trousers into position on the hassock; his uncle's cellar was famous, and you could always rely on Aunt Julia to provide a tip-top do. Poor old Aunt Ju, two such beauties to bring out and they'd already turned down five titles between them, to his certain knowledge! Not to speak of that American millionaire who'd been hanging round May, all set to reverse the trade in transatlantic heiresses. And all to no avail: Emily had apparently only wanted steady old William from the moment she'd first set eyes on him, at a nursery tea party, while May – May didn't know what she did want.

Archie risked a glance over the bowed heads to May's white back and golden mass of hair under its demure wreath of roses. Who'd have thought chubby little May would turn into such a stunner!

She'd always been a good sport, though, up to anything, and never complaining or peaching; not even when he and Bertie had pushed her up that tree and left her stranded for hours. What a state her clothes had been in by the time the footman arrived with the ladder! Nanny had marched her straight off to Lady Clarence, and then what a telling-off! She'd kept mum, though, just stuck out her lower lip and refused to answer, even though mending her best dress had cost her a few afternoons confined to barracks in the nursery. Mind, she had got her own back; he still shuddered to think of his embarrassment over that business with the horse.

Yes, despite Lady Clarence being such a disciplinarian, she'd had a real tussle persuading May to toe the line; perhaps it was Emily's influence which had eventually taught May the wisdom of some degree of discretion, at least. Funny the two girls got on so well; Emmie was so different, never put a foot wrong – but she'd never split on the others, either. Pity

5

she was going to India, May would miss her. She wouldn't take kindly to being Aunt Ju's only ewe lamb – the 'distilled essence of chaperons', that was what Bertie had called their aunt once, and how right he'd been!

The bride, her veil thrown back from a face glowing with happiness, prepared to walk down the aisle on the arm of her chosen husband. In a single, graceful movement the chief bridesmaid shook out her train to lie, fully extended, on the carpet. The organ rang out and the ancient church quivered with the resounding peal of the bells. It had been a most pleasing wedding.

Chapter One

The streets shimmered in the heat of a London July; May felt stifled by the heavy atmosphere inside the enclosed brougham. Conscious of tendrils of hair clinging damply to the back of her neck she glanced resentfully at the regulation one-and-a-half inch of open window that was all Lady Clarence would allow in Town. It admitted not the slightest movement of air on this burning day.

'My dear, your hat is slightly disarranged.'

Lady Clarence, still as immaculately groomed as when they had set out, and apparently impervious to the heat, inclined her head towards her step-daughter. May, knowing it was hopeless before she spoke, nevertheless made her bid for freedom.

'Oh, Step-mamma, mayn't we just leave cards for the rest of our calls? It's so hot!'

Displeasure registered briefly on Lady Clarence's face.

'Certainly not, May. What has become of your manners? And please adjust your hat.'

May removed her gloves and re-settled the confection of roses, mimosa and lace atop its base of fine white straw so that it tilted forward at the angle decreed by Lady Clarence as becoming yet modest on an unmarried girl. When her step-mother had given a nod of satisfaction she resumed her gloves and sat still again, back held straight and facing forwards. Lady Clarence's lids were lowered, but May cast only side-long glances at the traffic outside: she knew from past experience that the slightest deviation in her behaviour would be instantly corrected.

Her step-mother's hat, of course, needed no adjustment. Indeed, thought May, it would be a very strong-minded hat which dared to shift one fraction of an inch from its position once placed there by the unbending Fenton and approved by Lady Clarence herself. Why, that very hat, which May had seen before its purchase, then gay and delicate on the head of a pretty model at Paquin's, had now taken on some of the stern immobility of Lady Clarence's Grecian features. The wide brim, flicked up on the left side so that the brown and pink velvet ribbons made a soft massy bow against the hair, had lost its light charm and now looked, in some curious way, as though it were fixed firmly onto a frame of whalebone. Poor Lady Clarence! May felt a flash of sympathy for her unyielding step-mother: she and Emily had long ago realised that her only lapse into anything approaching frivolity was in the choosing of her hats; but it was no use, however delightful her choices for May and Emily her own selections were defeated as soon as they were set on the iron-rigid waves of her coiffure.

At this thought May turned instinctively to catch the eye of her accustomed companion, only to be jolted into the unpleasant realisation that there was no Emily beside her now. Her step-sister was at the other end of the country. Even Lady Clarence had had to bow to the exigencies of the Indian Army and arrange an unfashionably early wedding so that William's mother could present her new daughter-in-law at the first of the May Courts, thus leaving the bride time to fulfil her duties to her new relatives before quitting the country. As soon as the round of visits was over there would be only a brief weekend in Suffolk before Emily and William left for India.

India! A wave of loneliness swept over May. So far away, for years, and the climate – Amy Talbot's sister had died in India, just wasted away in the heat, they said, and here she was, complaining about the temperature of an English summer. She spoke impulsively.

'It will be so hot for Emily, in India, and she always found this weather so trying!'

Lady Clarence blinked, and May realised that her daughter would not have been far from her thoughts either; she sensed a rare moment of sympathy between them. In an unusual gesture Lady Clarence leant forward and placed her gloved hand over May's.

'Captain Target assured me that he would send her up to the hill stations the minute the temperature went up, my dear. He said the climate in Simla was like a fresh spring day in England, and the scenery as beautiful. She will be completely safe there.'

Having waited so long to marry her William, May could not easily imagine Emily allowing herself to be packed off to the hills while her husband stayed behind on the plains, but perhaps it was different when you turned into a wife.

May smiled at her step-mother in reply.

'She looked radiant on her wedding day. William will be a devoted husband.'

Lady Clarence withdrew her hand and sighed.

'Ah, I wish I could see you well settled, too, May.'

At this moment, to May's relief, the brougham drew up at Lady Bertram's front door and Lady Clarence's attention was distracted as James came back down the steps with the message that her ladyship was at home. In the little flurry of alighting from the carriage the moment of intimacy evaporated.

May followed her step-mother into the cool hall, up the wide staircase and through the double doors of the drawing room as the footman announced:

'Lady Clarence Winton.'

With a rustle of silken skirts Lady Bertram rose to greet Lady Clarence; the latter then drew May forward.

'My step-daughter, May, Lady Bertram. I believe you have met her before.'

Her ladyship extended a limp hand to May who pressed it with care: she had been warned before of her too vigorous grasp in social gatherings. There was a murmured: 'Will you sit here?' to Lady Clarence and the two older ladies gracefully arranged themselves in the correct posture of discomfort on the yellow brocade armchairs. Once they were seated May withdrew to a high-backed chair by the window, thus earning a wan smile of approval from their hostess, and a murmured commendation.

9

'So nice to see a well brought-up young girl, Lady Clarence, in these days. Really, some of them are so forward, especially once they're out of their first Season.' She directed a carefully arranged smile towards May. 'Let me see, is it May's second Season? Surely it can't be her third, she looks so fresh and young!'

Behind her answering smile May's thoughts simmered: 'You old harridan, you know full well I came out three years ago, since it was at the same time as your youngest daughter!'

As Lady Clarence deftly turned the conversation into less provocative channels a silent May remembered giggly little Phyllis, so much nicer than her mother. She'd fallen in love with a handsome young Guardsman – Egerton, had that been his name? No chance of a love-match there, though. Lady Bertram had bullied poor Phyllis unmercifully: she and Emily had found her in the conservatory one day, weeping behind the potted palms, and it had all come out. While Emily patted her gently on the shoulder and counselled patience, May had advised immediate elopement. Phyllis had sobbed harder.

'It's all right for you, May, you'll have all that money, but Henry only has three hundred a year, and Mamma says Papa will cut me off without a penny if I marry him.'

Prudence, or Lady Bertram, had prevailed, and three months later Phyllis had married Lord Poole's eldest son, at whom she'd always poked fun because he had spots and could talk of nothing but his dogs. Phyllis never giggled now, May noticed; she only hoped she had come to like dogs.

As these thoughts flitted through her mind the exchange of meaningless platitudes continued to flow inexorably on until the allotted time of the call was up. Lady Clarence's sense of timing had always been a source of wonderment to her daughters: there was no covert glance at her watch, but May knew from careful checks kept by Emily and herself in the past that exactly fifteen minutes would have elapsed between her seating herself and her rising, and this without any awkward break in the conversation. May could only marvel at the sense of discipline which had brought such precision

10

and skill to the pointless ritual of calling. She and Emily had speculated that when other women were relaxing in their boudoirs idly turning the pages of the latest issue of 'The Lady's Realm', Lady Clarence must have been sitting, upright on a chair, watch in hand, learning how to time herself to exactly fifteen minutes.

Now, as in some carefully rehearsed ballet, the three women rose as one; Lady Clarence and Lady Bertram touched hands again; May moved forward and took her hostess' soft fingers, squeezing them firmly this time – third Season, indeed, and what of poor Phyllis – noting with pleasure her Ladyship's faint *moue* of distaste. Lady Bertram advanced with her guests the regulation one step towards the door, now held open by the footman; May followed her step-mother out, down the staircase and into the hall, where there was only the briefest of pauses while Lady Clarence with practised ease produced her husband's cards from somewhere about her person and dropped them onto the waiting table. Then they were through the wide front doorway, out into the pulsating heat of the afternoon and back inside the stuffy brougham.

As soon as James had shut the door Lady Clarence spoke in her low but clear tones.

'May, I thought you had got over that childish habit of shaking hands too energetically.'

May retorted, 'I suppose I should have done, by my *third* Season!'

Lady Clarence frowned.

'It is not for you to question the words of your elders. Besides, it is entirely your own decision that you are still unmarried at twenty-one. Your father has had offers for your hand, some of them eminently suitable. It is time you realised the responsibilities of a girl in your position.'

May made no reply: her thoughts were mutinous. What was the point, married or not, of a lifetime spent paying calls and attending receptions and never saying what you really thought and having to spend hours dressing and undressing and dressing again every day because one had a position in

11

Society and that was how one filled it? At least men could go off and join the Army or sit in Parliament in between the boring dinner parties. Dinner parties, thought May, with a mounting sense of grievance, where you hardly had time to enjoy the food because you had to make polite conversation first with your neighbour on the right, and then, when the courses changed, with your left-hand neighbour, even if you hadn't the slightest interest in him or he in you.

There was a loud shout outside and the brougham jolted to a sudden halt. May defied Lady Clarence's stony looks to peer out of the window. A large wagon passed too close to the off-side and May heard a volley of curses. But their carriage merely jerked forward again and resumed its sedate clip-clop to the Countess of Woodbridge's London home. Disappointed, May sat back again and returned to her thoughts.

More cheerfully now she recollected that no one could bully her to marry money, like poor Phyllis Ainsley, the future Lady Poole. Either on marriage or at the age of twenty-five she would come into the control not only of her dead mother's considerable personal fortune, but also a three-quarter share of the income from one of the most profitable shipyards in Britain; then she could do exactly as she pleased. But could she, even then? With another plunge of her spirits May realised that she did not know one spinster, wealthy or otherwise, who was not as closely bound into the rules of Society as her step-mother; and certainly no young woman of her class could set up an independent establishment while she had a family and connections alive; and relatives of the ancient line of Winton were spread like a web all over East Anglia.

Perhaps she could go abroad? May's one stay on the Riviera had been exciting at first, but Lady Clarence had soon met like-minded companions, and she and her ilk had then imposed their own constricting pattern. Even the forbidden territory of the Casino soon palled, according to Archie.

'Lots of old fogies sitting round a table, eyes glued to the black and the red; you wouldn't like it May, no real action, not your style at all.' Nevertheless he'd seemed to spend quite a few evenings there, and May had had to beg ten pounds 'for trinkets' off her surprised father on Archie's behalf. May cheered up slightly, remembering that Archie had said he would be going with them to Lady Hindlesham's ball this evening.

She was even more cheered later when it became apparent from certain low-voiced utterances passing between Lady Clarence and her hostess at their next port of call that Lady Hindlesham's was not quite the kind of house to which Lady Clarence would normally choose to take her daughter. May was rather puzzled by this, since she had heard Lord Hindlesham spoken of with respect – and why, if Lady Clarence had scruples, were they going there at all? But all became clear as they were leaving. Lady Woodbridge turned kindly to May.

'I am so pleased to have met you, my dear. I trust that you will allow me to present my son to you this evening, he is just come down from Oxford. I don't believe you have made his acquaintance before.'

May indicated the correct degree of pleasure at this suggestion, but Lady Clarence's obviously genuine smile of approval did not bode well for the probable liveliness of Lord Woodbridge's heir. However, May was intrigued, and the prospect of the evening's entertainment began to hold more interest for her.

Chapter Two

The hour dedicated to afternoon tea was over; the fragile porcelain cups had been removed and the equally brittle conversation had ceased. Lady Clarence was resting in her boudoir to prepare herself for the rigours of an evening's chaperonage, and May had come up to her bedroom. She had pulled her chair close to the open window, but the quiet square in front of the Winton's London house offered little in the way of distraction, so she was desultorily turning the pages of a novel.

Even the knowledge that she would certainly incur Lady Clarence's displeasure if the latter discovered that she was reading Miss Cholmondeley's *Red Pottage* failed to arouse May's enthusiasm this afternoon. Shallow and unattractive as the character of Lady Newhaven was, May still felt a definite sympathy for her in her lapse into marital infidelity after ten long years of London Seasons.

In any case, May was missing Emily. Her interest in reading novels needed the stimulus of discussion: not about the subtleties of literary style, but on the endless question of what the characters actually did every day between their appearances in the plot, and, even more engrossing, after the book had ended.

May was constantly fascinated by the thought of other people's lives. She had spent her early childhood eluding Nurse and trying to insinuate herself into the kitchen quarters or the stable yard in a determined effort to find out exactly how things were done. The stables had been further away, and the head groom more patient than the short-tempered cook, so May knew more about cleaning tack and mucking out horses than she did about cooking; though a kindly scullery maid had one day initiated her into the

14

mysteries of drawing poultry, and even allowed her to disembowl one herself. Unfortunately, May had been caught red-handed by perspiring Nurse, her clean pinafore liberally bespattered with chicken's blood; but she had felt the resulting tirade well worth the experience, and had insisted defiantly throughout the following week that she really preferred her bread without butter.

Her father's remarriage had changed all that. Lady Clarence had imported a succession of stern-visaged and firm-handed governesses, and May's visits to scullery and stable yard became few and far between and dearly paid for in long lists of the most irregular German verbs. Still, Lady Clarence had not come into the household alone; she had brought with her Emily. With Emily as a constant companion it had been possible to substitute talk of action for the activity itself. Long whispered tales of adventurous heroines who made their way from one end of the country to the other had passed between their beds in the old night nursery, and later enlivened their interminable perambulations through London Parks when they had been dragged unwillingly from Allingham Place or Stemhalton up to Town.

May stared at her novel again. What exactly had Rachel West done to support herself in her years of poverty? Vague hints of typewriting were all that could be gleaned; and then, when restored by her fortunate inheritance to London Society, what exactly had she done when she made those tantalisingly brief visits to the East End, to relieve the poor? What was it like to be 'poor' anyway – really poor, that is? May tried to visualise the practical details but failed. She tossed the book to one side in exasperation and rang for her maid.

Bella tapped lightly at the door and came in.

'Good evening, Miss May.'

She was too well-trained to allow more than a faint hint of a question to show on her face, though May knew it was unusually early for her to start dressing; she generally put this off until the last moment, so that Fenton would arrive at the door: 'Lady Clarence wishes to know if Miss May is quite ready?' And then there would be a flurry of

15

pearls and hairpins as last-minute adjustments were made.

'Good evening, Bella. Oh, Bella, I'm so bored! I wish we were going down to Allingham tomorrow – at least I can go out for a walk on my own there!'

For a moment Bella looked hurt, and May realised she had been tactless.

'Bella, I didn't mean that, exactly. It's not that I don't like you coming with me, it's just that there's nowhere to go in Town. Only boring shops and dress-makers and milliners; and never going anywhere without Lady Clarence saying I can, and wanting to know exactly where I'm going, and how long for – then when we get back she insists on knowing whom I saw on the way. I'm surprised she doesn't make us count every cab and omnibus that went past so that she can check on our route!'

Bella moved across to the adjoining bathroom and turned on the taps.

'It's just her way, Miss May, you know that. Besides, young ladies have to be protected, especially in London.'

'Oh come on, Bella, there aren't villainous men in big floppy hats hiding round every corner, waiting to seize hold of me and drag me off to, to – to an opium den!' May started to laugh. 'I wish there were, I'd rush out and offer to go, this very minute, just for something different to do.'

Bella smiled, but shook her head.

'You know it's not that, Miss May, it's your reputation. What would people think if they saw you out in the street unaccompanied?'

May was silenced. She knew exactly what people would think because she had heard Lady Clarence on the subject on more than one occasion. When Lady Clarence expressed herself on such a matter it was with a clarity and precision which left no room for argument; though May, slow to realise when she was beaten, had frequently tried to find some.

Opening the door of the wardrobe Bella indicated a full-skirted dress of pale pink soie-de-Chine.

'Lady Clarence suggested the shell pink for this evening, Miss May. Will that be satisfactory?'

16

'I suppose so.'

The apparently endless procession of lace, lawn and silk undergarments appeared from the drawers of the mahogany chest and were laid in a fluffy array on the blue satin bedspread. Bella closed the light curtains and May stood up, went over to the bed and waited to be unhooked. Bella drew her afternoon dress over her head, loosened her petticoats for May to step out of, and then unlaced her corset. Reduced to her light shift and the silken wrapper Bella had slipped over her shoulders May moved towards the bathroom. Bella was there before her, turning off the taps, always timed to have filled the bath at the precise moment that May was undressed. Bella shut the door behind her and went back to her preparations.

May lay back in the bath and tried to float; wondering if Lady Clarence would let her go to the Bath Club the following morning. She had nearly succeeded in swimming a full length underwater, and Miss Lewin had promised to practise the double somersault with her next time she came. She slid down in the bath, raised herself on her elbows and stretched her long legs up to see if she could touch the edge of the lampshade with her toes. She had almost done it when her elbow slipped against the soap and she fell back with a resounding bang and sent the water fountaining up before it cascaded over the edge of the bath and onto the floor.

'Miss May, are you all right?' She heard Bella's anxious voice from the other side of the door.

'Yes, Bella, I just slipped as I was getting out.' May hastily leapt onto the sodden rug and began to towel herself vigorously. She threw on the clean shift which Bella had put ready, dragged her wrapper round her and squelched out. Bella, going in to empty the bath, stared at the floor then looked reproachfully at May.

'I'm sorry, Bella. Have you got your feet wet? I nearly touched the shade with my toes!'

'I'll ring for Mabel to clear it up. Come along Miss May, you spent too long in the bath. Miss Fenton will be here in a minute.'

17

By the time May had her camisole on, the housemaid had arrived with her mop and bucket. May spoke to her over her shoulder as Bella arranged her petticoats.

'How is your brother, Mabel? Bella said he's getting married. Is she someone you know?'

'No, Miss May. She's in service over Beccles way. Me Mam wrote she's a pert little thing with red hair. But then, me Mam always wanted him to marry Molly Sugden, her who works for the schoolmaster in the village.'

May automatically shook out her flounces.

'I think I know who you mean – she takes the children out, doesn't she? A dark girl with rather a low forehead.'

'And her chin sticks out.' Mabel emerged from the bathroom with her bucket. 'Our Tom said he'd as soon marry a witch! She's all right, Molly, and a dab hand with the pastry, but you know what men are, they're only interested in looks before they're married.'

'Oh well, let's hope the redhead can make pastry, too. Have they decided when it's to be?'

'Not for ages yet, Miss May, they want to put a bit by for furniture and things first.'

'Then perhaps your mother will have time to come round, then. Thank you, Mabel, I hope I haven't held you up.'

'Not so's you'd notice, thank you, Miss May.'

The door closed with a gentle click. May turned back to Bella, now ready with the ball dress in her arms. It slipped smoothly over May's golden head and fell in a silken swirl to the floor. Layer upon soft layer rustled gently as she moved towards the dressing table. Bella gazed with pride at the reflection: glowing pink shoulders rose from the chemisette of delicate ruched tulle, arranged so as to give a discreet emphasis to the roundness of her full breasts above her narrow waist. But May scarcely glanced in the mirror as she sat down and waited for her hair to be attended to.

Bella was a swift, deft worker, and May's hair was too long and thick to need the cunning addition of pads and wires. The elaborate coils and swirls were soon arranged and secured with invisible underpinnings; a circlet of the same small

18

rosebuds as those Bella had sewn onto the flounces of her skirt was placed on her shining hair, and a single string of pearls was being clasped round May's slender neck when the expected summons came. At the call, 'Come in,' Fenton's narrow face appeared in the doorway.

'Lady Clarence wishes to know whether Miss May is ready yet?'

'Of course, Miss Fenton; quite ready.' Bella's tone was surprised.

May caught her own maid's eye in the mirror and lowered one eyelid in a barely perceptible wink.

May gathered her full skirts in her left hand, and, barely touching the banister as she went, ran down the stairs to the first floor hall. Here she adopted a more decorous pace as she approached the drawing room, but her step-mother had not yet come down, and she found her father alone, reading the 'Morning Post'. As he rose on her entrance she noticed that he was wearing full evening dress. He gazed at her affectionately.

'My dear, you look a picture!'

'And you look very elegant, Papa.' She moved across to kiss his cheek. 'I didn't know you were escorting us tonight.'

A slightly hangdog look passed over Lord Clarence Winton's handsome features.

'Your Mamma particularly requested it.'

May carefully spread out her skirts as she sat down.

'I think she does not altogether approve of Lady Hindlesham, Papa; why is that?'

'And I think she would not at all approve of my telling you the reason, Miss.' But his smile was indulgent.

'Oh, Papa, surely . . .'

The door opened, and Lady Clarence, in her evening finery, glided through. Father and daughter fell silent. Lady Clarence looked searchingly from one to the other, then smiled.

'You look charming, May. Bella has turned you out very nicely.'

'I was ready on time, too. Step-mamma, may I go to the

19

Bath Club tomorrow? It's a Ladies' Morning; if I arrive there by nine I can be back in good time for luncheon.'

'Goodness, May, we will be very late tonight. Surely you will be too tired?'

'I'm never tired, Step-mamma, you know I'm not. I always wake up early, however late we've been.'

'An overabundance of energy can cause problems, May. It is time you grew out of it. However, if you do wake up in time you may go – but remember that Bella will have had a late night as well as you.'

'She won't mind, Step-mamma, she likes the Bath Club. She takes her sewing with her and has a good gossip with the other ladies' maids.' May had already told Bella she was to lie down on the day bed in her room while waiting up for her, but she knew better than to tell this to Lady Clarence.

'Remember, May, if you do go, you may rest in the ladies' drawing room after swimming, but I do not wish you to go into the billiard room.'

'But Step-mamma, it is for the use of the Lady Members!'

'I have heard,' Lady Clarence's voice was heavy with displeasure, 'I have heard that certain of the Lady Members invite male guests to play with them.'

May persisted. 'But it is allowed in the rules of the Club.'

Lady Clarence drew herself up to her full height. 'There are Club rules, and there are my rules. While you remain an unmarried daughter under your father's roof you will obey my rules. Your father expressly forbids you to use the Bath Club billiard room, is that not so, Clarence?'

'Certainly, my dear, certainly.'

Lord Clarence tugged at his moustaches, and as Lady Clarence swept towards the door he glanced at May with a look of commiseration.

'Better settle for the swimming, May old girl. We don't want ructions, do we?'

May felt she had no objection at all to ructions, but she was fond of her father so she merely smiled at him and kept silent.

Chapter Three

May and her parents were to dine at the Marquis of Andover's London house. The Dowager Marchioness had acted as her elder son's hostess since the death of his wife, four years earlier. Aunt Dora, whom May remembered only as a querulous, sofa-bound invalid in whose presence one had always to be quiet as a mouse, had died as inconveniently as she had lived – just before the onset of May's first Season. Lady Clarence, correct as always, had cancelled all arrangements and withdrawn her daughters to black gloves and crape in the seclusion of the countryside. As a consequence of this delay, coupled with Lady Clarence's earlier insistence that girls of seventeen should still be in the schoolroom, May had been a full nineteen years of age before she had made her curtsey to the King and embarked on that round of dances, dinner parties and calls which had marked her Coming Out. She had forgiven Aunt Dora her ill-timed demise as soon as she had realised that the result would be the joint presentation of Emily and herself: the two girls had derived great pleasure and much mutual support from each other's company, a support which May now sorely missed.

The heat of the afternoon had barely lessened, and as the carriage drew up in Arlington Street May noticed that her step-mother's normal high colour had drained away, leaving her face white and taut, and she swayed slightly as she rose to leave the brougham; but her back was as straight as ever as she preceded May up the wide staircase.

Despite the long summer evening, the drawing room was ablaze with artificial light which shone on the gleaming white shoulders of the women and struck sparks off their jewellery. Lady Andover greeted her son and daughter-in-law, then turned to May, who bent to kiss her scented, delicately powdered cheek.

'My dear, how lovely you look.'

'And so do you, Grandmamma.'

May's reply was sincere; Melicent Andover was now well past her sixtieth year but her face had not lost the deceptively fragile beauty which in her youth had captivated the then Lord Canfield, and in her maturity, so it was rumoured, the Prince of Wales himself.

Lady Andover turned to the next arrival and May's eyes followed her, admiring the graceful economy of her movements and the smiling ease with which she inserted her guests into the appropriate groups, while simultaneously sending Cousin Bertie, with a barely perceptible gesture, to the rescue of gauche Louise Dumer standing alone and awkward by the piano, without even the wit to make a pretence of studying the music.

May found herself manoeuvred in her turn into one of those all-too-common conversational situations where she knew well that the duty of a young girl was to gaze with rapt attention, interspersed with the occasional hushed exclamation, at an elder statesman whose experience in Parliament had only confirmed him in his long-held belief in the efficacy of the monologue. Widening her eyes in simulated interest May allowed her mind to wander as 'excise duties', 'amended income tax schedules' and 'new tariffs' reverberated inexorably around her. She knew that Lady Andover, who normally surrounded herself with the witty and urbane, had recently conceived political ambitions for her younger grandson, and her guest list had been ruthlessly amended as a consequence. May trusted that Archie would be suitably grateful for her unwitting sacrifice on his behalf, though this seemed unlikely, since a covert survey of the drawing room under her lashes failed to reveal any sign of the would-be MP.

Sir Robert, perhaps sensing a certain lack of interest in his audience, decided to toss in a note of gallantry.

'Still, I can't expect a charming young lady like yourself to be concerned about dull old affairs of State, now can I?'

22

'Why, Sir Robert, you make these financial matters sound quite, quite . . .' The appropriate word eluded May, but she saw it did not matter, since Sir Robert, a satisfied smile on his face, was clearing his throat preparatory to a fresh onslaught. At this point May decided she had had enough; besides she had caught a glimpse of a familiar pair of shoulders over by the door.

'Please do excuse me, Sir Robert, but I believe my grandmother is trying to attract my attention.' With a parting smile May moved swiftly across the room.

'Quick, engage me in animated conversation, I'm escaping from Sir Robert!'

Archie burst out laughing. 'Gad, he's fearsome, isn't he? If Grandmamma wants to persuade me into politics then she'd do better to keep men like that away. But I must say, May, you were putting on a marvellous show just now, Aunt Ju would have been proud of you; you looked absolutely fascinated by the old b– bore.'

May arranged her face into an expression of vapid insipidity, and simpered prettily at her cousin.

'Well, you know it was all for your sake, Archie.' She paused. 'After all, if you're ever to reach even the back benches you'll need all the help you can get.'

Archie bowed exaggeratedly. 'Many thanks, sweet coz – but you really needn't try so hard next time. Look at him, in full flight again, and obviously delighted with his audience – yet it's only Louise Dumer doing her "I am a rabbit, you must be a stoat" act.' Somewhat to her chagrin May noticed that this was indeed the case. Archie continued, 'Wonder where Bertie's wriggled off to? Grandmamma has hopes of the Dumer dollars you know. She says Louise is a very nice girl when you get to know her, and her mother can't help being American.'

'Oh, so Sir Robert won't have the pleasure of her company at dinner, then, if she's reserved for Bertie.'

Archie grinned. 'No, I've had a peek at the dining plan – Sir Robert is booked for a luckier girl!'

'No, Archie, not again!'

''Fraid so, and Lord Oulton's on your other side. Still, look at it this way: when your voice is hoarse from shouting down old Oulton's ear then you can turn and rest it listening to dear Sir Robert's views on tariff reform! Grandmamma's got very clear ideas about the duties of Family at her dinner parties.'

May sighed. 'If it weren't for the thought of Chef's wonderful food I'd be wishing I'd stayed at home with a headache.'

'Come on, May, you never have headaches – besides there's La Belle Hindlesham's Ball to look forward to, now there's a treat.'

May was just about to ask Archie why her step-mother disapproved of Lady Hindlesham when she realised that Lady Andover was deftly marshalling her guests into the order for dining; without any obvious chivying the pre-arranged pairs were formed and began to move towards the door. Sir Robert laid claim and she put her hand on his arm and took her place in the procession.

Despite the excellence of the oyster bisque, May soon felt that the meal was going to be as much of an ordeal as Archie had predicted. Sir Robert had long ago mastered the art of swallowing and talking simultaneously, while Lord Oulton, a pleasant old man whom May had met before, had great difficulty with his lip-reading at the dining table, so she was forced to swivel round in her chair and enunciate as clearly as possible every time she replied to his questions.

Meanwhile, May could not help but notice that things were a lot livelier on the other side of the table: Louise Dumer's plain face was unusually animated as she listened to the conversational sallies of Bertie, while further down a giggly red-head was so taken by Archie's quips that she felt it necessary to rap his knuckles with her fan; Archie hastily moved his wine glass to a safer place and winked across at May before turning back to his companion with unruffled good humour.

May suppressed a pang of envy and redoubled her efforts to communicate with her elderly neighbour, who was asking her

24

about her activities at the Bath Club. Despite the difficulties May found herself describing her failures and triumphs with enthusiasm; Lord Oulton did seem genuinely interested, and before the arrival of the fish she had invited him to the Lady Members' End of Season Display, an invitation which was accepted with every sign of pleasure.

He patted her hand. 'It's delightful to talk to a young girl whose pursuits range more widely than just parties and dances, m'dear.'

As she smiled back May felt a twinge of guilt – after all, swimming was as much of an indulgence to her as dancing was to other girls, and she might feel rather differently if she could only dance as well as she could swim; but all Madame Mantoni's efforts had failed to turn her into more than a mediocre performer. 'Poor little Miss May, she has no sense of rhythm; sometimes I despair of her, Lady Clarence!' had been an all-too frequent refrain.

With the arrival of the Soles Moulées May's attention was claimed by Sir Robert. He now chose to inform her why no right-minded individual, male or female, could possibly contemplate the enfranchisement of women.

'Why, I'd sooner see my bassethound voting, he has more sense!'

As his laughter boomed out, spraying the surrounding air with minute particles of coconut sauce, May gritted her teeth and maintained the necessary polite smile with some difficulty. She felt that her views on the Suffrage question, which had been entirely neutral, might be due for a revision. She turned back to Lord Oulton with relief when Sir Robert's opinion was loudly demanded by the lady on his other hand.

'What do you feel about the Suffragist movement, Lord Oulton?'

He watched her lips carefully, then nodded. 'I feel, Miss Winton, that since many households in this country are wholly or partially maintained by the earnings of women, then it must surely be unjust that these same women are denied the political rights of their brothers. Yes, my dear, where a woman makes a worthwhile contribution to the good

25

of her fellows or of her country, then I personally would give her the full responsibilities of citizenship.'

May was pleased by the old man's reply, though she reflected wryly that his criteria would leave her unenfranchised. Still, on that basis, some men would lose their right to vote as well! Look at Cousin Archie for instance – amusing flirtatious red-heads could scarcely be counted as a worthwhile contribution to society.

The dessert had been served and May was still savouring the sharp tang of a fresh orange when she saw her grandmother glance round the table. She hastily put down her fruit knife and Lady Andover then smiled at Lady Leamington, on her son's right. At this signal the ladies rose as one and moved, in a soft rustle of skirts, to the drawing room.

Lady Clarence was already sitting down by the time May arrived, and the latter noticed again her unusual pallor: her face had a greenish tinge. May walked across and spoke softly.

'Have you one of your headaches, Step-mamma?'

Lady Clarence's smile was strained. 'Just a slight twinge, my dear, nothing more. How was Lord Oulton? He appeared to take pleasure in your conversation, you must have spoken clearly.'

May flushed; she knew this was as near to paying a compliment as her step-mother would ever get. 'We talked of the Bath Club, Step-mamma, and Women's Suffrage – and he asked after Emily.'

'That was thoughtful of him. Lady Oulton was a kind friend to me when I came out; he must miss her greatly. Lady Leamington, how are you? You know my daughter, I believe.'

May could not pursue the matter of her step-mother's headache then, but when the gentlemen joined them later she approached her father and suggested that he ask her grandmother to look after May at Lady Hindlesham's ball, and so enable Lady Clarence to return home early. Lord Clarence immediately agreed and spoke to his wife with unusual firmness; although clearly unhappy at what she saw as a

26

dereliction of duty, Lady Clarence could scarcely refuse to deliver her step-daughter to the care of her own mother-in-law; besides, she was far from well.

May felt both guilty and pleased: Lady Andover's idea of chaperonage was a great deal more easy-going than Lady Clarence's; even in a crowded ballroom the latter was aware of May's every movement, whereas Melicent Andover would be much too engrossed in her own pleasure to cast more than an occasional glance in May's direction. The rest of the evening began to assume a more lively aspect, and May and her father, having seen Lady Clarence safely into the care of Fenton, set off again in the brougham in the light-hearted mood of a pair of children granted unexpected deliverance from the supervision of a strict governess.

Chapter Four

The chimes of a nearby church clock were striking the quarter after eleven as they reached Grosvenor Square. May had often seen Lady Hindlesham from a distance at the opera, but she had never before come face to face with this famous beauty, though she knew she and her grandmother moved in the same circles. Now she gazed with interest at the woman greeting her guests at the head of the magnificent curved staircase. Others had arrived just before them, so she had ample time to study the sinuous line of Della Hindlesham's shapely form as she turned gracefully from one guest to the next. May knew that the elder Hindlesham girl had recently given birth to her second child, but it was impossible to believe that the vision above them was already a grandmother – even allowing for the fact that she had been married straight out of the schoolroom, in a boy-and-girl romance. Now she dared to wear a Princess frock, with its clinging lines which so mercilessly exposed any fault of the figure: the silky grey panne velvet was embroidered with medallions of silver sequins and a myriad tiny pearls which outlined the low-cut décolletage in a style which contrived to be both subtle and yet suggestive. The diamonds of her tiara shimmered in the rich black mass of satin-smooth hair, and seemed to be mirrored in the sparkle of her eyes; and May felt herself suddenly childish in her debutante's pink frills.

As they drew nearer May was aware of her father pulling his shoulders back even further, and surreptitiously smoothing a nonexistent wrinkle in the set of his jacket, but May noticed now the delicate tracery of lines below the lustrous dark eyes, and surmised that the fashionable, many-tiered dog collar of pearls and diamonds was as much a disguise as a decoration.

Lady Hindlesham greeted Melicent Andover as an old friend, then turned to her granddaughter.

'So this is Mary's daughter. Welcome, my dear.'

Her voice with its curiously husky timbre did sound welcoming, but May sensed a measure of reservation in the searching gaze which swept over her from head to foot: Della Hindlesham seemed almost displeased by her appearance, so that May raised a doubting hand to her hairstyle, but she could feel nothing amiss.

At the entrance to the ballroom May paused a moment, absorbing the brightly-lit scene below. Flashes of white, rose-pink and Romney blue betrayed the presence of the débutantes, intermingled with the deeper shades of the married women: orange and sapphire, gold and silver; and everywhere the black and white of the men, twirling their partners under the blazing chandeliers. And all around the edge of the dance floor the dove greys, soft mauves and dark burgundies of the watchful chaperons.

Then the lilting strains of a waltz gave way to the vigorous rhythm of a galop and Archie seized her hand. 'Come on May, stop wasting good dancing time,' and they were on the floor and whirling round and round. May felt her cheeks glow with the swiftness of their movements and she relaxed and enjoyed the brisk exercise. Archie was well familiar with her defects as a dancer and had no compunction about pulling her into step when the need arose. As they rounded the corner of the room at a spanking pace May saw their grandmother smile benignly in their direction.

'You wouldn't have rushed me off like that if Step-mamma had been here.'

'But she isn't,' Archie replied. 'You played a neat trick there, Maysie old girl.'

'Don't call me Maysie – besides,' she blushed, 'it wasn't deliberate, she really was ill.'

'Good.'

May took advantage of a twist in the dance to kick his shin for his heartlessness, and then spun rapidly out of range. 'Anyway, shouldn't you be dancing with the Dumer dollars?'

'No, no, they're for Bertie. Younger sons have to make do with the Frears frigates.' Archie leered ostentatiously at May while neatly dodging a second kick.

'You haven't a hope! If you were the only man left in the world . . .'

'. . . you'd get mown down in the rush!' Archie finished triumphantly, and they burst out laughing.

When the music brought them to the far end again May caught a glimpse of their hostess, and remembered the scene on the stairs.

'Archie, has there ever been any quarrel between Stepmamma and Lady Hindlesham? She gave me such a strange look, she seemed almost, well . . . hostile.'

'Yes, I noticed that myself. Obviously Aunt Ju disapproves of the fair Della, but that wouldn't worry her. On the contrary, the disapproval of a woman like Lady Clarence is meat and drink to the Lady Hindleshams of this world. No, it was you she didn't take to.'

'But she doesn't know me!'

'You are naïve, May. She sees you as a rival, but with a good twenty years' lead.'

'Oh come on, Archie, don't be silly. Emily is the beauty in our family.'

'Maybe, but she wouldn't see Emily as a challenge. Della Hindlesham is a beauty all right, but she attracts the men because of something else, and that's what she recognised in you, May.'

May felt her face crimson. Archie grinned down at her.

'Be your age, May, you must be the lousiest dancer in London, but when do you ever have to sit one out?'

'Why, only last week,' May retorted. 'Jonny Yoxford said he'd rather not dance the quadrille.'

'So what did you do instead?'

'He offered to show me some particularly fine camellias, in their conservatory.'

'And did Aunt Julia enjoy the camellias?' Archie's tone was guileless.

'She said she did – how ever did you know she came with us?'

Archie threw back his head and roared with laughter.

'I knew we could rely on her!'

May tapped her foot on the floor. 'Stop making that ridiculous whooping noise and take me back to Grandmamma; the dance has finished, in case you haven't noticed!'

As soon as they were back amongst the chaperons May sat down and stealthily eased her right foot partly out of its shoe; she had stubbed her toe in the attack on Archie and her dancing slippers were tight-fitting. Just as she was wriggling her cramped toes she had to jump up again: Lady Woodbridge had arrived, fussy as a small tugboat and towing behind her a solidly built, heavy faced young man whom she introduced as her eldest son, Lord Alcester. While explanations and commiserations were being exchanged over the absence of Lady Clarence he stared at May, who began to feel that she was being looked over by a man thinking of buying a new horse. Archie had, of course, melted into the crowd on the arrival of the Woodbridges and May now had to sustain a one-sided conversation in which her gambits were met with a wall of 'Yes. No. Really?' and a species of grunt. But eventually it appeared that Lord Alcester thought this particular horse might be the bargain he was looking for, since he finally muttered, 'D'ye care to dance?' and dragged her off into a waltz without waiting for a reply.

Even through her silk glove May was unpleasantly aware of the sweatiness of his palm, while it was soon apparent that his talent for dancing was even less than her own. Her heart sank. She reflected grimly that they might have had some chance in the lancers, but their progression round the floor to the tune of the lilting 'Schönbrunn Valse' rapidly deteriorated into an ungainly scramble. When one moved up, the other moved down; both pulled back simultaneously then cannoned into each other with a thud whereupon Lord Alcester seized control of the situation by clamping May to his chest. May, hot and uncomfortable, braced her left hand against his shoulder and gave a fierce push. She thrust herself free just as

31

her partner tried to execute a complicated turn and the result was disastrous. She collided with the couple behind them and her right shoe flew from her foot and was lost in the surrounding mêlée.

Lord Alcester's face reddened with fury, May's with embarrassment; she breathed a fervent prayer that the floor would open up and swallow her where she stood. At that moment the man she had crashed into reappeared, her shoe dangling nonchalantly from one hand. 'Allow me,' and in one polished movement he was kneeling at her feet, had taken hold of her ankle in a firm grasp and had slipped her shoe back onto her foot. In seconds he was upright again, there was a smiling bow, a murmured 'My pleasure', and he caught up his waiting partner and was away. May had only a fleeting impression of a bony face, a flashing smile and an unruly lock of hair falling down over his forehead. With a feeling of fervent gratitude to her unknown rescuer she followed his example, seized hold of the awkward young man in front of her and, deciding that her dancing was marginally better than his, began to steer him firmly round the floor.

He muttered in protest: 'Hey, you're pushing me around. *I'm* supposed to lead.'

May, her composure now partly restored, hissed back, while smiling sweetly, 'Not after what happened last time.'

'That wasn't my fault, you pushed me!'

'A lady shouldn't *need* to push a gentleman.'

'Well, how was I to know that ass Cussons was so close behind? It was all his fault.'

May disdained to argue further, and they waltzed clumsily on in acrimonious silence.

When a sulky Lord Alcester had propelled her back to her grandmother and made a rapid escape, May turned and saw Archie leaning against the wall, with a wide grin on his face.

'Well, May, that was priceless – what a performance! I know Alcester's not the most exciting of partners, but to go and throw yourself at Harry Cussons like that. Some women will stop at nothing!'

'It wasn't my mistake, he shouldn't have grabbed me like

he did. And I don't know who it was I bumped into, but I was jolly grateful to get my shoe back – I didn't notice you rushing to my rescue with it!'

'What? Me? Try and compete with old Harry, the ladykiller himself – I'd have no chance. Why, he could put a lady's stocking back on, let alone her shoe, in the time it'd take me just to kneel down!'

'Archibald, that's quite enough.' Lady Andover spoke sharply to her grandson and rapped his hand with her fan. 'Go and find Bertie, I wish to speak to him.'

Archie, unrepentant, bounded off, and Lady Andover turned to May.

'Don't worry, my dear, Archie only happened to notice because he was dancing nearby. I'm sure most people were quite unaware of your little contretemps.'

'I do hope so, Grandmamma. I was so embarrassed, I just didn't know what to do, and Lord Alcester just stood there, gobbling like an angry rooster.'

'Yes, he takes after his father, they're quite a trial to poor dear Mabel – but May, you really should not have slipped off your shoe like that. I tried to attract your attention, I could see you had not got it on again properly, but you left so suddenly.'

'I won't do it again,' May promised fervently, thankful that her step-mother was safely at home.

Her hand was claimed next by the persistent Jonny Yoxford, and they moved off into a lively quadrille. Jonny kept up a lighthearted banter, apparently unaffected by May's refusal of his hand and heart a mere two months ago, and she relaxed gratefully in his arms.

As she returned to her grandmother May noticed a tall figure leaning over her chair in close conversation; there was something familiar about the set of his shoulders and when he turned and smiled May's heart jumped as she realised it was her recent deliverer. Jonny's greetings were restrained, and he soon left to find his next partner.

'My dear, Mr Cussons wishes to be presented to you.' And amid May's confusion the introductions were made.

33

'Are you free later in the evening – perhaps we could dance before supper?' His voice was low-pitched and attractive. May murmured an acquiescence.

'Good, I shall be looking forward to our dance. Good evening Miss Winton, Lady Andover.'

He strode off, just as May's next partner came for her; but half an hour later he was at her grandmother's side again, and had swept her on to the floor before she had time to draw breath. She soon realised that besides being an expert dancer he was strong enough to pilot her without mishap; when she did lose the rhythm his tactic was simply to lift her off her feet and then deposit her again in time to the music – and this with a smile which, while acknowledging her slip, made it seem of little consequence. Indeed, May soon began to suspect that he found her occasional lapses amusing, and she laughed with him.

He seemed in no hurry to open the conversation, but once May had relaxed in his arms he grinned, and spoke teasingly.

'So, Cinderella, you've come to the ball at last?'

May smiled back, replying candidly, 'I'm afraid my foot would never have squeezed into her tiny slipper – you would have exposed me as one of the ugly sisters!'

He threw back his head and laughed aloud. 'But you are Cinderella, because I've never met you at a ball before. However have you escaped tonight?'

'I'm sure we must have been in the same company sometimes, perhaps at a squash, but my step-mother is very strict about whom I meet.'

As soon as the words were out May could have bitten off her tongue, and she felt the crimson rise from her throat. Her partner pulled down the corners of his mouth in an exaggerated gesture, but his eyes sparkled.

'I am silenced – utterly!' But within seconds he whispered, 'You blush beautifully, Miss Winton,' then louder, 'So where is your step-mother tonight?'

In further confusion May murmured, 'At home, she had a headache. She sent me with Grandmamma.'

'. . . who is an old friend of mine, and so we met.' The note of satisfaction in his final statement was unmistakable.

He was silent for a few bars, then, to the mingled relief and disappointment of May, he turned the conversation into more conventional channels. The dance seemed to flash by, and so did their supper interlude. However, May was not so bewitched by her new partner as to fail to do justice to the excellent refreshments, and she exclaimed with delight over the table.

'I never tire of lobster mayonnnaise – why, there are truffles in this partridge pie – do try the mousse, Mr Cussons, it's delicious, and a little of the salad? – oh, quails, I never feel quite happy about them, they are such small birds.'

'But I notice you have no objection to eating *large* birds, since you've selected the chicken galantine.'

May smiled. 'One is never totally consistent, Mr Cussons.'

He looked down at her. 'How true, Miss Winton, how very true.'

The tiny meringues, coffee eclairs and Neapolitan ices were all sampled and eaten with pleasure, then he whisked her off to the dance floor again. May, well aware that Lady Clarence would certainly have been annoyed at her spending so long with one partner, made a half-hearted protest, but the lively strains of the polka, one dance she genuinely enjoyed, seduced her into compliance, and they pranced happily round the room in an amicable silence, Mr Cussons only venturing one question.

'Tell me, Miss Winton, do you ever suffer from indigestion?'

May widened her eyes in surprise. 'No, why ever should I?' Which made him laugh again.

Towards the end of the dance she saw a slight frown cross his face as he glanced towards the side of the room; she followed his gaze but could see only their hostess, Lady Hindlesham, in conversation with her grandmother.

This time, when the music ended he led her straight back to Lady Andover. Lady Hindlesham's face was smooth and unruffled as they approached, but May still sensed a coolness in her polite query.

'I trust you are enjoying yourself, Miss Winton?'

35

'Yes, thank you Lady Hindlesham, very much. And supper was absolutely delicious.'

At this last remark Lady Hindlesham seemed to relax slightly, and her smile almost reached her eyes. Then she turned to the tall man at her side and laid her slender hand on his arm.

'Come along Harry, I need you. Good evening, Melicent my dear. Good evening Miss Winton.'

As they moved away Harry Cussons turned back for a moment and murmured to May, 'Farewell, Cinderella.'

May could not resist it; she smiled up at him and whispered, 'Goodbye, – Buttons!'

He blinked, then laughed aloud. A look of distaste crossed Lady Hindlesham's face as she led him off.

The rest of the evening was an anti-climax, and May barely protested when Lord Clarence, a guilty expression on his face, almost seized her from the arms of her last partner, muttering, 'Come along, my dear, it's nearly twenty past three, whatever will your mother think? You know her views on young women who stay dancing until the servants are ready to sweep up!'

'But Papa, hardly anyone else has left yet,' but she allowed herself to be taken away.

Outside the night air was blessedly cool and clear, and May leant back gratefully on the cushions as they drove through the quiet streets. The steady clip-clop of the horses' hooves was pleasantly soothing, and when they alighted outside the house she paused a moment to gaze at the fluttering leaves of the trees in the square, silhouetted against the dawn sky.

'Come along, May, don't dawdle.'

She followed her father up the steps and through the open front door.

Chapter Five

Three weeks later May and her parents were on their way to Stemhalton, the Marquis of Andover's country seat in Norfolk. The London Season had ended and the round of summer visits begun. May missed her sessions at the Bath Club, but otherwise she felt relief at finishing the never-ending round of calls and tea parties, of dances and receptions, interleaved with stately strolls beside Rotten Row or in the Park. And all the time there had been the constant preoccupation with dress: standing immobile, transfixed by pins, at Konski's; inspecting a long procession of hats at Paquin's; and day after day, the continual changes of costume.

As she gazed out of the compartment window at the golden fields and green woodland of East Anglia May became aware of a certain stiffness in the low-toned conversation between her parents.

'Had I known that Lady Hindlesham was to be among the guests I would have pleaded an alternative engagement.'

'Come now, Julia, Hindlesham's a good chap, y'know.'

'I have no objection to meeting Lord Hindlesham.' Her voice lowered still further and May only caught the words 'Cussons' and, a little later, 'openly known'.

Lord Clarence spoke more loudly, 'I'm sure my mother knows what she's about.' He glanced at May. 'We won't discuss it further.'

Lady Clarence subsided into a thin-lipped silence, while her husband applied himself to his 'Morning Post'.

'Stemhalton Market, Stemhalton Market.'

May jumped down from the railway carriage and looked around her at the familiar brightly painted station buildings with their sentinel rows of hollyhocks. At the rear of the train Bella and Fenton, and Makins, Lord Clarence's valet, were standing over a pile of luggage, directing the energies of a couple of porters. May turned towards the barrier and saw her uncle's coachman, advancing with a beaming smile.

'Hello, Saunders, what a beautiful day; are we the only people on the train?'

'Good afternoon, Miss May; yes, the other guests mostly came on the two forty-five, and one of the gentlemen, a Mr Cussons, why, he motored over!'

'Goodness, that was adventurous of him.' May spoke calmly, but she felt her heart miss a beat. She had not seen Harry Cussons since the night of Lady Hindlesham's ball, but she remembered his strong features and commanding manner.

Lofthouse, the Marquis' butler, met them at the door; he had been with the family for years and was an old friend of May's. She felt the familiar lift of excitement as she crossed the spacious hall and entered the drawing room. Her childhood holidays at Stemhalton had always seemed golden times, especially when she and Emily had been packed off with just old Nanny, leaving their parents behind. Aunt Dora had exercised only minimal supervision from her sofa and the four children had ranged at will over the estate, May and Emily tagging along behind their older cousins, determined not to be left out. It had been worth the penalty of a scolding from Nanny, 'Your frock, Miss May, what have you done! And it's all stained with green at the back!' Later, even the governesses had seemed to relax a little at Stemhalton, although May well remembered the formidable Miss Worth, who had insisted on all rents and tears being summarily mended by the one who'd done the rending. Still, it had been a small price to pay for weeks of near freedom. May felt very old as she sighed for the lost days of youth, but she rapidly brightened when she spotted a pair of well-tailored shoulders outside on the terrace – so it was that Mr Cussons!

'Good afternoon, Grandmamma.' She bent to kiss the scented cheek. 'Hello Archie, don't scoff all the cake, leave some for me.'

'You should be as fat as a pig, the amount you eat!'

May made a face at her cousin.

'Nineteen inches, and that's without my corset,' she replied complacently.

'Stop squabbling, children.' Their grandmother's tone was goodnatured but firm. 'What would your mother say if she heard you speaking of undergarments at the tea table – and to a gentleman!'

'It's not a gentleman, it's Archie.' But May sat down and obediently began to play the young lady.

Harry Cussons had not come in from the terrace by the time Lady Clarence sent May upstairs for her obligatory quiet hour before dinner. May roamed restlessly round the light airy bedroom, missing Emily; then rang for Bella too early. Stemhalton had been built long before the days of bathrooms, and although two cavernous apartments had since been converted these were generally reserved for the gentlemen, so two housemaids struggled in with the hip bath and large cans of hot water, and arranged the screens around the rug in front of the fireplace. Splashing in the water on a warm August evening was pleasant enough, but May remembered shivering in the icy draughts of December when the roaring fire barely warmed even the area in front of it.

This evening May took more interest than usual in her toilette. She gazed critically at her reflection in the long glass, contrasting herself unfavourably with the remembered elegance of Lady Hindlesham. The frills which crossed over on her bosom, and were themselves ornamented with ribbons and tiny tulle roses, seemed over-ornate and fussy; she turned away, tugging impatiently at the spangled tulle of the heavily flounced overskirt.

'I'm so bored with pale colours, Bella: nothing but pastel shades. I'd love a dress in a deep, dark blue, or olive – or black, even!'

'When you are married you will be able to choose whatever colour you like,' Bella said placidly.

May sighed, then thought of Emily. Only the previous week she had said a final goodbye to her sister, after the young couple's fleeting visit to Allingham Place; but she felt that

Emily had been taken from her earlier, at the wedding ceremony: she belonged to William now, and had looked pale and drawn and dependent. The whispered confidence, 'If all goes well you will be an aunt next year, May, in early January,' had only seemed to emphasise the gulf.

May felt a shiver of excitement as she swept down the wide staircase in the wake of her step-mother, but when they entered the outer drawing room a quick glance showed her that Harry Cussons was already holding court amidst a flock of elegantly clad women, among whom she saw the distinctive long neck and raven-black hair of Della Hindlesham; so she knew that Lady Clarence would remain firmly at the other end of the room.

When the company began to move towards the dining room Mr Cussons glanced over the heads of his entourage, and for a moment smiled in May's direction; then he was lost to view in the shifting crowd.

At the dinner table May was interested to discover that one of her neighbours was Lord Hindlesham. As they were introduced she looked with some curiosity at the husband of the famous beauty; he was certainly no match for his wife in looks, being a small, slight man with a rather wizened face and the dark, sad eyes of an organ grinder's monkey. Yet as the meal progressed she warmed to him: he proved a witty and informative companion, and they soon discovered a shared enthusiasm for food; he confided in May that one of his reasons for accepting Lady Andover's invitation had been the well-known skill of Chef.

'I remember a capital dinner I had in Arlington Street, back in June. The ortolans, my dear,' leaning forward confidentially, 'were out of this world – pure poetry!'

May warmed to him even further.

'You must visit the kitchens while you are here, Lord Hindlesham: Chef loves the appreciation of a truly informed palate. Perhaps you would care to accompany me tomorrow?'

'With pleasure, my dear Miss Winton, with great pleasure.' He glanced along the table to where his wife was chasing a fragment of turbot round her plate while courting Harry

Cussons' sallies, then leant forward and whispered, 'Della bants, you know – she is terrified of becoming heavy! I tell her to eat up; when you're middle-aged, I say, like we two, a little heaviness is quite forgivable – but she seems almost annoyed by my advice.' And Lord Hindlesham's monkey face crinkled up into a mischievous grin, as he gave the ghost of a wink in May's direction. 'But, my dear, we were discussing the relative merits of oysters. I respect your preference for your Colchester native, but do you not feel that those from Falmouth have just that touch more lightness of flavour?'

After dinner the gentlemen seemed to May to spend an unusually long time over their port and cigars; then, when they did arrive, Lady Andover arranged the tables for bridge, while Archie called on the younger members of the party to join him in a spirited game of charades. May had to accept that Harry Cussons, being well into his thirties, was inevitably a bridge player, and although she enjoyed the dressing up and general quick-wittedness needed to satisfy Archie's artistic ambitions, she nevertheless did feel that just a few minutes' conversation with Mr Cussons would have been pleasant.

On the stroke of twelve Lady Clarence appeared in the outer drawing room to summon May, so breaking up the party. As they ascended the staircase May spoke in a casual tone to her step-mother.

'The tall, fair-haired gentleman, Step-mamma, was that not Mr Cussons, who Saunders said drove himself here by motor car?'

'So I believe, May.' Lady Clarence's reply was cool. 'We did exchange a few words, since I knew his mother, Lady Violet.'

Lady Clarence seemed disinclined to pursue the subject further, so May said no more.

41

Chapter Six

The bedroom was full of light when May woke up the next morning. She reached for her watch on the bedside table; the hands stood at five to seven. She put it to her ear, but it was ticking steadily, so she lay back impatiently against the soft pillows; it would be another hour or more before Bella came in with her early morning tea tray, and outside the sun was shining! Coming to a rapid decision she threw back the covers, pulled her nightgown over her head and tugged on a shift and her lightest morning frock. Having hastily replaited her hair and wound it round her head she hesitated over her stockings, then pushed them to one side – well, they wouldn't stay up without her corset, and in any case she would be back in her room long before anyone else was about. She slipped on her shoes, seized a plain straw boater and was through the door and scampering along the corridor in seconds. A housemaid clutching a pair of newly polished boots breathed a startled 'Good morning, Miss.' May flashed her an answering smile and bounded down the wide staircase. The heavy oak front door was locked and bolted, but she remembered the convenient small entrance between the gun room and the butler's pantry, and, sure enough, the knob turned at her touch.

Outside the air was fresh and sweet-smelling, every leaf pearled by the early morning dew. May ran straight across the wide level lawn, swung round the sentinel elm and then plunged headlong down the steep grassy bank to the smooth, still lake. She tracked back along the shore until she came to the swift-flowing stream which fed it, then crouched down to splash the silver water onto her face. Gasping with the shock she shook her head and laughed aloud as the drops showered over her bare arms. Then, walking purposefully, she set off for a circuit of the grounds.

A farmer herding milch cows in one of the home farm meadows touched his cap, but there was no one else around: at this time of day the gardeners were busy near the house, so the estate was her own. May moved with confidence, remembering each hollow and hillock from her childhood. She approached the graceful little folly, perched on its bell-shaped mound with the winding path; but they had always run straight up the steep side, and now May did the same, arriving panting at the top. Then she was plunging down again and on to the dark hidden pond where they used to hunt for newts; a quick glance and she was away again and into the small mossy wood, in reality quite near the house, but always seeming so far away. She spotted the big central oak, a special favourite of theirs in childhood because, due to some arboreal peculiarity, the branches grew lower down than on most oak trees so it could be scaled more easily.

May stood and eyed the branches speculatively; she had not climbed a tree since she had put her hair up. She glanced swiftly round: only the distant figure of a gardener pushing a wheelbarrow could be glimpsed through the trees. She took a deep breath, tossed her hat to the ground and reached up for the first two branches and braced her feet against the trunk. For a second she hung there, the next moves forgotten, then her muscles remembered and she was swinging herself up agilely. The branches shook and the leaves rustled around her as she climbed further and further up the tree, until eventually she came to the point where the trunk narrowed and bent against her weight. Panting and triumphant she gazed through the flickering green screen at the colonnaded length of the house, at one with the landscaped parkland behind it. Time hung suspended; then clear and sweet came the chimes of the stable clock. Reluctantly she began to edge her way down, more hesitant now, remembering that, in trees, the descent was always harder than the ascent: but she took a firm grip on the branches and moved down steadily. With her attention fixed on her hand and foot holds it was only as she reached the lowest branches that she glanced down and noticed the upturned face of a figure standing a few feet from the base of the tree. May stopped, poised in mid-movement, and stared down. Harry Cussons smiled up at her.

'So, my Cinderella has metamorphosed into a dryad! Clearly you are a young woman of many parts, Miss Winton; you never cease to surprise me.'

May unfroze and completed her movement, then slid down into a sitting position on the bottom branch. She strove to regain her composure, thinking wildly that Lady Clarence's exhaustive instructions on the rules of proper behaviour had entirely failed to prepare her for this eventuality: how did a lady address a gentleman from the boughs of a large oak tree, and, more to the point, how did a lady make a graceful descent from such a position in front of the laughing eyes of a decidedly attractive man of the world like Harry Cussons? She looked down to check the state of her dress and noticed a long green stain; as she shifted her leg to conceal this she realised to her horror that her bare ankles were in full view. A quick glance at her companion's face as she tugged ineffectually at her skirt told her only too plainly that she was merely drawing attention to her lack of stockings; she felt herself turning crimson from head to foot.

He continued smoothly, covering her confusion, 'Like you, I felt this fine morning was too good to be wasted, and so came out for an early stroll. I'm delighted to find I have company.'

May finally managed to pull herself together.

'Mr Cussons, I think it is nearly time for breakfast; perhaps you would be so kind as to – turn your back while I finish my descent.'

'But you might slip and break an arm, or an ankle, and then how guilty I should feel!' He strode up to the tree and stood beneath her. 'Come, nymph, jump!'

And May jumped into his outstretched arms. In seconds he had set her firmly on the ground, retrieved her hat and begun to usher her towards the house.

'Let's go and enjoy one of Melicent's excellent breakfasts in the smug knowledge that we alone, by our early morning exercise, have truly deserved it.'

44

May seized the proffered boater, set it on her head and followed him out of the woodland and up the sloping lawns to the main door.

As May entered her bedroom she saw to her surprise that Fenton was there, as well as Bella.

'Good morning, Bella. Good morning Fenton. What a beautiful day!'

She looked enquiringly at her step-mother's maid.

'Lady Clarence wishes to speak to you, at once, Miss May.' Fenton's voice was heavy with disapproval, her expression tight-lipped.

May glanced at Bella, who looked uncomfortable and gave a tiny shrug of her shoulders and a shake of the head.

Puzzled, May followed Fenton's rigid back along the corridor to her step-mother's room.

Lady Clarence, fully dressed, was sitting in a straight-backed chair beside the empty hearth; her nostrils were pinched and her step-daughter realised, with dawning dismay, that she was very angry.

'Thank you, Fenton, that will be all.'

The maid retreated noiselessly. Lady Clarence did not invite May to be seated. There was a charged silence as her gaze raked her step-daughter from head to foot. May began to feel acutely conscious of her untidy appearance.

'I'm sorry I'm rather dishevelled, Step-mamma. It was such a lovely morning I got up early and went out for a walk . . .' Her voice trailed off in the face of Lady Clarence's withering look.

'Yes, I saw you outside, walking – with a young gentleman! Just the two of you, alone, together!' Her tone was spiked with ice.

May had often incurred her step-mother's displeasure before, but she realised that Lady Clarence was angrier than she had ever known her.

'I didn't go out with him, Step-mamma. I had been walking by myself. I met Mr Cussons just before I came in, quite accidentally.'

45

'That is the kind of "accident" that no young lady should ever allow to occur.'

'But Step-mamma, I couldn't help it. I climbed a tree and he came along while I was up it.'

'You climbed a tree!' Lady Clarence's eyes were bulging with horror. 'You climbed a tree, at your age! The more you tell me the more appalled I become.'

May realised at last that silence was the only sensible course. She stood, head bowed, under the weight of Lady Clarence's censures. These finally rose in a crescendo with, 'And I have not failed to notice that your ankles are bare. Not only have you committed a major impropriety, you have committed it improperly dressed!'

By this time May felt nearly as angry as her step-mother. She had met Harry Cussons purely by chance; having once met him it would have been discourteous and hypocritical to have refused to walk back with him. But despite her sense of bitter injustice she knew better than to try and argue with Lady Clarence in this mood. She merely asked, 'May I go and dress now, Step-mamma?'

Lady Clarence made a gesture of dismissal, but insisted on the last word.

'You would have done better to have dressed before you left the house this morning. I am thoroughly ashamed of you.'

With cheeks ablaze May stalked back along the corridor. Bella was waiting with a sympathetic expression and day clothes at the ready. She dressed her mistress in silence. As the last hairpin was driven home May exclaimed, 'I can't do anything! I am as restricted and controlled as those wretched slaves in *Uncle Tom's Cabin*, but there are no Northern States for me to escape to – and don't tell me I should get married: I'd only finish up under the thumb of a husband instead.'

'Husbands are easier to manage,' Bella replied. 'Lots of wives twist their menfolk round their little finger.'

'I wouldn't want to marry that sort of man and have to wheedle for trifles. Oh, Bella, I wasn't doing anything wrong!'

46

May felt the gentle pressure of Bella's hand on her shoulder. She turned to her maid.

'I do miss Emily, and in November I shall lose you as well; I dread to think who Lady Clarence will find to maid me when you leave to get married.'

'That's a long way off Miss May, she'll come round. There now, that's the breakfast bell.'

May felt she scarcely had the appetite for breakfast, but once she got downstairs the appetising aroma of grilled kidneys and devilled bones made her think again, and she filled her plate from the hot dishes before sitting down at the end of the table with the other young girls. When Harry Cussons came in she scarcely glanced in his direction and instead applied herself to chatting to Louise Dumer, who seemed so painfully grateful for the attention that May felt quite guilty about her previous neglect.

After breakfast the men went out for what was described as a stiff ride, and the ladies composed themselves to their usual occupations of letter-writing, fancy work, sketching and most engrossing of all, gossip. Lady Andover and Lady Clarence had retired to their rooms, so the conversation soon became livelier. Lottie Dones, a vivacious, rather pert girl whom May had always found amusing in a casual way came and sat down beside May and Louise.

'Goodness, May, you have made a name for yourself! Fancy roaming round the grounds with the most eligible bachelor of the weekend – unless you count Bertie, which I don't suppose you do, since he's your cousin' – with a sly look at Louise, who reddened unattractively, – 'rich, handsome, and oh, so charming – how did you manage it my dear? You really are clever, why you hardly spoke to him last night, and yet you contrived an assignation for this morning, when we good little girls were all still in bed! You are a sly one, May.'

Louise was staring at May in astonishment. The latter replied through gritted teeth.

'I met Mr Cussons purely by chance. I was out for an early morning stroll, alone, and so was he. We only exchanged a few words.'

47

Lottie emitted a high-pitched trill.

'Oh really, May, we're not as naïve as all that!' She leant forward confidentially. 'And I shouldn't bother making that excuse to dear Della Hindlesham, they say she's blazing.'

May stared at the other girl in bewilderment.

'What on earth has it got to do with her? It wasn't Lord Hindlesham I met in the grounds.'

Further trills were at once forthcoming.

'Oh May, you are so droll! I must go now, Mamma's beckoning me.'

May glared at her retreating back. There was an agitated voice at her side.

'Don't take any notice of her, Miss Winton, she's only jealous. I expect if Mr Cussons had seen her in the grounds he would have walked off in the other direction.'

May felt momentarily warmed by Louise's championship; however, apart from the visit to Chef which Lord Hindlesham insisted on their making, this was the only bright spot of the day. On the wagonette expedition to a deservedly lesser-known local ruin May felt only too conscious of the barely-veiled hostility of Lady Hindlesham and the knowing whispers of the other women. She kept well clear of Harry Cussons, and when he approached her on the terrace at teatime she felt acutely embarrassed, could only manage monosyllabic replies to his comments and soon retreated back to the shelter of Louise, whom she had begun to think of as a quite acceptable cousin-in-law. Indeed, she decided that since her own affairs were in disarray she might as well do someone else some good: to this end she engaged Bertie in a triangular conversation and then, when Louise appeared to be holding her own, melted into the background. Her grandmother signed her over and patted her hand.

'That was kindly done, my dear.' May felt her eyes fill at the unaccustomed praise.

Lord Hindlesham then approached and suggested a visit to the kitchens in the lull before the preparations for dinner got under way. The footman returned with the message that Chef would be pleased to welcome Miss Winton and her guest, so they set off through the green baize door. Chef and Lord Hindlesham were soon absorbed in a welter of technicalities and May stood amazed at this other side to a man spoken of as an up-and-coming politician, who had made his mark in the Lower House before his father's death and now held junior office in the Upper. Both men were too courteous to leave her long out of the conversation, and she was cheered by Chef's: 'She 'as a natural talent for flavours, Mees May, eet iz instinct with 'er – ah, she could 'ave been a superb cook, what a waste.' May blushed and disclaimed, but felt duly flattered by this praise from a master of his art.

However, when she returned to her room before dinner she felt distressed and depressed. She could not feel that she had deserved Lady Clarence's strictures, yet the behaviour of Lottie Dones and of several of the other women seemed to suggest that there had perhaps been some sense in them. But what had she done wrong?

At dinner May was taken in by an elderly bachelor uncle whom she had never known well, while her father was on her other side. Lord Clarence had obviously been given a full account of his daughter's misdemeanours by his wife and alternated between sympathetic glances and attempts to look stern whenever Lady Clarence caught his eye.

In the drawing room conversation in the region of Lady Clarence was stilted, but May felt she preferred this to the murmurs at Lady Hindlesham's court, which sounded decidedly malicious. The first arrivals from the dining room proved to be Archie and an inarticulate young guardsman with whom he was friendly. They collected Louise, and the trio held a brief consultation before approaching Lady Clarence.

'Perhaps we could persuade May to come with us, Aunt Julia?' Archie's voice was deferential. 'We left the charades trunk in rather a state last night, and we really should tidy it up – the servants always try and organise it too thoroughly, and then we can never find a thing we want.'

Lady Clarence inclined her head graciously and May,

feeling rather like a prisoner on ticket-of-leave retreated with them to the little room behind the ballroom.

Once the box was sorted out Archie suggested a game of billiards, and they sauntered off to the modern wing, Louise ahead with the guardsman.

'Thanks for rescuing me Archie: it's been a grim day.'

'Well, you certainly don't do things by halves, do you, May? Walking back in broad daylight in front of all the main bedrooms, with Harry Cussons of all people – and with your hair half down as well!'

'But that was only because I'd been climbing the old centre oak.'

Archie threw back his head and laughed.

'I believe you May, because I know you, but there's plenty of tittle-tattlers around who don't. I know Aunt Ju lays it on a bit strong at times, but she's not completely off-beam. You know, I like Cussons, he's good company – but he is rather a cad with the ladies.'

'Oh Archie, you're just being narrowminded and prejudiced. Don't you turn against me as well.' May's voice trembled.

Archie looked quite alarmed. He reached for May's hand and squeezed it quickly.

'Sorry, old girl; 'nuff said.'

Several hard-fought games later May was feeling more cheerful; Bertie had arrived with a friend of his and the atmosphere was thick with cigar smoke and goodnatured banter. May had just executed a neat double hazard when the door opened, and to her surprise she saw her step-mother on the threshold.

'Evening, Aunt Julia,' said Bertie. 'Have you come for a game?'

'No, thank you Bertram,' Lady Clarence replied levelly. 'I have come for May; I wish to have a word with her. Perhaps you would care to accompany us back to the drawing room as well, Miss Dumer?'

Louise looked up in surprise and put down her cue; then, to May's eternal admiration she picked it up again, gripped it firmly and said, with a touch of her mother's transatlantic twang, 'Thanks awfully, Lady Clarence, but I guess I'll just finish my game.'

May barely had time to notice the look of surprised approval on Bertie's face before she was whisked out of the door. It soon became clear that their destination was not the drawing room at all but her step-mother's bedroom. With a sinking heart May prepared to endure her second homily of the day.

This time Lady Clarence fired her first salvo by pointing out that she had warned May before of the inadvisability of a young lady playing billiards later than noon. 'It is not an elegant game at the best of times, though I accept that on a rainy day in the country it might be a means of passing the odd recreational hour; but to play after dinner! After dinner the billiard room is the preserve of the young men, especially when they are smoking. Your cousins should have known better, since you yourself appear to have lost all sense of propriety today' – and there was considerably more in the same vein.

After an initial protest May closed her lips and listened in silence. Lady Clarence eventually wound up with: 'It gives me no pleasure to have to speak to you like this May, no pleasure at all.' May reflected mutinously that, since it certainly gave her no pleasure to listen perhaps they should dispense with the entire operation, but she realised anew the futility of arguing with Lady Clarence when she was in this mood, or indeed, in any other mood.

With a murmured, 'I am sorry you are displeased, Step-mamma,' – and that at least was true, she thought – she left the bedroom and returned to her own room. Bella came at once, and made no comment on May's early bedtime, merely wishing her a good night after she had finished brushing and plaiting her hair.

Chapter Seven

The next morning, May again woke to a room filled with sunlight, but she stayed in bed. The events of the previous day coursed through her mind, but she still failed to see how she could have acted any differently. At last Bella arrived with her early morning tea tray. As her maid moved between the wardrobe and the dressing table she murmured, without looking in May's direction, 'The gentleman who motored over, Mr Cussons, wasn't it? His valet, ever such a lively man, he kept us in stitches in Hall last night, he said they're leaving this morning. Apparently he should really be staying in Lincolnshire with his uncle, the Duke. He just made a special effort to run over here, now he's got to get back.' May's spirits plummeted even further; not that she would have dared to even speak to Harry Cussons again, still, he had seemed to enjoy her company.

After breakfast May and Louise sat in the inner drawing room with Lady Andover. While they were chatting idly, Harry Cussons came in to take leave of his hostess, so the two girls withdrew to the window seat. After a few minutes Lady Andover looked over at May, smiled, and called Louise to the piano to discuss some music. Harry Cussons approached May.

'May I sit beside you for a moment, Miss Winton?' He was seated before her confused assent had been given. He leant towards her, confidentially.

'I gather I have been the unwitting cause of some distress for you.'

May blushed; he gave a broad smile.

'I really should have remembered the oh-so-strict step-mother, shouldn't I?' His expression was rueful, and May could not restrain an answering smile.

52

'Don't worry, Mr Cussons, it's not the first lecture I've been given, and I don't suppose it will be the last.'

'You know, I rather hope not,' he said as he rose. 'I must say goodbye now, but I trust we shall be in each other's company again before long: and then I shall endeavour to behave with more discretion – in the sight of the Dragoness, at least!'

He laughed and was gone. May felt her cheeks burning; yet the sensation was not unpleasant. But, as her heartbeats slowed, she realised with dismay that it was quite likely that she never would be in Harry Cussons' company again. After all, they had only met recently, and then only because Lady Clarence had been tempted by Lady Woodbridge's matchmaking schemes; she was unlikely to make such a mistake again. May was very sure that the guest list would be carefully vetted before any further visit to Stemhalton; Lady Clarence was absolutely inflexible where she believed herself to be in the right. In any case did she, May, really want to see more of Harry Cussons? He was very attractive and amusing, but sometimes he seemed almost to have been laughing at her, as if he could not take her quite seriously. She certainly did not feel as at ease with him as she did with Archie, for instance, or even Jonny Yoxford. May bent her head and gloomily stabbed her embroidery.

A few minutes later her attention was aroused by her grandmother.

'Would you like to come up to my room for a little while, my dear? I seem scarcely to have spoken to you since you arrived.'

Melicent Andover's boudoir was as pretty, fresh and feminine as its occupant; May wandered round the room, exclaiming at familiar treasures.

'I remember Archie bringing that back for you after we'd spent that holiday in Cromer – and the delicious little fan, how fascinated Emily and I were by the pictures! We used to make up stories about their picnic and why the little brown lady was sitting all alone – we thought she must be the governess. And the ivory elephant! It's so tiny, but it has such old, wise eyes.'

Melicent Andover smiled indulgently.

'Come and sit down, May,' patting the low, chintz-covered ottoman. 'I'm afraid Julia has been rather annoyed with you, my dear, and she was quite right to speak to you.' May's heart sank. 'You were indiscreet: a young girl cannot be too careful of her reputation. But don't look so downcast, things will be different when you're married.'

'I don't want to get married, Grandmamma, I'm not in love with anyone.'

'Nonsense, of course you do, all girls want to get married, and you will have more freedom then.'

'But my husband might not like my climbing trees and walking in the early morning with Mr Cussons either!'

Lady Andover gave a peal of laughter and playfully rapped May's knuckles with the little ivory fan.

'You are so amusing, May, but so naïve; that's why I decided to have this little chat with you. Julia has sheltered you far too much; you're nearly twenty-two and a girl with your spirit needs to know more of the world. Now, my dear, it is silly to talk about falling in love in relation to marriage. You are an heiress and you are a very attractive girl. Settle for a young man whom you find pleasing, and who has a good position in society. Do your duty by him, give him the heirs he needs – then you can relax and enjoy yourself.' She smiled reminiscently. 'You wouldn't need to go walking with young Harry in the full daylight then! There are ways of arranging these things – discreetly, of course.'

May stared at her grandmother; Lottie's comments about Lady Hindlesham fell painfully into place. What a fool she'd been! But her grandmother had not finished.

'Mind, May, I'm not saying you will have to settle for one of those rather callow youngsters who dance attendance on you. No, it seems to me that a most enviable prize might be within your reach.' She leant forward confidentially. 'I have never known Mr Cussons show so much admiration for a young girl, my dear.'

May's thoughts were in a whirl.

'But,' she faltered, 'but Step-mamma will never let me meet him again.'

Lady Andover's eyes gleamed naughtily.

'There are ways of arranging that, my dear; but remember, you must always behave with total discretion – until your fish is well and truly landed.'

Melicent Andover's silvery laugh rang out again. She smiled at May's astonished face.

'I've shocked you, May, but think over what I've said carefully. You will soon see the sense in it. You do look rather discomposed at the moment: you had better stay up here until you feel calmer.' She picked up a pile of magazines from her bureau and handed them to May. 'Here, my dear, glance through my copies of "The Lady's Realm" until you are ready to come downstairs again.'

Unthinkingly, May opened the magazine on her lap. She felt totally bewildered. Her grandmother appeared to be encouraging her to deceive her step-mother, yet Lady Clarence, whatever her faults, had always been rigidly fair. May shuddered at the thought of being detected in a falsehood by her; indeed she felt a sense of revulsion at the thought – no, it just wasn't honest. Yet if she didn't hoodwink her step-mother she would probably never see Harry Cussons again! But did she want to? Since he was clearly some kind of – her mind groped for words – some kind of close friend of Lady Hindlesham's. And he had come into her life like a breath of fresh air; if she didn't follow her grandmother's suggestion then she would slip back into the same dull routine: endless calls and stuffy dinner parties and boring receptions. On the other hand, the idea of accepting say, Jonny Yoxford, then deliberately setting out to deceive him, that was too much – besides, suppose he did the same to her! May felt her throat thickening and the tears rising. She gripped the magazine firmly and forced herself to begin reading.

It was the June issue, and she dimly remembered leafing casually through it in London; now she made herself concentrate. The pictures on the fashion pages blurred and danced before her eyes, then slowly came into focus. She read, 'Some quietly chic toilettes are being made of a new silk grass lawn, decorated with the palest ciel blue, with parasols ensuite' but

55

this seemed of little interest to May; nor could she care that 'Paris has been curiously faithful to browns and yellows' – what was curious about any French fashion? She turned the pages, pausing briefly at the large picture of a laughing Billie Burke; she remembered how flattered she'd been when Archie, peering over her shoulder, had exclaimed, 'Why, she's the spitting image of you, May. I noticed it the other night. But you don't look quite such a flirt.'

'I should hope not, indeed.' Lady Clarence's voice had been scandalised. 'Comparing your cousin to an actress, Archibald, you should have more discretion. Come, May, we have calls to make.'

May sighed now, and listlessly turned on. Frescoes, she would read about frescoes; that seemed a sufficiently calming subject. But before she began she glanced idly at the full-page photograph of a society lady on the page opposite. The face seemed vaguely familiar, she must have seen her somewhere before. 'Lady Hermione Blackwood' – she had met a Blackwood once. She read the caption below: 'Who has acted as a trained nurse in one of the London hospitals. Her father was the late Marquis of Dufferin and Ava.' May looked at the pictured face with more interest. Fancy, a marquis' daughter, and yet she'd trained as a nurse. May had never heard of aristocratic young ladies acting as nurses, except those ladies who'd rushed off to South Africa in a blaze of patriotic fervour, and apparently been a thorough nuisance to the professional nurses when they arrived. It must have been a big change for Lady Hermione: very different from her normal round of calling and dinner parties and . . . May gasped and gripped the magazine more firmly; all the boredom and frustrations of the last few months boiled up and crystallised into one solid idea. That was it, that was the answer – she would cut the Gordian knot, and go to be a nurse!

She sat very still, testing out the sudden decision in her mind, like a tongue exploring a newly-arrived wisdom tooth. She could remember a trained nurse coming into the house once, when she and Emily had both had scarlet fever; Nanny

56

had been indignant but exhausted, Emily was delirious. May had watched the nurse rearranging the heavy nursery screen with practised ease. 'You are strong, Nurse. Nanny always gets Betty to help her with those.' The nurse had smiled. 'Nurses have to be strong, so that they can lift heavy patients when they're in bed.' May, who'd only come across 'patience' as something everybody said she hadn't got, had been puzzled then. Now she thought – well, I am strong, and I never catch cold. That should be worth something.

Suddenly her mind was made up. She sprang out of the chair, let the door bang behind her in her excitement and ran down the stairs. She found her step-mother sitting with her embroidery in the corner of the drawing room. May marched in before her courage faltered.

'Step-mamma, may I have a word with you?'

'Certainly my dear.' Lady Clarence looked surprised as she laid down her work. 'Sit down.'

May sat down and took a deep breath. 'Step-mamma, I wish to tell you that I have decided to train as a nurse, in a hospital in London.'

For once in her life May saw her step-mother flabbergasted. For a moment Lady Clarence's jaw actually dropped. Then her mouth clamped shut.

'Nonsense, May, young ladies in your position do not act as hospital nurses!'

It was a moment of exquisite triumph. May thrust 'The Lady's Realm' beneath her step-mother's eyes. 'Oh, yes they do, read this.' As Lady Clarence stared at the caption May continued vigorously, 'If a marquis' daughter can train to be a hospital nurse, then a marquis' grand-daughter certainly can!'

Chapter Eight

In the late afternoon of the second Friday in September May stepped down from a growler outside the long grey barracks of St Katharine's Hospital in the East India Dock Road. A mere four weeks ago she had announced her new ambition at Stemhalton, and here she was, deposited with her trunk and hand luggage outside the main entrance of the biggest voluntary hospital in the East End of London.

Events had moved more rapidly than even May had anticipated. Having made her announcement to Lady Clarence, she had listened to her comments in silence. May knew her step-mother was, though rigid in outlook, a just woman: she had expressed strong doubts on the question of May's motives, but could not castigate such an aim as immoral. She told her step-daughter she would give the matter careful consideration, but May, when she left her step-mother, went straight down to the library to find a directory of voluntary hospitals. She was bemused by the sheer number of them, but decided, after a quick survey, to write to St Katharine's, since it was listed as having the most beds which, she reasoned, must mean that they needed the largest number of nurses; in addition the address was given as the East India Dock Road, which seemed somehow appropriate to her Frears shipyard inheritance. A letter to the Matron was written and delivered personally into Lofthouse's hands, to go in the next post. On her father's return for lunch she informed him of the *fait accompli*.

Lord Clarence was stunned; but caught between the conflicting wills of his wife and his daughter he wisely said little, contenting himself with, 'It's, humph, – a big step – never knew you were interested in that sort of thing.'

Archie laughed; Bertie raised his monocle and his eyebrows;

her grandmother said she was disappointed; the Marquis said 'Really?' and talked of the weather. The general opinion of the house party was of incredulous disapproval, though Lady Hindlesham formed a surprising, and temporary alliance with Lady Clarence by giving the latter the reassuring information that some London hospitals took lady pupils. 'Paying probationers, I believe they call them now, just for a few months, Lady Clarence, some girls from very good families have gained a little nursing experience in this way – under the particular supervision of the Matron, of course.'

May said firmly: 'I wish to be a proper nurse, Step-mamma,' and Lady Clarence sighed.

Welcome support came from Lord Hindlesham. 'I am on the governing boards of several hospitals, Miss Winton, but I always feel the patients are spruced up for our annual visits. You must let me know what really goes on when you've been nursing for a while.' May was relieved that someone, at least, thought she was capable of staying the course. Then Louise Dumer said that although she personally couldn't stand the sight of blood, Lord Canfield – with a blush – had told her how May had bound up his cut hand with a handkerchief when he'd once fallen headlong out of the dog cart, and she was sure May would be a very good nurse. May, mentally commending Bertie's diplomacy, since she distinctly remem-bered ripping up her petticoat for this piece of first aid – and after all, she had pushed Bertie out in the first place – warmly thanked Louise for her confidence.

A letter was awaiting May at Allingham on their return, with an imminent interview date. May telegraphed an acceptance before she informed Lady Clarence, who im-mediately pointed out that May could not possibly go on that date since she was not herself free, having a houseful of guests. May insisted that she could stay with Great Aunt Ursula, who was now too old and infirm to leave her London home in the summer. Lord Clarence, when appealed to, finally gave his decision in favour of his daughter, and May and Bella set off for St Katharine's on a scorching August afternoon. May's impressions of her interview visit were of a confused medley of strange sounds and even stranger smells, and of looming grey buildings surrounding darkly shadowed courtyards.

A horse-faced woman wearing a severely cut dress of dark blue and with an improbably frilly housemaid's cap on her head looked May up and down and commanded her to enter an inner sanctum – 'Your maid will wait here.'

Matron proved to be a surprisingly young-looking woman with an even more improbable confection of lacy frills perched on her neat smooth hair.

'Sit down, Miss Winton. How old are you?'

May jumped at the abrupt opening, but replied swiftly, 'I'm twenty-two next week, Miss Anderson.'

'Only just old enough. We do not accept nurses for training below that age, as you will know.'

May had not known, but thought it politic to conceal this ignorance.

'Why do you wish to become a nurse?' The question was fired at her with the velocity of a rifle bullet, and May hesitated before blurting out her answer.

'I want something to do, I'm bored.' As soon as she had said it May realised how lame her explanation sounded, but it was the truth, so she let it stand.

Matron had raised her eyebrows; now she subjected May to a searching scrutiny, and the latter was suddenly conscious of the expensive texture of her costume, and the tailored elegance of its fit – yet she had deliberately chosen the plainest outfit in her wardrobe.

'So you were bored – yet many girls would have given their eyeteeth for your opportunities.'

May could think of no correct reply to this comment; she remained silent.

'What skills have you to offer me if I should choose to accept you?'

May thought rapidly. 'I was well taught by my governesses, I am fluent in French and German,' Matron did not look impressed, so May plunged on. 'I can sew, I'm very strong – and I can swim a full length underwater at the Bath Club.'

For the first time Matron smiled. 'We do not expect our

60

nurses to carry out their duties underwater, Miss Winton; and unlike Guy's we do not have a swimming pool in our Nurses' Home – perhaps you should have applied there. Why *did* you apply to St Katharine's?' Another rapid shot. 'We don't take lady pupils here, you know.'

'I do not wish to be a lady pupil. I wrote to St Katharine's because of its situation.'

The matron looked rather surprised. 'Indeed? Despite the proximity of the River, Poplar is not generally considered a salubrious area of London.'

'I should like to be near the Docks – you see, my grandfather built ships, though not in London, on the Tyne.'

'Oh, and what was his name?'

'Frears,' May murmured, looking down at her gloves.

'*The* Frears?'

'Yes, Miss Anderson.'

'Well, at this stage in an interview I usually point out to applicants that although nursing has its rewards, the financial are not amongst them. But I assume I may omit this in your case, Miss Winton.' May nodded; Matron leant forward. 'However, I should tell you that we have girls from a variety of different backgrounds at St Katharine's – if you come here you would be wise to be discreet about your personal circumstances. Do you understand?'

'Yes, Miss Anderson, I do.'

'Address me as "Matron" please, Miss Winton.'

It took May a moment to realise the significance of this last request. She stared at the woman behind the desk. 'You're accepting me?'

'Subject to a satisfactory medical report from your own doctor, and on probation for the first six weeks, yes. You appear to be a tall, healthy girl, and you obviously have a strong pair of lungs.' Matron leant forward and smiled winningly; inexperienced as she was, May felt a twinge of apprehension at the sight. 'As it happens, Miss Winton, one of our intending probationers, who was due to start in September, is unable to begin for family reasons. So we have an immediate vacancy for you; how very fortunate. Send us your measurements by return of post and we will have your uniform dresses waiting for you – charged to your account, of course. Good afternoon, Miss Winton.'

The interview was over. May was in such a daze that she saw little of the hospital; she and Bella climbed back into Aunt Ursula's landau and the coachman steered carefully into the stream of traffic along the Dock Road. When she thought over events later she could not decide what she had said to gain a place so rapidly: was it the mention of the Frears fortune; or her boast that she could swim a length underwater – or had Matron simply accepted her because she was short-handed? May rather suspected the latter, much though she would have preferred to believe that it was some sterling quality which Matron had instantly discerned beneath her frivolous exterior. Well, she had made her bid for independence, she would try her hardest to stick at it. But she felt her enthusiasm drain away as she stood again in front of the grimy portals of St Katharine's.

'Where do you want your trunk, Miss?'

The cab driver's voice shook May out of her reverie. She was on her own now. Lord Clarence, reluctantly abandoning his partridges for the day, had escorted her to London on the early train, and taken her to lunch at his Club. But May insisted on saying goodbye there and making the final stage of her journey alone: 'After all, I must learn to look after myself now, Papa,' and her father, looking suddenly stunned, had acquiesced. She squared her shoulders, took a deep breath and marched towards a pair of beady eyes fixed on her from the porter's cubbyhole.

'Would you be so kind as to show me the way to the Nurses' Home? I have my luggage with me.'

The porter's head poked forward, like a tortoise coming out of its shell. He subjected May and her luggage to a searching scrutiny. May smiled at him, and his leathery features softened fractionally in response. He gestured into the recesses of his lair: 'Jack.' A gangling lad with a cheerful smile and a bush of red hair appeared from the shadows: 'Evening, Miss.'

62

'Nusses' 'Ome – 'and luggage, trunk later.' And the tortoise subsided into immobility, and resumed his steady stare across the archway.

May turned and paid the driver, who had fetched her luggage and was now staring in horrified fascination at the looming bulk of the hospital.

'Rather you than me, Miss. I reckon 'Olloway Jail 'ud be more cosy.'

He grinned when he saw the size of his tip, leant forward and muttered confidentially, 'Any time yer wants to escape, you let me know. I'll be round wiv the files and a rope ladder.' Chuckling to himself he left.

May gazed after him, feeling totally bereft: her last contact with the outside world had gone.

'This way, Miss.' The obliging Jack had already picked up her baggage and now he set off at a brisk pace round the courtyard. 'You'll like the Nurses' 'Ome, it's new, just finished last year – opened by 'Er Majesty 'erself, it was.'

May remembered the Queen, elegant and beautiful in the drawing room at Stemhalton, and could scarcely imagine her in these grimy surroundings. Still, they had probably cleaned the place up a bit – planted some flowers, perhaps. Jack was still chatting; he seemed to need no answers – no doubt association with the tortoise had taught him to dispense with these. 'Course, there's still the old Nurses' 'Ome, round the back, that's used too, but not for the new nurses – Matron likes them to start off nice.' By this time they were approaching a high, bare frontage of raw red brick, pierced with row upon row of oblong windows and totally devoid of ornamentation. May wondered fleetingly what the old Nurses' Home could be like if this was 'nice'. But her guide had not finished. 'I ain't bin in myself, but,' in an awed voice, 'they say every room's got 'lectric light, with its own switch.'

May gulped. 'What is the lighting in the wards, then?'

'Well, some of 'em's electric, but others is gas and Abel Block, well, that's still lamps and candles. 'Ere we are, Miss.' He beat a tattoo on the door, which was instantly opened by a thin-faced elderly maid. She looked harassed.

'Good afternoon, Nurse. Don't waste time Jack, give me the bags. Is that all?'

'I have a trunk as well,' May said hastily.

'Fetch it Jack, don't dawdle, may I have your name, Nurse? This way, follow me.' May gasped 'Winton', and was already rushing to keep up, along the corridor, breasting a flight of stairs at top speed, then up again, and again, right, left – May was lost long before the maid skidded to a halt outside one of a row of identical doors and flung it open.

'In here, Nurse Winton. Go down to Home Sister's room in ten minutes.' She turned away.

'Where is . . .' Before May had finished the maid had interrupted.

'Sanitary facilities at the end of the corridor.' And she was off.

May closed the door, then stood in front of it surveying her new domain. It was a narrow, high room with an iron bedstead down one side, a peculiar piece of furniture that was half wardrobe, half chest on the other, and, in front of the window, a small table and high backed chair. That was all; and May noticed that the lower pane of the window was of frosted glass. The only concessions to comfort were a minute square rug on the polished linoleum floor and a brown speckled mirror hanging over the washstand, with its plain white jug and basin.

With hands that were suddenly shaking May unfastened her handbag and took out her brush and comb. By the time she had visited the 'sanitary facilities', washed her hands and face and tidied her hair the ten minutes were up. She looked round for the bell to summon the maid, and did not find it; the full realisation of where she was and what she had done hit her with the force of a physical blow. She pulled herself together. 'Don't be a fool, May,' she chided herself. 'You came here because you wanted a change, well, you've certainly got one. Brace up and enjoy it.' She marched to the door, flung it open and set off down the corridor.

Five minutes and several flights of stairs later May found herself still no nearer Home Sister's room. A slight figure in a neat green costume appeared at the other end of the corridor. It was a pretty girl with brown curly hair and a worried expression. Each rushed forward with the same question.

'Could you tell me the way to . . .?' Both stopped at once. May spoke first.

'Are you new too?'

'Yes, and lost. I'm Alice Rydal.'

'How do you do? My name is May Winton.'

They solemnly shook hands, and then looked round for help. A door opened further down the corridor and a woman in blue stripes and a white cap shot out. May and Alice Rydal rushed forward with an urgent plea for directions.

'Down there, first right and second door on the left.' The nurse tossed the instructions over her shoulder as she scuttled off.

A sharp 'Come in', followed instantly on their knock. They opened the door and found themselves confronted by a tall, gaunt-featured woman in a plain dark blue dress sporting an incongruous display of white lace frills on her hair and a large white bow under her jutting chin.

'Nurses Winton and Rydal, I presume. You're late.' The voice was uncompromising. 'Too late for tea. Follow me, Nurses.' May just had time to notice that there were four other young women in the room before there was the clatter of cups hastily deposited on saucers and the formation of a small procession. May and Alice brought up the rear. This time the journey was shorter and ended in a large airy classroom well-lit by windows set high up in the wall, presumably to avoid the temptations of a view.

'Sit down, Nurses.'

As soon as they were seated Home Sister produced a piece of lace-edged muslin and proceeded to instruct them in the art of cap construction. More pieces were produced and they all made caps which Home Sister promptly ripped apart. It was some time later before the correct arrangements of tapes and ribbons had received grudging approval, whereupon Home Sister embarked on a lecture on their duties as probationers. As far as May could understand these involved cleanliness, fresh air – 'All nurses must walk out once a day – all nurses must sleep with windows open' – and the eating of regular meals. May cheered up on hearing of this last responsibility, and hopefully followed Home Sister and her other charges to supper.

Supper was served at one end of a big, empty room and May soon realised the necessity for Home Sister's order, since it appeared to consist of stewed leather in grey gravy with a helping of what might once have been cabbage. Fortunately the rice pudding was creamy and much more palatable, and the cocoa quite pleasant. The meal passed in silence, the presence of Home Sister at the head of the table effectively discouraging all conversation. May noticed that she did not partake herself – had she eaten already, or were Sisters above such humble needs as food?

As soon as the last cup had been set down they were off again, back to the bare classroom where they awaited the arrival of Matron herself, to address them on the subject of Nursing Ethics. She now seemed a much sterner and more remote figure than at May's interview, and the winning smile had vanished utterly.

Nursing Ethics were apparently embodied in the words obedience, punctuality, accuracy and cleanliness. It was becoming clear, May reflected, that in the hospital, Godliness came a very poor fifth. It further emerged that the new nurses would have to learn to look without flinching on repulsive sights, manage delirious patients by sheer force of personality and have an inexhaustible supply of patience. May's heart sank. Matron then moved on to etiquette. She assured them that hospital etiquette was very simple: nurses apparently must stand in the presence of the visiting medical staff, the governors, the treasurers, the superintendent and, of course, Matron herself. At this point one girl half rose from her seat, and had to be frowningly restrained by Home Sister; she subsided in a blushing heap. Nurses must also stand in the presence of the resident medical officers, the Sister, and the nurse who was in authority over them at the time. May had decided by now that if she ever did wish to sit down she would have to go and visit the tortoise in his cubby-hole, since there was clearly no one else in whose presence she could do so.

A gleam of humanity did show through when Matron pointed out that patients' visitors, however poor and ragged, were entitled to equal respect, and more consideration in the light of their obvious anxiety and distress – but only, she emphasised, at the properly alloted visiting times. Except for clergymen: Matron rounded off her speech with the information that, 'It is rarely wrong to admit a clergyman at once, unless there is some reason, obvious to everyone, that it is not possible.' And on this note Matron ended her speech and swept through the door held open by Home Sister.

On her departure Home Sister rounded up her flock and sent them off to their rooms, with a reminder that lights out was at ten-thirty and the rising bell would ring at a quarter to six. The girl next to May squealed at this news but was rapidly silenced by a minatory glare. Home Sister escorted each new nurse to her room and bade a frosty goodnight: 'Trunks outside before you retire, Nurses.'

May unpacked her trunk and took her clothes out from their tissue paper wrappings, uncreased as a result of Bella's skilful packing. Her dresses and costumes hung, looking distinctly subdued, in the strange, cramped wardrobe.

She struggled out of her clothes, her hands fumbling with their unaccustomed task of unfastening all the hooks and buttons, arranged her new uniform over the single chair, ready for the morning, and climbed into bed. She began to write letters announcing her arrival at St Katharine's to her parents, and then to Emily, in India. There was a rush of footsteps and voices in the corridor then the noise died down again. Just as she was engrossed in a description of the hospital supper for Emily the light abruptly went out. She stumbled to the switch and tugged at it, then noticed that all the other windows were dark too, though the corridor was still dimly lit. At last she realised that when Home Sister had said 'Lights out at ten-thirty', that was exactly what she had meant. May felt her way back to the bed, climbed in and fell asleep.

Chapter Nine

As she awoke the following morning May was aware of a sense of bubbling excitement: new places, new people, a totally different way of life lay in front of her. She jumped out of bed and seized her watch from the top of the chest of drawers – twenty minutes to six. She threw her dressing gown around her and set off in the direction of the baths and lavatories. The long, straight corridor was empty, every door tightly closed.

Back in her room she was drawn irresistibly towards the window, but the bottom pane of frosted glass defied all her efforts to see out. After a moment's hesitation she dragged the single, straight-backed chair into position and climbed onto it, looking out of the open top. Below the window was an enclosed courtyard: a smell of bacon and wisps of steam indicated the presence of the kitchen on the far side, and May heard the distinctive clatter of cutlery. By leaning to the right and peering along the lefthand wall she could just see the entrance to the court, wide enough for delivery vans, and the row of milk churns alongside a door opposite showed that one had already been and gone. Otherwise there was nothing but windows, row upon blank row: some, all frosted and framed with pipes, indicated the bathrooms at the righthand corner of each floor, others were identical with May's own. These differed markedly in their degrees of openness. Some were set as wide as they would go, like hers; others, the majority, appeared fixed at a standard aperture, a neat one quarter of an inch. A few made a bare concession to fresh air; and one, yes, low down in the lefthand corner there was one completely closed, with curtains tightly drawn. Who was daring to disobey Home Sister's vigorously expressed command of the previous evening? 'Remember, Nurses, fresh air is essential in our profession. You will sleep with an open window.'

As May craned further out, one of her thick plaits falling forward, staring in fascination at the blank, firmly-closed window, she gradually became conscious of a persistent rapping sound. From one of the lower windows opposite a white hand was waving; May waved back. The window then opened to its fullest extent with a bang. It now became clear that the hand was not waving at all, but gesturing indignantly; a narrow, angry face was mouthing what May rapidly recognised as, 'Get back in, Nurse, at once!'

She jumped back so quickly that she nearly missed her footing, and the chair swayed perilously. As she regained her balance the harsh clamour of the rising bell assaulted her ears. May blinked, and climbed carefully down, noticing as she did so that the front of her nightdress now bore a black, sooty mark down one side, where she had leant against the outer window frame. She tried to brush it off, but it only smeared further, so she took it off and folded it carefully so that the mark was inside; she had no idea how frequently personal linen was sent to the laundry: she would have to try and get the mark off later.

May was soon into her underclothes and corset, but the full-skirted dress of blue-striped galatea took longer: the material was stiff and unyielding and the sleeves were unfashionably full at the shoulder. The bodice was close-fitting and she just could not get the buttons at the back done up; she missed Bella's deft fingers. She managed to get the cuffs on and fastened, and then turned to her hair. Thank goodness she had practised a simple style at home; but it did not seem so easy now. The mirror was awkwardly placed for a girl of May's height, and the heavy twisted rope of hair began to slip and slide before all the pins were in position. At last it held, and she reached for the carefully made-up cap: of white starched muslin, with a very narrow edging of lace on the two goffered frills, it looked to May like nothing so much as the housemaid's second-best, early-morning, bring-the-hot-water version. She found herself wondering whether she would ever attain the lofty heights of Home Sister's white cambric with its four frills of Valenciennes – just the thing for a parlourmaid

69

in a good house where no footmen were kept. May giggled at the incongruous picture of the hawk-nosed, grim-faced woman opening the door and dropping a polite bob in the hallway. But the time – breakfast was at six-thirty and she wasn't dressed yet! She took a deep breath and was in the act of positioning the stiff cap when there was a tap at the door.

'Come in,' May called. A girl in striped blue entered the room, smiling.

'Good morning, Nurse Winton. Home Sister asked me to show you the way to the dining room. I'm Taylor.'

'Oh, I'm so glad you've come. I've been up for hours, and I'm still not properly dressed. Would you do up my buttons for me?'

Nurse Taylor quickly fastened them. 'Now your collar.' High and stiffly starched it encircled May's throat like an iron band. 'You'll have to learn you know. I suppose you're like me, brought up with lots of sisters who always helped each other.'

May decided it would be undiplomatic to mention personal maids; she remembered Matron's warning words at her interview.

'Just one sister. Please, how does this cap stay on?'

More pins went swiftly into place.

'That's something else you will have to practise. Now, quickly, your apron, there's the breakfast bell.'

May fastened the waistband and Taylor pulled up the bib, crossed the broad straps and, with a tug, buttoned them into the band at the back. The bib strained tightly over May's breasts, so that the apron band showed above the wide linen belt she was buckling into position.

'You'll have to get busy with your needle tonight, Winton. Take in the waistband, it's far too loose, and then move the buttons down on the straps, to give you room to breathe.'

May's face fell. 'Oh, I hate sewing.'

Nurse Taylor laughed. 'Come on, Winton, most of us would be delighted to have to make alterations like that!'

May blushed, then gave a wry smile. 'That's not the way my step-mother regarded it: she thought unmarried girls should be flat-chested and the same shape all the way down!'

Nurse Taylor shooed her through the door. 'Don't worry, there's plenty of Sisters here who feel the same way; you'll have to keep well clear of the doctors if you want a quiet life. Now, quickly, we get a black mark if we're more than five minutes late for breakfast.'

In the corridor Taylor rushed ahead; May scampered after her, panting, 'And what then?'

'What when?' Taylor called back over her shoulder.

'What happens if we get a black mark?'

'Five in a fortnight and you lose your half-day off.'

May was temporarily silenced.

At the entrance to the dining room sat Home Sister, back like a ramrod. On a table in front of her were a long list of names. 'Good morning, Sister,' said Taylor, 'Good morning, Sister,' echoed May; two neat ticks were duly entered.

The long dining room was a white sea of gently bobbing caps as May hesitated in the doorway. Her companion pointed to an empty chair at the table nearest the far wall.

'Sit there, with the other new pros.' She was off down the room to her own place.

As May sat down she recognised her five companions of the previous evening. Opposite was Alice Rydal, her brown curly hair now pulled tightly back from a pale face; she smiled fleetingly at May, then stared down at the table. For the first time that morning May felt apprehensive.

A maid placed a plate in front of May; on it was one rasher of bacon. May turned to her neighbour.

'Is this all, do you think?' A murmur came from the left, 'I'm afraid I don't know.'

May studied the table and noticed, to her relief, plates piled high with thick slices of bread and butter. She leant towards the girl on her left.

'Shall we have some bread?'

Her neighbour's pale face turned to gaze at her; the big brown eyes were full of tears, and small white teeth were fastened over her lower lip. She handed the plate of bread to May with a shaky whisper.

71

'You have some, I couldn't eat a thing.' A sharp-featured woman at the head of the table glared down at her.

'All breakfasts must be eaten, or Home Sister will be angry.'

Two tears splashed onto the plate; the girl's shoulders quivered.

'I'll eat it for you, if you like,' offered May.

'Oh, please.' With a deft flick of her fork May had the bacon on her own plate; three mouthfuls and both portions had vanished. But as she put down her fork and picked up another slice of bread she became conscious of a cold silence emanating from the head of the table. The sharp-featured woman, who, May noted, bore a distinct resemblance to a ferret, was glaring at her now. The woman bent her head to a crony on her right and gave vent to an audible rebuke.

'There's someone who thinks she can do as she pleases. Matron will soon see to that!' Ferret-face then leant forward and looked at May directly. 'And wasn't it you I saw making a disgraceful exhibition of yourself this morning?' May froze with her fourth piece of bread halfway to her mouth; before she could reply her accuser had turned to her neighbour again. 'She was hanging right out of the window, in her nightgown! Sister Elijah saw her and was very annoyed, I could tell.'

For once May managed to control her tongue; what could she have replied anyway? She had indeed committed the crime, since crime it evidently was. She picked up her cup of dark-brown liquid and forced it down. The girl on her left reached for her handkerchief and began to dab at her eyes. Ferret-face, baulked of one victim, turned in her direction.

'You're not going to last long here, I can see that. Pull yourself together!'

May had had enough; she put down her tea cup and leaned towards the head of the table.

'May I ask,' every word was bitingly clear, 'who exactly you are to judge what we should or should not do?'

There was an appalled silence. Ferret-face was submerged in an angry tide of red: she drew breath, but the impending

72

verbal massacre was averted. Suddenly all the nurses began to get to their feet simultaneously, with a subdued scraping of chairs. May looked round, bewildered, and saw that Home Sister had risen from her seat. Nurses with cups halfway to their lips had returned them to their saucers. May's neighbour made a faint moaning noise and began to tremble.

'For the good food we have received, we give thanks to the Lord,' was intoned from the dais. Still no one moved.

'New probationer nurses will go to the following wards: Nurse Allen, Athanasius Ward; Nurse Carter, Martha Ward; Nurse Emms, Matthew Ward; Nurse Farrar, Rachel Ward; Nurse Rydal, Miriam Ward; Nurse Winton, Simeon Ward. You may go now, Nurses.'

Home Sister sat down and the nurses began to file out. A particularly violent shudder from May's left at the words 'Nurse Carter' had alerted May to the identity of her neighbour; she almost felt inclined to follow Nurse Carter's example, for excitement was giving way to anxiety. Anxiety gave way to downright dismay as she realised that Ferret-face was waiting for her.

'Are you Winton?'

'Yes.'

'Yes, *Nurse*,' through gritted teeth. 'You're Simeon Pro Five, I'm Simeon Pro Four. Well, don't shilly-shally, look sharp.'

Pro Four was halfway down the corridor before May realised that the older girl must be her guide. She rushed forward, pushing past fast-moving groups of nurses.

'Would you be so kind – I am so sorry – please forgive me – thank you.'

May fastened her eyes grimly on the narrow shoulders and sandy bun ahead; after what seemed like endless corridors and steps they came out into the open air, and began to crunch their way along a gravel path. The shoulders halted at the door of what appeared to be a small church; other nurses were streaming in. Bewildered, May risked a question.

'Is this Simeon Ward, Nurse?'

'Don't try to be clever with me, of course it's not!' The

voice was by now in a state of barely controlled fury. 'Be quiet and follow me.'

May followed, into a stained glass interior and onto a narrow pew. A hymn book was thrust in front of her, and the assembled nurses began to sing. The minute the hymn ended they were all down on their knees, May scrambling down last of all, and a man's voice began intoning prayers. May, feeling by this stage that she needed all the help she could get, prayed with fervour. At the words: 'That it may please Thee to forgive our enemies, persecutors and slanderers, and to turn their hearts,' May risked a glance through her fingers at Simeon Pro Four; the rigid posture showed no signs of a turning heart so, with a sigh, May redoubled her own pleas for divine intervention. As suddenly as it had begun the service was over: out into the sunlight again. Some nurses were standing in groups, chatting to each other, but Simeon Pro Four was off, and May renewed her pursuit.

They cantered into a high, looming building, up a flight of stone steps, down a passageway, and in through a pair of imposing, half-glass doors with gleaming brass knobs. Four other nurses were ahead, one more brought up the rear as they hastened down the corridor and into a high, long room. May had a confused impression of seemingly endless rows of red-check covered beds and a bright fire surprisingly burning in a central pillar before a voice hissed: 'Into line, face Sister,' and she was prodded round. A woman in the distinctive four-tiered, lace-frilled cap and dark blue dress was sitting behind a large table, writing. A nurse leant across and pulled May's hands behind her back, not ungently, but firmly. For half a minute they stood to attention, then the woman looked up.

'Good morning, Nurses.'

'Good morning, Sister.' May managed to join the chorus, albeit belatedly.

Sister Simeon began to speak to the nurse at the end of the row who was wearing a dress of purple stripes and a wide black belt. Although she listened intently, the conversation meant little to May, consisting as it did of unfamiliar names and terms. The sister appeared to be quite young: her hair

74

was still brown and her unsmiling face barely lined; a handsome woman. It was the tone of her voice which struck May: it was firm, incisive and rather loud; definitely not the voice of a woman who spent her life in a drawing room murmuring social pleasantries and indulging in flattering chitchat.

'You may go, Nurses; not you, Nurse Winton. Staff, remain please.'

May stood straight while Sister Simeon looked her up and down; she felt ridiculously like a scullery maid applying for a new position.

'Your first day, Nurse Winton.'

It was a statement, but Sister Simeon appeared to be waiting for a reply, so May ventured a response.

'Yes, I arrived yesterday, – Sister.'

She felt as if her individuality was being stripped away. Miss May Winton, granddaughter of the Marquis of Andover, heiress and débutante, was being inexorably reduced to Probationer Five under the considering gaze of this formidable woman.

'Have you any previous nursing experience?'

'No, Sister.'

'You have helped your mother with her household duties?'

'No, Sister.'

'Can you cook?'

'No, Sister.'

'Have you ever visited a hospital before?'

'No, Sister.'

'Do you know how to scrub mackintoshes?'

May, whose feelings of inadequacy had been mounting with every negative she uttered, noticed a very faint curve in Sister Simeon's lips as she asked this last question.

'No, Sister, but I'm sure I will soon learn how to.'

Sister's lips curved slightly more.

'Indeed you will, Nurse Winton; this very day. Now, Nurse,' the lips set in a firm line again, 'There is one thing you must understand. I expect obedience, total obedience, from all my nurses.'

75

For once in her life May felt absolutely no inclination to argue.

'Yes, Sister. Please may I ask a question?'

Sister Simeon looked surprised, but answered politely.

'If you are quick, Nurse.'

'Why are there mackintoshes to be cleaned? I thought the patients stayed in all day.'

Sister raised her eyebrows, and glanced quickly at Staff Nurse; May saw a faint flicker pass between them.

'I think, Nurse Winton, that the nature of their usage will become quite apparent to you once you start your task. You may go now.'

Staff Nurse, who was tall and dark, whisked May along the corridor with a flurry of purple stripes and ushered her into a white-tiled room. It smelt strongly of carbolic, and of something else rather unpleasant. Pro Four was at the sink.

'Winton will take over from you here, Bates. Show her what to do, and then start making the beds with Evans. As soon as you've finished these, Winton, you must sweep the ward and dust all surfaces. Fetch the broom and dusters from the kitchen.'

Bates directed a look of dislike at May. 'There's the brush, there's the soap. Get a move on.' She whisked through the door.

May picked up the first red mackintosh sheet from the pile. She sniffed; the meaning of Sister Simeon's reply was now all too apparent. There was a large table in the centre of the room so May spread the mackintosh out on it. Then she found a bowl on the draining board, filled it with hot water, picked up the brush, soaped it and began to pull it towards her over the sheet. Both the sheet and May's apron were soon covered with a film of soapy water, but the dark stain in the centre of the mackintosh was unchanged. May pushed harder; there was a faint blurring round the edges of the stain. She gripped the brush and began to force it backwards and forwards with all her strength; at last the dark patch began to lighten. Within minutes May, in her tight bodice and high collar, was hot and panting, and she felt the damp trickles of sweat run from her armpits; but the mackintosh was noticeably cleaner. She hauled it off the table and onto the floor and started on the next one. As she worked she felt her skirt dampen and cling to her legs and realised that her apron was soaking from neck to hem. Doggedly, she started on the third sheet.

'Nurse, what are you doing? You're soaking wet – and just look at the floor?'

A dark haired girl in a blue-striped dress stood in the doorway. May recognised her from the morning's parade in front of Sister.

'I'm scrubbing mackintoshes.'

'That's not the way to do it, no wonder you're drenched. Don't pull the brush towards you all the time – here, wait a moment.' She disappeared and came back with a sheet. 'Put this under the mackintosh, it'll absorb some of the water. Scrub away from yourself, and put a piece of jaconet round your waist to protect your apron.'

She was off again as swiftly as she had arrived, so May had no chance to ask what jaconet was, or where it could be found; but the sheet underneath did help. Working as fast as she could May soon had a pile of neatly folded mackintoshes on the floor beside her; she lifted them up and put them proudly on the table; now for the sweeping and dusting.

May set off down the corridor, peering in open doors until she found the kitchen. A short, squat maid in a sacking apron was chopping cabbage with staccato thumps of the knife. She looked May up and down.

'Cor, you aint 'arf in a mess duck – what you been doing? 'Aving a bath wiv one o' the patients? You should've took your clothes off first!' She gurgled at her own joke.

'I've not even seen a patient yet, I've been scrubbing mackintoshes. Now I've got to sweep.'

The woman gurgled again then pointed behind the door. 'There's the broom, dusters in the box, tealeaves in the bucket.'

May had opened her mouth to ask what on earth she was supposed to do with the tealeaves when a loud and angry voice rang down the corridor.

'Who, may I ask, has been in the sluice?'

A voice muttered, 'Nurse Winton, Sister.'

'Send Nurse Winton to me, at once.'

Bates' nose appeared round the door. 'Sister wants you, Winton,' she delivered her message to the floor.

The maid grimaced in commiseration and shook her head.

'You young ones, allus in trouble. You better look sharpish, she's a tartar when she's roused.'

With a sinking heart May followed Bates into the ward. She stood to attention in front of Sister's table. There was a long pause while Sister Simeon's eyes raked May from head to foot. She obviously did not like what she saw. She drew breath.

'Nurse, just look at the state of yourself. Your shoes are filthy, your apron is sodden – whatever possessed you to do a job like that without taking your cuffs off! Your cap is crooked and,' her voice rose, 'your hair is coming down. Never have I seen such an appalling spectacle; you only started this morning and already you look a disgrace to the profession! I am ashamed to have you on my ward, ashamed, Nurse!'

Sister Simeon did not look ashamed, she looked blazing with anger.

'But, that is not the worst, there is the damage to valuable hospital property!'

May stared at her in astonishment, surely not, the scrubbing brush had already been rather battered.

'You folded the wet mackintoshes, how utterly careless of you, Nurse. Have you any idea of following instructions?'

May felt her jaw begin to drop. Sister looked at her sharply, then glanced at Bates. A degree of comprehension began to dawn on May.

'Nurse Bates did give you full instructions, did she not, Nurse Winton?' Sister's tone was ominous. Out of the corner of her eye May saw Bates give a convulsive gulp; the girl's hands were tightly clenched and the knuckles as white as her face. May knew fear when she saw it. From far back there flashed through her mind a memory of Archie hacking her viciously on the shin under the table when she had told

78

Nanny: 'Please, Nanny, it was Archie who threw the milk over the cat, not me.' – 'Tell-tale, May, little tell-tale tit. Gentlemen don't snitch.' Soundly bruised, May had tried to be a gentleman ever since. She took a deep breath and spoke firmly.

'I'm afraid I misunderstood Nurse Bates' instructions, Sister. The fault was mine; I sincerely apologise.'

Sister was still very angry. 'It is your job to do exactly as you are told, Nurse, not to think for yourself. Go back at once to deal with those mackintoshes, then go over to the Home and change yourself completely. Since that will take you at least fifteen minutes you must come back from your off-duty this afternoon a quarter of an hour early. Do you understand?'

'Yes, Sister. I'm sorry, Sister.'

'Nurse Bates, take Nurse Winton back to the sluice and instruct her in words of one syllable, please.' She picked up her pen.

May followed Bates out, feeling very subdued. Fortunately Bates was equally subdued; she showed May how to dry off the mackintoshes with a clean cloth and hang them over a clothes horse. As she went out of the door she muttered, 'When you come back, go and report to Sister. Always do that when you've been off the ward.'

'Thanks, I'll remember.'

Bates vanished. May finished her task as quickly as possible, then rushed out and back to the Nurses' Home. She lost her way once, but managed to re-orientate herself from the small chapel. In her room she found a note on her chest of drawers: 'Beds must always be left fully stripped. Home Sister.' May sighed, changed as quickly as possible, skewered her hair with all her remaining hairpins and then set off again for Simeon Ward.

Chapter Ten

Mindful of Bates' warning May presented herself to Sister, who was rustling down from the far end of the ward. She was subjected to a tight-lipped scrutiny, but thankfully Sister merely informed her that she was well behind with her work and she must sweep and dust the ward at once, then report to Staff Nurse. May rushed back clutching broom, box of dusters, shovel and bucket of tealeaves in an unwieldy bundle. Earlier, May's imagination had dwelt excitedly on the moment of her first entry on to a hospital ward as a fully-fledged nurse; it would be a dramatic and significant occasion. Instead she felt hot, flustered and awkward. Everything had been such a rush and her dress was tight and her starched collar bit into her neck as she bent down and dumped her tools on to the floor. She picked up her bucket, tipped it and threw a sweeping arc of tea leaves in front of her and began to savage them with the broom. Almost at once a hoarse voice called from her right.

'Nurse, Nurse.'

At first this made no impression on May at all; then suddenly she realised that the prone figure in the second bed was beckoning to her. Her heart sank; what could he want that she would possibly be able to do for him? She looked round, but all the other nurses were out of sight behind screens further up the ward. May was sorely tempted to rush up and tug at someone's skirts and beg them to come in her place, but the old man's gestures were becoming more frantic, and visions of delirium raced through her mind – he might fall out of bed while she was away. Squaring her shoulders she put down the broom and marched over to him.

'Yes? What can I do for you?'

To her relief it was obvious from the expression in the patient's eyes that he was alert and fully conscious; indeed, he appeared to be trying not to laugh.

'New, are yer, gal?'

May hesitated, then admitted, 'Yes, it is my first day. Can I help you?'

'No, lass, I can help you. Yer doin' it wrong.'

May bridled. 'Doing what wrong?'

'Everythin', so far. Ain't that right, 'Arold?'

May turned to the next bed. A blue-chinned individual with a squashed nose gave a faint nod as he lay propped up on his pillows. He panted, ' 'Sright. You tell 'er, Dad. She's only young.'

'I'm twenty-two!' May said indignantly.

'That's wrong, too,' the old man was chortling. 'You didn't oughter tell us personal things like that – Sister'd 'ave yer guts fer garters.'

'She already has done,' May rejoined gloomily.

'Right then, you listen to us. Yer gotter dust first, before yer sweeps.'

'Why?'

'Cor blimey, yer worse than a new recruit. 'Cos they always does it that way, that's why. Dust first, everywhere yer can find ter dust, dust it, fast. 'Ere, 'and me that glass, duck, Staff's looking this way. Now, put yer tools neat-like next the fire, don't leave 'em about like that – 'cos someone'll trip over 'em, that's why,' forestalling May's interjection. 'Yer'll 'ave ter move now, she's lookin' again. When yer done what I told yer come back and 'and me me glass again and I'll tell yer what to do next. Right, 'Arold?'

'Right, Dad.'

With a hurried word of thanks May stacked her utensils near the hearth, picked up her duster and began to rub everything she could see with it. Halfway up the ward a hollow-cheeked grey-faced man pushed himself up off the pillow and called her over.

'Aspidistra,' he gasped, then fell back exhausted. May looked wildly round, then rushed back to the centre table and

81

passed her duster over the glossy leaves. Then she was off again on her headlong charge.

'You are nearly running, Nurse Winton,' came the carrying tones of Sister stationed at the far bed. 'Nurses do not run other than in the case of fire or haemorrhage.'

'No, Sister, thank you, Sister,' a flustered May tossed the apology over her shoulder. Down the far side, back to the entrance, dusting frantically as she went, May felt the beginnings of a stitch, and was aware of her corset digging uncomfortably into her ribs. She trotted over to the old man; on her circuit she had noted the charts over the beds, and now with a quick flick upwards she read his name.

'Good morning Mr Tomkins. Would you like a drink of water?'

He grinned his approval as he took the glass. 'Thank yer, Nurse,' loudly, then, dropping to a conspiratorial tone, 'Now, get yer broom and put the end with the bristles on the floor.' Harold gave a sycophantic chuckle from the next bed, and May glared at Mr Tomkins. 'I have seen a broom used before!'

'I wouldn't ever've believed it. Throw an 'andful o' tea leaves on the floor, they lays the dust, see, then push the broom forrards – away from you, what yer was doing before put dirt all over yer shoes and stockings. Up this side, down the other, and keep level. If yer doing it wrong 'Arold an' me'll shake our 'eads. Orlright?'

'All right,' May echoed. She flashed a smile of thanks at him and then was off for her broom. Apart from banging into a trolley and earning a glance of reproof from Staff Nurse she got round the ward without mishap. Scrambling her implements together she returned them to the kitchen.

'Give 'em 'ere, Nurse. I'll empty yer shovel for you, just this once.'

'Thank you, I'm afraid I don't know your name – I'm Nurse Winton.'

The maid looked surprised, but pleased. She wiped her hand on her apron and held it out to May.

'Pleased ter meet yer, I'm sure. Me name's Roberts, Missus

82

Roberts, but you can call me Maudie, like the others.'

They shook hands and then May pounded back to the ward and thankfully noticed Staff Nurse at the centre table.

She put her hands behind her back and reported: 'I've dusted and swept, Staff.'

Staff Nurse's practised gaze scoured the ward. 'Fluff, third bed from the end, Nurse Winton, and the fourth locker on the right is crooked.' May panted off to rectify the faults. 'Well, it'll have to do, since it's your first day, but tomorrow Sister will run her finger over every ledge; it must be perfect. The bedpans are waiting for you in the sluice; wash them, and then bottles, test glasses and spitting mugs.' May swallowed, but as Staff moved away she hastily asked, 'Please, Nurse, would you show me the right way to do them?'

Staff Nurse gave an exasperated sigh, then, obviously having heard of the mackintosh episode said, 'Well, you are new. I'll send Pro Three to help you.'

May's spirits lifted when Pro Three turned out to be the helpful, dark-haired girl. She whisked down the ward with a smile, and the words, 'I'm Sellers, by the way,' as they went into the sluice. 'Bates didn't tell you what to do this morning, did she?'

May shook her head.

Sellers continued, 'Sister scares her stiff, and she takes it out on everyone else, if she gets the chance. She can't help it.'

'Well, I did upset her at breakfast, and my step-mother has often told me how tactless I am.'

Sellers grinned at May. 'Oh, so that was you, was it? You're certainly making an impression on your first day. Now for goodness' sake listen carefully and do just as I tell you – I haven't got long.'

Sellers reeled off her instructions; May listened intently.

'Lysol, this bottle here, put about that much,' finger held against the bottle, 'in the sink. Use this tow, and watch for the handles, they're hollow and you must get them absolutely clean inside, Staff will have a squint down them when you've finished. Bottles, urinals, that is, some of them get a bit smelly, put a piece of bicarb in and pour really hot water down their necks.'

It was obvious from the smell what these funnel-mouthed objects were used for, but May was puzzled. 'Why don't they just use bedpans, Nurse Sellers?'

'They do on a women's ward, but the men use bottles, it's really much easier.'

May still didn't understand. 'But however do they use them – isn't it rather awkward? And why only men?'

Sellers turned and stared at May. 'Have you no baby brothers, Winton?'

May shook her head.

'Oh dear,' Sellers hesitated, then her face cleared. 'You must have noticed male horses, what they do – well, men are the same. Only smaller, of course,' she added hastily.

May looked at Sellers in amazement. 'How very odd!'

Sellers was obviously trying not to smile. She said kindly, 'You'll see odder things than that in hospital. Now, these are spitting cups, you do know how they're used?'

'Yes, Nurse.' May peered inside. 'Ugh, how revolting!'

'Yes, I prefer bedpans myself, but actually you can learn a lot about a patient's condition from these, Winton. But just wash them out now, and put turps in the bottom when you've finished. Here it is. Test glasses, for urine, you know – don't touch them until you're sure they're finished with. If they're stained you can use some nitric acid, but only a few drops, mind, and be careful, it can give you a nasty burn. I must go now – if you're really in difficulties come and find me or Bates, but don't go near the ward while the honoraries are there, whatever you do though they mostly come round in the afternoon.'

Sellers was gone before May could ask who or what the honoraries were – they sounded like a variety of geranium, but presumably were something more important.

May marched resolutely over to the sink, turned on the hot tap and reached gingerly for the first bedpan. Suddenly Sellers was back; she opened a cupboard and handed May a piece of waterproof sheeting. 'Jaconet, pin that round you, otherwise you'll have no aprons left by the end of the week.'

'Thank you, Nurse.'

May picked up the lysol bottle and poured the recommended quantity into the sink.

Once she had overcome the initial feelings of nausea May found a certain satisfaction in attacking the bedpans; at least you knew where you were with bedpans, there was no pretence about them: and she had remembered to fill the urinals first so they could soak in their bicarb. She paused for a moment and stared at them in wonderment. Well, she had learnt something today, at least!

At ten o'clock Staff Nurse appeared at the sluice door. 'Haven't you finished yet, Winton? Really, you'll have to learn to work faster. Report to Sister at once.'

May's heart jumped. 'Why, what have I done wrong now?'

'Everything, very likely,' Staff Nurse replied, then relenting, 'She will send you off duty for half an hour to dust and sweep your own room and make your bed; and if you move quickly you'll have time to snatch a glass of milk in the dining room before you come back.'

May sped along the corridor to Sister's table and found Pro Two already there, being dismissed as well. She raced off and May panted after her, determined to find out the whereabouts of the brooms and dusters in the Nurses' Home. Having asked this May continued, 'Wouldn't it be easier for the maids to do our rooms?'

Pro Two, who had a rather unpleasant flat-vowelled accent replied tersely, 'We're cheaper. Do get a move on, Winton, otherwise I'm not waiting for you.'

It struck May that after years of being told to walk in a more decorous and ladylike manner she was now being constantly scolded for her slowness! She quickened into a trot, only to be told, 'Don't run, we aren't allowed to run except in cases of fire and haemorrhage – you'll get into trouble with Sister.'

'Which Sister?'

'Every Sister,' was the repressive reply, and May lapsed into silence and concentrated on copying Pro Two's scuttle – ungainly, but definitely fast.

Pro Two, though not particularly friendly, did give May

85

the help she needed, and twenty minutes later chivvied her down to the dining room where large pitchers of milk stood waiting and, to May's delight, piled slices of bread and basins of dripping. She spread a slice and then noticed one of the new probationers watching her.

'Hello, I'm May Winton. You started yesterday as well, didn't you?'

The girl nodded; she was tall and bony, but with striking features. Her voice was clear, 'Ada Farrar.' She shot out her hand.

May, perilously balancing glass and plate in her left hand shook it firmly. 'How are you getting on?' she asked.

Ada Farrar emitted a sound somewhere between a laugh and a snarl. 'Do you know, some little pipsqueak of a doctor, barely wet behind the ears, came into the ward this morning and we had to practically get down on our knees and salaam to him! Fancy, the Sister must be well into her fifties, she must know a thousand times more than he does, and yet she kowtows to him – just because he's a man!' She put down her glass with a bang and added, unnecessarily, May thought, 'I'm a suffragist, myself. Well, I suppose I'd better get back, I don't want another shouting match,' and flashing a smile surprising in its charm and vivacity she was off. May, cheered by the encounter, followed suit.

The rest of the morning passed in a whirl. May cleaned all the baths and basins and polished the taps, then she polished the taps again, since Staff Nurse said they were smeary. After this a great pile of soiled linen had to be sorted out, and the worst stained drawsheets rinsed out, since the laundry maids were apparently more fastidious than the nurses. As soon as the linen was neatly folded in its baskets, it all had to be taken out again while she searched for a patient's personal shirt that she had put in by mistake. By this stage May felt that she was spending as long undoing her tasks as she was doing them, and it was clear from Staff Nurse's terse comments that she shared this view.

Then she was back on the bedpans and bottles. 'But I did the bedpans this morning, Staff Nurse.'

'They've been used again, Winton.'

'Oh.'

'And there's the bandages to be washed, they're soaking in carbolic over there. Do get a move on, Winton.'

When she saw the bandages May felt sick – she thought she could have faced the bloodstains with stoicism, but the foul, yellow-green streaks of pus were another matter altogether, and she had to force herself to pick up the reeking slimy mass. She closed her eyes tightly and threw them into a sink full of hot soapy water. But eventually they had been scrubbed and hung out to dry and there was the exquisite relief of leaving the smelly sluice and being sent to cut bread for the patients' dinners. Once in the kitchen May would have been in further trouble had not Maudie come to her rescue and shown her the correct way to handle the knife – and even then the slices were either too thick or too thin.

Still, Staff Nurse's rebuke was followed by a summons to the ward, and May spent a hectic but interesting half hour rushing round with trays and plates of dinner, soon realising her worst mistakes would be either put right or concealed by the patients themselves: the more Sister harangued the junior pros the more the men closed ranks on their behalf. After dinner May scurried round the ward again with her broom, and then was sent to Sister to be dismissed for her own dinner.

'Nurses Sellers and Winton, you will be off-duty until five. You may go now.'

May's face lit up – three and a half hours without any scrubbing, sweeping or dusting, what bliss!

As they left the ward she said to Sellers: 'I was expecting another dressing-down from Sister. I seem to have made one mistake after another today.'

Sellers was reassuring. 'Well, it's obvious you've never done much housework but you'll learn. And you're really very lucky to be starting on Simeon – Sister's very fair, she only tells you off for what you have done wrong.'

'Well, I seem to have given her plenty of scope.' May's voice was rather downcast.

'Don't worry. Sister Simeon is a good teacher, she really

looks after her pros – after all, she came on early today specially, because it was your first day.'

May tried to look grateful, but privately she felt that she would prefer rather less consideration from Sister in future. She changed the subject.

'Nurse Sellers, are we allowed to go outside this afternoon?'

Sellers stared at her. 'Of course we are! This isn't a prison.'

'But I suppose we have to have a companion if we do go out?'

'Goodness – wherever do you come from? This is London, you know, not Casablanca. There are some areas, Limehouse, for instance, the Chinese quarter, that people say are dangerous at night, but personally I've always found them very respectful. I don't suppose you'll get dragged into an opium den in the middle of the afternoon. No, there's no problem about going out – it's if you don't get back by five o'clock that the trouble starts!'

By now they were at the dining room, and separated, May taking her place at her lowly table where she looked in dismay at the plate of watery stew and soggy potato that was slapped down in front of her. But she felt positively hollow inside, so she raised her knife and fork, remembering as she did so the delicious lunches sent up by Chef at Stemhalton. A wave of homesickness threatened to engulf her, but she fought it down and reached for the bread.

Chapter Eleven

As she came out of the dining room May caught sight of Alice
Rydal slowly climbing the stairs; she hurried after her and
caught her up.

'Were you thinking of going out for a walk this afternoon,
Miss Rydal?'

Alice looked horrified. 'I wouldn't dream of it! My feet are
on fire and my legs ache; I'm going to lie down and have a rest
until I have to drag myself back at five. I'm not walking a step
further than I have to. I've had the most disastrous morning:
if it wasn't Sister nagging me it was that awful Staff Nurse,
and the wretched wardmaid - I only asked her to clean the
broom properly next time!' Her voice was one long wail of
protest.

May commiserated, but although her calves were feeling a
little strained, her determination to venture outside and
sample the delights of three hours of freedom in the East End
was unshaken.

In her room she pulled her uniform cloak around her and
tied the strings of the curious little bonnet under her chin. Her
face looked back at her from the mirror as though decked in
fancy dress and she stepped out of the door and set off down
the corridor feeling like an actress in a play - 'Madam, the
nurse has arrived' - a domestic melodrama, perhaps? By the
time she had reached the main door she felt stifled in her
cloak, but unless she clutched it tightly round her it slid off her
shoulders and flapped around her skirts.

There were lots of people moving purposefully about the
large courtyards, and at first May expected any minute to be
the subject of a stern challenge - 'Nurse, wherever do you
think you're going? - but no one showed the slightest interest
in her, and she realised with a jolt that she was just another

anonymous uniformed figure. Yet mingled with this new and disconcerting awareness of her lowly status there was a sense of emancipation: to be just one more scurrying figure among seven hundred had its compensations. She saw the main entrance ahead and, like a hound heading for open country she rushed under the archway and out onto the pavement. Outside the noise was deafening. Loaded drays and wagons piled high with goods clattered and rumbled over the granite setts, their cargoes swaying perilously, while a tram sped whining down the centre of the road. May stood quite still and stared.

''Scuse us, ducks.' A woman carrying two large baskets elbowed her out of the way, and May jumped back flattening herself against the hospital railings. She looked up; directly in front of her, suspended against the blue, smoke-smeared sky was a tracery of masts and yards and soaring crane jibs, rising above the long, blank wall of the docks. Before, all her attention had been focused on the hospital; now she began to take in its surroundings.

May looked to the left – the dock wall was unbroken; she turned in the other direction and saw it curve away from her, and the distinctive shape of a clock tower. She took a firm hold on her cloak, waited for a second tram to pass and then stepped out into the road, dodged through a gap in the traffic and made for that promising curve. Just beyond it was the dock entrance. She peered through the open gates and spotted men trundling loaded trolleys and boxes hanging suspended, swaying in the air beside the looming bulk of a hull. But as she leant forward there was a clatter of hooves and she hastily jumped aside as a laden cart bore down on the entrance. The driver grinned and touched his cap, and May was surprised, then realised he was saluting her uniform and smiled quickly back.

She looked around her: the high dock wall continued on the other side of the gateway, but across the road were the grey-green leaves of shrubs in a public garden, with a stream of traffic turning down beyond it. She walked along the main road to see more and there was the steep incline running down to the dark mouth of the tunnel – the tunnel which ran under the Thames itself. The Thames! Crossing the tunnel road May took the next turning and walked briskly down. She negotiated a junction and found herself passing under the iron balconies of several ugly blocks of flats; but the road continued to slope down, so she was convinced she was heading in the right direction. There was a sharp turn left and then, quite suddenly, the road stopped and the river began.

The water moved gently against the stones with a soft, slapping noise, and as she watched a sailing barge glided past, closely followed by the panting, puffing disturbance of a little paddle steamer which sent ripples up the causeway. May gazed entranced at the shining river. Then a cloud crossed the sun, the water turned leaden and dull, and the spell was broken. She turned away and walked back up the street, more slowly now, and her legs began to remind her of their busy morning.

When she came in sight of the clock above the centre arch of the dock gate she saw that it was still only half past two, so she veered away from the hospital entrance and set off down the East India Dock Road. She was fascinated by the variety of the shops and buildings and eating houses, and was constantly getting in people's way and being jostled as she stopped to stare, already convinced that the East End was an altogether livelier and more exciting place than the West.

She paused to read the menu emblazoned across the front of one eating house: 'Meat pie, Pie crust and potatoes' – that was plain enough, but whatever were 'Saveloys'? And were German sausages different from British ones? And why did you eat them with Pudding, and Black Pudding, at that? She must ask Chef to explain when she next saw him. A most appetising smell was drifting out of the doorway, and May's mouth began to water. She peeped in, but the room was dark and crowded with men and women talking in high Cockney voices and gesticulating with their knives and forks – it seemed like a foreign world and May felt suddenly very shy and out of place. Her nerve failed her, and she was stepping back from the threshold when a voice from inside called:

91

'Miss Winton, over here!' Astounded, she peered into the gloom and saw a blue-bonneted figure waving from a small table in the corner – it was her sad-faced companion of breakfast, Nurse Carter!

May stepped inside and threaded past the busy tables.

'How very lucky, a girl's just left, there's a spare seat – I was *so* hungry this morning, and that cabbage was nasty, wasn't it? I'm Ellen Carter, by the way.' The words came out in a rush.

May murmured, 'How do you do? My name is May Winton,' and sat down. Ellen Carter was working her way through a piled-up plate of round brown objects accompanied by mashed potato and peas, all liberally doused with thick gravy. May gazed at the plate longingly and decided to waste no more time.

'How do I order?'

'There's a man,' said Ellen vaguely. 'He tells you what's good today – these are faggots, apparently, they're very tasty, but they cost more if they're hot, so if you haven't much money . . .' She looked at May, suddenly worried. 'Oh, I didn't think perhaps that's why you weren't coming in!'

May hastily reassured her and, the waiter appearing at that moment, ordered the same as her companion.

The faggots, though lacking the subtlety of the food May was accustomed to, were a great improvement on their lunchtime stew, and although she and Ellen could not actually identify the meat used they decided there were onions in them somewhere. Since the waiter recommended the Currant Roly Poly as well as the Jam Pudding they compromised on both and washed them down with strong sweet tea.

'How did you get on this morning?' May asked.

Ellen's face fell, and her eyes filled with tears. 'Oh, it was dreadful, that wretched Sister just shouted at me all morning – and when she wasn't shouting the Staff Nurse hissed – you know, she was just like a gander we've got at home,' Ellen lengthened her neck and flapped her arms in a parody, while hissing loudly across the table. Embarrassed, May looked round at their fellow diners, but they seemed oblivious to Ellen's antics, and May reddened at her own embarrassment. Ellen, rapidly restored to cheerfulness, reached for her purse. 'We've still got some time left, shall we explore? This is the first time I've ever been in London, except for my interview with Matron. I must say, it's very interesting. Have you ever been here before?'

'Not to this area,' May said cautiously. 'I live in the country, most of the year.'

'So do I, all the year. My father's a stationmaster in Devon. It's only a very small station, but very pretty. I helped out at the cottage hospital nearby, but I felt like a change. What does your father do?'

May hesitated, then said, 'He doesn't do anything, actually, – well he rides round to see the tenant farmers sometimes, but only when he feels like it.'

Ellen's eyes widened. 'Goodness, are your family some of the Idle Rich?'

May said apologetically, 'I suppose we are.'

'Oh, you don't have a *title*, do you?'

'I don't, but my father does.'

'What a shame, I was hoping you might be Lady May – it would have sounded impressive in my letter home!' Then she leant forward and whispered, 'Really, it's just as well – my father's a Socialist, though he wouldn't want the Railway Company to know, so he wouldn't at all approve of my dining out with the aristocracy – even if it was only on faggots and peas!' Ellen threw back her head and laughed out loud, and after a moment May joined her.

The next hour passed rapidly. May found it far pleasanter walking with a companion, and Ellen shared her enthusiasm for all the new sights. They stopped, and stared, and tripped over the paving stones because they weren't looking where they were going, and generally got in people's way. But the East Enders, although they pushed their way past, seemed mostly easy-going and friendly, and several times they were addressed as 'Nurse' to their great pride. They looked in shop doorways and gazed at the puffs of steam escaping from

Poplar Baths, speculating on what 'slipper baths' were, Ellen maintaining people must get into the bath wearing their slippers, while May contended it must mean that you actually bathed your slippers, instead of yourself. Then May read out the legend on the statue of Mr George Green, Shipbuilder, only to find Ellen, eyes brimming, gazing at the sculpted dog at the foot of the statue, wailing softly.

'Oh his dog, it's the image of our Sammy at home!'

May, who had begun to understand the mercurial nature of Ellen's temperament, hastily seized her arm and whisked her across the road in search of distraction.

They were just tasting the delights of the edge of the Chinese quarter – 'Oh, May – pigtails, a man with a *pigtail*!' – when they saw a clock and May remembered that she had to be back on duty fifteen minutes early, so they started trotting, May in her anxiety setting a spanking pace. Ellen clasped her side and complained of a stitch, but May noticed that she had no difficulty in keeping up, and still had eyes for her surroundings, so she decided that Ellen's frail appearance must be deceptive.

Gasping for breath and sweating under their long cloaks they swept past the gloomy gaze of the tortoise and up to their rooms to tidy themselves. Then May headed for Simeon Ward, and left Ellen to enjoy whatever St Katharine's chose to offer their nurses in the way of tea. Ellen's hopes were not high but the unscheduled meal on the Dock Road had obviously not damped down her appetite, and May felt a pang of envy – she was hungry again too. But the thought of an angry Sister Simeon was amazingly invigorating, and she ran up the stairs to the ward as fast as she dared.

Hot, clammy air enveloped May as she entered the ward; the high collar, which she had scarcely noticed over the afternoon, cut into her neck, and her shoes began to feel several sizes too small. May had a sudden vision of the airy, cool drawing room at Allingham, windows flung open to the terrace; and she thought of the pleasure of strolling in the gardens on a warm evening such as this. The ward windows were open, but the air was heavy and still; it had the stale, used-up feel of the city. The fire had been allowed to die down, but it still glowed sullenly in the central pillar, adding unwanted warmth to the atmosphere.

Sister's chair was empty, and May stood irresolute until she saw her emerge from the screens round a bed further up the ward. She was followed by Bates, pushing a trolley and looking utterly miserable. Sister was as erect as ever, her apron smooth and white, her cap crisp and fresh; she seemed totally unscathed by the heat. The sight stiffened May's pride and she stood to attention by the table.

Sister Simeon looked her up and down, said: 'Your cap is crooked, Nurse Winton,' then sent her off to Staff Nurse, who directed her into the sluice.

'There's a lot of cleaning to do, Nurse, just get on with it.'

Besides the inevitable bottles and bedpans there was a pile of dirty bowls and slimy rubber tubes, and the smell was nauseating. May gazed up at the tightly closed high window, then made up her mind. She pushed the table across to the sink, clambered up and over the draining board to the window sill. She stretched up and tugged the latch; at first it would not budge, then it gave with a sudden jerk and almost tipped her into the sink full of bedpans. Despite the still evening the atmosphere immediately smelt less foul. As she turned to climb down she saw a red-haired young man in a white coat grinning at her from the doorway. May did not return his smile.

'Would you like some help, Nurse?'

Before he could move, May, mindful of Home Sister's warnings and remembering the last time she had been assisted in her climbing, spoke coldly.

'No, thank you. Please close the door as you leave.'

He blinked, opened his mouth, then closed it again and went out, shutting the door behind him. Relieved, May jumped down to the floor and began to attack the bed-pans.

A couple of minutes later the door opened and Sister looked in.

'Who opened that window, Nurse Winton?'

95

May felt slightly apprehensive, but was determined to stand firm on this issue.

'I did, Sister. It smelt in here.'

'Did you open it by yourself?'

'Yes, Sister, entirely.'

Sister Simeon actually smiled. 'Then make sure you close it again before you go off duty: the night nurses are not so athletic. Now, as soon as you've finished in here and helped with the patients' suppers and done the washing up, come to me on the ward. I want you to assist with the evening dressings.'

May assented eagerly. That sounded much more interesting than washing bedpans.

Apart from a lecture from Staff Nurse on the stupidity of trying to wash greasy knives and forks before the cups and glasses – 'Any one would think you'd never washed up in your life before, Winton!' – May managed to get through the next hour without mishap, and to present herself to Sister as commanded. Sister ushered her into the ward entrance, away from the nearest beds, but where she could still see the whole ward.

'Now, Nurse Winton, this is a surgical ward, which means that all our patients have had, or are about to have, an operation, and as a result they are left with open wounds. You will need much more experience before you are able to deal with these wounds yourself, but I make a practice of taking all my new probationers on a dressing round with me, so that they understand the condition of the patients. You will make beds with more care when you have seen what lies under the bandages,' she added grimly. 'Left to itself the body tissues have the power to heal cleanly, but if germs invade, then the wound does not heal, it suppurates.' May raised her eyebrows in a question. 'The flesh around the wound rots, Nurse, and there is pus. It is our job to fight a battle against the invasion of germs, so we clean and disinfect constantly – that has been the purpose of your work in the sluice today, Nurse Winton.' May nodded in dawning comprehension. 'But everything we use for dressing the wound itself must be better than that, it must be sterilized – boiled – to kill the germs. My hands are not sterile, so I will use instruments which are; and your hands are not sterile either, remember that, Nurse Winton; however much you scrub them, your hands are dangerous.'

May jumped, and gave an involuntary glance down at her hands, reddened by the day's work but looking quite innocuous to the naked eye.

'Unfortunately,' Sister continued, 'we rarely succeed in banishing all germs, and so the wound becomes septic, or poisoned. Now you will know that rotten meat has a disagreeable odour – so does rotting flesh, Nurse Winton, and you cannot open a window on a living patient, so you will have to endure the stench.' Sister paused, and looked enquiringly at May.

'I will try to do so, Sister.'

Sister Simeon's tone hardened. 'You will not *try* to do so, you *will* do so, and you will do it with a smile on your face. Do you understand?' she rapped out the question.

May gulped. 'Yes Sister,' her voice squeaked.

Sister Simeon's tone softened a fraction. 'Remember, if you were lying there feeling wretched with a stinking wound you would not want to see a nurse wrinkling up her nose and looking disgusted. Now come with me.'

May, by now heartily wishing that she had found out rather more about nursing before she had plunged into this new and now frightening world, duly followed.

Sister's hands worked swiftly and surely as she assembled her dressing trolley, explaining clearly and concisely the purpose of every object. May stood nodding like a puppet doll, repeating her 'Yes Sisters' every time Sister Simeon's voice rose in interrogation. As Sellers had said this morning, Sister was a good teacher; but May began to wish for a less enthusiastic superior who would have let her lurk in the sluice for the evening – even those dreadful bandages would have been preferable, at least you didn't have to smile at them.

All too soon they were rattling up the ward, and at the bedside of the first victim.

'Screens, Nurse – no, not like that, another two inches to

97

the right – a screen is a *screen*, Nurse Winton.' May understood then, and positioned them more carefully.

'Good evening, Mr Hawkins. I have come to do your dressing myself this evening, and Nurse Winton is assisting me.'

The man in the bed whispered a response. May, already aware of a pervasive and unpleasant scent smiled weakly at his hands, which were calloused and grey. Sister twitched back the bedclothes and began to undo the bandage round his middle.

'Hold that receiver just there, Nurse Winton, where I can reach it easily – come nearer.'

As the bandage came away green streaks began to appear, and the smell grew stronger. Wielding her forceps Sister dumped the sodden mass into the bowl right under May's nose. She felt her smile become a rictus as she gripped the enamel rim, remembering Sister's final warning words before they had started up the ward: 'Don't forget, a poisoned wound is a danger to you, Nurse. Never touch septic dressings with your hands if you can possibly avoid it.' She felt her skin crawl. Sister deposited the last sodden piece of gauze, said, 'Brace yourself, Mr Hawkins, this will hurt,' and with a deft flick of the wrist pulled out a wriggling red worm. May swayed, but Sister Simeon's brisk voice steadied her. 'This is the drainage tube, Nurse Winton. The other receiver, please.' May dumped one bowl down with a clatter and picked up the other to take its disgusting cargo.

Sister paused, her face a mask of concentration. Then she said, 'I think your wound looks a little healthier today, Mr Hawkins, but I'm afraid I shall have to get more of the poison out. Mr Hawkins has had a damaged kidney removed, Nurse Winton. Now, hold that dish near the wound.' The wound was actually a largish hole in the man's side, and Sister proceeded to place both hands on his stomach and flank and squeeze firmly; a thin stream of green pus oozed out. May stared in horror, and felt the bile rise in her throat; but just before she gagged she heard a slight mewling sound. She turned her head and looked fully at the man on the bed. The veins on his forehead stood out, and his jaw was clenched; his eyes were staring straight at her – and there was a desperate question in them. A flood of pity and comprehension washed over May: the stench faded into the background, she looked directly into the pain-wracked eyes and spoke in a firm and cheerful voice.

'Don't worry, Mr Hawkins, it's nearly over now – not much longer, you've been very brave,' and she felt her face blossom into a smile as easily and naturally as breathing. The thin lips quivered in response, and then, thankfully, Sister Simeon's assured voice rang out.

'The worst's over, Mr Hawkins, you can relax now,' and incredibly the man did relax, while Sister's nimble fingers re-packed the wound with a clean rubber tube and yards of gauze, cottonwool and lint. Sister explained her actions clearly, but May was hardly listening: her legs were trembling and her forehead damp with sweat. Once the binder was fastened into position with a large safety-pin Sister straightened up.

'Move the screens back, Nurse.' May did so, hoping that Sister could not see that her hands were shaking uncontrollably. 'Now take the trolley back into the sluice, I'll be along in a few minutes to tell you what to do next.'

May managed to get the trolley out of the ward and into the sluice, then she leapt for the sink and was thoroughly sick. A slight breeze had sprung up and cooled her flushed face as she sagged weakly against the draining board. She had coped, but it had been a close-run thing and she felt no exultation in the victory. Then she heard Sister's brisk footsteps in the corridor, and reached for the carbolic.

An hour later she had been initiated into the mysteries of the steriliser and had helped Sister with four more dressings, none as bad as the first. She decided that Sister Simeon was an exponent of Lady Clarence's philosophy: always tackle the worst task first, then what comes after is, if not easy, at least bearable. As she helped Sister settle each patient down after their dressing, and saw the relief, even contentment, on their faces as they lay back on their pillows she began to feel a sense

99

of satisfaction at her share in their tending. The last man, an elderly Scot far from home, murmured, 'Ah, you're a guid wee lassie, and a bonny one,' and made May blush with pleasure.

At ten minutes to eight the lights were shaded, all the nurses grouped themselves around the centre table and got down on their knees on the hard floor, to hear Sister read prayers. May glanced through her lashes at the silent ward, the patients lying still in their beds, their serious faces turned towards the small group of women kneeling under the dimmed light. Sister's voice was as fresh and clear as it had been at seven o'clock that morning, and as May scrambled to her feet, legs stiff and aching, she felt a profound admiration for this formidable woman. While the nurses stood to attention Sister, lamp in hand, made her round of the calm ward, speaking quietly to each patient in turn.

Then Sellers took May into the kitchen and instructed her on the art of making custards and jellies for the next day, but May was slow and clumsy, and Sellers did most of the work.

'I expect you're tired, Winton. The first day is pure hell, I'll never forget it.'

'Nor will I,' May agreed fervently.

At nine o'clock the two night nurses arrived, each with a basket on her arm, and while Staff Nurse reported on the patients Sister dismissed the day staff one by one. When she finally came to May she looked her up and down then said, 'You have a lot to learn, Nurse Winton.'

May bent her head as she murmured, 'Yes, Sister.'

'Still, at least you don't repeat your mistakes. You've done well enough for the first day, I suppose.'

To May this qualified approval seemed like an accolade; she set her shoulders further back and said a firm, 'Thank you, Sister, good night,' before marching out of the ward with head held high.

Chapter Twelve

For May, the next two months were a flurry of activity. Learning new skills and absorbing new ideas took all her energies. Her experience was a mixture of discoveries, mistakes, humiliations and the occasional hard-won triumph.

A week after their arrival the six new probationers attended their first lecture. May listened with rapt attention to the consultant surgeon's tales of staphylococci and streptococci; she wrestled with the concepts of asepsis and antisepsis, and slowly assembled the assorted pieces of the jigsaw until they formed the pattern of Sister Simeon's deft hands as she prepared the dressings trolley and cleansed the patients' wounds.

The following day May stepped eagerly onto the ward, determined to put her newfound knowledge to the test – and was banished to the sluice and the bedpans. But as she mechanically scrubbed she repeated to herself the words she had learnt: tetanus, erysipelas, cellulitis; and, less euphonious, gangrene – mysteriously both dry and wet. However Staff Nurse rapidly brought her down to earth again by seizing her bedpans, squinting down the handles with a practised eye and instantly rejecting two: 'Really, Winton, have you no sense of pride in your work?' May forced her attention back into more mundane channels.

The following week she managed to achieve minor notoriety in the hospital by burning a whole panful of boiled eggs, and was forced to sit at the dining table with cheeks on fire while the story went the rounds of her fellow nurses – 'How can anyone burn boiled eggs?' 'Don't ask me, ask Winton, she knows how,' and there were squeals of delighted laughter until Home Sister half-rose ominously from her chair and the merriment subsided into whispered giggles. Yet this embarrassment was less upsetting than the carefully emphatic assurances of the eggs' owners that they had not really felt like one today, anyway. The next morning, having discovered from Maudie the whereabouts of a reliable dairy, May rushed out in her two hours off-duty and bought replacements, carrying them carefully back together with a lame tale of an anonymous lady donor who just happened to have had a surplus of eggs. But she could see that the men had guessed the truth and were uncomfortable at the idea of her spending her meagre salary on them, so in the end she wondered whether it would have been better to accept their generous understanding and simply swallow her own feelings of guilt. Sister Simeon, who was clearly aware of the existence of the Frears fortune, let May flounder on with her explanations to the patients, and seemed to derive a sardonic amusement from her discomfiture.

Yet there were compensations in the continuous back-breaking round: she had learnt to make a bed so that the undersheet was satin-smooth and there were exactly ten squares of the checked bedspread hanging from the foot – 'Not, nine, Nurse Winton, not eleven, but *ten*!' And she was at last allowed to wash a bedridden patient single-handed. Anxiously muttering to herself a litany composed of: 'Hot water, bowls, soap, screens, *two* pieces of flannel, don't forget to close the windows,' she had approached the elderly patient with what she hoped was a fair imitation of professional confidence. So intense had been her concentration on doing everything in the right order that the embarrassment of washing a naked male had completely passed her by. When she had finished, the tired, lined face had smiled at her, murmuring, 'Thanks, Nurse. I feel really freshened up,' and he had settled back on his pillows and dropped off to sleep. May felt ten feet tall as she almost waltzed back to the sluice with her bowls of dirty water – only to be met with: 'You must speed up, Nurse Winton, you've taken far too long,' as she passed Sister's desk. Then Sister Simeon had smiled at her crestfallen face and added, 'But otherwise you managed very well, and I was pleased to see that you took the trouble to

102

warm the towel as well as the change of clothing.' May sang tunelessly to herself as she attacked the mackintoshes that morning.

Then the new pros had discovered the little recess in the corridor of the Nurses' Home fitted out with two gas rings, a kettle and saucepan. Using the sturdy white earthenware cups and saucers which they bought in Chrisp Street market, they made drinks after supper and took them into each other's rooms and capped each other's tales of the day's disasters. May thought Alice Rydal too ready to whine her complaints, but Ellen's odd mixture of ingenuousness and self-mockery made them all laugh, while they were alternately impressed and shocked by Ada Farrar's trenchant criticisms of public institutions in general and St Katharine's Hospital in particular.

As they shared stories of aching backs and sore feet and tired legs May realised that she was lucky; after the first few days she rarely reached the point of exhaustion. Some of their duties were boring and repetitive, but they did not drain her physical strength as seemed to be the case with Alice Rydal, Minnie Emms and tiny Flossy Allen; while Ellen, and even Ada, sometimes came off duty with white faces and dark rings round their eyes. Also, the enforced punctuality and petty restrictions of life in the Nurses' Home sat more easily on her shoulders; after years of having every move monitored by Lady Clarence it could only be to her advantage that now the attentions of Home Sister and her three acolytes were dispersed among a crowd of probationers. Even her step-mother's homilies, bitterly resented at the time, could be viewed philosophically as useful preparation for the relentless barrage of criticism delivered by Sisters and Staff Nurses.

One Tuesday evening in late November, May and Ellen discovered to their mutual pleasure that they had both been granted a half-day off the following afternoon; even Ada's reminder that they would have to be back for an evening lecture failed to damp their anticipation, and they made plans for a rapid exit immediately after dinner.

103

The next day was dull and rather cold, with a blustery wind which whipped grit into their faces as they came off-duty, but May and Ellen were undaunted – it was their holiday and they were determined to enjoy it. They wasted no time on changing but simply threw on cloaks and bonnets and headed for the front door. Home Sister emerged from her lair nearby, looked them over and barked, 'Where are your umbrellas, Nurses? The weather is inclement.'

Ellen hesitated but May retorted firmly, 'It will not rain on our half-day, Sister,' and took Ellen's arm to steer her past.

'Remember you must return by six o'clock for Dr Colson's lecture.' Home Sister fired her parting shot as they crossed the threshold.

Ellen sighed. 'They always get the last word, don't they?'

May was bracing. 'Never mind. Just think, one day it will be our turn!'

Ellen's face was doubtful. 'I'm not sure I can see myself as ever being a Sister, May. I don't much like the idea of bossing other people around.'

As they raced for the main gate May had to admit to herself that she longed to move up the ladder and be able to tell other people what to do; even being Pro Four would be an improvement on her present lowly position. Obviously Ellen had a much nicer nature than she had.

Once outside they realised they had given no thought as to where they were going to go, but as they skidded to a halt, uncertain, May saw a tram coming, heading westwards. Calling to Ellen to follow she dodged a cursing van driver and in seconds they were both scrambling aboard.

'Upstairs, May, we'll see more.'

May hesitated, then seized her skirts and climbed up – after all, Lady Clarence was not around to notice.

'All the way, please,' Ellen told the conductor. Then, as they paid their fares, 'By the way, where do you go?'

'Terminus is Aldgate – 'Eart of the Empire!' The man winked and passed on.

'Oh May, let's go to the Houses of Parliament – I know they're not in session, but there's bound to be someone around. My father's said so much about this government – and I would love to see if all the Lords really do have cloven hooves and forked tails! – Not *your* father, of course,' she added hastily.

'My father doesn't sit in the Lords, his is only a courtesy title,' May said. 'And Uncle Bertie's far too lazy to go very often.'

'Well, never mind, we'll just stand outside and gawp, like a pair of country cousins – and I'll send my father a postcard to show we've been.'

They jumped off at Aldgate Pump and went in search of further directions. After a confused stream of instructions they decided on a horse bus and stepped onto the platform and clambered up the stairs. After the swift, smooth roar of the electric tram it seemed quite old-fashioned to watch the driver cracking his whip or skilfully checking his horses with a touch on the reins, as they sat high up in the front seat, glad of the strong ribbons on their bonnets in the gusting wind.

A change of buses found them outside Blackfriars Station, where they selected another tram and whirred down the broad, tree-lined sweep of the Victoria Embankment. They were so engrossed in looking about them that they nearly missed their stop, and barely had time to leap off before the tram turned sharp left and clanked across Westminster Bridge.

May pointed out the imposing blocks of St Thomas' Hospital on the other side of the river. Ellen gazed with interest, then spoke firmly.

'Well, it looks more impressive than ours, but I'm sure St Katharine's is better. Now, which House is which? I do wish we could go inside – I suppose you've been in, you are lucky, May!'

They circled round the Palace of Westminster, Ellen moving in a series of quick rushes and sudden stops, neck craned, quite impervious to where she was going. May stood still to have a good look at the Westminster Hospital opposite – after all, she had seen the Houses of Parliament before. At the moment she found hospitals far more interesting – it did look very cramped, it must be quite dark inside some of the

105

wards. Just then she heard Ellen's clear, light voice raised in a flurry of apologies.

'Oh dear, I am so sorry, it was entirely my fault – do let me brush your hat down for you, it's only a little mud.'

With a sinking heart May realised that her friend had cannoned into a gentleman alighting from a hansom, and instead of passing on with a slight bow she was actually chattering to him! Ellen really was far too countrified sometimes. May was stepping forward to take charge when she realised that there was something familiar about the slight, well-groomed back in front of her, and as he turned in her direction she recognised the small, neat features and saw that the man politely struggling with Ellen for the control of his headwear was Lord Hindlesham. Good, she might be able to make Ellen's wish come true after all, providing the latter had done no irreparable damage to his glossy black top hat! May moved forward with hand outstretched.

'Lord Hindlesham, what a pleasant surprise.'

Lord Hindlesham momentarily released his hold on the hat, which Ellen seized triumphantly and began to dust down with her pocket handkerchief, and stared in amazement at May for a second; then his good manners reasserted themselves and he seized her gloved hand and shook it heartily.

'Miss Winton – I didn't recognise you at first in your uniform. So you went ahead with your decision: you really are nursing!'

May blushed. 'Well, I'm doing the work of a scullerymaid at the moment, though I am occasionally allowed near a patient! But please, do let me introduce my friend, Miss Ellen Carter, who is also a probationer at St Katharine's – Miss Carter, Lord Hindlesham.'

Ellen's eyes were a rounded 'Oh' as she heard the title, and for a dreadful moment May thought she was going to ask Lord Hindlesham to remove his glossy boots so that she could inspect his feet for cloven hooves, but she restrained herself, smiled prettily and held out her hand.

'Good afternoon – would you like your hat back? The dent is only a very little one.'

May noticed Lord Hindlesham's lips twitch, but his voice was quite steady as he replied, 'It's of no consequence. Indeed, I'm grateful for the mischance which has brought us all together. And now, please, may I escort you anywhere?'

Ellen looked hopefully at May and the latter replied with decision.

'Yes, if you would be so kind. Miss Carter would very much like to see inside the House of Lords.' She could not resist adding, 'She has made a particular study of the subject.'

Ellen blushed, then leant forward and spoke confidingly to Lord Hindlesham.

'My father often talks of you all, he thinks your House should be abolished and all peers should be banished utterly from the counsels of government – in the interests of democracy, of course; he has no personal animosity,' she added reassuringly.

May could only be thankful that it was Lord Hindlesham they had bumped into, rather than Uncle Bertie who, though rarely gracing the Upper Chamber with his presence, would have gone to the guillotine in defence of his right to do so. Nor was the Marquis of Andover noted for his sense of humour, whereas Lord Hindlesham appeared to be amused by Ellen's wholesale condemnation. He beamed at her, saying, 'Then, Miss Carter, I insist on showing you round while there is still time, since imminent dissolution is threatened. Perhaps I may even be able to overcome your principles and prevail on you to take tea with me? Come along.'

As Lord Hindlesham led the way in, Ellen turned to May and whispered, 'What sort of Lord is he?'

May hissed back, 'An Earl.'

'Goodness, yet he seems so nice!'

Lord Hindlesham had clearly overheard. He looked back with a smiling face. 'I shall have to point out a Duke to you, Miss Carter, so you can see that even he has neither horns nor a forked tail!'

May was pleased to see that at this uncanny prescience Ellen went beetroot red and was temporarily silenced.

Their tour completed, Lord Hindlesham took them for the

promised tea. Over their cups of fragrant Earl Grey he became more serious, and began to question them more closely about their recent experiences.

'St Katharine's is in Poplar, isn't it? The Labour Member for Woolwich, Mr Crooks, has often spoken in the Lower House of the conditions there. What has struck you particularly, as newcomers to the East End?'

May hesitated. 'We've only been there a couple of months, you know.'

'Nevertheless, that is two months longer than any of us here.' His gesture encompassed the small number of his fellow peers who were placidly occupied in chewing their way through buttered crumpets and strawberry jam. 'What are your first impressions? I don't suppose you've stayed in the hospital all day.'

May and Ellen glanced at each other, then in turn they painted verbal pictures of what they had seen in their off-duty times. May had tended to walk westward: she described the looming walls of the London Dock, overshadowing and cutting off light from all the streets around, in which drunken men lurched from one dingy public house to another; and where she had once peered into an opium den – a dull, dispiriting place, but an opium den nonetheless.

Ellen had not gone so far afield; she had ventured down the narrow streets near the hospital. 'Some are quite nice, you know, with flowers in window boxes and friendly cats sitting sunning themselves on doorsteps, but others,' – she shuddered, – 'the children look so pinched and pale, and they have no coats, or even shoes, sometimes, and their noses run and they have sores on their faces.' Then she stopped, and her face was serious as she gazed straight at their host.

'I don't know whether you are a Liberal or a Tory, Lord Hindlesham, but I am a Socialist, and I don't think either of you care much for these people.'

There was a silence, and May held her breath.

Lord Hindlesham's face was as grave as Ellen's as he looked back at her. But when he spoke his voice was gentle.

'Believe me, Miss Carter, some of us do care. But the

108

machinery of government is complicated, and there are many conflicting interests to be reconciled.'

Then Ellen said, the country burr in her voice very pronounced, 'But I don't suppose your children go hungry to school.' She pushed her chair back and was on her feet before Lord Hindlesham could rise, and with a muttered, 'I'm sorry, it's rather hot in here, I will go and look at the river,' she slipped through the door and out onto the terrace.

May felt acute embarrassment. Lord Hindlesham was gazing after the retreating figure, his face unreadable. As he slowly resumed his seat, May spoke.

'I am so sorry, I must apologise for Ellen, she comes from a different background, her father is only a country station-master, she does not always realise . . .' May's voice trailed off as Lord Hindlesham turned and leant towards her.

'Miss Winton, May, until very recently you have lived amongst a very small group of people, a highly privileged group who think that they are right, and those who differ from them are wrong. Now, since by your own courage and initiative you have broken away, don't spoil this opportunity by clinging to the same narrow prejudices. Don't be ashamed of your friend: her views are valid ones, and she has the right to express them openly, whatever company she is in.'

May bowed her head over her empty plate.

Lord Hindlesham's voice was kind. 'Dear me, now I have distressed two young ladies. Come along, let's go and find your friend on the terrace.'

May forced a smile. 'We had better, before she overbalances and falls into the river in her anxiety not to miss any detail of each passing tugboat.'

As soon as they were outside Ellen came running to meet them, her face alight. 'Do look, May, you can see the little white caps of the nurses in the windows of St Thomas'. Do you think the men working in the Docks can see us in the same way?' Then she turned to Lord Hindlesham. 'First I almost knock you over, then I kidnap your hat, and now I have insulted your political beliefs – and you have been so kind – can you forgive me?'

Lord Hindlesham's serious mood evaporated in seconds. 'Political insults are meat and drink to us peers, you know; this is the place for them.' He smiled at Ellen. 'The pleasure has been mine, Miss Carter, and in return – yes, there he is, look, that gentleman who's just come out of the far door – there is a real live Duke for you!'

May recognised the short, fat, red-faced figure of the Duke of Dorset, clutching a cigar almost as fat as himself. Ellen gazed at him intently.

'Which one is he?' she whispered to Lord Hindlesham. When he told her she looked again. 'He's rather small, isn't he?'

Lord Hindlesham drew himself up and balanced on the balls of his feet, murmuring, 'Some of us lords aren't quite full size, you know,' then laughed at Ellen's confusion. 'Shall I introduce you? I think May has met him before.'

Ellen shook her head. 'No, I think an Earl is quite enough for one day – my father would never forgive me if I spoke to a Duke as well. Oh, May, the time!' as Big Ben boomed above them. 'We'll be late for the lecture!'

'Goodness, it took us ages to get here.' May pulled her cloak around her. 'I'm so sorry, Lord Hindlesham, we must rush off – you've no idea how strict they are – we get black marks if we're just a minute late for breakfast.'

Lord Hindlesham ushered them swiftly through the House. At the front entrance he said, 'I'll ask the man to call a cab to take you back, then you'll be in good time.'

But as May opened her mouth to give a grateful assent Ellen broke in, 'Thank you very much, but that would be rather poor-spirited of us, we must learn to find our own way about. I shall ask the policeman.' And she approached the enormous moustached bobby on duty outside the door.

May and Lord Hindlesham exchanged rueful grins and waited.

Ellen was soon back, her face cheerful. 'It's all right, May, we can go on the underground railway, all the way to Aldgate.'

110

May immediately perked up. 'Oh, good – I've never been on one of those. But won't we get horribly dirty?'

Ellen shook her head. 'No, that's the best of it. He says all the trains on that route are electric now, and it's nice and clean. Thank you so much, Lord Hindlesham, I have enjoyed our visit.'

Lord Hindlesham insisted on escorting them across the road and into the station and buying their tickets, then there was a subterranean rumble and May jumped for the stairs, closely followed by a panting Ellen.

As they collapsed onto their seats Ellen turned to May. 'Well, what an exciting afternoon, you do have some interesting friends. Isn't Lord Hindlesham kind? Do you know his wife as well? Is she as nice as he is?'

'I know her slightly,' May replied cautiously. 'She is very beautiful.'

'Oh, he isn't good looking at all, is he? But he's got a nice smile, just like a friendly monkey.' Ellen glanced sideways at May. 'But you haven't answered my question about her – or have you?' And May remembered that for all her ingenuousness Ellen could be disconcertingly shrewd at times.

Ellen said now, 'I'm sorry, he deserves better. Look, May, we've come out into the daylight – what a cheat, it's supposed to be an underground railway!'

May laughed aloud at Ellen's indignation, and realised that she had not enjoyed herself so much since before Emily's marriage.

111

Chapter Thirteen

By early December a whole tableful of new probationers had arrived and May and her friends no longer ate next to the wall. Bates had been sent to the Nurses' Sick Bay with a poisoned finger – Sister Simeon had been very annoyed about this and had berated poor Bates for her carelessness – but May felt a guilty pleasure on hearing the news since she knew it would mean her promotion to Pro Four.

Smith, the new Pro Five duly arrived and proved to be a stolid, freckle-faced girl who was the eldest of a large family and already knew how to use a broom and tealeaves. May's efforts to be patronisingly helpful were met with blank stares, but so, she noticed, was the friendly banter of the men, and May was incensed one day when Smith, unusually communicative, said that she could have managed to get through the work very well if only there were no patients. 'They seem to expect us to run round after them all the time!' Her voice was aggrieved. May's retort, 'But that's what we're here for!' was met with a look of incomprehension and Smith turned back to her brass taps which, May had to admit, gleamed with a glassy sparkle she had never been able to achieve.

The world outside the East End consisted almost entirely of letters: letters from India which were so resolutely cheerful that May shut herself in the Nurses' Library for a whole afternoon, and came out feeling coldly apprehensive. And it was clear from Lady Clarence's weekly epistles that some of the same fears were in her mind. There was a scrawl from Archie, written on a wet day in the Shires, to say that the hunting was disappointing this year, how was she going on, and had she chopped off any legs yet? Old George was here and said he'd seen May at the House with her pretty friend and when was he, Archie, going to meet all those pretty friends?!! May laughed and tossed it to Ellen to read. The latter had blushed and returned it without comment.

Then Lady Andover had written to say that she would be in Town for a few days from the third and she was looking forward to seeing May. May was delighted; she had seen nothing of her family, apart from a hurried hour with her father, when he had come up on business and been totally uncomprehending as to why his daughter's presence was required back in Poplar, when he thought she should have been available to lunch with him. As always in the autumn, London had been empty, while the annual round of shooting parties and Scottish visits had gone on without her; she had had no time for more than the odd regret, though she rather wished Ariche had run into 'old Harry' instead of 'old George'. Now, however, the sight of her grandmother's elegant, spiky handwriting suddenly brought her life before September back into sharp focus and put her quite out of patience with the usual Monday supper of porridge and cold sausage.

Her half-day off was due and Sister Simeon, unlike some of the other Sisters, always tried to give good notice of the event, and then keep to it, so May was able to write back to her grandmother with a firm date for an afternoon visit followed by a quiet family dinner. The very thought of one of Chef's meals made her mouth water; the Dock Road faggots were more satisfying to the stomach than the palate.

As she changed for her visit, the soft material of her dress felt strange under her roughened fingertips, and she scarcely recognised herself in her close-fitting gown of blue silk; while the upward sweep of her velvet brim, with the long ostrich feather nestling against her shining hair below it gave her face a delicate fragility, so that in the mirror she saw a stranger, elegant and pampered. She strolled over to the main entrance in the thin December sun, the ungainly scuttle of the last three months put aside with her blue striped galatea, and sat straight-backed and demure in the cab which the tortoise himself had summoned for her. It was delightful to feel like a young lady of leisure again.

Lady Andover was gracefully welcoming, but her gaze was searching as she surveyed May from head to foot.

'At least you have not lost your looks, my dear, living in that terrible slum, but,' as May removed her gloves, '*what* have you been doing with your hands?'

'Washing hundreds of bedpans, Grandmamma.' May's answer was short and to the point.

Melicent Andover raised her eyebrows in horror. 'My dear, you can't be serious, suppose you catch something!'

'Well, I haven't done yet,' May replied cheerfully. 'Now, tell me how everyone's getting on – is Bertie any nearer to proposing to Louise yet? And has Archie finally decided whether to join the Guards? I'm sure he'll never really do it, he's too lazy – and how is Papa, and Step-mamma?'

The afternoon passed in an agreeable sparkle of gossip while May enjoyed to the full the pleasures of being waited upon. She noticed as she never had before the noiseless drawing of the curtains, the unobtrusive feeding of the fire and the silent arrival of the tea equipage. She was savouring the delicate smoky fragrance of the Lapsang Souchong in its porcelain cup – how terribly fragile the fine china seemed! – when her sharp ears caught the distant ring of the doorbell and the subdued bustle of a visitor being admitted. She glanced in surprise at her grandmother, who had certainly given her the impression that they would have an undisturbed afternoon together – 'Just the two of us my dear, so we can have a nice feminine gossip' – and noticed an expression of innocence which was so carefully assumed as to arouse all May's suspicions. The mystery was soon solved when Lofthouse himself announced: 'Mr Cussons, M'lady,' and a familiar, broad-shouldered figure appeared in the doorway.

'Why, Harry, what a surprise!' Lady Andover's tone of amazement would have done credit to an experienced actress, but May was not deceived –especially as Harry Cussons, when coming forward to greet her grandmother, winked in her direction.

'Melicent, how do you do it? While the rest of us add years, you shed them! And Miss Winton, why, you have become quite the mystery maiden amongst us, dire rumours of durance vile in foreign climes have reached our ears – were it not for Hindlesham's reported sighting last month we would have quite given you up for lost!' He held her hand a fraction longer than was necessary before releasing it. 'Certainly your incarceration seems not to have had any ill effects, quite the contrary, she looks blooming, doesn't she Melicent?'

May felt her face glowing, and turned to the fire. She was disconcerted by Harry Cussons' bold gaze – yet she felt little flutters of excitement, and the room seemed dominated by his masculine presence.

The next hour flew by. May chatted and was lively, yet scarcely knew what she replied to Harry's sallies. Then he rose to his feet.

'I have trespassed too long already on your time together, I will leave you now. Good evening, Melicent, goodbye, Miss Winton.' His tone was formal but his eyes danced and again his handshake was a little too protracted, yet so carefully judged that no one could say it was too long. He leaned forward, his voice low but confident. 'Now I know where you are hiding, it will not be so long before we meet again.' He was gone, and the drawing room seemed suddenly empty without his vibrant personality.

'I'm so glad Harry happened to drop in while you were here, May.' Melicent Andover's voice was complacent.

May shook her head reprovingly at her. 'Oh Grandmamma, don't think I'm fooled, you know you arranged it beforehand!'

Lady Andover's voice was tinged with amusement. 'It didn't take much arranging, May. Young Harry needed only the barest hint of your presence here today.' She leant forward confidentially. 'There is no doubt, my dear, he is seriously thinking of settling down; he needs a mistress for his house and a mother for his children. It will be a wrench for him, of course, but I am sure Harry is wise enough to realise that a man cannot play the blithe bachelor forever.'

May was not at all sure that she liked the picture which Lady Andover's words conjured up. Was she then no more than an appetising morsel laid out for Harry Cussons' approval, so that he could decide whether she was sufficiently delectable to be worth his sacrificing himself in marriage? As if sensing her disquiet her grandmother continued.

'Think of the advantages to you, my dear: such an attractive man, always so amusing, so much charm. Harry knows just how to please a woman!'

May dropped her eyes and toyed with the tasselled fringe of the low lamp beside her chair.

'Is Lady Hindlesham in Town at the moment?' Her voice was carefully casual.

'Don't be silly, May. You are a child sometimes.' The hint of irritation behind her grandmother's indulgent tone gave May the answer she did not want.

May returned home in her grandmother's brougham, feeling delightfully cossetted with the footwarmer under her shoes and a thick rug wrapped closely around her. Uncle Bertie had been his usual urbane self, and Archie had teased her unmercifully about her skivvying, saying in mock serious tones, 'There are rumours that the second scullerymaid is looking for advancement – now you always got on so well with Chef, why don't you consider it? The hours aren't so long, the pay can't be much worse, and you must admit the food is better!' May could only agree with this last comment, as she ate her way from the Filets de Sole à la Bisque, through the Vol-au-vent de Foie gras à la Talleyrand to the final triumphant conclusion of the Bombes Surprises.

'Chef insisted on sending up all his specialities tonight, May,' Lady Andover smiled. 'He is convinced that the East End is a gastronomic desert.'

'As far as the hospital's concerned he's absolutely right.' May carefully selected a plump purple grape with the bloom still on it. 'But there are the jellied eels, they're not quite like anything else I've ever tasted – they keep them live, you know, in big tanks, and skin them at the back of the shop.'

Archie gave a loud guffaw, while Lady Andover made a *moue* of distaste.

116

'Really, May, don't let yourself become coarse.'

After the meal May insisted on descending to the subterranean kitchens of Arlington Street to thank Chef in person. His round red face gleamed and his waxed moustaches quivered with pleasure at her appearance. He was fascinated to hear of her experiences in the eel and pie shops, but raised his hands in horror at her description of the food served in the hospital. 'Tinned sardines for breakfast, and porridge in ze evening – it's barbaric, an inzult to zee taste buds, Mees May, I feel for you, 'ow I feel for you,' and his conker brown eyes were misty with sympathy.

As May was taking her leave Lofthouse came forward with a large basket under a snowy white cloth. 'With Chef's compliments, Miss May,' and he carried it out in person and bestowed it on the seat.

The carriage swayed gently to a halt. The footman's face was a mask as he pulled out the steps and helped May to alight onto a pavement alive with the tapping heels of cheap boots and high-pitched Cockney voices. A group of women stopped to stare at the gleaming horses and the polished brougham with the Andover crest on its side. May recognised one of them, a tired-faced girl with a bundled baby in her arms, shivering in a threadbare shawl. She was a regular visitor to Simeon Ward, where she sat patiently twice a week, holding the hand of a young man whose leg had been crushed by a falling crate in the docks. They hardly ever spoke, but the girl was always at the head of the queue on visiting days, and one of the last to leave. Now May smiled in her direction.

'Good evening, Mrs Jackson.'

But the girl gasped and shrank back, suspicious and wary, and May realised that she could not see the familiar nurse in the wealthy stranger; and before she could identify herself the woman had seized the arm of her companion and melted into the shadows. The little incident, so soon over that it was not even noticed by the escorting footman, was oddly disconcerting; May felt suddenly ashamed of her strong, well-fed body and warm furs. Then the hospital clock struck the half hour and she quickened her pace; her special late leave ended at ten-thirty and Home Sister was standing in the doorway, a stern, gaunt figure. May seized the basket from the bemused footman with a murmured, 'Thank you, Robert,' and stepped in.

'Good evening, Sister.'

'Good evening, Nurse Winton, you are only just in time.'

'I'm sorry, Sister.' May made the automatic apology, and set off up the steep stairs.

When she awoke the next morning she felt a sudden surge of excitement, and for the next few days she was careful to collect her letters after each meal. But it was the following week, as she dashed across to sweep and dust her room, that she picked up the envelope with its bold masculine scrawl dashing across it, so that there was scarcely room for the 'E' in the bottom corner. May smiled to herself, thinking that it must surely be the first time Harry Cussons had ever put that superscription on one of his letters. She stood with it in her hand, hesitating, but Simeon Ward was on accident take-in this week, and May knew that even an extra five minutes would put her behind until dinner time, so she thrust the letter unopened into her dress pocket where it rustled tantalisingly as she moved about her morning routine.

When she did open it in her room after dinner it was disappointingly short, yet as she swiftly scanned the lines she realised it was very much to the point. He wrote that his sister had come up ahead of her family and would be in London for several weeks, as he would be himself. Could he prevail on her to dine one evening? Although couched as a mere proposal he had clearly been in no doubt as to her response, since he stated that he would call for her at St Katharine's on the following evening, at seven-thirty. May felt disconcerted; had the spell he cast over her been so obvious? She had thought her behaviour more discreet. But then she reflected wryly that Harry Cussons, of all men, had the experience to judge whether a woman was interested or not, and since it seemed that they mostly were he could afford to be presumptuous.

118

She read the letter again, and felt a sudden surge of dismay – whatever would Lady Clarence think if she heard that she had dined with Harry Cussons? Then she pulled herself together: she was an independent woman now, and entitled to lead her own life as long as it did not conflict with the duties of her profession. Besides, she had heard Lady Beddows spoken of as a woman of unimpeachable reputation: no harm could come in her company – perhaps she was hoping to see her brother safely settled?

May hastily thrust this thought aside, together with the letter, and began to plan how she would ask Sister Simeon to grant her off-duty for the following evening, and, even more formidable, persuade Home Sister to allow her a second late pass, so soon after the last one.

Sister Simeon had been reasonable. 'Well, you have never asked for specific off-duty time before, Nurse Winton, so I suppose I can make a concession this time, despite the short notice. I trust you do not hope to make a habit of dining out in Town?' She looked sharply at May who replied mendaciously, 'No Sister, of course not, Sister,' her hands neatly behind her back, her spine straight. 'Thank you so much, Sister.'

Home Sister proved a more redoubtable obstacle, as May had feared, but she eventually yielded to the justice of May's argument that Matron had said they could have one late pass a month and she had been here three months and had had only a single late pass so far. 'But remember, Nurse, that late passes are not intended to be banked, like money. In future if you don't use one during the month then you have lost it for good.' May privately resolved that from now on she certainly would use it, even if she had to spend the last evening of every month lurking in Harris' Eel and Pie Restaurant consuming mounds of mash and gravy. But she merely nodded her head in agreement.

'Yes, Sister, certainly not, Sister. Thank you, Sister, no, not a minute after ten-thirty by the hospital clock, Sister. Good afternoon, Sister.'

Tuesday was one of Simeon ward's operation days. May

119

usually enjoyed these, and found the extra work more than compensated for by the flurry and excitement, but now she just wanted to get the day over and done with, so that she could relax in a hot bath and linger over her preparations for the evening.

She rushed along beside the trolley carrying her patient, a teenage boy who was determined to show he was grown up, and cracked stupid tasteless jokes until May spoke sharply to him, whereupon he relapsed into silence and she saw the naked fear in his eyes and was ashamed; but there was no time for a reassuring word before the anaesthetist pounced. As she watched the surgeon cut and cut again so that the blood gushed up before the forceps could be applied, and she prayed that the boy would not die there, on the table, with the last voice in his ears that of an impatient nurse. Her calves ached as she fetched and carried, and the sickly-sweet smell of ether was over-powering amidst the persistent humming sound of the theatre.

The boy did not die, of course. May had seen the surgeons pause, and shake their heads over a prone form, but they always managed to sew things up somehow and get the patient back to the ward. Ada Farrar, in the equivalent women's surgical, had once had to gallop all the way back with a dying patient – 'I thought the lift would never come, May' – but she had got there in time and the grim-faced Sister had stood by the bed with her finger on the fading pulse saying to Ada, 'At St Katharine's nobody dies in the theatre, remember that, Nurse Farrar. Surgeons' reputations are more precious than ours.' But this boy was breathing normally, and the healthy pink returned to his cheeks as May trotted beside him with a firm hand clutching his jaw, and she was able to assuage her guilt by settling him comfortably in bed before she sped off with the next patient.

The day dragged on and the long awaited six o'clock found May beside an appendectomy who was vomiting helplessly into the bowl she held for him. Staff Nurse appeared at her elbow. 'Sister says you may go now, Winton, you'll have to leave a clean bowl wedged by his pillow, everyone else is busy.'

May looked down at the shivering, whey-faced man on the bed, wiped his lips gently with a piece of flannel and said, 'Tell Sister I can stay a little longer if she wishes, I'm not in any hurry.' Staff Nurse nodded and vanished.

It was beyond the half hour before the patient stopped retching and sagged back on the pillows. May washed his face and hands, took her bowl into the sluice for emptying and cleaning, and reported to Sister. Sister Simeon nodded her dismissal.

'Enjoy your evening, Nurse Winton.'

'Thank you, Sister.' And May left the ward.

Chapter Fourteen

The cold air outside was blessedly reviving. May took several deep breaths, sniffing the tang of salt from beyond the dock walls. Refreshed, she dashed across the courtyards and into the Nurses' Home. Reaching the bathroom she turned on the taps on her way to her room; and was back, and in and out of her bath in minutes – regretfully remembering her plans for a long, hot soak. She dressed with care. Her most elaborate gowns had been left at Allingham, but she selected a dinner dress of the palest green miroir velvet, with a delicate froth of creamy lace around the low neckline, and hooked herself into it. Her hair took longer: she wanted to show it off to its best advantage, and was struggling with it when Minnie Emms, back from her half-day off, looked in and lent a helping hand. Minnie slid in the final pin.

'My, May, you do look swish, where are you going?'

'I'm not sure yet.' May felt the beginnings of a blush. Minnie raised a pair of questioning eyebrows.

'I'm dining with a family friend,' May added quickly.

'When is he picking you up?' Minnie asked slyly.

'At half-past seven – oh, you wretch, Minnie!'

'Well, you'd better get a move on, it's gone twenty-five past already.'

'Oh, my cloak, my gloves – Minnie, do help me with the buttons.'

Minnie attacked May's long white kid gloves, managing to fasten a piece of the skin of May's wrist along with one of the tiny pearl buttons – but there was no time to put it right. May threw her cloak around her, checked her hat in the mirror and was off down the stairs, pursued by Minnie's cries of, 'Enjoy yourself, and don't be late back!'

A smart carriage was parked outside the main entrance,

looking out of place in the Dock Road; the glossy-coated horse tossed its head disdainfully. The liveried attendant jumped down and held the door open, and May tumbled in. The soft darkness of the interior was redolent of the upper class male: she caught the mingled aroma of shaving soap and good cigars, and the underlying tang of sweat. For a panicky moment May wondered whether she had jumped into the wrong carriage, then the deep tones of Harry Cussons' voice broke the silence. He sounded amused.

'You are always in such a rush, Miss Winton. What can you possibly have been doing all day to be in this flurry now?'

For a brief moment the vision of the surgeon's knife poised above the blood-beaded incision flashed before her eyes, and the face of the shaking, vomiting wretch on the bed. She opened her mouth to tell him, then commonsense reasserted itself. Lord Hindlesham might be interested in the details of a nurse's daily life, but she knew Harry Cussons would not be – he expected entertainment from his companions.

'Oh, we keep busy,' her tone was light. 'But I'm off duty now. Tell me, how is the Little Season?'

Harry Cussons' gossip was lively, amusing, and tinged with a spice of malice. May was soon relaxed and laughing in the warm intimacy of the carriage. As they talked she tugged at her left glove, trying to ease the pinch, though she knew from past experience how difficult it was to put this right. Why did long gloves have to be so tight? But they always were; fashion and Lady Clarence decreed it so. As they passed under a street lamp her companion noticed her fidgeting. He reached across and picked up her hand.

'What's the matter? Ah, you have trapped your skin – how well I remember my younger sister doing the same thing when she first Came Out. You are a careless nymph, you know!' He inspected her wrist in another passing light. 'I'm afraid you won't get this right without taking your glove off and starting again.'

'I've got out of the habit of wearing these,' May replied. 'Bella, my maid, always used to put them on for me.'

'Then let me be your lady's maid for this evening.'

There was amusement in his voice, and an elusive hint of something May could not recognise. His grasp on her wrist was firm, and she could not have broken free without a sharp tug; besides, she knew she did not want to break free.

Harry Cussons' hand glided lightly up to her elbow, and with strong yet gentle fingers he began to undo the small loops, one by one. He lingered over each tiny button in turn, his touch caressing and intimate. May sat unprotesting, as though mesmerised. She gazed at his bony profile, a dark outline in the light of the passing lamps, and felt an overwhelming urge to reach out and delicately touch his face and gently push back the rebellious lock of hair which flopped forward over his forehead. But she did not.

Then the glove was drawn slowly off her hand, and the small red patch of skin disclosed. Harry Cussons touched it tenderly with his fingertip.

'There is the cause of the mischief. Now I must do as my old Nanny always did when I fell and hurt myself.' And before May could move he had bent his head and kissed her wrist, not once, but twice. With an effort May removed her hand from his grasp and recovering herself said, 'But I have not yet fallen, Mr Cussons.'

At this he threw back his head and roared with laughter, and May felt uncertain and ill-at-ease; her companion, as if sensing this, picked up the glove, said, 'Hold your hand out, we're nearly there,' and refastened the buttons swiftly and deftly.

'There, now you are ready to face the world.'

May wondered where he had learnt to handle tiny buttons so skilfully, and could not resist saying as he finished, 'Clearly you are an experienced lady's maid, Mr Cussons', and he looked at her sharply for a moment so that she felt she had scored a hit.

Then the carriage drew up and there was all the bustle of alighting. May recognised Claridge's; she had never dined in an hotel before, and only lunched in the company of her parents. But she did not know the circumstances of Harry Cussons' life in London, only that he had a place in the country. Since Lady Beddows had come up ahead of her family she was possibly staying here.

Having left her cloak May preceded Harry Cussons into the dining room, where a black-garbed manager escorted them to a small table in a secluded corner and drew back her chair. She gathered her skirts in her hand and was on the point of sitting down when she froze in mid-movement. The table was set for two. She glanced up at Harry. There was a look of smug confidence on his face, like a man who has seen his horse first past the post and now puts down his binoculars in anticipation of enjoying the fruits of his wager. May slowly straightened herself. She looked at the manager – his face was politely enquiring. She surveyed the public restaurant: there were several girls of her own age, but they were all with family parties. The women seated à deux were all older, or had that indefinable air of – May could not quite express it to herself but years of Lady Clarence's tutelage had left her well able to recognise it. Her mind was made up. She turned to the manager.

'How foolish of me. I have left my handkerchief in the pocket of my cloak. Mr Cussons, perhaps you would accompany me?'

Unsuspecting, Harry Cussons ushered her out, wearing the sleek assurance of a well-fed tom cat whose next meal is temporarily delayed, but who knows it will come, as surely as night follows day. As soon as the manager left them in the foyer May turned and faced her escort.

'I thought Lady Beddows was to dine with us?'

He smiled. 'Dear me, what gave you that impression, Miss Winton?'

'You did, in your letter.'

'I am sure I did not say that.'

May thought back to the well-perused letter – no, he had not said that. She, gullible fool, had made her own deduction. But her anger was rising now, and her confidence with it.

'You lied, by implication you lied.'

'Oh, come now, that's too strong.'

125

'You know I would never have agreed to dine with you alone, in a public restaurant.'

He smiled engagingly. 'Then I will cancel the table here. Come back to my rooms, my man will soon rustle something up for us. That would be much nicer.'

May felt her colour deepening. 'I do not wish to dine with you alone – anywhere.'

'Miss Winton, you're a woman of the world now, you're free of your duenna.' His voice was coaxing. 'Relax, enjoy your evening.' His tone lowered. 'You know, you look very beautiful when you're angry.'

May had had enough. 'I am leaving, now.'

She marched over to the cloakroom, retrieved her cloak and put it on with shaking hands. When she came out Harry Cussons was still waiting, his composure barely ruffled. She moved swiftly to the door; he followed rapidly behind. She ran down the steps and out onto the pavement. With several long strides he overtook her and barred her way.

'Miss Winton, stop a minute. Now calm yourself,' he spoke as though to a rather tiresome child.

May broke in through gritted teeth. 'Will you get out of my way?'

'No.' He was becoming impatient. 'You're behaving like a spoilt child. I deserve a hearing.'

May erupted. 'You deserve *this*!' and raising her right hand she brought it with all her strength in a stinging slap across his face. 'Now will you get out of my way?'

Involuntarily he stepped aside and she carried away a last glimpse of his sagging jaw and the look of stupefaction on his handsome face.

May pulled her cloak around her and ran. Fortunately there were few people about as the evening was cold, and she made good speed down the street and round the next corner. She stopped, panting. There was no sound of pursuing footsteps. A blue-uniformed figure approached her.

'Are you all right, Miss?'

May steadied her breathing. 'Yes, thank you, Officer. But perhaps you could direct me to the nearest cab rank?'

'Certainly, Miss. Just down there, on the right.' And he pointed to the blessed sight of a row of hansoms, each behind its drooping horse.

'Thank you so much.'

May stepped briskly forward. It was just as she reached the foremost horse that realisation hit her – she had no money! She had got used to carrying a purse when walking in the East End, but she never had taken money with her when going out to dine; it had never crossed her mind to bring any tonight.

The cab driver, sensing a fare, sat up straight and tugged at the slack reins. May lifted her chin in the air and walked past.

The events of the evening had left her mind in a whirl. She couldn't think straight – she would walk back – but it was much too far, and her feet were already cold in her light evening slippers – besides, how could she walk through Poplar in a velvet cloak trimmed with sables? Her thoughts raced. She was, after all, in the West End, she must know many people within a hundred yards of where she was now – but to whom could she go and ask for money, alone and unattended on a freezing night in December? Whatever would they think? What tale would go the rounds later?

A carriage drew up ahead of her and for a childish moment she believed that the stately, straight-backed woman alighting from it was Lady Clarence, and she broke into a run. Then the woman turned her head and she remembered that her step-mother was far away in Stemhalton, with all the rest of the Andover clan; her grandmother and uncle had left Town two days ago.

Tears spilled over and trickled down her face, but she dashed them away. She must calm down and think, at least find out where she was. If only she'd been more observant when Lady Clarence had taken her on those interminable calls. Then, all of a sudden, a memory reasserted itself: surely this was Grosvenor Square – she remembered coming here at the end of July to Lady Hindlesham's ball. She looked along the terrace. There it was – and there were lights on in the front rooms.

May stopped, uncertain. How could she ask Della Hindlesham for help? Della of all people asked to lend her the fare to get home after she had walked out on Harry Cussons! In a tiny corner of her mind she began to unfreeze: he had looked so surprised – perhaps he'd never had his face slapped before, or at least, probably not with such force. But here she was, still stranded in the middle of London without the wherewithal to get back to St Katharine's – perhaps she could manage to walk, after all.

Then, just as she was about to turn away, she saw a shadow pass across the blind of the window to the right of the front door. It was small and slight, yet unmistakably male. May paused; she would feel no compunction about begging her cab fare from Lord Hindlesham – were they not both the victims of Harry Cussons? Before she could lose her nerve she marched forward to the railings, reached into the window box for a handful of small gravel and threw it at the window. The shadow's head rose for a moment, then bent again. May picked up more gravel, and threw a second time. The figure moved forward and the blind began to rise. May stood poised for flight in case the man should prove to be a stranger; but it was Lord Hindlesham.

He stared out into the darkness and she moved into the circle of light cast by the street lamp and waved. He nodded his head in comprehension and turned away from the window. May waited in an agony of impatience – suppose the butler came out? But as the door opened she heard a familiar voice.

'It's all right, Ellis, I'm just stepping outside for a moment for a breath of air.' The door was firmly shut and the slight form came lightly down the steps.

'Miss Winton! What on earth are you doing out alone? And on a night like this! Do come inside. Della is upstairs, I will send for her to come down.'

'No!' May's voice was too quick, she slowed it down. 'No, please don't disturb Lady Hindlesham. I just want to borrow my cab fare home – back to St Katharine's.'

Lord Hindlesham did not reply at once. He took May by the elbow and propelled her gently round until the light from

128

the lamp fell full on her face. May, conscious of her tear-stained cheeks stared fixedly over his shoulder.

'I'll take you back, now.'

'No, please, it's very kind, but if you'll just lend me the fare I'll be quite all right.'

His voice was firm. 'Miss Winton, you are little older than my two daughters. You are not going back alone, not tonight.' He checked her protest. 'I often go out for a stroll before dinner, my absence will cause no comment – Della will not even notice.' His tone was dry, and May said nothing further.

He walked her briskly round to the nearest cab rank – 'A growler I think, you are cold enough already' – and in a few minutes May was sitting with her feet in the musty straw, listening to the steady clip-clop in front. She felt totally miserable – whatever must Lord Hindlesham be thinking of her?

He broke the silence.

'Have you been on duty today? Tell me what you have been doing, May.'

May began to speak, slowly at first, then the words tumbled out as she told him about Sister Simeon and Bates and the new Pro Five and the boy she'd spoken sharply to and the man who was dying from drink, delirious in the end bed, screaming for his morphia with a high-pitched keening sound that only Sister Simeon could stop. And for a short time she forgot Harry Cussons and the débâcle of her evening.

Aware of the sympathetic concern of her companion she spoke more slowly of the all too apparent poverty and distress of so many of their patients, and of her own inadequacy in coping with these. Lord Hindlesham's voice was serious as he replied, saying that at least the evils she grappled with were openly recognisable and could be battled with directly, and as he compared the two Societies, the one May had now entered with the one she had left, she wondered if his wife were in his thoughts.

Then the cab drew up at the hospital gates. Lord Hindlesham helped her down.

'I've enjoyed talking to you, May. Give my best wishes to Miss Carter, and tell her I think the election may go her way, rather than mine. I will wait until you are inside.'

May thanked him then walked through the archway. She looked back and waved to the slim figure which raised its hat in reply, muttering under her breath as she turned away, in the language of the East End: 'Della is a bitch!'

Ada and Ellen burst in as she was sitting at her table, trying to distract herself by writing to Emily.

'We saw your light on, you're back early,' then, 'May, what's the matter?'

May bent her head and put her hands to her eyes to stop the telltale tears. Ellen came quickly across and put her arm round May. She spoke back over her shoulder, 'Ada, go and make us all some cocoa,' and the door closed. May poured out her tale to Ellen, who murmured, 'The beast – how thoughtless – oh, I hope you hit him hard May!' 'I think I did,' May said with simple pride – telling her story was cheering her up. She felt Ellen's arm stiffen slightly, then relax again as she explained how she had recognised Lord Hindlesham's house –'How fortunate he was in, May, he was quite right to bring you back,' and May, now hiccuping gently, was imparting Lord Hindlesham's message when Ada returned, bearing three cups on a tray and a face of thunder. 'Really, those Second Years have gone too far, they'd taken *all* the milk – I had to go right down to the kitchen and *abase* myself before the cook to get some more. I wouldn't have done it if it hadn't been for you being in such a state, May. Now tell me, what did this brute do to you?'

Ellen related the story, omitting, May noticed with interest, precise reference to Lord Hindlesham – he was translated simply to 'a friend'. Ada was loud in her commendations of May's attack on Harry Cussons, though she seemed rather sorry that she had not gone further – 'Only one slap, May? Still, I'm glad to hear it, I've always thought of you as rather soft with men.'

'But Ada, all the men here are patients, I couldn't hurt them.'

130

'They still need to be kept in their places. Sister Simeon lets them roam around far too much – flat on their backs in bed, that's where men should be!'

At this Ellen gave a little gasp, and put her hand to her lips, then started laughing. May began to giggle weakly, and even Ada gave a reluctant chuckle.

'Well, when they're ill, I meant. But seriously, May, I don't know why you got so hot under the collar at the idea of dining with him. After all, you were in a public place. I suppose he was a bit deceitful, but it is a ridiculous convention whereby an adult man and woman can't enjoy a meal together on their own. I've certainly spent the evening out without a chaperon, not with just one man, admittedly, but in a mixed group of my own age.'

'And so have I,' said Ellen softly. 'But we come from backgrounds where this is accepted, May doesn't.'

'But that doesn't stop her changing now. She doesn't live at home any longer,' Ada argued.

Ellen shook her head. 'That would be true if, say, young Dr Wade and his ginger-haired friend asked us to accompany them out for a meal,' – 'We'd be thrown out if we went!' Ada interjected forcefully – 'Well, two doctors from a different hospital, then. But you see what I mean, it would be natural for them to do so, because they wouldn't see it as improper – but this Mr Cussons, he knew that May would never normally dine alone in a public restaurant without a chaperon – so I think he was wrong. He tried to take advantage of her being younger and less experienced than himself to bluff her into doing something she would be unhappy about later.'

'Well, he won't try again in a hurry,' said Ada in a tone of satisfaction.

May recognised the truth of this and winced. Had she been too proper? After all, Harry Cussons was used to experienced women of the world, perhaps she had been rather childish. She remembered the caressing touch of his hands in the carriage and shivered – was Ada right? Had she made a terrible mistake? And yet there was good sense in Ellen's

131

words – he should not have taken her alone to a public restaurant.

Ellen, noticing the shiver, stood up.

'Come along May, it's time you went to bed. I'll fill your hot water bottle for you. It's a busy day tomorrow.'

Ada retorted, 'It's always a busy day tomorrow,' and collected up the empty cups.

Chapter Fifteen

The rising bell jarred May into wakefulness the next morning. She pushed herself heavily out of bed and began slowly to dress. As she did her hair, her reflection in the mirror stared back, strained and heavy-eyed. She went over the scene with Harry Cussons again in her mind, and now that her anger had evaporated she felt wretchedly depressed. Had he really meant to be so careless of her reputation? And, if he had, was not the fault at least partly hers? – Lady Clarence would certainly say so. After this débâcle, would she ever see him again? Did she want to? The unanswered questions chased round her brain until there was a brisk tattoo on the door, and Ada's voice said, 'May, you'll be late – I can't wait for you.'

May forced herself into a burst of feverish activity and rushed out, bed left unstripped, down the endless stairs to the dining room.

When Sister Simeon arrived, after the morning routine of breakfast dishes and bed-making had been completed, she called May to her table. May waited, hands clasped behind her back, to be told her latest faults.

'Don't look so chastened, Nurse Winton, I am not going to chide you – though I am not completely certain you are paying adequate attention to my prize aspidistra. Now, as soon as Christmas is over you will be moved from this ward, probably to a medical one, so I think that before you go you should take sole charge of a patient's daily dressings.' May's head jerked up. 'The appendectomy whom you took down to the theatre yesterday – Mr Tyrrell – his case was without complications, and he looks quite well this morning, so you shall do all his dressings yourself.'

May's depression began to lift. She knew this was a sign that Sister Simeon was satisfied with her work, and she felt a stirring of pride.

The pleasant faced, blue-eyed young man in the bed looked very different from the shivering creature of the day before. As soon as May approached with the dressing trolley he smiled broadly at her.

'Feelin' a bit more meself, today, Nurse. Cor, I thought I were a gonner yesterday, keep throwin' up like that – don't know 'ow you nurses stand this job, straight I don't.'

'Oh, it's all in a day's work, Mr Tyrrell. Now, I'm just going to change your dressing. It will feel a little sore, but I'll try not to hurt you too much.' May kept her voice firm and level, and hoped that her nervousness was not showing in her face. It seemed strange to be acting without Sister or Staff Nurse standing by to supervise. But as soon as she began unwinding the binder her confidence returned. As Sister had said, the dressing was uncomplicated, and apart from the occasional gasp or flinch Mr Tyrrell chatted gamely on, telling May about his wife and small son, and how they were hoping for a daughter in the New Year – 'As pretty as 'er mother, she'll be, that's what I tells my Betty.' As he talked May recalled Sister Tutor's words: 'Remember, Nurses, that worrying about his family will often impede a patient's recovery. The Lady Almoner has access to some limited charitable help, a tactful enquiry may sometimes be in order.' Now May said, her voice level,

'It must be difficult for your wife at the moment, without you.'

'Cried 'er eyes out when the old Doc says I 'ad to come in 'ere,' Mr Tyrrell replied with simple pride. 'But I told 'er not to be so silly. They carves 'em up by the 'undreds in St Katharine's, I says. You just cut along the Friendly Society and claim me sick benefit and 'ave a rest while I'm out the way. At least I'll not be dragging 'orse muck into the 'ouse every day for you to clean up, I says. Anyway, me old Mum lives just round the corner, 'er'll keep an eye on Betty for me. Thursday visiting, ennit, Nurse?'

'That's right, your wife can come tomorrow. So you work with horses, do you, Mr Tyrrell?'

'Allus 'ave done, since I were a nipper. Us'ter go round and

134

muck 'em out in the evenings for a few 'apence, so Mr Jones – 'e's the foreman at the Brewery – 'e offered me a job, soon as I left school. I likes 'osses. You treat 'em right and they'll behave back – mind, you get the odd bad 'un, just like 'umans. One we've got, Danny, 'e's called, a mean brute 'e is. Didn't get out of 'is way fast enough, and 'e didn't 'arf land me one, broke the skin of me leg, it did, you can see the bruise. I swore, I can tell you, then the very next day I gets this orful pain and I'm in 'ere – wouldn't put it past the b –, oops, sorry, Nurse, the brute, to 'ave give me appendywhatsit as well!'

May laughed. 'Well, if he did, it'll be the first recorded case. Is that quite comfortable now?' She fastened the last safety-pin.

'Lovely, Nurse – ta, ducks.'

Glowing with pride May pushed her trolley back down the ward.

Mr Tyrrell's wound was healing well, and May found him a very easy patient to nurse: anxious to do what he could to help himself, and always bright and cheerful. Even when May, in her rush to give half a dozen enemas at speed, failed to completely fill the bulb of the Higginson's syringe with soapy water and so squeezed a little air into his rectum, he made light of the pain, merely grunting, 'Way you girls 'ave to work a little 'iccup's not to be wondered at, think nothin' of it, ducks.'

When 'My Betty' arrived on Thursday May was introduced as, 'Me Special Nurse, wot keeps me under control' with a wink in May's direction. Mrs Tyrrell looked very young. She moved slowly with the ungainly gait of the heavily pregnant, and her smile was shy as she took May's proffered hand and murmured a word of thanks. But as she turned back to her husband her thin face lit up and she looked suddenly beautiful as she took his hand and gently stroked it, gazing at him with such open adoration that May felt quite bereft, and Harry Cussons' face, never far from her mind recently, swam sharply into focus before her. What had she lost by her childish and impetuous behaviour?

'Winton, what on earth do you think you're doing? Get out

135

of my way and into the kitchen – you haven't even started cutting the bread and butter yet!' Staff Nurse's voice was sharp, and her face harassed, so May, with a 'Sorry, Staff,' moved smartly in the direction of the corridor. Useless day-dreaming, she scolded herself, was a luxury far beyond the reach of a lowly pro, not that Sister seemed to spend much time on it either, as her voice rang out, 'Nurse Winton, your cap!' and in a carrying aside: 'Some young women have no pride in their appearance!' May thought that she must say, 'Sorry, Sister,' in her sleep at night, she said it so often in the daytime. She was reaching for the bread knife even as she tumbled through the kitchen door.

''Ere, Nurse, mind yer plates of meat' – and an indignant Maudie reared up from her kneeler brandishing her scrubbing brush.

'Sorry, Maudie.' May positioned her knife and cut the first slice crooked, and heard herself mutter, 'Sorry, loaf.' She began to laugh.

Maudie looked round. 'What's tickled yer fancy, duck? Come into a fortune, 'ave you?' She cackled at her own joke. 'Well, if you 'as, Hi wouldn't spend another minnit in this dump, 'swelp me I wouldn't.'

May said, 'Well, I suppose I might as well stay for tea, since it's currant buns today,' and sawed furiously away at the loaf. 'I'm all behind, Maudie, will you put the butter to warm for me, there's a dear.'

'I suppose in the h'absence of a fortune we'll 'ave to 'ang together.' Maudie shuffled over to the stove. 'But don't you leave it to melt, like you did yesterdiy.'

On Sunday afternoon Betty Tyrrell visited again. May saw her coming down the ward after Sister had rung the bell to signal the end of visiting time. There had been a serious accident in the Docks the previous day; extra beds had been set up in the centre of the ward and all the nurses were frantically busy, but something about Betty Tyrrell's expression made May pause and smile. The girl hesitated then waddled slowly up to her.

136

'Nurse,' her voice was shy. 'Bob, seems – seems a bit low today.' She flushed and stopped a moment, disturbed at her own temerity, yet determined to ask. 'Is he all right?'

May said, 'His operation has been a complete success, Mrs Tyrrell. His wound is healing nicely. I expect he's missing you, and his son.'

The girl looked slightly relieved, yet it was clear she was still worried. ''Is face looked a bit funny, Nurse, and 'e didn't say much – that's not like 'im.'

May spoke reassuringly, 'I'll ask him how he feels this evening, and if there's any doubt Sister will send for the Doctor.'

'Thank you, Nurse.' Then she burst out, 'It's a long time till Thursday.' She turned her face away and swayed off down the corridor.

When May went to collect the tea things she noticed that Bob Tyrrell had only drunk half a cup, and barely touched his bread and butter.

'This tea is cold. Would you like a fresh cup, Mr Tyrrell? Perhaps you could try a little more bread?'

'No thanks, Nurse, ta all the same. It seems to be an effort to get me mouth open to chew proper like.'

On pretence of adjusting the bedclothes May glanced at his temperature chart. It did show a slight rise – but surely she would have noticed if the wound had become infected? If only she knew more: Betty Tyrrell was right, he wasn't himself, but what did it mean? She made up her mind; she would have to risk a rebuff. She marched down the ward to lay her story before Sister Simeon.

Her evidence seemed very feeble as she related it, and she waited to be sent about her business with a flea in her ear, but Sister was silent for a moment, then said, 'I'll speak to Dr Barnes when he does his round this evening. You may go now, Nurse.' Relieved, May escaped to her washing up.

Just after seven she was summoned to Sister's room. Dr Barnes looked impatient, Sister Simeon determined.

'Nurse Winton,' she began, 'Do you happen to know the nature of Mr Tyrrell's employment?'

137

May was surprised. 'He's some sort of groom, Sister. He works at the Brewery, with the horses.'

Dr Barnes broke in impatiently. 'Really, Sister, I am extremely busy . . .'

Sister Simeon silenced him with an upraised hand. 'When you have washed him, Nurse, did you notice any injury – a cut or abrasion? Sustained before he entered St Katharine's?'

May was becoming more and more bewildered. 'Well, Sister, he did tell me he had been kicked by a horse, just before he went down with appendicitis. It did break the skin on his shin.'

Sister Simeon expelled her breath sharply. Her lips tightened.

Dr Barnes broke in again. 'Sister, I'm sure this is all very interesting, but I really must . . .'

'I suggest you go and consult your copy of *Fenwick* on the causes and symptoms of tetanus, Dr Barnes; then come back and examine my patient again.'

Dr Barnes was angry. 'Diagnosis is the province of the medical staff, Sister Simeon.'

Sister Simeon's voice was icy. 'Certainly, Dr Barnes; and the sooner you diagnose the better. Tetanus is highly infectious.'

Muttering imprecations under his breath the young man flounced out. Sister Simeon's lips appeared to be forming the words, 'Bumptious young pipsqueak,' but May could hardly believe she had read them aright. As soon as the door closed she risked a question. 'Sister, what is tetanus? I've heard the name before, but I don't really know . . .'

Sister looked tired. 'It's lockjaw, Nurse. We will leave it at that for the present. I may be wrong, I hope I am – say nothing to the patient, of course.' She rapped out these last words. 'You may go now.'

Dr Barnes came back with his immediate superior, and the two white-coated men prodded and poked Bob Tyrrell and listened to his chest, but May went off duty no wiser.

Next morning Sister was already on the ward when the day nurses arrived. After the report she kept May back, called her into her sitting room and closed the door.

Sister's voice was grave. 'Dr Anderson confirmed Dr Barnes' diagnosis.' May blinked, but Sister Simeon continued smoothly. 'I am afraid Mr Tyrrell has contracted tetanus. He will need constant attendance from now on, and as you have already been dealing with his daily dressings I have decided that you shall nurse him alone. It will be safer for the other patients – this is a surgical ward, so however careful we are, there is always a risk of infecting them. Hold your hands out.' Startled, May did as she was told. 'Good, no sign of any broken skin. You must tell me immediately if you damage your hands in any way. This is not a task I would normally give to a probationer of only three months' experience, but we are exceptionally busy at the moment, and the hospital is always under-staffed, so Matron has agreed. The patient is used to you, and you are a level-headed girl.'

Before she could continue May burst out, 'But Sister, suppose I do something wrong – and he dies!'

Sister Simeon paused, then said steadily, 'Nurse Winton, he is going to die anyway, whatever you do.'

May said, 'No, no he can't, he's such a nice man, his wife . . .' her voice trailed away in the face of Sister Simeon's implacable gaze. 'Is there no hope?' She spoke in a small voice.

Sister Simeon's tone was brisk, but not unsympathetic. 'Very little, I'm afraid, Nurse.' – Then why tell me now, May thought rebelliously, but Sister Simeon, seeming to read her mind, went on, 'It's better that you face up to this at once, otherwise you might be tempted to blame yourself later, and no good nurse allows herself to indulge in useless self-reproach.' – But I'm not a good nurse, May's mind screamed silently, only a raw probationer, a stupid girl who came because she was bored, what have I done? Yet another part of her brain stayed calm, and accepted the harsh truth of Sister's words, though almost crushed under the weight of her knowledge.

Sister Simeon reached back to a bookshelf behind her chair, and took out a small volume. After finding the page she handed it to May.

'Stay in here and read this carefully. I will come back in fifteen minutes to see if you have any questions. You may sit down.'

It felt very odd to be sitting alone in Sister's room during the morning rush. She handled the book gingerly, as though it might explode, then, bracing herself, began to read the section on nursing patients with tetanus.

By the time Sister returned fifteen minutes later she knew what she was supposed to do, but quailed at the thought of having to do it. Sister Simeon questioned her closely, seemed satisfied with her answers, and added further instructions of her own. She told May that she would be nursing Bob Tyrrell in the small linen room, which could be emptied and used as a side ward when the need arose. They went in; Maudie had already lit the fire, which was burning brightly in the small grate, and Sister stood over May while she practised a silent manipulation of tongs and poker.

'Remember, Nurse Winton, any noise at all, even a movement of air, like a draught, is liable to bring on a convulsion in a tetanus patient. Now go to the door; open and shut it until you can do it silently.' When Sister was satisfied on this point she made a final check of the room, then said, 'Don't forget, Nurse, you are not to leave him under any circumstances. You must always wait for a relief.' May nodded, then suddenly remembering Betty Tyrrell's loving face: 'Sister, his wife, she'll want to be with him – she's expecting a child soon.'

Sister asked, 'Do you think she can be relied on to stay calm and quiet?'

May thought wildly, can I be relied on to do that? But after a moment's consideration she said, 'I think so, Sister.'

'Very well, I will send a message and arrange for her to visit today.'

It was at this point that May finally accepted what was going to happen to lively, friendly, cheerful Bob Tyrrell. Today was Monday; visitors on Monday could have only one meaning.

Chapter Sixteen

The next four days were a nightmare. Although clearly feeling ill and apprehensive at first Bob Tyrrell tried to keep a cheerful face. As his jaw gradually clenched he still tried to crack little jokes, which May smiled and laughed at. Then the jokes became smaller and sadder, and ceased altogether once the spasms laid hold of him like a giant hand and forced his body into a rigid arch, so that only the back of his head and the heels of his feet still touched the bed. As Sister had predicted, his stitches tore apart and his stomach wound gaped; May padded and bound it as loosely as she dared and as gently as she could, bending across so that her body hid the exposed gut from his tortured gaze.

May had to fight for control of herself, repeating like a litany, 'Slow and rhythmical movements, be slow and rhythmical, don't hurry, touch him gently, warm your hands and be gentle.' Then, as he collapsed back on the mattress exhausted she tried, oh so carefully, to spoon a little liquid through the gap they had made by pulling out his front teeth. And all the time he lay there with his mouth twisted up, his eyebrows raised and his whole face fixed and rigid in a travesty of a grin. But his eyes, despairing and hopeless, were fixed on May's, so that she felt her own facial muscles stiffen and contract as she kept her face smiling and her expression calm.

In a corner of her mind May remembered Lady Clarence's patient, tireless training. 'Walk more slowly, May, do not bob up and down, move smoothly, be graceful. You must sit absolutely still in your chair, do not ever fidget.' Now May was grateful as she sat quite still and did not fidget and moved so slowly and smoothly – yet still he went into violent contortions, and once she knew it was her fault, when the

141

door slipped in her hand and banged as she came back from her half-hour at dinner; she watched helpless, consumed with guilt as his body reared up and hung suspended.

Betty Tyrrell, and Bob's tiny wrinkled mother slipped in and crouched motionless in the corner. The two women's hands were clasped and May sensed their desperate longing, willing him to survive, to recover. May made herself believe he would; she forced her mind to blank out Sister Simeon's predictions and kept repeating to herself only, 'He will get better, he will get better,' and fancied she saw a faint glimmer of reassurance in the eyes staring up into hers.

Dr Barnes and Sister came and went. At mealtimes Staff Nurse slipped in and sent May out; she ate mechanically, grateful for Ellen's fierce unspoken protectiveness, which allowed her to sit in silence and pull herself together for the inevitable return. At night, when Grayson came to take over, May did not want to leave, convinced that the stolid Grayson with flat white face and boot button eyes could not under-stand and anticipate as she could do; though she knew that the other nurse was tireless and efficient.

At the end of four days it was clear that willpower was not enough: Bob Tyrrell was dying. He was gasping for breath, his skin was cold and wet with sweat as May touched him, and his face livid and swollen with the oedema of incipient heart failure. Yet his eyes were still alive, and he gazed imploringly at his wife as she bent over him, whispering her love and her devotion. May watched with breaking heart, and saw intensity give way to resignation; she knew he could fight no longer.

She helped Betty Tyrrell back to her chair before closing the eyelids of the body, relaxed at last. Then she went to the door and summoned assistance, her voice still even and low-pitched, although the man on the bed would suffer no more convulsions now.

After Staff came she led the two women out and listened to their broken words of thanks as she swallowed the bitter taste of defeat. Sister came, and May realised she was offering her a choice: she did not have to lay out the body if she did not wish

142

it. But feeling that she must complete her duty to Bob Tyrrell to the end she said she would prefer to do so. Sister nodded, and left Staff to help her, for which May was grateful.

By late morning the body had been removed, the bedding bundled up and sent down to be sterilised, the mattress and bed carbolised, and the room thoroughly scrubbed out. May reported to Sister Simeon in the ward; the latter ordered her to go and wash in a bath laced with disinfectant and to send all her own clothes for fumigation. 'Then you may go off duty until five, Nurse Winton.' As she heard these last words, and realised she was no longer needed in the small side ward, May felt the threatening tears well up, but Sister Simeon's stern voice telling her to pull herself together held them poised on her lids, and they did not spill over. Then came her dismissal.

'That is all, Nurse Winton, you have done everything that was necessary.'

But despite her shock and grief May knew that this was not true; there was still something more she must do. Hesitant, groping for words and worried by her own presumption in the face of the inexorable hospital system she reminded Sister Simeon that she, May Winton, was a woman of considerable means – would it be possible? – Betty Tyrrell's baby was due soon, she had another young child, no husband now, could Sister arrange discreetly, so that no one need know? . . . Sister inclined her head in agreement. She would speak to the Lady Almoner herself, if May would visit her in her office tomorrow – a convenient Charity would be used. May bowed her head, murmured 'Thank you, Sister,' and left the ward.

As soon as she was disinfected May went back to her bedroom, threw herself on her bed and wept. At one o'clock Ellen rushed up and dragged her off to dinner, then had to leave her to go back on duty. May tramped round the streets of the East End until she had tired her legs and regained some degree of composure, then for lack of any alternative, came back to her room.

She had only been there for a few minutes, sitting at the table trying to compose a careful letter to Emily, when a maid tapped at the door.

143

'There's a gentleman to see you, Miss, waiting at the porter's lodge.'

May stared blankly at the maid before she spoke. 'Thank you, Ethel, I will be down in a few minutes.'

Even curiosity seemed deadened as she mechanically pulled her cloak round her shoulders and drew on her gloves.

As she walked across the busy courtyard she saw the man waiting at the main entrance – tall, broad-shouldered, immaculately turned out, gold-knobbed cane held casually in one hand – it was Harry Cussons. He came forward, right hand extended.

'Miss Winton, I feared I would never run you to earth, you seemed to be held captive in this convent – or prison!' She watched the remembered muscles ripple in his throat as he laughed. 'May we go somewhere more private to talk?'

'Across the road, there are public gardens, above the tunnel entrance. We can go there.'

She walked ahead of him out into the bustle and noise of the Dock Road. He took her elbow as they threaded between the traffic, but released it as soon as they reached the other side. The gardens were deserted, except for a few wizened old men, huddled on the benches on the far side, soaking up the meagre rays of the winter sun. May turned and faced her companion.

'I do not advise the seats, they harbour bugs.'

For the first time since they had met Harry Cussons looked discomfited, but he rapidly recovered himself.

'Miss Winton, May, the last time we met, I forgot myself. I was so impatient for your company I just did not think – I failed to realise the implications of taking you to a public restaurant. Please do forgive me.'

He waited expectantly. As she looked at him May had a strange sensation of unreality. The cold wind whipping her skirts around her ankles, the gusts of grit blowing into her face, the roar and clatter of the traffic running down the steep slope to the tunnel – that was all real enough. But it was as

144

though the man standing in front of her were the other side of a thick sheet of plate glass: he smiled, he spoke – she saw his smiles, she heard his voice, but they did not touch her.

He seemed to be waiting for an answer, so she replied, 'We all make mistakes, Mr Cussons.'

He beamed in relief, and said gallantly, 'I do, Miss Winton, but you, I'm sure, never!'

May thought of Sister Simeon's many rebukes, and a bleak smile passed over her lips. Harry Cussons seemed to interpret this as encouragement.

'Miss Winton, this is hardly the appropriate time or place, but I wish to ask you – as I have never asked any woman before,' he paused, then pressed on. 'Will you do me the honour of becoming my wife?' He gathered momentum. 'I find you so beautiful, so high-spirited, so witty, so charming. Let me,' and he made a sweeping gesture that encompassed their drab surroundings, 'let me take you away from all this ugliness and grime, let me take you back to that life of gaiety and elegance and luxury where you belong. I do love you, May, and I think you feel something for me.'

As he spoke these last words May felt the sheet of glass begin to shiver and soften. The dusty grey shrubs around them receded and she seemed to be peering down the tube of a kaleidoscope, a child's toy in which there, in the distance, were the brightly-coloured patterns, forming and re-forming before her eyes: the glittering ballrooms, the shining summer sun at Ascot, the white napery and gleaming silver of a long table arrayed for dinner. They were tiny and far away, but they were there, sharply etched, jewel-bright, and infinitely desirable. But then, as she bent nearer, she saw another picture: Lord Hindlesham's sad, monkey face in the shadows of the cab, and she heard again his low, serious voice, 'You are lucky, my dear. You see the evils that you wrestle with – the dirt and the disease and the poverty. They are all clear before you, too clear, perhaps, but you know your enemy and can fight it face to face. There is evil and weakness and corruption in Society, too, but it hides itself under a dazzling exterior, and its creeping rottenness is hard to grasp and harder still to battle with.' And as she listened, the pictures in the kaleidoscope became smaller and smaller, and shrank to the size of a pin's head, and went out.

May pulled her cloak more tightly around her against the cold wind and asked, 'What of your mistress, Mr Cussons. What of Lady Hindlesham?'

He flinched, as though she had struck him; then took hold of himself again. 'Of course, if we were married, I would break the association completely.'

May looked at him, and the betraying conditional hung in the air between them. Then he began to try and regain his lost ground, his voice gentle and persuasive.

'I know you value your calling, you feel you are useful here; but, seriously, May, there must be many other women with a talent for nursing, while there is only one woman I could ever marry, and that is you.'

And May saw the sincerity in his eyes and knew that that was true, for the moment, anyway. And what was her task here, but to watch helplessly by as young men arched their backs in agony and died too slowly? But as the wave of easy surrender reared up and hung poised, waiting to sweep down and overwhelm her, she remembered other voices: 'Pull yourself together, Nurse Winton, there are other patients. We will have a heavy ward this evening.' And the sobbing: 'You tried, Nurse, you tried. Thank you for trying.'

May shuddered, pulled herself up straight and raised her chin. She spoke in a level tone.

'You are right, Mr Cussons. I am not indispensable here, but there is some benefit to others in what I do, however little. I will not give up now. Besides,' she hesitated, then plunged on, 'though it is true, as you said, that I do feel something for you, I do not respect you as a woman should respect the man who is to be her husband. Thank you, but I cannot marry you.'

She turned away from his stricken face and moved swiftly along the gravel walk. She ran between the jostling traffic and under the archway, fleeing inside the high, prison-like walls as though into a refuge.

146

Home Sister was crossing the courtyard. 'Is that you, Nurse Winton?' she called. 'Hurry along, girl, and have your tea, or you'll be late back on duty.'

'I'm sorry, Sister. I'm quite ready.'

Chapter Seventeen

'Seven-thirty, Nurse.'

Head aching, body heavy and unrested, May dragged herself out of bed and across to the water jug. She pressed damp fingers into her eyes, and then, with slow, clumsy movements, began to dress.

The Christmas period had passed in a daze for May, alternately haunted by Bob Tyrrell's agonising death and the disturbing scene in the Tunnel Gardens. On Boxing Day ward changes were announced and May was told to come off duty at midday so that she could report to Isaiah Ward that night. She made her farewells to Sister Simeon, moved her belongings to the top floor, reserved for night nurses, then undressed and lay sleepless in bed over the long afternoon.

She had been on night duty for ten days now, and felt as though she had entered another life – a life where the previous comfortable, unthinking acceptance of her body was a barely remembered dream; now every movement demanded a constant exercise of willpower. As she came off duty in the morning she felt like a broken-winded cab horse, which needed whips and curses to goad it into activity. May bitterly recalled her former pride in her strength, her stamina, her ability to sleep deeply and well and rise refreshed and full of energy in the morning. Now, the needs of the institution had caused her to be picked up and turned upside down, and she had to face the humiliating truth that she could not properly function so; only endure, and that with difficulty.

In the morning she felt she might perhaps have been able to collapse into the oblivion which both her mind and body craved; but the system and Home Sister would not allow this. By the time the approved hour came round she was beyond sleep, and could only toss, restless and tormented between brief snatches of unconsciousness, until the maid's call came, when she dragged herself to her feet to start the whole punishing cycle again.

To compound the nightmare, fog had descended on the city. For five days now the dense, sulphur-yellow cloud had clasped the hospital in its cold, clammy embrace. The noisy Dock traffic was reduced to a muffled, kerb-hugging crawl, and oily brown drops coated and smeared every surface. Inside the wards the weaker patients gasped and choked, slowly losing their unequal fight for breath, while May watched helplessly; and each day the death toll mounted.

Isaiah Ward was in the basement, next to the mortuary. This was the oldest part of the hospital, where the ceilings were low, the windows small and the rooms gloomy even at midday; at night the shadows barely retreated from the flickering light of the oil lamp. Despite the never-ending round of scrubbing and cleaning, the wards here smelt sour and musty, and the ill-ventilated sluice rooms stank. Isaiah was not one single large ward, but a scattered collection of different-sized rooms, so that, despite her inexperience May was often left to govern her own empire, while the senior ruled elsewhere. Her unwilling sway was exercised over cases whose infected wounds stubbornly refused to heal; they had been moved down from other wards to lurk, delirious or despairing, as an evil-smelling decay in the bowels of the hospital. They were not forgotten; Sister Isaiah, round-faced and determinedly optimistic, laboured over them all day, and left May and her colleague a full programme of fomentations to be carried out all through the night: some four-hourly, some two-hourly, a few every hour. And this was as well as the normal routine of giving drinks, washing, turning and preparing for the day staff.

At three in the morning there was a short break; each nurse was allowed to sit down and drink a cup of tea – prepared in their own special pot and drunk from their own, hopefully uncontaminated, crockery. On this night May did not bother with the tea. She decided that the effort of making it would outweigh the reviving effects of the drink. So she simply sat

149

down in the ward and gazed from under heavy lids at her unwelcome kingdom. As she sat there, the air around her began to take on substance and shift unnervingly before her eyes; then she was floating, light-headed, yet weighed down. She felt as if she were about to tip forward off the chair, yet was powerless to stop herself. She tried rubbing her eyes, blinking rapidly, concentrating on her breathing, pinching the pad of her thumb – but it was no use, unconsciousness was overtaking her in irresistible waves. The two lines of white beds danced into the shadows; she was cushioned by the seductiveness of sleep. With a last mighty effort she forced herself to her feet and staggered off down the endless ward. She thrust open the kitchen door and fell against the sink; then she managed to turn on the tap and bend down and push her face into the icy flow. The shock brought her round. Face dripping, she filled the palms of her hands with cold water and lapped it up.

Full consciousness came back, as she stood shivering in the draughty kitchen, cap awry and apron damp. 'Whatever am I doing here? It's the middle of the night, I should be in bed, warm and asleep!' She felt the outrage in her voice as she spoke aloud. Like an exile she remembered other nights when it had been a pleasure to be woken by the cry of a dog fox, for the sheer joy of turning over and snuggling down again into her soft enveloping bed.

A cockroach scuttled out from under the sink and headed busily across to the darkness under the dresser. May lacked the energy even to stamp on it. Rather, she felt a faint sense of relief that some other creature was awake and alert. The cold, the harsh, starched edge of her stiff collar biting into her neck, and the pounding ache beginning to engulf her temples all combined into a feeling of such utter wretchedness as she had never before known. Misery and self-pity washed over her.

She would go, now. She would walk out of the kitchen door, into the passage and through the ward entrance. She would pass along the dark stone corridor, up into the foggy courtyard, and find her way up, up, to her narrow bedroom with its hard bed. There she would throw herself down, shoes

150

and all, and sink into oblivion. And in the morning she would leave; break free from the high prison walls and the filthy streets and the yellow, sulphurous air, and go to crisp, clean, calm Suffolk.

May recognised that she had been defeated. She did not care. One foot had actually been placed in front of the other on the worn linoleum when she heard it: the feeble, whining cry, 'Nurse'. Deliberately May hunched her shoulder against the direction of the ward, and began to move, crablike, towards freedom. '*Nurse*', the note was higher, keening now. Dimly there formed in May's consciousness the sullen awareness that that meant her; there was no other nurse within earshot. Her reason, huddled in the corner of her mind, argued that old Mrs Slinger was safe in bed – if she soiled the linen, what did it matter? Just another set of sheets to keep the fallen girls in the laundry busy. But another, painfully learned response was taking over. Night Sister's rasping voice echoed in her memory: 'You will attend to the patient first, Nurse. You are here for her benefit, not she for yours. Go now.'

So, back into the dark, malodorous ward, feet leaden and heart unwilling, May went.

Night duty dragged on interminably. After her crisis May forced herself into a rigid routine: she made herself walk briskly every morning, whatever the weather, and then came back and sat in front of her medical textbooks, compelling herself to concentrate on every word until she had bludgeoned herself into sleep. But it was never more than bare endurance. A moment's inattention on her part and she knew she would slip back into surrender: she was fighting a war in which the only hope of survival was constant vigilance, and this took a heavy physical toll.

Yet there were some rewards. Gradually she learnt to push out of her mind the despair and hopelessness generated by her basement patients, and to recognise that the few emaciated figures who finally left their beds were a kind of victory.

Her senior nurse was the stolid Grayson, with whom she

151

could at first make no relationship; but slowly she began to respect the woman for her competence and sheer stamina, and she got used to her expressionless face and long silences. Indeed, she grew to understand them after one night, when she had turned to Grayson as they waited for the mortuary trolley and burst out, 'Don't you hate this job, sometimes?'

Grayson deliberated, slowly, then said, 'No.' Seeing May's downcast expression she had made an effort to explain. 'I was brought up in an institution, a school for orphaned clergy daughters. The High Mistress was vicious and spiteful to us, and to the younger teachers. We hated her, and we feared her.'

May waited, half-repelled, half-fascinated, for some ghastly revelation, but none followed. Grayson added simply, 'You can stand anything, you know, if you have to.' She went to attend a restless patient. May began to recognise the stolidity as stoicism, and to feel ashamed of her own squeamishness.

Sometimes, when her hands were occupied with a mechanical task, May's mind would wander and ask the unanswerable question. Would she have refused Harry Cussons so abruptly if she had not been so stunned by Bob Tyrrell's tragic death? Where would she be now if she had said 'Yes'? Certainly not in this dark insect-ridden basement, where one had to bang the door as one went into the kitchen, to frighten away lurking rats. Marriage to Harry Cussons would have been an honourable escape; even Matron could scarcely have objected. Nursing seemed to offer little at present. It took all her energies just to keep going; there was no enjoyment in it in Isaiah, and scant satisfaction. He had come to seek her out; he had forgiven her resounding slap and impetuous departure that evening. Dimly, May recognised that she had had reasons for her actions, but the weeks underground were blunting her critical faculties. Like a tongue prodding an aching tooth she tormented herself with visions of being escorted round Harry's relatives – introduced as his affianced bride – made welcome, as she would have been, being young, of good family, and an heiress too. To be squired by Harry Cussons, debonair and amusing, and to be touched by him!

May shied away from the thought, blushing even in the privacy of the damp kitchen, remembering his hand on hers, and the feel of his lips on her wrist.

Perhaps he would not take no for an answer, and would come to find her again – no, May thought of her face in the telltale mirror, eyes dark-shadowed by exhaustion, staring out from under hair that was dull and lifeless, showing all too clearly the ravages wrought by nights – no, not yet, he might disdain her now. But perhaps, later, when London filled up again and the Season began, then she might see him. He would come towards her, his hands held out, his voice warm and alive: 'Miss Winton, May,' but beyond this point May could never imagine what would be said, or what would happen. In any case, she was usually interrupted by Grayson's phlegmatic yet authoritative voice, 'You must work faster, Winton, we have a lot to get through, tonight.'

It was halfway through March that May realised that the end of her sentence was finally in sight. Her monthly days off could at last be claimed, and she would have three glorious nights in bed – not in the narrow iron bedstead at St Katharine's but lapped in the luxury of feathers and linen, behind velvet curtains with a crackling fire in the grate, at the Winton's Town house. Lord and Lady Clarence were coming up ahead of the Season especially so that May could spend the time with them.

The last week, the last night – it had finally come; now May no longer thought of Harry Cussons, she could think of nothing but the rest in front of her for her leaden limbs and heavy head. Then, as she and Grayson sat in the largest ward over their midnight meal May realised that the ache in her neck, with which she had woken, was getting worse. When she tried to swallow the toast rasped her throat, and left it on fire. By the morning she felt burning hot, yet could not stop shivering; the floor seemed to recede and waver as she put her foot on it. She could barely croak and her throat was agonisingly painful. Night Sister looked at her sharply, and when May barely managed to reply to her question she tipped May's chin up and held her lamp high so that she could look into her mouth. What she saw made her shake her head.

'You must report sick to Home Sister as soon as you go off, Nurse Winton.'

May squeaked frantically, 'But I'm going home today, it's my nights off.'

Night Sister was kind but firm. 'I'm sorry, Nurse Winton, but you are not going anywhere with a throat like that. You might spread infection.'

May refused to believe it. Surely Home Sister would let her go?

By the time she reached Home Sister she was light-headed. A doctor was called, another inspection held, then sentence was passed: 'Over to the sick bay, at once.' May tried to speak, but no voice would come. She shook her head and her eyes filled with tears. Dr Calne patted her hand gently.

'Hospital throat is inevitable, my dear. All you young nurses come down with it at some time, especially after a spell in the septic ward. Don't worry, we'll look after you.'

May looked despairingly at Home Sister. There was no trace of sympathy in her face, she said merely, 'Illness among the nursing staff is always a nuisance, Dr Calne, but fortunately Nurse Winton has just finished her period of night duty, so it's not too inconvenient.'

May felt the mingled anger and distress well up. She turned her head away as the childish tears spilled over and ran down her cheeks.

As she lay in bed the pain was like sharp knives sawing at her throat. When she was forced to swallow the knives became red-hot. Whenever Nurse Sampson insisted on more drinks, or, 'A little arrowroot, dear, ever so nourishing,' the red-hot knives grew larger and larger and slashed across her palate. Nor was her misery confined to this: her neck was swollen and exquisitely tender, the slightest awkwardness on the part of the ham-fisted Farrell made her feel like screaming. She lay rigid, afraid to move, listening anxiously to the rhythm of the feet approaching. Farrell's light pattering

154

steps, a charming sound in themselves, reminiscent of lively ballrooms and country house parties, filled her with dread as she braced herself for the well-meant but clumsy ministrations which would follow. When the tread was that of Sampson's flat feet, large and dropped at the arches, she relaxed, secure in the knowledge that her aches and pains would be deftly eased, and even, for a moment, charmed away under the influence of Sampson's warm, reassuring presence.

The doctor and Sister gazed down at her, as she lay hot with fever, her legs shaking uncontrollably. They pursed their lips and looked grave, and May felt the despair of weakness rise in her, and force tears to her eyes, so that she turned her swollen neck painfully away to hide them. But as soon as their measured tread had moved away down the ward, the heavy, padding footfalls were approaching, a gentle hand whisked away her tears and a cool palm rested on her forehead, while the adenoidal, common voice murmured words of comfort.

'You're doing very well, Nurse Winton, very well indeed. Just stick it out, dear, it's always darkest before the dawn.' The commonplace clichés took on the character of inspired prophecies through the medium of Nurse Sampson's personality.

May remembered how she had winced at the girl's accent and blowsy looks when she'd met her before in the Nurses' Sitting Room; now any twinge of shame was swallowed up in the determination that when she got back to the patients she would be a Sampson instead of a Farrell – so much of Sister Simeon's painstaking teaching now made sense. Such was the power of Nurse Sampson's faith that in her presence May had no doubts but that she soon would be back on the wards, ill though she knew she was. 'You'll be all right, dear, you're a strong girl,' were the words she heard, and Sampson was right. The shivering fits and the hot, drenching sweats began to decline, and a week after her arrival in Rachel Ward May found herself waiting impatiently for her dinner, disappointed that it was only rice pudding. Now Sister herself said, 'Of course, you've got a sound constitution Nurse Winton – a severe attack, but we knew we'd soon pull you through.' But

155

May thought that she hadn't said it last week, while Nurse Sampson had.

They sent her home for ten days' convalescence. Lord Clarence came himself in the brougham, and fidgeted with the window to ensure that not a breath of cold air blew on his daughter. May, swathed in her furs, felt warm and weak and very tired.

She slept all the nights and long into the mornings. Lady Clarence made her round of calls without her. But two days before May was due to return to St Katharine's her step-mother suggested, tentatively, that May might like to ac-company her parents to a squash – 'Just a small reception, May, your cousins will be there, you will enjoy a little chat with them.'

May did not much want to go, but Lady Clarence had been very kind, and it was unusual to see her tentative; also she knew her step-mother was anxiously awaiting her next letter from Emily, so it seemed needlessly cruel to disappoint her over such a relatively small matter. Her agreement was willingly given.

Fenton dressed her and she was escorted to the coach as though she were a piece of Dresden china. Her father almost carried her up the stairs when they arrived, although she really felt quite well again. Archie was there, and Bertie, and Louise Dumer. May was beginning to enjoy herself when the crowd around her suddenly shifted and parted – and there was Harry Cussons. May gasped, and he was staring straight at her. She smiled at him, and raised her hand – his face was cold and resentful. He turned ostentatiously to the woman at his side and slid his hand possessively up her arm and whispered something in her ear. Della Hindlesham glanced round and stared at May, made a little half bow then turned back to Harry and gave a tiny shrug of her exquisite shoulders. She tapped his cheek with her fan, spoke softly to him, and they both laughed in shared intimacy. It was skilfully done. May felt the burning blush of humiliation rise in her cheeks and the easy tears of convalescence fill her eyes. She would have stood

there, exposed, had not Archie put his arm around her waist
and guided her into a window recess, shielding her from the
curious looks of the crowd with his body.

'So you did turn him down, then.'

May, unable to speak, just nodded.

'Grandmamma dropped hints – she was annoyed.'

May shook her head, and felt her control slipping. 'I wish I
hadn't, now.'

'Well, it's no use crying over spilt milk – plenty more fish in
the sea, and all that.'

Archie's attempts at comfort were so like him that May
managed a shaky smile, but the tears were still threatening;
she looked down and bit her lip. Then another male form
appeared beside them, and Archie's voice was relieved.

'I say, George old fellow, d'you think you could locate my
aunt? Poor old May's quite done up; been ill, y'know, first
day out, and all that.'

'Of course, I'll find her at once.' May recognised Lord
Hindlesham's collected tones.

'That'll be all right then, May, we'll soon have you home.'

In a very short time Lord Hindlesham was back. 'She was
downstairs. She's sending for the carriage; I told her we'd
bring May down.'

Lord Hindlesham forced a pathway through the throng
and May followed, grateful for Archie's arm. Her father came
up the stairs to meet them, his face concerned. Lady Clarence's
voice was anxious. 'I should not have brought you, May.
Thank you so much, Lord Hindlesham.'

May's father reiterated, 'Thanks, old man – didn't expect
to see you here tonight.'

'I leave for the Continent in the morning,' Lord Hindlesham
replied. 'Goodbye, Lady Clarence, Miss Winton. I hope the
nursing is not too exhausting.'

May managed a proper smile at last. 'I'm afraid night duty
is, rather. I'm glad my three months of that is over for the
year.'

Lord Hindlesham said, 'It is strange, is it not, that we
legislate against women in factories working the night shift,

157

yet expect it of young girls in hospitals – still, I'm sure your friend Miss Carter would be able to explain that!' He smiled and left them.

Next morning May came down to breakfast late, still shaken by the memory of Harry Cussons' open resentment. She found Lady Clarence sitting, her toast untouched, with a letter in her hand and a drawn expression on her face. She pulled herself together with a visible effort and turned to May.

'Are you quite recovered, my dear?'

'Yes, thank you Step-mamma. Is that a letter from Emily? How is the baby?'

Lady Clarence abruptly thrust the letter into May's hands. 'May, read it, please. Tell me what it means.'

May read the anxious words Emily had carefully penned far away in the heat of India. In her time on night duty, when she had forced her way through volume after volume from the Nurses' Library, she had learnt a lot. As she read Emily's account of her son an ominous picture rose up in her mind. She made herself re-read the letter, carefully, conscious of her step-mother's anxious gaze, then she looked up and said firmly, 'I think you should go to India, Step-mamma. Emily will be needing you.'

Lady Clarence blinked, her usually impassive face betraying a mixture of emotions.

The door opened and May turned to greet her father. 'Papa, I think it would be as well if you escorted Step-mamma to India.'

Lord Clarence looked startled, but soon recovered himself. 'If you say so, my dear.'

Lady Clarence began to protest, but May silenced her with a glance. 'You could book the tickets today, Papa. You could be there in less than a month.'

Lord Clarence was visibly brightening. 'Always fancied a tiger shoot, m'dear – splendid idea, why didn't I think of it myself? I know you've been fretting about Emily, Julia my love; we'll go and see her. You must come too, May.'

May felt a little burst of excitement, and a longing to see

158

Emily, but she resolutely shook her head. Her duty lay elsewhere now.

'No, Matron is expecting me back. You must both go.'

'But May, you will have no home while we are away.' Lady Clarence's voice was concerned.

'I shall spend my free time with Grandmamma.' Her heart sank a little at the thought of whom she might meet in her grandmother's social circle, but she smiled reassuringly at her step-mother. 'If our positions were reversed then Emily would be the first to tell you to go, you know that. Of course you must go to her.'

Lady Clarence stood up. 'Then I will go and speak to Fenton.' She turned to May and put out her hand. 'Thank you, my dear.' She left the room with unusual haste.

As her father displayed his hazy knowledge of Indian geography over his breakfast – 'Old Tim Schofield said at Simla, or was it Poona? – all those places sound alike – still, I daresay we'll sort them out when we get there,' May sat quiet, feeling very alone. Then she took a deep breath, reached for her cup and drank steadily. She had made her bed and now she must lie on it, even though it were narrow and hard and made of iron. Why, this fine Darjeeling seemed positively anaemic after the strong hospital brew – she would soon get used to life in St Katharine's again.

Chapter Eighteen

On her return May was sent to Naomi, a women's medical ward. The patients were ill and the nursing heavy, but Sister Naomi was elderly and experienced. Although strict with her nurses she was invariably fair, and she had endless patience with the sick women. Staff Nurse was a good teacher, so May, learning to deal with new problems and to carry out different treatments, felt a sense of discovery, and growing confidence. By the time Lady Clarence's telegram announced her parents' safe arrival in India she had settled back into the routine of St Katharine's. She did not forget Harry Cussons' snub, but it mattered less to her. After all, he was a man who had spent a lifetime getting exactly what he wanted, and she had had the temerity to refuse him – no wonder he had been angry and resentful.

One fine evening in late spring May and Ellen found themselves at Victoria Station, with three full hours ahead of them before the doors of the Nurses' Home shut at ten. They had just waved goodbye to Ada, who was one of the lucky probationers whose parents lived near enough to London for her to get home on the evening before her monthly day off and so enjoy a whole twenty-eight hours of family life. The three of them had rushed off duty together and Ada had changed while the other two packed her bag; then they had hurried by train and underground to the terminus of the Brighton Line. Ada, festooned with an assortment of badly-wrapped parcels – it was her twin sisters' birthday that week – had been bundled onto the Redhill train with seconds to spare, and May and Ellen, pleasantly conscious of having fulfilled their duty as friends, now had the evening in front of them.

'Where shall we go now, May? It's a lovely evening.'

May thought for a moment, then suggested, 'I think we're

160

quite near St James' Park – we could walk up past the Palace.'

Ellen was immediately interested. 'Oh, do let's – we might see the King and Queen!'

May laughed. 'I must say, for someone who disapproves of inherited wealth you're uncommonly interested in royalty and the aristocracy!'

Ellen grinned. 'Well, you're all such a novelty to a country bumpkin like me. Come on, let's go and see what we can.'

As they neared the Palace the traffic began to slow down, then it stopped altogether. Beyond the cursing, swearing cab drivers they saw a long queue of private carriages. As they gazed at them May was transported back in time, to when she and Emily had sat, side by side and still as statues under the watchful eye of Lady Clarence, in just such a queue on just such a fine spring evening. She remembered the endless tiresome hours at the dressmaker, while a tuck had been taken here, or a seam altered there; Bella's pride as she had carefully lifted the ostrich plumes to set them on their hair – three apiece and stiffly white; the strange sensation of the long unmanageable train fastened to her shoulders, dragging her back as she walked; the slow, stately procession down the stairs to where the servants waited in the hall, whispering in excited admiration. The whole scene was suddenly as bright and vivid before her eyes as though it were only yesterday. How pale and set Emily's face had been in the carriage – May had begun to feel frightened herself, until she had looked up at her step-mother, so stern and imposing. The sight had given May immediate reassurance: nothing would go wrong because Lady Clarence would not allow it to go wrong. So they had waited in the coach, just as these young girls were waiting, grateful for once for Lady Clarence's formal conversation and the formidable bearing which had driven away even the curious Cockneys who thronged the streets and pressed their noses against the very windows of the carriage.

'What's happening, May? What are they waiting for?'

Ellen's fingers pressed her arm, and her voice was insistent.

'It's a Court. They're waiting to be presented.'

Ellen's face was alive with excitement. She tugged at May's cloak, pulling her along. 'Do let's get closer, I want to see.'

Ellen, thin as a lath, pushed and wriggled her way through the crowd. May followed, unresisting. A friendly policeman saw them and cried, 'Make way there, please, let the nurses through,' and the crowd parted good-humouredly so that May and Ellen found themselves suddenly at the front, within inches of the rounded hindquarters of a glossy chestnut. They shifted slightly sideways and saw the face of the débutante, a pale blur through the misted glass, surrounded by the billowing white froth of dress and train.

The policeman turned his head. 'Can you see them, ladies? Take a good look at how the nobs live, while you've got the chance. When you're rushing around with your pills and potions first thing tomorrow they'll still be lying abed, thinking what a busy time they've had this evening!' He chuckled. 'But we know better, don't we? You and me, we have to work for our living.' Imperturbable, but watchful, he paced off amongst the crowd.

May whispered, 'I feel rather warm – shall we step back a little, Ellen?'

Ellen obediently stepped back, until they stood alone on the grass, still gazing at the line of carriages, stretching all the way to the Palace gates.

'What do they do when they get inside, May?'

May said slowly, 'You sit down on little gold chairs and you wait. It seems to be nothing but waiting, the whole evening. Then, when they tell you to, you have to join another long queue and move forward, oh, so slowly, through endless big rooms until you get to the ballroom – where the lights are dazzling and you want to blink but you know you mustn't – then suddenly it all goes deathly quiet and you hear your name, sounding very loud in the silence, as you walk forward, and you realise you're directly in front of Their Majesties.' May paused, remembering the total isolation of that moment.

'Then what do you do, May?' Ellen prompted.

162

'Then you curtsey, once to the King and once to the Queen.'

'What next?'

'Nothing, that's it.'

'All this, just for a curtsey!' Ellen's voice was stunned as she stared at the long procession of carriages, each with its liveried attendants. 'It's incredible.'

'Two curtseys, Ellen,' May corrected. Then she began to laugh, and Ellen joined her, until they were doubled up and gasping for breath.

Slowly the line crept forward, then stopped again. Ellen, still giggling a little, said, 'All the same, I'd like to go in, just once, and see it all happening. If only Lord Hindlesham would jump out of a cab and whisk us inside!'

'He can't, Ellen, he's in Italy. My grandmother told me when I had lunch with her last week. He'll be away the whole of the Season, she said.'

Ellen made no reply, but her expression was questioning, so May explained.

'His younger daughter married an Italian Duke, or Marchese, or something, and she's been very homesick, so her father's gone out there until after the baby is born.'

'So there will be no dazzling balls at Hindlesham House this year, like the one where you met Mr Cussons?'

May retorted swiftly, 'Oh, I'm sure there will be! Lady Hindlesham hasn't gone, she's in London as usual.'

Ellen sounded surprised. 'But if her daughter . . .'

May's tone was cold. 'Dear Della would never, but never, miss the Season. Besides, the last thing she wants is to be reminded that her daughters are grown up. Archie had quite a penchant for Helen Hindlesham, the younger girl, and I remember him saying how amusing it was to watch them. Helen is the image of her mother, only twenty years younger, of course, and apparently Della could hardly bear to be seen in the same room as her. Lord Hindlesham's sister virtually brought the two girls out, with her own three – except for the Presentation, of course, she'd have to do that.'

Ellen was still upset. 'But fancy not going to visit her own

163

daughter if she's unhappy! Italy's not that far away, and your step-mother's gone right to India – whatever must the poor girl feel?'

May grimaced at the very idea of comparing two such different women as Della Hindlesham and Lady Clarence Winton. She reassured Ellen. 'Don't worry about Helen, Archie said she idolised her father; he took them everywhere as children. I'm sure she'd rather see him, any day. And I've no doubt it suits Della very well indeed – with her husband away she can amuse herself how she pleases.' May recognised the leaven of bitterness in her own voice, and so did Ellen. The latter spoke firmly.

'You were absolutely right to reject that man, May. You at least, are free of the whole miserable tangle. But Lord Hindlesham – why ever did he marry a woman like her? He seems so kind – and so honest.'

'Ada's right, all men are fools at heart, even the best of them.' May spoke almost savagely.

'But he was very young, May.' Ellen's voice was soft, and May, glancing quickly at her, saw the tell-tale glint under her eyelashes. Dear Ellen, with her ready sympathy: May felt ashamed of her harshness. After all, Lord Hindlesham had been so kind to her, and why should she expend her anger on Harry Cussons now? She had made her own choice.

She took Ellen's arm. 'Come, it's a lovely evening, and we've got plenty of time before we have to start back. Let's stroll in the Park like ladies of leisure, and think of Ada. She'll be home by now, tying her fingers in knots to get those parcels open, with her sisters shouting and squealing and falling over the dog and teasing the cat – weren't they little horrors!'

Ellen smiled, and they began to chat about other things as they sauntered across the grass in the balmy evening air.

Chapter Nineteen

In the third week of September May received a summons to Matron's office. As soon as she was dismissed for her morning's off-duty she raced across to her room, put on a clean apron and set her cap firmly in position on her tidied hair. There were three other nurses already waiting on the row of hard chairs outside the main office. The first in the queue was weeping copiously, while the other two looked strained and apprehensive. May wracked her brains, but could think of no recent sins of omission or commission on her part – at least, none that Matron could possibly have discovered; but the scent of fear from her three companions began to affect her too.

She was most grateful when a stout, red-faced probationer sat down on her other side and said loudly to the corridor, 'If that old cow thinks I'm going to grovel over a broken thermometer she can think again.'

May was sympathetic.

'How did you come to break it?'

'I'd just rammed it up the patient's backside when the old fool turned over and sat on it,' a jolly laugh rang out. 'You should have seen Sister Barnabas, she was in a taking.'

At this point the door opened and an immaculate Office Sister beckoned in the weeping girl. Five minutes later the girl came out, still weeping. The other two went in, one after the other, and one after the other came out again, handkerchiefs to faces, sobbing piteously. May stood up, squared her shoulders and marched in.

'You wished to see me, Matron?' her voice was cold.

Matron glanced up from her papers. 'Oh yes, Nurse Winton, did you not realise your fortnight's holiday was due? You girls are so thoughtless – it takes time to arrange replacements, you know.'

165

May's jaw tightened. Ada had already asked about her holiday and been told in no uncertain terms that this would be taken at Matron's command and at Matron's pleasure – it was no business of the probationer concerned. Matron opened her mouth to continue but May slid in smoothly, seconds before her.

'I would not dream of presuming on my annual leave without a personal directive from you, Matron.' Her eyes were round and innocent. Matron looked at her suspiciously, but May's expression was guileless.

'Your fortnight's holiday starts on Friday.'

May, thinking of her parents' absence overseas and her grandmother's busy social life exclaimed, 'But suppose that's not convenient?'

Matron gave her a level stare. 'It is quite convenient to me, Nurse Winton. Send in the next nurse, please.' She bent her head over her desk.

As usual May left Matron's office vowing that she would get the better of her next time. She was interested to see that the red-faced probationer was now sniffing dismally and trying to wipe her nose surreptitiously on the corner of her apron. May silently handed her a clean handkerchief, gestured towards the office door and passed on.

Naturally it was not convenient. A brisk exchange of telegrams elicited the information that Lady Andover was at present staying in a remote area of Scotland. May was quite welcome, of course, though the house was rather small . . . Marvelling at her grandmother's ability to convey the most delicate nuances by telegram May dispatched a terse: 'Arrive Stemhalton Friday. Await your eventual return.' and began to pack her bags.

When she got to Stemhalton the servants were welcoming and old Nanny toddled up from the lodge where she had been pensioned off, to weep tears of joy over her nursling. For a week May roamed round the estate in the morning, alternately slept and read the afternoons away on the sunny terrace with a cup of fragrant China tea and a plate of the stillroom maid's feather-light scones beside her, and then strolled down to a delicious dinner prepared by Chef's own hands. 'Bettair cook for one who respects food zan for a dozen gulpers, Mees May.' May suspected he enjoyed the excuse, and the upper servants lived royally from the surplus of her meals. She only wished she could have joined them, but knew they would have been scandalised at the suggestion.

Just as May was beginning to feel in need of a little mild distraction Lady Andover arrived with her house party. As each lady entered the drawing room May noticed the signs of a barely suppressed excitement. Conversation was strained in the presence of the gentlemen, and the longing for their absence was imperfectly concealed.

As soon as the old Duchess of Portchester had steered her bewildered and resisting husband to the doorway with a firm 'Shut the door behind you, Cedric,' there was a convergence into two parties. The young girls moved reluctantly to the far end of the drawing room while the married women began to regroup round the hearth. May hesitated, then firmly sat down with the latter. There was a look of surprise on one or two faces, but her presence was accepted. On the few occasions she had been in society over the Season, May had realised that, without benefit of that magic gold circlet, she had crossed the invisible barrier between girlhood and woman-hood. Although obviously not having any clear idea of a nurse's duties there was a general recognition that it con-stituted experience; and, May reflected, what could be more of an experience than giving eight soap and water enemas to eight recumbent males in thirty minutes flat?

There was a momentary pause while the ladies waited for one of their number to break the silence. With an innate awareness of rank they glanced expectantly at the Duchess of Portchester; daughter, sister and wife of Dukes, she did not disappoint them. Planting two large feet side by side under the dusty hem of her tweed skirt she spoke in her usual harsh croak.

'Even I never expected Della Hindlesham to be such a fool.'

There were excited anticipatory twitters.

'But Mr Cussons is of a good family, and very wealthy.'

'Any woman who leaves her husband is a fool – what did she need to elope for? George would never have taken a horse whip to her, more's the pity.' Her Grace was trenchant.

A lady tittered. 'Poor George would have been exhausted if he'd taken a horse whip to her every time . . .' the voice trailed off. Mrs Jermyne subsided, realising she had gone too far too soon. Conventional exclamations of horror and dismay were called for before a full character assassination could begin. Murmurs of – 'Dear Della must have had a brainstorm' – 'Surely she would never . . .' and, in a voice tinged with regret, 'Perhaps it is only a rumour . . .'

'Nonsense.' The Duchess soon dismissed this one. 'The woman's halfway to the Continent by now, with that blue-eyed Casanova.'

It struck May at this point that one or two of the younger ladies looked almost wistful as they contemplated the vision of Della Hindlesham setting off on a life of sin with Harry Cussons. May herself was shocked, but not, she knew, as shocked as she would have been a year ago. She was well aware now of the casual exchange of partners which was customary in certain areas of the East End – why should the denizens of Mayfair be any different? And yet it was surprising: she had had a higher opinion of Della's hypocrisy. Since she had clearly been enjoying all the benefits of her position in Society while indulging in the pleasures of a lover – why should she have taken this irrevocable step? And it was irrevocable, May knew that. The erring husband or wife of Dockland might have some chance of being reinstated, but Della's only hope lay in eventual marriage to Harry Cussons, and even then she would be excluded from much of Society as the guilty party in a divorce. But the gossip continued.

'Of course, George Hindlesham is such a chivalrous fool he'll probably do the decent thing and give her grounds himself.' The Duchess spoke with regret.

'No, no, Your Grace,' young Mrs Dalbany was blushing at her own temerity in daring to correct a Duchess, but she ploughed on. 'That would not do; she is already compromised. If both parties have, have . . .' she faltered.

'Committed adultery, you mean,' her Grace said helpfully. Mrs Dalbany was crimson; she knew full well that only her elderly husband's status as a High Court Judge had secured her inclusion in this house party and she was aware of being rather too genteel for the company. 'Yes, your Grace, well in that situation there can be no divorce – perhaps you remember the Allison case.' Several ladies nodded, they did indeed.

'So poor Della's affairs will be splashed all over the newspapers – how shocking!' Lady Canning sounded as if she could scarcely wait. May was sickened by her tone, but determined to keep her place and hear any further details. After all, she of all people had a right to be interested in the affairs of Harry Cussons.

But there was little more to be added. With the best will the ladies had exhausted their information, and only the bare bones were known. Della Hindlesham had left her home, and so had Harry Cussons. A sharp-eyed acquaintance returning from the Riviera had seen them both at Dover, boarding the cross channel steamer. The whys, the wherefores and all the explanations beyond the simple facts remained a matter for speculation. However, before they dispersed Lady Canning cheered the party by reminding them of the expected arrival the following day of Mrs Anstruther – 'Connie Anstruther's maid comes from the same village as Della's, she will know more.'

Connie Anstruther arrived on the two o'clock train. If she was surprised at the reception committee awaiting her in the drawing room she showed no sign of it. May, slightly ashamed of herself but burning with curiosity was there with them. One glance at Connie Anstruther's smug face as she sat down was enough to indicate that she could end their suspense. The conventions were dealt with with almost indecent haste, then the Duchess set the ball rolling. Mrs Anstruther began.

'My dear, never was I so surprised as when Barnes told me' – a significant pause – 'but I had noticed that dear Della was becoming just a fraction "embonpoint" – I thought it was middle age, how easily one can be deceived!'

169

A glimmering of understanding could be seen on several faces. May tried to wrestle with the idea, what a terrible mess! Connie Anstruther continued.

'Barnes tells me Easton had found her mistress unwell on several occasions recently, in the morning.' The last word was underlined.

'You mean, Della's in foal!' The Duchess' voice was astounded.

Connie Anstruther smiled. 'It would appear so, Your Grace. Yes, she is enceinte.'

There was a stunned silence. May noticed one or two of the ladies surreptitiously counting on their fingers; two months on a gynae ward had given her the answer already.

'But George Hindlesham was away for the whole Season, in Italy.' Lady Canning put into words what the others were thinking. 'How could Della have been so careless!'

Connie Anstruther still held the stage. 'Oh, whether he had been away or not he would have known. Barnes says it's common knowledge among the servants that he's not been inside her bedroom door for years.'

'I suppose there was hardly room for him as well,' said Mrs Jermyne.

There was a chorus of half-hearted reproof. 'Come now, Maud, she has been quite faithful to Harry, more so than he to her, I suspect. And then there was that young fair-haired boy, Alton's heir, just the same. Della was always faithful to her lovers.' There were approving murmurs.

May felt like shouting, 'And what of her husband? Did he not deserve her fidelity?' With an effort she held her tongue. But she had misjudged the ladies. A voice spoke out.

'Suppose the child is a boy? Della and George only had the two daughters.'

There was an appalled silence; the affair became suddenly serious now property and titles were seen to be at risk. The Duchess was the first to recover.

'Typical of Della, she should have done her duty earlier. No proper wife gives up after two girls.'

'No indeed,' Lady Langdale, mother of five daughters,

spoke with feeling. 'Poor, poor George. Do let us hope the child is female.'

With that sentiment at least May found herself in whole-hearted agreement, but she could stand no more. She got up and walked out into the fresh air of the terrace. How shocked middle-class Ellen would be when she told her. It was clear that Lord Hindlesham would have to take divorce proceedings for Della's sake. May had no doubts that he would eschew revenge and set his erring wife free. How would he endure the publicity? And then, would Harry Cussons actually marry Della? May supposed he would. After all, he was a gentleman, and it was his child she was carrying. Despite herself May felt a stirring of sympathy for the absconding Della: an acknowledged beauty who craved adulation and flattery, yet was no longer young. Had she feared to lose her handsome, charming lover and so hazarded all in this last, dangerous throw? And suppose May had given another answer to Harry Cussons in December, as she so nearly had, what difference would it have made? Probably there would have been no elopement, but perhaps the rest of the sorry story would have been little changed. She winced at her own cynicism, yet took a sombre satisfaction in recognising that she was no Lord Hindlesham, to play the complaisant husband; she would have acted, whatever the cost.

Chapter Twenty

May felt a quickening of the pulse as she jumped down from the cab outside St Katharine's at the end of September. As soon as her bags were upstairs she rushed to the Nurses' Sitting Room, where Minnie Emms squealed with pleasure at her return, and made haste to regale her with the latest gossip, amid constant interruptions from several other pros who had even better tales to tell.

Ada and Ellen had just gone off for their annual holiday, but news had arrived that Alice Rydal was not returning. May was hardly surprised: she only wondered that the girl had stayed as long as she had done. She was always complaining and had frequently threatened to leave. More unexpected was the announcement by quiet Flossy Allen that she was breaking her contract in order to be married at Christmas to a young man who worked in her father's grocery shop. 'Better be a slave to one man than to forty.' Her voice was resigned and May wondered whether she really wanted to marry at all – or did it just seem the less unacceptable of two alternatives? But Flossy insisted her mind was made up, and May knew she had found the persistent, harping correction by Sisters and Staff Nurses hard to bear. May fortified herself by planning mutiny, while Ellen was too mercurial of temperament to stay depressed for long, but it had obviously been too much for Flossy. Then she confided to May one night that she was frightened of greater responsibility, 'I'm terrified of making a mistake, and killing someone.' Her face was grey as she spoke and May stopped trying to persuade her to think again. So only trenchant, argumentative Ada, gentle Ellen and cheerful, slapdash Minnie remained with May of the original six.

May enjoyed her work on the gynae ward. Sister Dorcas was a law unto herself. Totally committed to her patients, she fought for them through thick and thin, and she never judged the women in her care. At first May had been deeply shocked at the arrival of self-induced miscarriages: women obviously determined not to bear more children and risking their lives to avoid it. But Sister Dorcas, sensing her recoil, called her away from one patient's bedside and spoke to her privately.

'Of course it's wrong to set out to deliberately destroy life with a knitting needle – and a dirty one at that – but before you pass judgment try and imagine the state of mind a woman must be in to attempt something so unnatural and so dangerous. Look at their faces, Nurse Winton, look at their exhausted bodies, listen to them talking amongst themselves; then ask yourself how you would feed and clothe and shelter a dozen children on a pound a week – that is, if you're quick enough to get it out of your husband's hands before it's spent at the pub!'

May recognised the truth of what Sister Dorcas was saying, but she still argued. 'But why do they do it then? I mean,' she floundered, then ploughed on. 'They must know if they do certain things, well, what causes . . .'

Sister looked at her pityingly. 'You have a very romantic view of men, Nurse Winton. Oh, there are some who will restrain themselves if their wife's health is at stake, but the great majority – well, they're stronger, they earn the wages, even if they don't always part with them, and if they don't get what they want at home they'll find some poor creature of the streets, and what wife wants that to happen?'

May was shocked to the core, but she made an effort to understand, though she said to Ellen that evening, after they came off duty, 'But what about the young girls, who aren't married, why do they allow themselves to get into that situation?'

Ellen was more tolerant. 'Remember their lives have not been as sheltered as ours – who knows what pressures have been brought to bear? Besides,' she hesitated, and her pale skin flushed pink, 'if they loved the man they were with – it is not just men who feel desire, May.'

May blinked, then remembered how she had felt when

173

Harry Cussons had so caressingly unbuttoned her glove, how would she have felt if . . . Feeling suddenly at sea she opened her mouth to question Ellen further, then hastily closed it again as she recollected that Ellen had been engaged – her fiancé had died of pneumonia the year before she had come to St Katharine's. She couldn't talk of this to her, it would revive painful memories. She began to speak instead of the projected Royal Visit, which had just been announced.

By the time May was due to leave Dorcas she had faced up to the shattering of many long-held prejudices, and had learned things which would have appalled Lady Clarence. On the last day before she was due to change, Sister Dorcas expanded her knowledge even further. Sister called her into her sitting room and posed a direct question:

'Nurse Winton, in future years you may find yourself, as a nurse, faced with a desperate woman who has just given birth, and to whom the possibility of yet another pregnancy is a nightmare – what would you do?'

Three months ago May would have had no difficulty in answering. Now she paused, looked at Sister Dorcas, and eventually admitted, 'I just don't know, Sister. I don't know.'

This admission of defeat appeared to satisfy Sister Dorcas. She leant forward. 'In that situation I advise the use of a sponge, well soaked in vinegar, placed in the appropriate position – at the appropriate time.' May stared at her, with dawning comprehension. 'For medical reasons, of course. Remember that, Nurse Winton, always for medical reasons, otherwise you will have the whole weight of the establishment descending on your head. And don't, under any circumstances, give this advice while still in training, leave that to me. Come now, Nurse, don't look so surprised. How many women in your rank of society give birth to more children than they wish? And they have all the money and domestic assistance that they need. You may go now, Nurse.'

As she left May remembered Lady Canning's cry, 'How could Della have been so careless!' and another piece of the jigsaw fell into place. So it had been deliberate – had Della

Hindlesham known of Harry Cussons' proposal to herself and decided not to risk losing him in the future?

May's next ward was a men's medical, and May told Ellen privately that it was just as well. 'After three months on Dorcas I'd begun to think of the male of the species as nothing more than a selfish, vicious brute; but I suppose men are only like us really, just a little different.'

Ellen's eyes danced. 'Oh, they're certainly different, May, even you must have noticed that!' May laughed at herself.

Still, she was glad she was no longer on Dorcas when Lady Clarence's letter arrived telling of the death of her little grandson, and of Emily's heartbroken grief. May wrote long letters of grieving sympathy to her step-sister. Emily replied herself, saying how grateful she had been for her mother and step-father's presence over the long exhausting summer months. 'Mamma has been a tower of strength, May, I could not have continued without her. I am so glad you told her to come in the spring – she admits she would never have taken such a step of her own accord; we are both grateful to you.'

At the end of November preparations got under way for the Royal Visit. A new wing was to be opened by the Queen herself. Matron decreed that every part of the hospital must be scrubbed and re-scrubbed.

'Though I just can't believe,' Ada exclaimed one evening, 'that Her Majesty will stick her august nostrils into the "dirty" sink in Job's sluice room, yet Staff Nurse said to me today, "I'm sure I detect a stain around that plughole – remember, Nurse Farrar, your work must be fit for the gracious lady herself to inspect!"' The spectacle of Ada, hands on hips, elbows akimbo, trying to imitate Staff Robson's genteel tones was too much for May and Ellen – they rolled on the bed, helpless with laughter.

Ada said indignantly, 'Well, *I* don't think she'll go in there, do you? You know how Job sluice smells when the wind's in the north.'

Ellen mopped her eyes and said soothingly, 'I'm sure you're right, Ada. But I suppose Sister Job keeps on hoping.'

175

Hosea, May's own ward, was in the new wing, and so definitely due for an inspection. The nurses' hands were red and raw from scrubbing and cleaning, while the elderly ward maid had claimed republican sentiments and refused to do a stroke more than usual. This had left May with the job of dismantling and cleaning the gas stove, and she incurred Sister Hosea's wrath when she failed to reassemble it correctly. May, hot, filthy, and exhausted, had finally suggested to Aggie that she might just possibly find herself able to discover some lurking monarchical tendencies in return for a pound of winkles from the stall near the main gate. The addition of jellied eels to the bribe sealed the bargain, and on May recklessly throwing in a jar of cockles Aggie managed a toothless rendering of the National Anthem as she reassembled the stove.

'You're an old hypocrite, Aggie.'

Aggie winked at May and licked her lips. 'I've allus bin partial to shellfish.'

The great day finally arrived. Sister Hosea, her collar so stiffly starched that she could not lower her chin, lectured the men into abject submission and arranged her minions in ranks behind her.

The Queen was as unpunctual as May remembered from her visits to Stemhalton, and Sister Hosea was quivering like a jelly by the time the retinue entered the ward. The nurses bobbed respectfully. Her Majesty uttered a few gracious words to Sister, listened with her sweet smile to the stammered reply, then prepared to cast her glow over the patients. But just as she was about to move her eye alighted upon May; she paused, turned to Matron and spoke softly to her. Matron's voice was clear.

'Nurse Winton, step forward please.'

May moved forward and dropped into her court curtsey, feeling very strange as her blue-striped galatea swept the shiny linoleum floor of Hosea Ward. The Queen was gracious.

'Your grandmother told me I might see you here, Miss Winton. How are you enjoying nursing?'

May, conscious of Sister Hosea's barely suppressed gasp of

176

astonishment, replied, 'Very well indeed, Your Majesty.'

'But not, I think, the meals at St Katharine's!' The Queen laughed, a clear silvery peal. May, aware of Matron's raised eyebrows and the furious glare of the Hospital Chairman, wished the floor would open up beneath her, but it remained rock solid and the Queen was waiting for a reply.

'The nature of our nursing duties is such as to encourage an appetite, Ma'am.' The answer was the best compromise between diplomacy and truth that May could manage on the spur of the moment.

The Queen turned to the red-faced Chairman. 'Miss Winton begs for food hampers, you know, from her grandmother's chef. You really must feed your nurses better in future, Sir James.' Sir James looked apoplectic, but the Queen did not choose to notice. With a last kindly word to May she moved on to the first patient.

After the procession had left the ward the other Hosea pros looked at May with mingled awe and compassion.

'My God,' said outspoken Evans, 'You certainly move in exalted circles, Winton, but I wouldn't like to be in your shoes when Matron sends for you tomorrow morning.' A sentiment with which May could only agree.

The expected summons came the next morning, delivered in a biting voice by Sister Hosea, who had obviously recovered her composure and was determined to show May that hobnobbing with the royal family cut no ice on her ward.

As May entered Matron's office she noticed that the Hospital Chairman was present. Matron merely told her that Sir James wished to speak to her, then sat back in silence. The Chairman fixed his basilisk gaze on May and launched into an oration in which he informed her that every luxury was lavished on the nurses of St Katharine's, and that she had been guilty of base ingratitude and shameful disloyalty in daring to complain. As soon as he had brought his tirade to a resounding conclusion he turned to Matron and indicated that he had finished with her probationer. May was absolutely furious, and determined not to leave the field of battle without firing her own fusillade. Who did this man think he

177

was? How dare he sit there and treat her like a naughty child out of a schoolroom? She acted quickly. Before Matron had time to dismiss her she had launched into her reply, her voice cold and her tone controlled.

'Since you were present, Sir James, you must be well aware that I did *not* complain. However, as you have given me this opportunity to expand on the situation,' at this point Sir James appeared to be trying to indicate that he was not, in fact, offering any such opportunity, but May merely raised her voice slightly and continued as if he had not spoken, 'I must say that it is true that I, and all the other nurses who can afford to do so, supplement our rations here.' By now the Chairman had given up expostulating and was staring at May with a bemused expression on his face; she was encouraged to further flights of rhetoric. 'How would you like to scrub forty bedpans on one sardine, Sir James? And come off duty tired and hungry after a long day to be faced with gristly mince and porridge, *cold* porridge? And on nights, why, not only do we have to cook for ourselves, but to make anything like a reasonable meal we have to buy extra food – whereas at Guy's the night staff are served with a freshly cooked meal in the dining room, halfway through their duty – and they have a swimming pool! Why can't we have one?' May's voice rose indignantly on this last demand. She paused for breath and Sir James seized his chance, and his hat.

'Swimming has nothing whatsoever to do with nursing! Matron, I have an urgent appointment, but I trust you will endeavour to make this young lady see the error of her ways. Good morning.' He had surged through the door before either of the women could reply.

May was flushed with triumph at the rout of her opponent – until she looked at Matron's impassive face. Her spirits sank, but she seized the initiative again, smiled sweetly and said quickly, 'Thank you so much, Matron, for allowing me to present the nurses' case to the Chairman in person.'

Matron gave her a level stare, then said, 'The pleasure was mine, Nurse Winton. I have frequently expressed my concern on this matter to the Board, though not, I admit, with quite

178

your fervour. Maybe you will have more success. However, I do feel it was perhaps a mistake of strategy to demand a swimming bath at this juncture – it is generally better to concentrate on one theme only in a situation like this. Still, you're young yet, you will learn. Possibly you could mention the pool next time you dine at the Palace? Will you send in the nurse waiting outside, please?'

A week later two sardines were served for breakfast, and the supper porridge was offered hot, with a choice of an apple or an orange. It was generally agreed that, between them, May and the Queen had scored a major victory; but May felt she never would understand Matron.

Chapter Twenty-One

Although Ellen, Ada and May were the best of friends there was one clear difference between them – dress. Ada, for all her suffragette convictions, had a keen interest in clothes: she invariably changed out of uniform for even the shortest of off-duty periods. May, despite her sense of relief when she arrived at the hospital and found she was at last somewhere where she did not have to change her clothing four or five times a day, still enjoyed dressing up for special occasions. She had spent too much of her life in fashionable dress-makers to be totally immune now. But Ellen was different: Ellen would not or could not care tuppence about her appearance. Her face was pretty, her figure slender, but she always looked dowdy. Indeed, May strongly suspected that she would have cheerfully gone out with buttons missing and hem dangling, had not the other two kept a sharp eye on her.

Matters reached a head in the New Year. Ellen's parents, well aware of her failings, had sent the money for a new outfit, in good time for Christmas. By the third week in January Ellen had respected their wishes to the extent of having neither given it away nor bought books with it, but the sum remained unspent. In desperation May and Ada embarked on a concerted campaign of coaxing and bullying, and eventually extracted a promise that Ellen would go up to Town on her very next half day, and not come back without a purchase.

Ellen set off after dinner looking, as Ada reported to May, more like a candidate for rack and thumbscrew than a young woman about to enjoy a pleasant afternoon's shopping. It was May, coming off duty at six, who caught her slinking into her room in her old shabby coat and hat, looking much more cheerful but with no sign of parcels or boxes. She gave a guilty

180

gasp as May pounced, but insisted that she had an excuse. May felt she should be severe, but as she could not help noticing Ellen's heightened colour, curiosity won the day and she made a pot of tea and settled down for a good gossip.

The explanation was all too typical of Ellen. 'I went, just as I said I would, May, and I got off at Hyde Park Corner and I was going to go straight to Harrods – honestly May – but the sun was shining, and that's so unusual in January, and I had to go past the Albert Gate, so I thought, well, a short walk in the Park, there'd still be plenty of time for shopping, it would have been criminal to waste the fine weather . . .' Ellen's story spilled out. Once in the Park who should she see but Lord Hindlesham, over the other side of the Row. 'He was walking so slowly, and he looked so sad – not at all bouncy like he was when we met him in the House of Lords.' Ellen, being Ellen, had rushed across in ready sympathy and introduced herself. 'I thought for one awful moment he hadn't recognised me out of uniform, then he realised who I was – he does have a nice smile, May.' Ellen had admitted to playing truant whereupon Lord Hindlesham had claimed to be doing the same and suggested a further stroll round the Park. May tried to look stern.

'Really, Ellen, he just aided and abetted you – I don't know what Ada will say!'

Ellen looked momentarily horrified. 'Oh, don't tell her it was a man, May, she'd never forgive me!'

But May was far too intrigued to scold Ellen further. Her friend's story had brought back to her a vivid picture of the drawing room at Stemhalton, and the gossip exchanged there in September. She exclaimed, 'Why, Della's baby must have been born by now – I wonder whether it was a boy or a girl?'

'It was a girl.'

May was startled. 'Surely he didn't tell you that?'

'Yes, he did.' Ellen was pink but definite. 'Obviously I didn't ask him, May, but we were talking about Elizabeth Ward, and I told him of that poor little Mary Jones who came in with pneumonia, after her mother abandoned her under the railway bridge because she came from a respectable family and couldn't face the shame of it, and Sister says she'll be put in prison and I think that's so wrong – anyway, after I'd told him he said he was acknowledging Della's baby as his, as it wasn't the child's fault, and obviously there hadn't been time for a divorce before the birth, so he'd not started proceedings until after. She wants one you see, and he'd written to Della and told her, and I think its very noble of him, May. But his mother is annoyed, and she never liked Della anyway.'

May said dryly, 'I'm sure she'd have been even more annoyed if the child had been a boy.'

Ellen nodded. 'Yes, he said it would have been more difficult then. I told him he was absolutely right and he'd quite restored my faith in the aristocracy, and he laughed. He seemed to cheer up after that, and we spent the rest of the time arguing about politics – you know he's far too good to be a Tory, I do hope he realises he's mistaken.' Ellen added rather wistfully, 'I must say, it was rather nice being escorted by someone so smart; I was glad I'd changed out of uniform.'

May gazed at Ellen's small figure and thought of her old coat and battered felt hat and wondered what on earth George Hindlesham must have thought of her after the beautifully groomed, Junoesque Della, but she thrust the disloyal comparison to one side – Ellen was worth a thousand Dellas – and stated firmly, 'But there was still time to buy your new outfit.'

'No, there wasn't, because you know I disapprove of shopping after five-thirty, I think it's so unfair on the assistants, whatever the law says.'

May's curiosity was further aroused. 'But you weren't walking in the Park until then – not in January?'

Ellen said no, she'd invited him to tea in the Corner House, and May gasped at the thought of Lord Hindlesham's fine palate being subjected to those bright yellow rock buns and the stewed Indian tea; but Ellen was more concerned by the fact that he had refused to let her pay the bill, and then insisted on sending her home in a cab. 'Ada will be furious with me about that, too, only it would have been discourteous to keep on refusing – but it was me who'd invited him to tea, and I did want to treat him.'

May laughed. 'Ellen, the Hindlesham estates are enormous! Besides, with your principles you should have been glad to relieve him of some of his inherited wealth.'

Ellen gave a mischievous grin. 'Actually, that's exactly what he said, so I gave in. Then he gave me ten pounds for Sister Elizabeth's Take Home Blanket and Baby Food Fund – she will be pleased. Did I tell you she's got some special cot blankets with stripes on now, and she's been round all the local pawnshops and they've agreed not to accept them, so they'll have to be used for the babies.'

Ellen had obviously said all she was going to about her meeting with Lord Hindlesham, so May picked up her cue and they turned to discussing hospital matters.

Lord and Lady Clarence came back to England in the early spring. William had been given a new posting, to a healthier area, and would be able to be more with his wife, so her mother felt it was time to return. But Lady Clarence's plans for taking her step-daughter more into Society in the coming Season were thwarted by Matron, who transferred May to nights on Elizabeth Ward. Apart from hurried trips to the West End for a second breakfast before going to bed May saw little of her parents, and less of the Season. Ellen was on nights as well, and May often invited her out to breakfast, and was surprised at how much more tolerant Lady Clarence was of Ellen's directness of speech than she ever had been of her own daughters. India seemed to have mellowed her a little.

May had been dreading the recurrence of nights, but Ellen being off duty at the same time helped, and May made a resolution to visit the Bath Club twice a week, to encourage sleep in the daytime. The main difference, however, was in the ward. Isaiah had been hard work and unrelentingly gloomy; Elizabeth was sometimes heart-breaking, but never ever gloomy. May became involved with her small patients. She laughed with the lively ones, cuddled the unhappy and played with the restless. Her deep sense of satisfaction was intensified by the fact that she was left in virtual charge at night, since her nominal superior was kept busy on the adjoining Obadaiah Ward.

Nevertheless, there was a fly in the ointment: House Surgeon O'Halloran. From their very first evening at the hospital, when Matron had implied that association with the medical staff was a crime on a par with the wilful neglect of patients, May had behaved towards the doctors with a circumspection which would have gladdened the heart of Lady Clarence. Not, she had to admit to herself, that this had been difficult, since the rules of conduct for nurses were drawn up with this express end in view. On days, only Sisters, Staff Nurses and Head Nurses ever spoke to the doctors and medical students, and Head Nurses only on sufferance. As Minnie Emms frequently pointed out, by the time you were senior enough to even pass the time of day, you were past it anyway. May had had looks cast in her direction, but frigid non-recognition had been adequate to repel approaches. But nights were rather different – not down in the septic ward, for there was only minimal medical supervision there at night since the best hope for the patients lay in good nursing care and the only regular male visitors there were the porters with the mortuary trolley. On Elizabeth, however, May found a rather different situation. It was accepted unofficially that house surgeons and physicians called out during the night should be fortified with cocoa and a sandwich in a convenient ward kitchen. Night Sister did not approve, but she and her assistants did not go out of their way to detect lurking males behind the door, providing that the ward probationer was clearly on the ward, being chaperoned by her patients. Certain wards were more popular ports of call than others, and Elizabeth was one such. The babies ensured the availability of milk in the kitchen, while the presence of the children made for a more homely, domestic atmosphere, with the firelight glinting through the tall mesh guard and the pleasant gurgles of toddlers asleep.

The House Physician responsible for Elizabeth was a quiet,

184

soft-spoken Scot. Devoted to the study of medicine and engrossed in his job he held long, whispered discussions with May on the progress of each child, and May looked forward to his visits and questioned him eagerly. He, in his turn, was pleased by her interest, and once told her she should have trained as a doctor – 'There are a guid few women students at Edinburgh, ye ken.'

May had swelled with pride, and held her chin very high for the next couple of hours, until young Elsie woke up screaming, and after being sick all down May's apron refused to go back to sleep until May had nursed her for an hour, as she sat by the fire sewing tiny shrouds with her free hand. Robert MacDougall was a joy to work with, and May felt that his sweet-faced fiancée, whose photograph she was privileged to view one night, would have a devoted husband one day – if he could only spare her some time from his patients.

No, the drawback was Jack O'Halloran. From what the theatre nurses told her he was a swift and competent surgeon, but the sight of his handsome face and knowing smile as he walked onto the ward at night sent May's heart down to the very tips of her soft-soled leather shoes. O'Halloran was a big, goodlooking man, and he knew it, and expected others to know it to, especially any young nurse who caught his roving eye. It was clear that May had caught his eye, as he set out to lay siege to her.

There was something attractive about his very confidence in his own charm, and at first May laughed with him, and half-unwillingly responded to his jokes, delivered in a soft brogue and with immaculate timing. But then she saw the predatory look in his eye, and began to feel uneasy when alone with him in the kitchen, and turned the gas up high to hurry the milk for his cocoa. When she overdid it, and the milk boiled over, he insisted on helping her clean up the mess and trapped her against the heavy cast iron stove, so that she had to thrust him aside. But whereas the men she had known would have apologised, and retreated abashed, O'Halloran seemed to derive pleasure from her anger. He moved towards her with a determined glint in his

185

eye so that May had to leap to the door and run to the ward, where she prodded little Albert Ferris awake. His howls gave her an excuse to refuse to boil up a second panful of milk. She felt guilty about Albert, but he was almost well, and had disturbed her often enough on previous nights, so she considered he owed her his protection now.

For the next few nights May felt like a mouse with a large cat sitting outside its hole, but she did manage to avoid being alone with Jack O'Halloran. Then, inevitably, he arrived as she was making a hot drink for a fractious child, just after the pro she shared with Obadaiah had left. O'Halloran advanced with a grin on his face. May was brisk.

'I have to attend to a patient.' She began to edge around the room, but he had positioned himself near the door, and cut off her escape.

His grin broadened. 'Ah, sure now, you can spare me a minute, a pretty girl like you!' He lunged in her direction.

May threw the mug of milk straight at him and dodged behind the table. He dashed the milk from his face, but her action seemed to have excited rather than angered him.

Murmuring, 'I like a girl with spirit,' he began to advance purposefully again. May wanted to slap his face, hard, but something in his expression made her hesitate. Harry Cussons had been stopped in his tracks by a slap, but Harry, for all his faults, was a gentleman. It was clear that O'Halloran was not, and he was bigger and stronger than her. As these thoughts were passing through her mind May continued to sidestep round the room, keeping the table between her and her assailant. The table! O'Halloran was at the other side, with his back to the stove. May called, 'Careful, that gas is alight!' and as he turned, momentarily distracted, she gripped the edge of the table and sent the whole heavy piece of furniture hurtling towards him. There was a loud thud followed by a volley of Irish curses, but May was through the door – and cannoning straight into an astounded Night Sister! May jumped back, pulled her cap straight and waited, speechless.

'Whatever is going on in this kitchen?'

May had no intention of telling her. She gulped, then managed a reply.

'Dr O'Halloran fell against the table, Sister.'

Night Sister stared at the heavy table, pinning the furious O'Halloran to the stove, then at May, hot and panting. She turned to the house surgeon.

'Dr O'Halloran, your presence is required on Simeon Ward, please go there at once. I trust you have sustained no permanent damage?'

O'Halloran, red-faced now, extricated himself, muttered, 'No, thank you, Sister,' and limped out of the kitchen without even a glance in May's direction.

May waited for the wrath to descend on her hapless shoulders.

'Really, Nurse, how careless of you – you might have broken Dr O'Halloran's leg! We're desperately short of house surgeons already, with Dr Simpson off sick.'

May bent her head. 'I'm sorry, Sister.'

'Why on earth did you have to throw the table at him? You're far too headstrong, Nurse Winton, I've noticed it before. A good clout with the large saucepan would have been quite adequate. If that table is damaged Matron will be annoyed, very annoyed.'

She marched into the ward, and May meekly followed.

Chapter Twenty-Two

May finished her spell on night duty at the beginning of July. She spent her three days off with her parents, in Town, but since she was making up her arrears of sleep there was only time for one social occasion: a small family dinner party on the day before her return to St Katharine's. The party was in honour of Louise Dumer. Bertie had finally brought himself to the sticking point and proposed and Louise's mother had accepted him with indecent haste. As Archie put it, a future Marquis in the hand was worth any number of Dukes in the bush. Besides, Duke's heirs were in short supply that Season.

Mrs Dumer looked radiant, Louise rather dazed. May seized a few moments alone with her after dinner, and after wishing her well, murmured reassuringly that Bertie would be a very easygoing husband. Louise brightened slightly and agreed. Then she glanced round, lowered her voice and spoke confidentially.

'There was this awful French Comte. Mamma said he was of a very old family,' she shuddered. 'He used to look at me as if he despised me, and there were rumours – boys, you know.' May didn't know and couldn't imagine, but she tried to look comprehending. 'He was quite broke, so I heard, and he approached Mamma . . . I was so relieved when Bertie proposed, you can't imagine, May. Mamma said I'd had quite long enough, and if I didn't bring it off this Season I'd just got to take the Comte. She's so determined, and it *is* her money. Oh, I am grateful to Bertie!'

When May congratulated her cousin later, he shrugged.

'Louise is a decent sort, you know. She won't interfere with a chap too much, too relieved to get away from that awful mother of hers. We can have central heating at Stemhalton now; it was so cold last winter, but Father wouldn't hear of it, spends all the money on the estate. We're getting married next month, as soon as the lawyers have done their stuff – no point hanging about, is there?'

May agreed that there was not. She felt saddened by the exchanges – yet were Bertie's and Louise's chances of happiness any worse than most? At least neither was under any illusions about the other's motives.

The next day May reported for duty in the Receiving Room. The enormous hall, with its high arched roof, seemed very alien after the warm cosiness of Elizabeth Ward, and it was odd to deal with patients in their outdoor clothes. Men and women were huddled on the hard wooden benches all day, waiting their turn. The endless procession of strange faces in and out of the treatment rooms was confusing and difficult to cope with after the wards, and it was sometimes hard for May to remember that she was dealing with individual human beings, rather than just numbers. But after a week or so a pattern began to emerge for her, and she tried to recognise, if not people, at least emotions, and so be able to respond.

Between the regular bouts of black eyes, crushed fingers and swallowed farthings there were the sudden, dramatic entrances of serious accidents. Sometimes the clattering hooves of a hard-driven ambulance gave warning, or a panting stevedore announced the imminent appearance of the creaking wheeled stretcher from the docks; but when the accident was nearby then shouting would be heard in the street, and May, sent to the doorway, would see the small crowd with the loaded shutter in their midst, the overhanging parts of the victim's anatomy supported by those around while an escort of excited boys raced ahead or climbed railings to get a glimpse of the horrible spectacle. It was May's job to separate the shutter bearers from the hangers-on and take them into an empty dressing room, where the full extent of the damage could be revealed. As soon as the reddened ends of bones poking through torn trousers appeared, or Sister uncovered the greasy, mangled flesh of an arm caught in a machine, then the medical students and nurses sprang

189

into action, while a hovering policeman waited for the full story of what had happened.

On other days distraught mothers rushed in clutching scalded babies, whose skin came off as their wounds were dressed. Or two burly policemen would bring in a drunk who had fallen and laid his scalp open, and who now slumped between them, head dangling and legs dragging along the pavement, often laughing or singing, still impervious to pain.

The nurses had to think quickly and act fast; the rigid daily routine of the wards had no place here. At first May was exhausted when she came off-duty at the end of the day, but the constant variety began to exert its own fascination over her, and she was quite sorry when her time there came to an end in mid-September. Still, her holiday was due, and the thought of leaving dirty, stifling London for two full weeks was very attractive.

She spent the holiday period quietly at Allingham, feeling as though a lifetime had passed since she had been at her home before, rather than a mere two years. May and her step-mother had to share the rather clumsy services of one of the housemaids, since Lady Clarence had allowed Fenton time off to look after the children of her sister during the latter's confinement, but May found that she scarcely knew how to make use of a maid these days.

In the second week of her holiday May decided to make the journey to see Bella, now living with her young husband on an estate some twenty miles away. When her former maid opened the door May was shocked at her appearance. Bella's once pretty face was drawn and haggard, and her body already swollen with her second pregnancy.

'Miss May – how nice to see you!' Then her face fell. 'But I'm all at sixes and sevens – and the baby just won't stop crying.' May, seeing her lips quivering and her eyes filling, acted quickly. She took Bella's elbow, steered her inside, sat her down in a chair and, improvising a footstool, lifted the girl's feet onto it, noticing the swollen ankles as she did so.

'You should be resting, Bella. Stay there, I'll see to the baby and make us both a cup of tea.'

190

It was like being back on Elizabeth Ward as she picked up the squalling infant, changed and fed him and gently rubbed his painful gums until he hiccupped into silence with a look of surprise on his damp red face. Dirty dishes were piled in the stone sink in the scullery, and May dealt with them while waiting for the tea to draw. She laid the tray with a plate of the delicate almond biscuits sent by the Allingham cook and carried it through into the kitchen.

'You must eat something, Bella, your face is far too thin. You'll need to keep your strength up.'

Bella looked almost stunned, but she ate and drank obediently while May attended to the range. Then the baby began to make ominous noises so May lifted him out again and nursed him into contentment while she sipped her own tea. A little of Bella's colour returned as she drank, and she began to tell May about her husband, and her bossy mother-in-law who lived in the village, becoming more like her old self. Then she suddenly broke off, and exclaimed:

'Miss May, you have changed – you've changed so much!'

May smiled. 'Well, I'm afraid living in London does dull the complexion.'

Bella shook her head. 'No, Miss May, you look as well as ever, that's not what I meant. When I maided you, you wouldn't have known one end of a baby from the other, leave alone what to do with it – or make tea, or wash up, or anything.'

May had to laugh at Bella's astonishment. 'Matron would soon give me my marching orders if I hadn't learnt something in two years. Anyway, I never complain about being bored, these days.'

May sent the coachmen down to the village pub for their lunch and stayed the rest of the day. She enjoyed her gossip with Bella, who shed tears for Emily's loss, and hugged her own son tightly as she did so. Even Harry Cussons came up for discussion, and it was clear that Bella had known all about his liaison with Della Hindlesham. It had been common gossip in the Servants' Hall, where feelings had run high on Lord Hindlesham's behalf. 'That kind of thing is common enough

191

among the gentry, we all know that, but it's usually six of one and half a dozen of the other; but her husband, he wasn't like that – so it didn't seem fair, somehow.' But May suspected the real reason for the partisanship was that George Hindlesham was a considerate and generous employer, while Della had been arrogant and thoughtless, except when restrained by her husband.

Bella continued, 'I'm glad you didn't marry that Mr Cussons, Miss May. We knew he had an eye for you, but Lady Hindlesham wasn't the only one, not by a long chalk. It serves him right, it really does.'

All in all, May felt she had learnt more about the goings-on in Society that day than she had ever known when she was involved herself. She wished Bella had told her more at the time – but young ladies had to be blinkered, especially when they were the daughters of Lady Clarence Winton.

Before she left Bella, May extracted a promise that she would sink her pride and call upon her mother-in-law for help. 'You must look after yourself, or the new baby will suffer.' When it became clear that Bella's worries extended beyond the next child May, blushing but determined, imparted Sister Dorcas' advice on sponges and vinegar, and felt her embarrassment well worth it when she saw the dawning relief in Bella's eyes.

The following day Lady Clarence was stricken with one of her sick headaches, and May found her hot and uncomfortable under the awkward ministrations of the young housemaid. Again May mentally reached for her cap and apron, and drew the curtains, remade the bed, produced cold compresses and administered medicines, until her step-mother relaxed against the pillows and fell asleep. Lady Clarence had recovered by the evening, but there was a subtle change in her manner towards May; May recognised it for what it was, respect.

Back in the East End the autumn passed in a rush. It was mid-December when Matron summoned May and told her she would be changing wards, and going to Martha. May was pleased. Martha was a large women's surgical, taking in accidents and emergencies, and always busy, but she wondered why Matron was taking the trouble to tell her in person; then she saw them, on the desk, two white tapes. Her heart jumped. Matron picked up the tapes.

'You will go to Martha as Probationer One, Nurse Winton. Here are your strings.'

'Thank you, Matron.' May's reply was formal, but she almost skipped out of the office. Some nurses had to wait three full years for their strings, most at least two and a half – she had been given hers already!

The next day she presented herself before Sister Martha, with the absurd little bow tickling her chin. Sister Martha was elderly, and severe of expression. She looked May up and down, then sent her about her duties.

For the next few days May was on tenterhooks. Sister Martha did leave the ward from time to time, but only when Staff Nurse was present. Then, two days after Christmas, Staff went off at twelve, for her half-day. At two o'clock Sister Martha beckoned May to her table.

'I am going off duty, now, until four. I leave you in charge, Head Nurse Winton.' Sister got up and left the ward.

May stood still, shaking slightly. She looked down the long rows of beds, at the slowly moving patients and the briskly moving nurses, and felt a mixture of acute apprehension and pure joy. For two hours the ward was hers. No matter that Sister had chosen the quietest day of the week to leave her, and that she would certainly be no further than the Sisters' Sitting Room. She, May, was in sole charge.

193

Chapter Twenty-Three

May soon discovered that being in charge of a large and busy ward, albeit for only two or three hours at a time, was not an unadulterated pleasure. She had taken responsibility on her previous night duty, but only for herself; now she seemed to be constantly pestered by subservient pros, all anxiously waiting to be told what to do next. In an emergency she had to make the immediate decision of whether to summon help or try to cope from her own resources. Inevitably, she made mistakes, especially in dealing with Pearson, the very inexperienced Pro Five. May began to feel a distinct sympathy with Sister Simeon in her own early days, and at least May only had to cope with the problem for a short time: Sister Simeon had had to face it continually.

In the first weeks May found herself watching the ward clock with mingled apprehension and longing: longing for the relief of being able to hand over the reins to Sister Martha or Staff Nurse Lee, apprehension about what they would find to criticise in her conduct of the ward. May had to admit that though she did not enjoy them, their criticisms were usually justified. However, she did learn by her mistakes, and the decisions she had at first made from panic became more calm and considered. A pattern began to emerge as she looked at the routine of a busy ward through the eyes of authority. Sister Martha was shrewd and competent, but there were certain moves which she made which May would have liked to alter, and she began to think tentatively about how she would run the ward if she were in control. Her fourth year at St Katharine's, when she would be a Staff Nurse and so in charge of much of the daily routine, became a goal to be anticipated.

By the end of January, May had ceased to watch for the

194

return of Staff or Sister when she was left as Head Nurse, and knew that soon she would be looking forward to their absences. Nevertheless, she was relieved that Sister Martha was in her sitting room when one of the porters arrived with a message to prepare a bed for a bad accident case.

'Cor, she's a real sight, Nurse, proper turned me stummick, and that don't turn easy. She's bin scalped, sure as I'm standin' 'ere, blood everywhere.'

May flew for Sister, and both were waiting with the necessary equipment by the screened bed when the stretcher came up, Dr Rawlings in hovering attendance.

'We stopped the haemorrhage in the Receiving Room, Sister, but we'll have to take the compress off again and do a thorough clean up before we can safely stitch it. Her hand's badly crushed as well.'

'How did it happen?' Sister asked as the woman was transferred.

'At work – she's a machine minder at the boneyard.'

Sister said, 'She caught her hair in the belting, I suppose?'

The house surgeon nodded. 'And then tried to free it with her hand – but we'll deal with that later.'

Sister stood back. 'I'll leave you to assist Dr Rawlings, Nurse Winton, I have to serve dinner. Call me if you need me.' She moved off.

As the house surgeon removed the temporary bandage it became clear that most of the woman's scalp had been literally torn off. When she saw the white skull showing through the blood May had to suppress a momentary surge of nausea. She had helped with similar cases in the Receiving Room, but never one as bad as this. Then the woman began to moan weakly and May had to take hold of herself. She spoke reassuringly to her, wiping the blood from her eyes with one hand while handing Dr Rawlings the instruments with the other. He was quick and confident; when the arteries began to spurt he transfixed each one in turn with a harelip pin, and twisted a suture round it. Then, 'Take the scissors, Nurse, we'll have to get this hair off.'

But as May reached to cut off the matted, bloody hanks of

195

hair the woman suddenly reared up in the bed and screamed.

'No, no, not me 'air, don't cut me 'air!'

May was astounded that she should have the energy to worry about her hair in such a state, while Dr Rawlings was impatient.

'Come along now, Missus, we can't get you cleaned up and mended with all this in the way.'

The woman tried to twist away and moaned. 'What will my Billy say? What will 'e say? All me luvely 'air.'

Rawlings placed firm hands on her shoulders and said, 'Get it off, Nurse.'

May wielded her scissors quickly. She knew it was necessary, yet felt like a traitor as she saw the woman shake with a series of convulsive shudders. The house surgeon nodded to the instrument tray and May reached for the razor and silently shaved as much as she could of the area around the wound. As soon as she had finished May spoke soothingly to her, but the woman lay limp and unresponsive, seeming to have lost heart with the loss of her hair. Dr Rawlings put out his hand and May gave him the threaded needle; with quick stabs the piece of scalp was sewn back on.

'Cyanide gauze, Nurse. I'll leave you to do the bandage, while I have a look at this hand.'

May wound the bandage firmly round the cranium, and put a turn or two under the chin to keep everything tight. Dr Rawlings glanced up as she finished and nodded approvingly. 'I expect Matron was pleased with your bandaging in the hospital exams, Nurse.'

May smiled at him and spoke clearly to the woman. 'We've finished your head now, my dear, Doctor's just making your hand more comfortable and then we'll get you undressed and into bed properly for a nice sleep.'

The woman twitched, but made no sound. May was worried by her torpor.

'I think we'll try irrigation, with carbolised water, Nurse, for this hand.'

May groaned to herself. Dr Rawlings was a great believer in irrigation, but it was a nuisance to the nurses. Unless everything was positioned precisely the bed became soaked and the sheets had to be constantly changed – still his patients did seem to heal better. She fetched the necessary equipment and assured the patient she would soon feel a soothing trickle on her injured hand. The woman's clothes were removed with the minimum of movement, and she was soon tucked in, with only her damaged arm and bandaged head exposed. Her face was as white as her bandages.

May reported back to Sister who listened to the details of the treatment, raised her eyebrows at the irrigation, then said, 'You or Staff Nurse had better do the daily dressings, Nurse Winton, as there's always a possibility of oedema in these cases – watch for any bogginess around the wound.'

May nodded, then ventured a comment. 'The patient seemed unduly disturbed at having her hair cut off, Sister.'

Sister Martha gave May an old-fashioned look. 'I don't suppose you'd be very enthusiastic about that, either, Nurse Winton.' Her voice was dry.

May flushed, but persevered. 'She seemed to be standing up to the pain very well, Sister, but when she heard the scissors she did appear to be excessively distressed. And then she just seemed to give up.'

Sister Martha was grudging. 'I'll bear that in mind, Nurse Winton, but when you've seen as many of these accidents as I have you'll know all women hate to lose their hair.'

May had to be satisfied with this.

An agitated woman appeared at the ward doorway half an hour later, claiming that her daughter had been carried in. It emerged that the scalped woman was a Mrs Dolly Hills, and that her mother had been minding her two babies for her while she was at work. Sister Martha allowed Mrs Jones a quick glimpse of Dolly and then shepherded her firmly out. Like her daughter, Mrs Jones bewailed the lost hair.

'Lovely 'air she 'ad, Sister, like spun gold it were, she could sit on it. Ever so proud of it, she was – ust'er spend 'ours brushin' it. I don't know what 'er Billy'll say, he worshipped 'er 'air, 'e did straight.'

197

Sister Martha was short. 'He's very lucky that his wife is still alive. Visiting is on Thursday, Mrs Jones.'

As the disconsolate mother left, Sister turned to May. 'Really, all this fuss about hair – if the woman had been less vain of it in the first place she'd have covered it up more securely, then the accident might never have happened.'

May suspected Sister was right, but could not help sympathising with Mrs Hill's despair. She would never admit to pride in her own golden mane since Archie had teased her unmercifully as a child. 'It's almost red, May, it's going red, I can tell – why don't you have normal hair like Emily's?' But she knew she would have shed bitter tears at its loss. She redoubled her efforts to reassure Mrs Hills that her crowning glory would grow again, and very likely with a nice curl in it: 'That's what often happens after accidents like yours.' Dolly Hills smiled wanly. May admired the woman's stoicism – she was very brave during the ordeal of her daily dressings – but the low-voiced lament for her lost locks continued.

May was off duty on the Thursday afternoon, but an indignant Staff Lee greeted her on her return.

'Honestly, Winton, we were furious! That wretched scalp woman's husband came in, and instead of saying, "How are you?" or thrusting a few wilting pansies into her hand before complaining about the kids like any normal husband would have done, he just stood there, staring at her, went quite white, then said, "You're not my Dolly any more," and walked out! Just like that, with all the other visitors there as well. I'll say this for Sister, she caught him at the entrance and gave him a good talking-to, but I don't think she made much impression. He kept saying, "She's not my wife, not with no hair," and marched off.'

For one fleeting moment May wondered whether Harry Cussons or even house surgeon O'Halloran would have paid her such assiduous attentions had she been completely bald, then she recollected herself and joined Lee in her paean of indignation. Lee finished with, 'Really, the more I see of them the more I wonder why women ever bother to marry men!'

May murmured, 'The lack of any alternative, I suppose,'

but Lee had already swept off. In any case May knew it was a waste of time arguing with her since Lee and Ada were firm disciples of Mrs Pankhurst; they had even informed Matron one day that they were going to chain themselves to the railings of No. 10 and they hoped she had no objection. Matron had apparently said none at all, since it was their day off, but when they came back she would order an immediate operation for the removal of their swallowed keys. 'She had quite a glint in her eye, May,' Ada had said afterwards, 'so we just helped to carry the banners.'

As was only to be expected, May found Dolly Hills very dismal that evening, and there was a worrying rise of temperature. However, her wounds were healing satisfactorily, and May even managed to raise a tremulous smile with an account of her activities on her afternoon off.

The next visiting day, though, May had cause to understand exactly why Dolly Hills was so disturbed at the loss of her hair. Staff was off and Sister had gone for her tea, leaving May in charge, during the latter half of visiting. May was in the kitchen checking the inventory, a hated Sunday task which explained Sister Martha's willingness to leave May in control, when she heard raised voices from the ward. She was already in the corridor when a flushed and panting Pearson arrived.

'Head Nurse, come quickly please, this awful woman visiting Mrs Hills . . .'

May rushed up the ward to be confronted with a scene more worthy of the music hall than a well-regulated hospital. Dolly Hills had flung herself back on her pillows, hands covering her face, her round bandaged head looking small and pitiful as she sobbed. Her mother was standing in front of her, one arm stretched protectively across her daughter, the other shaking in a fist at a brawny Amazon who stood, hands on hips, shouting a tirade.

''E's not your Billy now, 'e's mine, fer good! You snatched 'im off me, Dolly Jones, and wed 'im, right under my nose – Church an' all – well you've 'ad 'im now,' she leant forward. 'No man wants a woman 'oose bin scalped, 'oose 'airless!' The last word was spat out in a reptilian hiss.

199

Dolly gave an agonised moan and the visitors at the surrounding beds sat transfixed, mouths ajar and eyes agoggle, waiting avidly for the next round. May walked forward, placed her hand on the woman's arm, and spoke quietly.

'Excuse me, madam, but I think you are disturbing my patients, would you kindly leave?'

'No.' The woman swung her forearm and jerked May's hand away as though it were no more than a gnat. 'I'm 'aving my say. I got rights – 'e were in my bed last night, so I wants yer wedding ring!'

There were gasps from the women around. May, completely at a loss, prayed fervently for Sister Martha to come back. Then Dolly's hands shifted slightly and May caught a glimpse of her stricken face. It was enough. She drew herself up to her full height, pointed to the door and said, 'Out, *now*.'

The woman turned and glared straight at May. The issue hung in the balance as May held her gaze level. Then the woman's eyes dropped, she gave a defiant toss of her head and stamped off down the ward. May let out the breath she had been holding and felt her legs trembling with the reaction. But there was Dolly to be considered. She spoke firmly to Pearson.

'Fetch the screens, Nurse. Mrs Hills and her mother would like a little privacy. Then bring two cups of tea.'

The other visitors turned hastily back to their relatives, and there was a sudden obscuring buzz of conversation. Behind the screen Mrs Jones gripped her daughter's uninjured hand, while May supported the shaking shoulders. Much of May's own anger was directed against the absent Billy, but the two women seemed not to feel this.

''E's soft, Billy, allus 'as bin, an' Big Liza gets 'em drunk, she drinks sumfink awful, Nurse. She's done it with other women's 'usbands, too. But what about me kids? I won't be able ter work fer months, with me 'and like this!'

Mrs Jones calmed her. 'Me and yer Dad'll see ter them, don't you worry, Dolly.' She turned to May. 'It's 'er 'air, yer see, Nurse, 'e's funny about a woman's 'air, is Billy.' As she spoke May recalled the menacing figure in the ward, and the

200

great pile of improbably brassy but undeniably impressive hair under the bright red hat.

Dolly wailed, ''E wouldn't care tuppence fer 'er if she 'ad no 'air – 'e's got more sense than that!'

Privately, May had no such faith in the good sense of the errant Billy, but between them she and Mrs Jones managed to soothe Dolly, and May went back to the interrupted inventory. Pearson was in the kitchen washing up.

May sagged against the dresser and said, 'Thank goodness she went quietly.'

Pearson turned from the sink. 'Wasn't she awful? But I'm not surprised she went without a struggle, you should have seen your face, Nurse Winton, I was terrified, let alone her!'

But May wondered what she would have done if the woman had simply refused to leave – the thought of a physical set-to in the middle of the ward at visiting time was just too terrible to contemplate. Had she been wise to risk a direct confrontation?

However Ellen, when regaled with the whole story that evening, was reassuring.

'You had a perfect right to tell her to go, and you were in uniform, and on your own ground. She would have been very hard-faced to stand firm.'

'But Ellen, she was hard-faced – I almost feel sorry for that wretched Billy, though he seems such a sap. Dolly should tell him to go, and good riddance.'

Ellen disagreed. 'He is her husband, May, and the father of her children. They owe each other some loyalty – perhaps he'll come to his senses.'

'When I told Sister Martha about it she was furious; she'll never let Big Liza in again. She was particularly annoyed because Dolly's sprung a temperature now.'

May was off-duty the following Thursday, but she heard from Staff Lee what had happened. Big Liza had arrived at the ward entrance with a bottle of gin poorly hidden in her shawl – 'Already half-empty, Winton.' – Sister Martha had fortunately posted Pearson as look-out, so Sister and her lieutenants had barred the way. 'It was like the Battle of Thermopylae all over again, Winton, but with a very big female Xerxes.' But on this occasion victory had been with the Greeks, and Big Liza had turned tail and been escorted off the premises by a porter, who had instructions to lower the main portcullis against her in future. Mrs Jones had apparently been even more distressed than her daughter, and had vowed vengeance. As the top of her scrawny bun barely reached Big Liza's brawny shoulders this seemed unlikely of achievement, but feeling in the ward ran high on Dolly's behalf.

Chapter Twenty-Four

To the envy of her fellow nurses May was awarded the following Saturday as her half-day off. Feeling very virtuous she decided to make a dutiful visit to Great Aunt Ursula, now very frail, but still in full command of her wits. Great Aunt Ursula had been annoyed when May had once come to visit her in uniform, claiming she saw quite enough of nurses as it was, and expected her niece to look like a lady. Since this view was expressed with some force in front of one of her own private nurses May avoided further embarrassment by always wearing mufti on future occasions.

In any case, as she changed after lunch, May had to admit that it was very pleasant to dress up in her finery while the rest of the hospital was working. She had made several enjoyable trips to Paquin's and Konski's recently, and with the support of Ada she was leaving the excessive frills and pastel colours of the débutante behind and creating a style of her own. An arrangement with the maid who acted as caretaker at the Andovers' house in Arlington Street had secured her as much wardrobe space as she needed, as well as cleaning and refurbishing services; as a consequence May was now able to indulge herself as she wished.

The February day was mild, so she was able to wear her most recent purchase from Konski's: a little Persian lamb coatee, cut en sac at the back but fitted and belted at the front, with a trimming of fine silver embroidery. Her sapphire velvet skirt fell into graceful folds below it as she fastened the braided loops. Satisfied, she reached for her hat and positioned it far back on her head. She had had the matching toque of Persian lamb with its silver embroidered wings and echoing touch of sapphire blue made specially to her own design, and she was very pleased with it. She eased on her fine kid gloves,

203

picked up her muff and sauntered out, luxuriating in the transformation from flurried nurse to leisured lady of fashion.

Although so elderly, Great Aunt Ursula was at the centre of an intricate web of gossip. May had visions of her equally aged but more mobile friends infiltrating all the fashionable spots of England, and beyond. Great Aunt Ursula herself appeared to act as a clearing house. In the past Lady Clarence had regularly sent May off to the other end of the room, to look at the photograph albums, but now she was able to sit back and listen in amazement to the torrent of information which flowed over her

The child of a more outspoken age, her Great Aunt clearly had no fear of action for slander. May found herself feebly protesting, 'But surely, Great Aunt Ursula, they wouldn't . . .' but her objections were brushed aside as mealy-mouthed liberalism. 'I have it on the *best* authority, my dear,' and May subsided again, until brought up with a jerk by the words: 'They say the Cussons-Della Hindlesham affair is coming apart at the seams.'

May blinked.

Great Aunt Ursula peered at her from under hooded lids and said, in a tone of satisfaction, 'I knew *you'd* be interested to hear that, May.'

For one incredulous moment May wondered whether one of her Great Aunt's cronies had been crouching behind the dusty shrubs in the Tunnel Gardens that December day two years ago, then commonsense reasserted itself: the informant had obviously been Lady Andover. Rebuffed, Harry Cussons had poured out his indignation to her grandmother, who had made it abundantly clear to May that she held her personally responsible for the subsequent elopement. Now she remarked mildly, 'They have the child to consider.'

Great Aunt Ursula snorted. 'When did Della ever consider her children? Besides, their daughter's legally a Vane-Lawson, George played very fair there; and Della's hardly likely to breed again at her age, for all she's still besotted by him. Harry's got a roving eye, you know – and that's not all that roves!' Great Aunt Ursula cackled. May winced.

'You think they won't marry, then?'

Her Great Aunt shrugged. 'Who knows? She begged George to divorce her, the case was splashed all over the papers – you must have seen it, May, even in your slum – so it becomes Absolute this spring. I think Della will be a very worried woman by the summer.'

May was definite. 'I'm sure he'll behave chivalrously.'

'You youngsters are too starry-eyed.' Great Aunt Ursula's tone was robust. 'Why should he bother now? If it was chivalry she wanted, she should have stayed with George – though I admit he's not much to look at. Do you know, fond as I am of him, that man's been a great disappointment to me, over the years.' She leant forward and her small eyes glittered. 'He has never told me one item of scandal in all the time I've known him – and he must have heard plenty, being married to Della!'

'I don't think they spoke much.' May couldn't resist adding, 'But has he ever been involved in any scandal himself?'

Her Great Aunt shook her head regretfully. 'No.'

May was pleased – so there were some honourable men, after all. But Great Aunt Ursula had not quite finished. 'I did have hopes, you know, this time last year. He was seen in the Park with a strange young woman on his arm; we couldn't identify her, dressed like a governess, apparently.'

May felt her eyes widen with astonishment. Really, her Great Aunt was unbelievable. Then she thought, 'On his arm' indeed, Ellen didn't tell me that, and suppressed a smile. Great Aunt Ursula looked at her suspiciously.

'I suppose *you* don't know who she was?'

May felt it was cruel to deprive the old lady, but one had other loyalties.

'I've no idea, Aunt Ursula; perhaps she was a member of the suffragist movement? I believe he has sympathies in that direction.'

Her Great Aunt looked disappointed. 'I dropped hints, you know, when I saw him next, but one can't ask outright – I wouldn't wish to appear inquisitive.'

205

May murmured, 'No, of course not.'

'In any case, he's got too much sense to play around in the middle of a divorce – you remember the Allison case?'

At this point May had a strong sense of déjà vu. Fond as she was of the old lady she began to talk of having to be back. Great Aunt Ursula, who did tire, though she would not admit it, let her go, gratifying May by telling the footman to make a parcel of the rest of the cakes for Miss Winton. He looked down his nose at this but May, who thought that where food was concerned pride was an unnecessary luxury, smiled prettily, took her parcel and kissed her great aunt good-bye.

It was just after six when she arrived back at the hospital. She went along to Ellen's room, stretched herself out on the bed and waited for her friend to come off duty. Ellen arrived in a rush, as always, smiled, and said, 'May, you look an absolute fashion plate. Where shall we go?'

May suggested Chrisp Street market. 'It's very lively on Saturday nights.'

Ellen nodded her head and leapt for the wardrobe. 'Too lively, sometimes. We'd better go now, rather than later. Wait while I change, I can't go out in my uniform with you dressed like that.'

Within fifteen minutes they were out on the Dock Road and heading for Chrisp Street. Chrisp Street market had provided an endless source of amusement for May and Ellen since they had first come to St Katharine's. Now they heard the roar of voices: yelling, crying, calling, before they had turned the corner and saw the streaming naphtha flares, hissing, spluttering and fizzling above the stalls. The flares were blowing out wildly in the wind. Their mingled reds and oranges, yellows and blues, gave a strange unnatural light, so that the faces of the stallholders and their customers looked like carved wooden puppets, all lines and shadows, their normal expressions grotesquely exaggerated. It was a scene May never tired of: like a great, colourful pantomime, yet one you could take part in yourself.

The cheap furniture, which in daylight was tawdry and ill-made, now looked sturdy and strong, with bold clean lines. Other stalls were a blaze of colour from the strong violets, magentas and carmines of the drapery to the piles of glowing orange carrots, subtle white turnips, and purply green cabbages. All were mingled together in the light of the flares, like an enormous, shining palette.

Ellen tugged at May's sleeve. 'Come on, May, I feel as though those eels are winking at me.'

They edged away from the zinc trays of squirming black eels, past the doorway of the eel and pie shop, with its smells of vinegar, parsley sauce and sweaty bodies, and into the market. By unspoken mutual consent neither lingered by the blue-garbed butcher extolling his wares and waving his long knife over piles of brains and chitterlings, tripe and liver – there was just the hint of a reminder of the operating theatre here, and they were off duty. But they paused at the glowing red eyes of the chestnut seller's brazier, with its mouth-watering aroma, then moved on to admire the mounds of bright-skinned oranges and shiny polished apples. As they stood in the street May felt a tug at her skirt, and looked down to see Benji Rook, who had been a mischievous but likeable patient of hers on Elizabeth Ward.

''Ullo, Nurse.' His small face screwed up into a lopsided grin. 'You goin' ter buy some oranges? They sells the bruised ones cheaper.'

'Would you like an orange?'

Benji nodded. 'An' fer me bruvver?' His voice was hopeful. May felt for her purse in the depths of her muff and dropped a shilling into his grimy paw.

'Ta.' He flashed across to the stall. As soon as he was served he sank his teeth into one of the fruit and in seconds it had vanished, peel and all.

May turned to Ellen and laughed. 'Goodness, that was quick!' As she spoke she caught sight of a man's face, high-lighted by the glare of the flares. It was sharply etched in black and white: black hair and white face, the gleaming white band of a clerical collar above broad black shoulders, and, staring straight at her, deep dark eyes which, as the flare

207

blew up seemed to be burning in their sockets with an expression of anger and contempt. Then the crowd shifted and the face vanished. May suddenly shivered.

Ellen asked, 'Are you cold, May?'

May thrust her hands further into her muff. 'No, no of course not. These flares play strange tricks – they make people look so odd.'

'Yes, it's lovely, isn't it?' Ellen's voice was happy and May scolded herself for her too-vivid imagination.

They moved on to watch the gypsy with the enormous gold earrings and jangling coins sewn round her headscarf, who sold fortunes with her specially trained love-birds. She looked hopefully at May.

'Fortune, pretty lady?'

May handed her two coins and the gypsy put out her stick; a bird flew down and daintily picked out a small piece of coloured paper with its beak. The woman passed it to May, then repeated the performance for Ellen.

'Mine says I shall marry a lord,' said Ellen. 'Oh I've had that one before, what a fraud! What does yours say, May?'

'It's the one about meeting a tall, dark stranger who will be my fate – soon.'

'Gosh, I've had that one before as well, May. I do wish she'd change her slips occasionally. I say, I wonder what happens if a *man* asks for his fortune, I mean he'd scarcely want to marry a lord, would he? Can the bird tell?'

'Men don't ask their fortunes, Ellen, haven't you noticed? It's always women. Men go out and make their fortunes, they don't wait about for fate.'

Ellen laughed. 'You sound exactly like Ada! Come on, I want to see the man take his chains off – I do love his tattoos, they come alive when he wriggles.'

They strolled on, up towards the quieter end of Chrisp Street; but there were still plenty of people about, and a small crowd was forming near the entrance to a side street in front of them. May noticed an anticipatory shiver run through the group, and a purposeful shifting of bodies, then a woman's scream rang out. Instinctively May and Ellen pressed forward, and found themselves part of the throng. In a rough oval in the centre two women facing each other slowly circled round like a pair of dogs – it was a fight.

May gasped in surprise: she recognised both the combatants. She bent and whispered to Ellen, 'It's Big Liza – the woman who came into Martha and made that scene, and the other one is Dolly's mother, Mrs Jones. They must be fighting over that wretched Billy!'

Trapped in the crowd May and Ellen stood staring in horror – what chance had tiny Mrs Jones against Big Liza? But a man nearby shouted, 'Two to one on the littl'un – t'other's drunk,' and Big Liza did seem to be flailing with her fists, hitting Mrs Jones, but not hard enough to stop the smaller woman, who kept springing up like a bantam cock, hissing defiance to the other's hoarse shouts.

'But what can she do? She'll never get Big Liza down,' May gasped to Ellen.

Ellen's fingers tightened on May's arm. 'It's her hair, May, it's her hair she's after, don't you see?' And suddenly May recognised the purpose behind the smaller woman's jumps and lunges. A handful of Liza's incredible hair was already down, another tug and the rest tumbled. There was a flash of steel as Mrs Jones drew a large knife, seized a hank of Big Liza's hair and began sawing it off. The crowd roared approval at this novel move and May found herself crying out with the rest, 'Oh, well done, well done!'

'What a disgusting spectacle!' a deep male voice spoke from behind her. 'And you, Madam, in your position, you should know better!' The voice was outraged. May turned her head quickly and there, looking directly at her, were the dark burning eyes and pale face she had seen earlier; now there was no possibility of mistaking the expression: it was utter contempt. He shouted above the crowd, 'I am fetching a police constable, at once,' then turned and thrust his way out of the close-packed bodies.

Big Liza chose this moment to make another grab at her assailant; she caught her by the bun and punched her on the nose. The knife winked dangerously and a hefty man leapt forward and seized Liza by the arms. 'You 'eard, 'e's gorn fer the p'lice.' He dragged her away into the darkness. Mrs Jones still stood in the middle of the street: a small, bedraggled figure, clutching the wicked-looking knife, now stained with the blood from her nose – she seemed dazed and helpless. There was the ring of heavy boots on the cobbles and May, who had been paralysed by her encounter, sprang into action.

'Ellen, go and get her, take her away, hide her somewhere – I'll stop the policeman.'

At once Ellen was wriggling through the crowd. May wheeled round and ran across the road, towards the tall dark clergyman, who had a reluctant-looking policeman in tow. She dared not look back to see if Ellen had escaped with Mrs Jones. Instead, pushing her purse into the depths of her muff she held it well out of sight with one hand, while placing the other on the constable's arm, barring his way as she cried, 'Officer, officer – thank goodness you've come! My purse, I believe my purse has been stolen.'

The policeman stopped immediately, with a look of relief on his face as he turned away from the scene of the fight and the crowd melting into the shadows. He reached for his notebook.

'Perhaps you could give me the details, Madam?'

The clergyman, whom May could see now was young and still very angry, tugged at his sleeve. 'Officer, there is a woman over there attacking another with a knife – surely that is far more important?'

'All in good time, Sir, but this young lady has lost her property.'

'This young lady,' the tone was biting, 'would do well to go back where she belongs, and learn to stay away from street fights.'

May turned her back on him.

'Now, when did you last notice your purse, Madam?'

May faltered, 'I'm not quite sure – I bought our fortunes from the gypsy.' There was a furious exclamation from behind her, she ignored it, and gazed expectantly at the policeman. Then, just as the official notebook was being ponderously opened and the regulation pencil receiving its preparatory lick, she felt it – a sharp pull at her purse. She tightened her fingers over it and was aware of the pressure increasing. May kept her wide-open eyes firmly fixed on the policeman while for several seconds an absurd tug-of-war took place in the silky depths of her muff. She edged her hand forward and tried to prise apart the intruding fingers, but they were too strong for her and as she loosened her grip to manoeuvre, the purse suddenly vanished, only to immediately reappear in the hands of the young clergyman.

'Is this your purse, Madam? You must have mislaid it in your muff, it was just about to slip out.'

May breathed, 'You liar,' but her face, gazing at the policeman registered only pleased surprise.

The constable's countenance broke into a broad grin. 'Now isn't that nice, the gentleman finding it for you like that. All's well that ends well, I allus say. And it do seem that them female harpies have given up and gone away. I do hate to see females fighting, it fair turns me stomach.'

The clergyman muttered, 'So I noticed.'

May smiled sweetly and said, 'Yes, it was dreadful, wasn't it? Thank you so much, officer, you've been so kind.'

The policeman beamed at her. 'Well, if you don't mind me saying so, Miss, I'm not sure a young lady like you ought to be out alone in Chrisp Street. I'll just see you to the cab stand, in case you have any more fears about your purse.'

May said hastily, 'Oh, that's quite all right, officer . . .' but a voice broke in smoothly, 'I'll look after the lady, constable, and see she understands how to get home safely.'

'Thank you, Sir, then I'll be on my way.'

May's companion took her elbow: his grip was light, and she braced herself to break free, but at this his hold tightened, and sooner than face another tussle she began to walk forward, addressing the air in front of her.

'Please do not feel under any obligation to escort me, I know where I am.'

211

'I doubt very much whether you do.' His voice was level, but May could sense the suppressed anger in it. 'You fine young ladies, who think you can come down from the West End for an evening's entertainment laughing at the poor,' May gasped and half-turned towards him, but he continued without pause, his voice rising, '"Slumming" I believe you so delightfully put it – you have no conception of the lives these people lead, yet you think you can interfere whenever it pleases you! I saw you earlier, tossing coins to children . . .'

'One child,' May managed to get in.

'The number is immaterial. You're encouraging begging, undermining their self-respect, you patronise – and, what's more, you aided and abetted law-breaking! To you they're nothing but performing animals, putting on a show for your benefit. You're no better than an ancient Roman, cheering as they throw Christians to the lions! Can't you understand?'

This time he paused for a fraction too long; May had her chance. 'I understand one thing, Sir, and that is when they throw you to the lions I'll be cheering with the best of them! I will not stay here to be insulted, unhand me, now!'

For a moment the young man looked startled, then he drew breath for more, but suddenly a thin form materialised beside them.

May exclaimed, 'Ellen, wherever have you been?' Her voice was reproachful. Before Ellen could reply the clergyman dropped her elbow as though it were red-hot.

Raising his hat he said coldly, 'Since your maid has returned I will leave you, Madam.' He strode quickly off.

Ellen was indignant. 'Your maid! This is my best outfit – who does he think he is?'

The only reply May could think of was so near to blasphemy that she stayed silent, shaking with fury.

'You do look angry, May, your eyes are flashing and your bosom is actually heaving – just like the wronged heroine of a melodrama!'

'Then he's the villain,' was the reply through gritted teeth.

'He can't be, May, he's a clergyman – and very good-looking. He must be the hero, I'm sure – oh, May, perhaps he's the tall dark stranger promised in your fortune!'

May spoke fiercely. 'If he is, then that's the very last time I'm ever buying my fortune!'

Chapter Twenty-Five

During the next few weeks, as she bathed a collapsed old woman whose body had clearly not been touched by water for several years, chasing the jumping fleas with a bar of soap and a smart flick of her wrist; or as she carefully sieved the malodorous faeces of a patient whose recovery Dr Rawlings believed was being impeded by worms, May frequently thought of the angry words of the young clergyman. As she demonstrated to Nurse Pearson how to change the bedlinen of an incontinent patient, 'Don't worry at all, Mrs Adelman, it's quite normal after your operation – we'll soon have you clean and dry,' she composed witty and crushing ripostes in her mind, and imagined his mortified expression as she delivered them. And where had his suit been made, she asked herself angrily? If it hadn't come from the same tailor who was used by Cousin Bertie and Harry Cussons she would be very surprised. Whatever he'd done for the inhabitants of the East End she was sure he'd not emptied their bedpans or deloused their hair or nursed their dying children.

Sister Martha's voice interrupted. 'I like to see lockers clean, Nurse Winton, but there is no necessity to remove the varnish.'

May murmured, 'Sorry, Sister,' and moderated her energy.

At least she had the satisfaction of knowing that despite the young man's importunate rifling of her muff, her diversionary tactics had paid off. Ellen had got Mrs Jones clean away, and Dolly, discovering via the mysterious bush telegraph of the East End May's part in events had expressed her heart-felt gratitude. There had been a gleam of spirit in her eye as she told May of her mother's return home, clutching a fistful of Big Liza's hair. 'Dad was clean bowled over, Nurse, said 'e never believed she 'ad it in 'er.' Dolly didn't say

214

whether the rape of Liza's brassy locks had cooled Billy's ardour; May hoped for the best.

In any case, Dolly was definitely on the mend, her recovery aided by the unexpected collapse of the young girl in the next bed, who had come in for what should have been an uncomplicated appendix operation and had finished up with blood-poisoning. May and Staff Lee had spent some anxious times with Hetty Barnes. At one point the girl seemed to lose heart altogether and it was Dolly who had given constant encouragement, and persuaded Hetty to fight back. Now, though still very weak and often in pain, she was showing distinct signs of improvement, and May looked forward to a peaceful two hours on the Wednesday morning when Staff left her in charge on Sister's day off.

As she left, Staff Nurse Lee said, 'If you've got any time, perhaps you could try and knock some sense into Pearson, Winton. I'm fast losing patience with her, the girl seems all thumbs, and frightened of her own shadow.' May decided that when Pearson had finished scrubbing mackintoshes in the sluice she would teach her how to do a four-hourly temperature and pulse round of the more serious cases.

Ten minutes later May looked up from rearranging the pillows of fat Mrs Soames to see a worried Pearson appear at the ward entrance, clutching a scrubbing brush and dripping soapy water on the floor. May sighed, and went to her.

'Is anything the matter, Nurse Pearson?'

'Head Nurse,' as usual the words came out in an anxious rush, 'There's a man, a visitor, what shall I do?'

'It's not visiting today, Pearson, besides, it's the morning. Has he a particular reason for wishing to see his wife?'

The probationer, still looking worried, shook her head. 'It's not a relative, Nurse Winton, it's a gentleman, a clergyman.'

May frowned, would the girl never learn? She said sharply, 'You should know the rule by now, Nurse Pearson. Don't you remember Matron's lecture on ethics, on the day you arrived? "It is rarely wrong to admit a clergyman at once, unless there is some reason, obvious to everyone, why it is not possible."' May gestured back at the ward. 'Even you can see

215

there's no such reason at present, so you should have ushered him straight in. What have you done with him?'

Pearson reddened. 'I'm sorry, Nurse, I forgot. I put him outside and told him I'd have to go and ask Head Nurse, since she was in charge.'

May exclaimed, 'Really, Pearson, you don't "put clergymen outside"! I'll go and invite him in. Get rid of that scrubbing brush and come with me, now, so that you'll know how to do it next time.'

With a chastened Pearson trotting obediently at her heels May walked up to the big double doors and swung them open, a professional smile on her face. Her features froze. Outside stood the young clergyman of Chrisp Street market. May saw his jaw drop, and felt hers do the same: they both stood motionless, staring at each other.

He found his tongue first, his voice hoarse, 'You!' His gaze swept over her, from the tips of her stiffly starched muslin frills, down her all-enveloping apron, to the rounded toes of her sensible black shoes. Then he looked back at her face again. He seemed totally stunned.

May had remained speechless, then she became conscious of Pearson's earnest gaze beside her, and she managed to stammer out, 'What do you want?' Then, at last, her training reasserted itself. She beckoned him through the door and along the corridor, saying, 'I'm so sorry you've been kept waiting, but Nurse naturally wished to check that a visit was convenient. Which of our patients do you wish to speak to?'

He had regained his self-control as well. 'I'd like a few words with Hetty Barnes, if I may. Her grandmother is my cook; she has been unable to come herself, and is naturally anxious about her granddaughter.'

'I have heard her mention her grandmother – Mrs Lewis, isn't it?' He nodded. May continued, 'I'm sure Hetty will be pleased to hear of her.'

They reached the bed. Hetty looked up, her face flushed with pleasure.

'Hello, Mr Lisle. Gran wrote you'd try an' come an' see me.'

216

May swung a chair neatly into position and motioned to Mr Lisle. He hesitated, uneasy at the reversal of roles. May was firm.

'Do sit down, Mr Lisle. Nurse and I will fetch the screens.'

He said hastily, 'Please don't bother, that's really not necessary. My visit is purely a social one.'

May paused, then noticing Hetty's look of pride in her well-dressed visitor she decided to let the girl bask in the envy of the other patients – after all, Sister wouldn't be back for ages. She smiled at Hetty and withdrew, Pearson following. As she reached the ward entrance she realised she felt quite shaken – fancy that angry young clergyman being Hetty's grandmother's employer – 'My gran works for a vicar, Nurse, up Bromley way. He's a bachelor, and ever so handsome.' She remembered the words now, though barely listening to them at the time as she had been concentrating on the state of Hetty's wound. She stood still for a moment, forgetful of Pearson as the memory of the scene in Chrisp Street flooded over her, then a worried voice said,

'I watched ever so carefully, Nurse Winton, but I don't know if I can do it just like you – exactly how long do you have to stand and stare at clergymen before you let them in?'

May gulped. 'Actually, Pearson, I think you'd better watch Sister on another occasion – I don't think I got it quite right this time. Go and finish the mackintoshes, then come and fetch me and I'll show you how to do the four-hourly temps.'

Pearson's face lit up. 'Oh, thank you Nurse, I've nearly done.'

A few minutes later Pearson was back. May checked the mackintoshes – a supervision she never failed to exercise – then took her into the ward. They went over to Mrs Field in the first bed and May showed Pearson how to shake down the mercury in the thermometer to 95°, then insert the bulb under the tongue.

'Tell her to close her lips over it – I know you know what to do, Mrs Field, but another patient might not be so experienced – time it by your watch, five minutes it's got to stay in, now on to the next patient, a minute later, so you remember, we'll just do two at a time for the moment, to make it easier. Three fingers on the pulse, not just one, I'm sure you've practised this with Sister Tutor – why must you not use your thumb? That's right, Nurse, well done. Now enter it on the chart – good girl, that's very neat. Back to the thermometer, now, what must you do before you use it on another patient?'

By a careful mixture of chivvying and coaxing May got Pearson round. When they reached Hetty Barnes Mr Lisle began to rise, but seeing Hetty's look of disappointment May motioned him back.

'No need for you to go yet, Mr Lisle, you'll just have to do all the talking for the next five minutes, while Hetty holds the thermometer. I'm sure you can manage that without any difficulty.'

She smiled directly at him and was fascinated to see a red flush creep out from under the white band of his collar, and up over his face. But to be fair to the young man, he was obviously keeping Hetty entertained; she had quite a pretty colour in her cheeks.

'We'll do the axillary temps last, Pearson, all at once.' She took the probationer past the following five beds to the next acute case.

Finally they returned to the old lady in the next bed to Hetty. She plucked at her bedclothes and made a constant low muttering sound in her delirium; she could not be trusted with the thermometer in her mouth. As May showed Pearson how to take a temperature from the armpit she had a strong suspicion that Mr Lisle, though apparently taking a lively interest in Hetty's story about her brother's donkey, was, in fact, listening to her voice as she instructed the junior probationer. But she made herself concentrate on the matter in hand and watched Pearson narrowly. The girl was clearly nervous of the old woman, but she did as she was told. When the temperature had been registered May drew her back from the bed.

'You coped quite well, Nurse Pearson, but you did not speak to the patient.'

Pearson murmured, 'But she's delirious, Nurse Winton, she doesn't know us.'

May shook her head. 'Perhaps not, but there is always the possibility that she understands a little, and even if she doesn't, a soothing tone may help to reassure her and calm her – think of a delirious patient as a frightened one, Nurse, and it will help you. And remember, we can never know how much a patient understands – dying patients often look unconscious, but hearing is the last sense to go, so never say anything you would not wish them to hear.'

Pearson nodded solemnly, and May added for good measure, 'Don't forget, Nurse, you must never judge solely by appearances, they are often deceptive.'

As soon as the words were out of her mouth May realised their double-edged meaning. She glanced hastily at the grey-suited back, and saw another tide of red rise above his collar and lose itself in his thick black hair. She felt a pang of remorse, then hardened her heart – serve him right, that was exactly what he'd done. She turned back to Pearson and spoke briskly.

'Come along, Nurse, you've the dinner things to prepare. Report back to me when you've finished.' Pearson scuttled off.

May moved up the ward again to Mrs Green, a patient in the end bed, recovering well from her operation. She pretended to be checking the ventilation from the window above as she covertly studied the woman's colour. Why had she felt a stab of unease during the temperature round? Her reading had been a little high, and was her breathing slightly laboured?

'How are you feeling, Mrs Green?'

'Quite well, thank you, Nurse Winton.' Yet the woman's smile was strained.

May walked thoughtfully back down the ward. As she passed Hetty's bed her visitor stood up. He turned to May and said, his voice formal, 'I wonder if you would be so kind as to spare me the time for a few words, Miss Winton, before I leave.'

'Certainly, Mr Lisle.' May was curious.

He went back to shake Hetty by the hand and say his goodbyes, then he walked down the ward beside her.

'You seem very busy.'

'On the contrary,' May replied. 'Today is very quiet, otherwise I could not have spent the time teaching Nurse Pearson. Besides,' she added honestly, 'Sister and Staff would not both have been off-duty had the ward been very heavy. I am only in my third year, and still in training.'

He looked quickly at her, but stayed silent until they reached Sister's sitting room. May ushered him in, but left the door wide open; he glanced at it but May knew she must never ever shut this door when alone with a male doctor and she had no intention of taking chances in the case of another male, even though a clergyman – certainly not one still on the lower side of thirty as she judged Mr Lisle to be. She did not sit down, but stood with her hands neatly clasped in front of her apron, waiting for him to speak. He seemed to be having some difficulty finding the right phrases, and May felt a distinct pleasure in seeing her eloquent accuser of several weeks ago now apparently searching for words. At last he took a deep breath and began.

'Miss Winton, it is very clear that I owe you an apology. Obviously I totally misunderstood your position in the East End. I am deeply sorry.'

May saw that he really did look sorry: his expression was anxious.

She allowed herself a cool smile. 'Everyone makes mistakes sometimes, Mr Lisle.'

He looked relieved, but she remembered the expression of contempt on his Byronic features in Chrisp Street and could not resist adding, 'Though I would have thought that in your profession it was particularly important not to make hasty and ill-considered judgments.'

He flushed, then said, 'Be fair, Miss Winton. You were apparently inciting one woman to attack another in a street brawl.'

May glared at him. 'You know nothing of the circumstances!'

220

'I can think of no circumstances in which a woman of your class in Society,' May opened her mouth to protest, but he ploughed on, 'Very well, of your profession, then, should condone a skirmish like that in Chrisp Street. Men fighting is one thing, but to see women setting about each other on the streets is appalling!'

May drew a deep breath and burst out, 'So it's quite permissible for *men* to fight, but not women, because it offends your delicate sensibilities as a male. I suppose you're one of those hidebound reactionaries who would deny the franchise to mature, adult women!'

'Certainly not – I wholeheartedly support the enfranchisement of mature, adult, women.' The emphasis on the last three words was unmistakable.

May's anger was rising. 'You should come into the Receiving Room on a Saturday night and see the damage these males, these drunken lords of creation inflict on each other, and on their weaker wives and children. Surely, as a clergyman, you should be a man of peace?'

He said doggedly, 'I don't agree with fighting by either male or female, but I have a higher opinion of women. I expect the female of the species to exercise womanly restraint.'

They glared at each other like a pair of fighting cocks. Suddenly the absurdity of the whole situation hit May forcefully. Whatever must they look like! She took hold of herself.

In a voice as sweet as honey she said softly, 'Mr Lisle, I *am* exercising womanly restraint – now, at this very minute!'

He started, and looked at her closely. Then his mouth began very slightly to curve up at the corners. May felt hers twitch in response. He spoke.

'Touché, Miss Winton. I am sorry for Chrisp Street – believe me, I regretted my words long before I saw you here.'

May held out her hand, but before he could take it Pearson shot through the doorway.

'Head Nurse, come quickly – Dawes says she thinks Mrs Green's stitches have burst, she's collapsed!'

221

May rapped out, 'Tell Warner to fetch the emergency tray, then go and find Dr Rawlings, *at once*.'

Mr Lisle jumped out of her way. 'Goodbye, Miss Winton.'

May threw a hurried farewell over her shoulder and was off into the ward at top speed, her eyes on the far bed where Dawes was trying to calm the terrified woman.

Chapter Twenty-Six

It was a bright morning, and thin shafts of sunlight from the high windows lay across the tables in the centre of the ward. The freshly sponged leaves of the aspidistra, Sister Martha's pride and joy, resplendent in its ornate brass pot, gleamed a lighter green. Yesterday had been operating day, so breakfast had taken longer than usual. May and Pearson were whisking through the beds at speed, but they slowed down when they reached Hetty Barnes, handling her gently as they removed the drawsheet.

'How are you today, Hetty?' May asked. 'I'm afraid you'll feel the pain in your side for a while yet.'

'I'm fine, Nurse, really I am. I feel so lazy just lying in bed here, with you all working so hard.'

'It's our job, Hetty.' May's reply was firm. 'We'd soon get bored if all our patients were up and about, wouldn't we, Nurse Pearson?'

Pearson, who had already broken one thermometer that day and been harangued by Sister for failing to remove every trace of fluff from the inside rim of a trolley wheel, agreed without much conviction. May, determined to set the girl a good example, continued.

'Now, Hetty, if there's anything at all we can do for you, don't hesitate to tell us.'

Hetty's thin face brightened, but she spoke haltingly.

'Well, Nurse Winton, I were wondering . . . but I don't like to ask . . .'

'Anything, Hetty, now you just tell me. We can't have our patients worrying, can we, Nurse?'

Hetty became more cheerful. 'It's like this, Nurse Winton. Me Gran, she do worry something awful; me being the only girl, we've always been close, especially since me Mum died.

223

But she can't get to see me, her legs are that bad. Mr Lisle, he's been very kind, said he'd bring her in a cab, but it's still a long way, across the yard and up all them stairs, she didn't want to bother him. That's why he came himself, to tell her I was all right, like. Well, she told him her mind were at rest, cause he'd taken the trouble, but Sid says she's still fretting, him being a man, and Sid too, well she can't really ask him, like, can she . . .'

Hetty's voice trailed off, she was sweating with the effort of the long speech. By now May was heartily regretting her officiousness in insisting on hearing Hetty's problem, but she smiled into the anxious eyes.

'So you'd like me to call round and have a word with her?'

Hetty's face lit up. 'Oh, if you would, Nurse Winton, I'd be ever so grateful! You've told me how you go walking a lot, and you do know Mr Lisle don't you? 'Cause you had quite a chat when he came to see me.'

Recalling the precise nature of that 'chat' May felt her colour rising.

'I don't know him well, Hetty. But that won't matter as it's your grandmother I'm going to see. Staff Nurse is glaring at us now, we'll have to get on, but you can tell me exactly where the vicarage is later, and I'll go this very afternoon. I'm off two till five.'

'Thank you so much, I'm ever so grateful, I really am. I know you'll cheer her up.'

Hetty's relief was so transparent that May chided herself for her reluctance, and decided not to be silly. After all, it was highly unlikely that the vicar would be at home at that time of the day, and even if he were, there was no need for May to see him. Besides, they had achieved some sort of truce before she'd been called away to Mrs Green.

May kept her uniform on and set off immediately after dinner. As she walked up the Dock Road the sun came out again, and she felt her spirits rising at the thought of three hours off duty and a brisk walk ahead. She turned into St Leonard's Road and it struck her how very at home she now felt in the streets of Poplar. When Hetty had given her directions she had been able to visualise the greater part of the route, though she went northwards less often.

'Good afternoon, Nurse.'

The call broke into her thoughts. May turned, looked, and stepped quickly out into the street, jumping over a pile of horse dung to reach the huge dray drawn up on the other side. The driver beamed down at her.

'Why, Mr Thomas, isn't it? How's your leg, these days?'

'Almost as good as new, like you told me it would be, when I were on Simeon Ward. It's good ter see you agin, Nurse. I bin workin' over Whitechapel way, don't often get over this side, but the reg'lar drayman's sick. The wife'll be pleased I sin you, she remembers you well, from visitin' – that time you 'id the jug o' beer fer us! Cor, that Sister were a Tartar, and no mistake! When yer kept on droppin' things and gettin' behind, didn't she give yer wot for! And the way you used to look at 'er, all saucy like, an' tappin' yer foot – I didn't think yer'd stick it, Nurse, an' that's a fact.'

'Well, I'm still there, Mr Thomas – and not breaking quite as much, I hope.'

'Whoa, boys! I better git on, these lads is gettin' restive, an' I wouldn't want anuvver accident. But I'm glad I sin you agin, Nurse. Soon as I sees that yeller 'air and blue cloak I says ter meself, "Sure as I'm sittin' be'ind these 'osses it's Nurse Winton!"'

He flicked his whip, and May stood back. 'Please give my best wishes to Mrs Thomas.'

'I will, Nurse, I will.' The dray lumbered off.

May pressed on, looking for the spire of St Barnabas' Church. There it was: an ugly, new yellow-brick building, squatting too close to the road. Close behind it was a sizeable private house, which in this part of London could only mean the home of a doctor, or a vicarage. May slowed down and surveyed the scene. She had intended going to the back door, but there was a stout brick wall around the house, with apparently only one pair of gates, now standing open. The driver of a growler, waiting further up the road, was eyeing her with interest, so she stopped her uncharacteristic

225

dithering and marched boldly in. There had to be a path round the side of the house for tradesmen: annoyingly there were two, one in each direction. May stood, irresolute. Should she choose the route of the grimy laurels, or pass between the sooty rhododendrons? Really, she thought, the man might at least keep his shrubs clean! The hesitation proved her undoing. Before she could set out on the laurel path, chosen for no better reason than that she never had cared for rhododendrons, due to an early weakness in spelling, she was arrested by a tapping from inside the bay window. May saw the unmistakable flash of a clerical collar. She felt annoyed at being spotted, but moved at once towards the front door. It would have been exceedingly undignified to try and make her escape at this juncture. She rang the bell and awaited the arrival of the maid, determined to insist that her business was with the cook, and the cook alone. Her resolution was thrown into disarray when the master of the house opened the door in person.

'Miss Winton – what a pleasant surprise! How good of you to call.'

To be fair, thought May, as she walked into a dark and musty hall, he did look both surprised and pleased: a much warmer reception than she might have expected in the light of their previous exchanges.

She turned to explain her business, but before she could speak a ginger tornado launched itself from the floor straight at May's chest. She caught it instinctively, and found herself with a large cat in her arms; it began a thunderous purring.

'Miss Winton, I'm so sorry! Shadrak, get down.'

Shadrak opened one yellow eye in his direction, then rubbed his head against May. She took off her glove and began to stroke him. The purring intensified.

'It's quite all right, Mr Lisle, I like cats.'

'I'm afraid he's in a temper because he's been banished from the drawing room fire.'

'With a name like his he has every right to be,' May said with a smile.

The vicar looked at her and chuckled. 'I suppose so.'

226

May gently touched the ragged ear. 'I can see you've been in a fight recently.'

'Yes, he's descended on the neighbouring felines like Attila the Hun, and it's a rather one-sided war – he's twice their size.'

'Then you must stop sharing your breakfast kippers with him.' May saw from the young man's expression that she had scored a hit. Then he smiled.

'But Miss Winton, I'm forgetting my manners – do let me take your cloak.'

He lifted Shadrak from her arms and pushed him, protesting, through a door on the left. Unthinking, May slipped her cloak from her shoulders, then remembered where she was and twitched it quickly away from his outstretched hand.

'No, thank you Mr Lisle. I'm not paying a social call – not on you, at least. My business is with your cook. I have a message for her, from her granddaughter.' He looked quite crestfallen at her words, so May, deciding she had been too abrupt, relented, and smiled directly at him. 'After all, it would scarcely be proper for me to call on a young unmarried man in his own house without a chaperon, now would it?'

Mr Lisle seemed considerably cheered by this remark. His face broke into a broad answering grin.

'A very natural sentiment, Miss Winton. But then, your sense of propriety is so acute! However, as it happens, today there is no problem. We have a chaperon.'

May looked at him doubtfully. 'We do?'

'Why yes, an old friend of my mother's, the widow of the Bishop of Ludlow, has called on me, with her daughter.'

Mr Lisle looked rather conscious at the mention of the Bishop's daughter, and May was at once intrigued. So Mamma was match-making, was she, on behalf of her handsome bachelor son? May squared her shoulders, flicked back a loose tendril of hair, and allowed herself to be ushered into a gloomy plush drawing room.

'Mrs Tranter, may I present Miss Winton, who nurses at St Katharine's hospital, in the East India Dock Road.'

May moved forward, and waited for Mrs Tranter to extend her hand. She did not. Instead, her pale, prominent eyes slowly raked May from her windblown hair to her muddy boots.

'Does your Matron allow you to tramp the streets un-unaccompanied?'

The young vicar went rigid with embarrassment. May moved rapidly onto the offensive.

'In my profession it is essential to obtain regular exercise.'

'The dear Bishop always firmly believed that young women should stay at home, under the care of their mothers.'

'How, then, did he propose to staff the great hospitals?' May's voice was silky, but Mrs Tranter ignored the question.

'It is not fitting for young women to take responsibility for their own behaviour.'

May's reply was icy. 'Since as nurses, we regularly take responsibility for the lives of others, it would be strange indeed if we were not considered fit to conduct our own.'

Mrs Tranter drew a deep, angry breath, but before she could exhale it in speech Mr Lisle broke in, turning hastily to her daughter.

'Miss Tranter, Miss Winton.'

May turned to the young woman. She was about the same age as herself, with a pretty face spoiled by red-rimmed eyes and pale lashes. Miss Tranter's smile was uncertain. She was obviously torn between her desire to be friendly to any acquaintance of Mr Lisle, at whom she gazed adoringly, and her natural reluctance to do anything which would upset her formidable mother.

May felt sorry for the girl and asked her whether she had been in the East End of London before. Miss Tranter said she had not, found it very dirty and noisy and preferred the country, did not Miss Winton agree? Miss Winton agreed that she did agree, and the conversation then languished, despite the heroic attempts of Mr Lisle to divert the frigid glares Mrs Tranter was casting in May's direction.

May, deciding that she had done her duty socially, rose to her feet and announced that as her original intention had been to visit Mr Lisle's cook she would now like to be shown to the kitchen, if Mr Lisle would be so kind. Mr Lisle, looking both relieved and regretful, escorted her out of the drawing room, to an audible 'Humph!' from Mrs Tranter's corner.

As soon as they reached the hall they were greeted by a loud wail and the vicar released an indignant Shadrak from his captivity, with a 'Sorry, old man, but the lady in there doesn't like cats.'

May bent and stroked the arched back, murmuring, 'That's two of us beyond the pale, chum.' The ginger tom purred a loud agreement.

Mr Lisle took May to the top of the basement stairs, and then stopped.

'Miss Winton, I'm awfully sorry about that, that experience – I'm afraid Mrs Tranter has old-fashioned views.'

He looked upset, and May was sorry for him. He could hardly have expected such a broadside to be fired by his guest. In any case, May felt she had kept her flag flying in the encounter and could afford to be magnanimous.

'Don't worry, Mr Lisle, I quite understand. My stepmother can be just as freezing when she wishes.' Privately May knew this was a slander against Lady Clarence, who, unlike Mrs Tranter, understood the art of being frigid without descending into rudeness. But since the young vicar was unlikely ever to meet Lady Clarence Winton the white lie seemed immaterial.

He looked relieved and took her down the stairs and into the kitchen, explaining that it was the housemaid's afternoon off, and Mrs Lewis would be on her own. Hetty's grandmother was a thin, careworn woman, with a surprising shock of white hair, and a worried expression. She was obviously pleased to see May, and soon had her sitting in a chair in front of the glowing range, a cup of hot strong tea in her hand and a satisfied Shadrak on her lap.

Chapter Twenty-Seven

May passed a peaceful half hour in the kitchen with Mrs Lewis. Both the atmosphere and the temperature was noticeably warmer than upstairs. As she took her leave she edged towards the scullery, determined to slip out through the servants' door, but Mrs Lewis, realising her intention, hauled herself out of her basket chair and shuffled forward.

'No, no, Miss Winton, you musn't leave by the back door – the Vicar would never forgive me!'

'Now, Mrs Lewis, it will be much quicker. He has visitors, I wouldn't dream of disturbing him.'

May moved forward, but Mrs Lewis, her face puckered with distress, barred her way. Realising the old lady was genuinely upset, May gave in and turned instead towards the door leading to the hall stairs.

'Very well, Mrs Lewis, but I can't let you climb these steps, with your leg in the state it is. I'll say goodbye to Mr Lisle, and he'll see me out.'

May had no intention of doing any such thing. Shutting the kitchen door firmly but quietly behind her she stepped lightly up the drugget and into the back of the hall, intending to make a rush for the front door and to slip through it before either her host or his visitors were aware of her departure. But just before she reached the drawing room door on her left her attention was caught by the strident tones of Mrs Tranter, carrying through the ill-fitting panels. When she heard what she was saying May froze.

'Agnes, my dear, let that be an object lesson to you! The dreadful consequences of young women trying to be independent! That girl – so pert! The way she tried to answer me back! And her looks – red-faced, blowsy – did you see the state of her hands?' There was an assenting murmur from her daughter. May stood riveted, barely conscious of the click of a door opening across the hallway. Mrs Tranter's voice boomed out again. 'Agnes, I could scarcely believe my eyes, an unmarried girl,' the tone was lowered, but still clearly audible, 'her, her *chest*! So unrestrained, so prominent!'

May was transfixed. Then, as her anger rose, she became aware of a muffled snort to her right. Mr Lisle, his hand clasped over his mouth, was draped against the newel post, overcome by a paroxysm of suppressed laughter. May felt a wave of pure fury wash over her as she looked at his shaking shoulders. She marched across, seized his arm and wrenched it away from his face, hissing, 'How dare you – how dare you!'

He straightened up and made an obvious effort to pull himself together, then his glance fell on her heaving bosom; his lips began to curve again and, leaning forward, eyes alight with mischief, he whispered to her: 'But Miss Winton, she's right! Your, your . . . it is – but it's quite superb!'

May was too angry for speech. She seized his quivering shoulders, glared up into his face and shook him, hard. But he was stronger than she was. He put his hands to her waist and held her at arms length.

'Come now, Miss Winton, no violence, please, remember, I am a man of peace!' He smiled down into her infuriated eyes. Held fast, May was suddenly very conscious of her flushed face and disordered hair, but before she could break free from his restraining grasp she heard the door behind her open. Mrs Tranter, made suspicious by her host's overlong absence, was coming in quest of her prey. May stood paralysed.

'Walter, how could you! And you, you shameless hussy, take your hands off him, this instant!'

Her words broke the spell. May sprang back, collided with the outraged bosom of the bishop's relict and was summarily bounced to one side. There was a howl of anguish from Shadrak as she landed on his tail. Mrs Tranter ignored them both. She turned the full force of her fury onto the young vicar, on whose face May saw the dawning realisation of what their tableau must have looked like.

231

'Mrs Tranter, please, let me explain . . .'

But she would have none of it. 'When I see your poor dear mother, tomorrow, at the earliest opportunity,' each word was slowly and deliberately enunciated, 'I shall tell her,' there was a dramatic pause, 'All! Come, Agnes.' Then she turned back to Walter Lisle. 'We shall see you again, Sir, when you have come to your senses.' She swept out of the door. Agnes, pink rabbit nose aquiver and china blue eyes brimming with tears, darted a last agonised look at the young clergyman.

Walter Lisle gazed after them, his expression appalled. Then he suddenly remembered May's presence. 'Miss Winton' – May cut his words short.

'Goodbye, Mr Lisle.' She pulled the tattered remnants of her dignity around her together with her cloak and almost ran out of the open door and down the gravel path, her eyes stinging, her face burning.

She came out of the vicarage gate and turned instinctively away from the cab into which Mrs Tranter was climbing. Soon she was adrift in unfamiliar streets, all of which looked confusingly alike: she lost her sense of direction. The sun had gone in, and a damp, clammy fog was beginning to rise from the greasy pavements. She felt very alone. The emotions roused by the scene in the vicarage hall were taking their toll: a wave of nausea swept over her. She stopped and clutched her side, looking about her. She was completely lost.

She walked forward onto a bridge and looked down. It spanned a foul-smelling canal which she did not recognise at all. The road was deserted. While she stood hesitating a dark, bent figure appeared from a side alley beyond the bridge. May ran forward.

'Excuse me, would you be so good as to tell me the way back to the East India Dock Road?'

A seamed old face peered back at her. 'I couldn't tell yer, Miss,' moving on. 'This un's Limehouse Cut,' gesturing at the stinking water as he shuffled on.

May realised that she could not even find her way back to the vicarage, not that she would ever ask the help of Walter

Lisle, she thought with a small flash of spirit. The memory of his remarks in the hall brought back some warmth to May's cheeks. She must pull herself together, she was only in London, for goodness' sake – Limehouse Cut was hardly the Orinoco.

She took several deep breaths and tried to regain her self control. She must find a place where there were more people, then she could ask about public transport; fortunately she was carrying some small change. Her first priority was to get back to the hospital on time for her evening duty. The road beyond the Cut seemed wider – better take ·a gamble and press on.

May stepped forward briskly, hugging her cloak around her in the cold, dank air. Soon, there were more people about. She waited until she saw a respectable-looking woman dressed in black and went up to her, asking for the nearest railway station.

'Why, Miss, you're only a step from Bromley; keep going, it's straight ahead.'

With a sigh of relief May pressed on. Suddenly she heard the welcome hiss of escaping steam, and there were the station steps. She rushed up them and into the booking hall. The clerk was young, but efficient.

'East India Dock Road, Miss? St Katharine's? You really want the North London line to Poplar, that's Bromley South Station, but it's a tidy walk, especially in this weather. Best use the Great Eastern instead: go down to Stepney, there's one due in three minutes, you're in luck. Then catch the Blackwall train, watch for the board on the front. It'll drop you the wrong side of the Dock, but I'd say it was your best bet.'

May only had enough to pay for a third class ticket, but this was no time for niceties.

'Platform One, Miss.'

'Thank you, thank you so much.'

Once on the train she sank onto the narrow seat with a sigh of relief. The journey back was blessedly uneventful. On arriving at Stepney she found she only had ten minutes to wait for her connection. A glance at the clock and a quick calculation reassured her that, as long as she moved quickly, she would be back on the ward on time.

May had opened the door and leapt out of the carriage before the train had properly stopped. Ignoring an indignant: 'Mind yourself, Miss!' from a porter she raced for the exit, flew down the steps into Black Wall Way, dodged a grocer's van as she sped over the tunnel entrance and turned right into Robin Hood Lane. By the time she reached the Dock Road she was hot and panting, but her goal was in sight. There were no trams coming so she ran behind a cart, waited for a wagon to pass and then headed for the high arch-way.

Jenks was on duty. He beamed at her as she shot in. 'You'll make the Derby this year, Nurse Winton, sure you will.'

May gasped a greeting and slowed to a more decorous pace as she came within the hospital precincts. It wouldn't do to be stopped by an irate Sister at this stage. The hands of the big clock on the tower stood at five to five: she had just made it.

The worst ravages of her hair had been restored on the train, so with a quick splash to wash her hands and face and a hasty donning of apron and cap she was ready.

Sister Martha looked her over suspiciously. 'You seem a trifle heated, Nurse Winton.'

'I had to run from the station, Sister, I was a little late.'

Sister shook her head disapprovingly. 'You young nurses, travelling everywhere by train and omnibus – you should be out getting exercise, tramping the streets, like I did in my young days.'

'Yes, Sister.' May thought wryly that she just couldn't please anybody, today.

For the rest of the evening May felt dull and clumsy. She fumbled with the first fomentation, scalding her hands, and having to start again. When they came to dress old Carrie's leg the foetid odour of the pus seemed more foul than before, and as they took the bowls back to the steriliser Staff Nurse Lee voiced May's fears.

234

'I'm afraid she'll have to be transferred to Isaiah Ward, Winton.'

'Oh, Staff, she'll be so upset: she's made friends here.'

'She'll do no good to her friends if she stays here. It's too risky to keep her.' May knew that this was true, but felt very sorry for the uncomplaining old lady.

Hetty asked about her visit to the vicarage. May found it an effort to answer cheerfully, but Hetty seemed pleased that she had seen Mrs Lewis and chatted about her grand-mother's leg. 'It comes and goes, Nurse, sometimes it's there, and sometimes it's not.' May smiled and moved on.

Sister Martha was late dismissing them, and they all had to bolt their suppers, under the accusing glare of Home Sister. May sat next to Ellen, but for once she didn't feel the urge to confide in her. The scene with Mrs Tranter had hurt. She tried not to think of it.

'Cocoa, May?' Ellen asked when they got upstairs.

'No thanks, Ellen, I've got rather a headache. I think I'll go straight to bed.'

Ellen looked at her searchingly. Then she pressed May's hand and said, 'Well, you know where we are if you want us. Look after yourself, May.'

But once she was in bed, sleep would not come. The events of the afternoon crowded in upon her. With unpleasant clarity she heard again Mrs Tranter's condemnation: 'Pert – redfaced – blowsy – did you see the state of her hands?' Well, she was not ashamed of her hands, they were roughened by hard work, but 'pert', 'blowsy', – how dare she call her so! And Walter Lisle, how could he have laughed when she was being insulted? But as she re-played the scene in her head May remembered a tiny sound, ignored in the heat of the moment: the click of the other door opening. Suppose he hadn't heard the earlier strictures at all – only Mrs Tranter's comment on her bosom? He was still guilty of gross in-delicacy, May told herself firmly, but – but not of the unkindness she had been laying to his charge. And she should never have seized hold of him like that, whatever the provocation. What must he be thinking of her now? No

235

wonder the bishop's widow had called her a shameless hussy!

By now May felt cold and wretched. She pulled the hot water bottle up from her feet and clutched it to her chest. Fighting off the threatening tears she finally fell asleep.

Chapter Twenty-Eight

May knew that her distress over the scene in the vicarage had assumed ridiculous proportions. After all, Walter Lisle's parish was well to the north of St Katharine's. She was unlikely to come face to face with him again. And unpleasant though the confrontation with the Bishop's widow had been May felt that her behaviour, though unmaidenly in appearance had not been so in intent – surely Mr Lisle had realised this? In any case, what of his own comment, hadn't she been entitled to be angry at that? But reason alone did not calm her. She felt bruised by what had happened, and did not even tell Ellen, although she knew her friend's good sense would have helped her to regain her sense of proportion.

Fortunately for May the Staff Nurse on Elizabeth Ward chose this moment to go down with measles, and a severe attack at that. The only other available Staff Nurse with experience of nursing children announced that she was breaking her contract to marry a wealthy undertaker, and the pool of private nurses was fully engaged – the spring seemed a particularly sickly one. In consequence May found herself in Matron's office being informed that she, Nurse Winton, was, as a great concession, to be appointed temporary Acting Staff Nurse; not, of course, on Staff Nurses' pay, Matron added hastily. She was to stay on Elizabeth Ward until Jameson was fit for duty again. May was well aware of the chain of circumstances which had forced Matron's hand, but she was grateful. She liked Elizabeth, and knew the temporary promotion would delay the onset of nights – besides, she was flattered that she had been chosen. With this new interest, St Barnabas' Vicarage, together with its occupant, began to fade from the forefront of her thoughts.

On her second day on Elizabeth an anguished mother arrived, panting in the wake of a Receiving Room porter who was carrying her badly burned child.

The mother moaned, 'I'll never fergive meself – I fell asleep, I were so tired.' May glanced at her swollen belly heavy with pregnancy. 'She wanted ter cook the dinner, as a surprise, an' she fell in the fire. She's only seven, Sister, she were tryin' to 'elp. Oh, my Louie!'

Sister Elizabeth was soon busy with the child. May gently led the mother to a chair and whispered, 'Try to stay calm, Mrs Brown. We'll do all we can for Louie.'

The other children were hushed and round-eyed as Sister wrapped the little girl in a warmed blanket, and placed her near the fire, carefully dropping brandy and water into the small mouth twisted up on the left where the flames had licked up. May prepared a warm bath of boracic and behind the screens they floated off the charred remnants of clothing. Then May and the probationers attended to the other children while Sister and Dr Rawlings applied zinc-smeared lint and followed with fomentations.

They had little hope, since the area of the burn was extensive for such a young child, but Louie hung onto life with a desperate intensity. After three days the routine of daily changes of dressings had to begin, and however careful May and Sister were these had to be excruciatingly painful. But the child gritted her teeth and only whimpered, though her eyes were round and staring. May's respect for Sister Elizabeth went up by leaps and bounds. Her skill was such that the offensive smell so often met with in these cases was kept at bay, while by a judicious mixture of coaxing, pleading and nagging she persuaded Louie to take food into her distorted mouth.

As a prevention against contraction the little girl's arm was splinted, and they made her lie with her head overhanging the bed to stop the burns on her neck pulling her jaw down onto her shoulder. Yet somehow Louie survived, and unbelievably soon was showing a keen interest in the doings of the ward: whispering question after question of the nurses and holding furious hissing arguments with the other children from her upsidedown position.

Louie's mother staggered up the stairs every visiting day, 'Me man's good with the kids, Nurse, I'm very lucky,' and Louie confided in May one day that two babies were soon expected, not just one. May had long ceased to be surprised at the precocious knowledge of East End children. She was relieved that Louie appeared to be looking forward to this event – far more so, May suspected, than her mother was.

Babies came in – ill, emaciated, wounded. Some of them died, one with his thin chest still bearing the clear marks of his father's hob-nailed boots. ''E was drunk, Nurse, didn't know what 'e were doin' – 'e luvs the kids when 'e's sober, 'e's just not often sober.' May watched other parents slowly drag themselves away from small bedsides, and walk, defeated, from the ward; but Louie confounded the experts and set out on the road to an uneventful recovery. Somehow she avoided septicaemia and pneumonia, and even that common complication of children's burns, scarlet fever. Her body would be scarred for life, and the disfigurement of her face and neck could not be hidden, but she had an indomitable will, and May felt she would cope. Meanwhile, she was their living miracle, and May knew they needed her as much as she needed them.

In the West End the Season unrolled its luxurious carpet of balls and receptions, operas and concerts, dinners and theatres; but May's chances of stepping onto this carpet were few and far between. Many functions did not even start until after the time that Home Sister locked the doors of the Nurses' Home, and though she managed to get back from the odd short play, or miss the ending of the longer ones, her only opportunity of staying to the end of an event was on the evening before her monthly day off, when a sleeping-out pass could be obtained. Otherwise, as Archie pointed out, she did considerably less well than Cinderella.

But May did not waste much time in repining: the nurses had their own amusements, there was always somebody

239

around, or something going on, even if it were only a lively piano-playing session in the Nurses' Sitting Room. May found she was becoming more and more detached from the life of High Society – she felt it was like caviare – delightful in small quantities, but too much soon produced a surfeit.

Lady Clarence seemed to understand May's feelings, but Lady Andover bewailed her unavailability, 'My only unmarried granddaughter, an heiress, and your looks, incredibly, unaffected by all the awful people you mix with – yet I'm not able to show you off! You disappoint me, May, you really do.' But she laughed as she spoke, and May felt little compunction, as she knew her grandmother revelled in Society for its own sake; May would only have been the icing on the cake.

However, Lady Andover was well aware of May's Achilles' heel: her luncheon and dinner parties drew like a magnet. The hospital food, though more sustaining these days, was often dull. The promise of one of Chef's masterpieces made May reach for her diary. So on the Thursday of the last week in June May hurried off-duty and jumped into a cab with a quick, 'Arlington Street, please, Andover House.' Friday was her day off that month. She would be able to spend a leisured evening at Lady Andover's dinner party, followed by a night in feather-bedded luxury, with perhaps a session at the Bath Club, or a stroll in the dazzling mêlée of the Park to follow.

Her grandmother greeted May in her boudoir, already dressed.

'I've changed early, so that Collins can spend the time with you.' May was touched by her thoughtfulness.

Collins, plump and cheerful, ran May's bath for her and sent her along to it while she laid out the dress for the evening. May lay back and soaked the cares of the day away in the scented bath water. She stretched out and raised her feet in the air, and as she did so the memory came to her of lying in the bath at her parents' house, before another of Lady Andover's dinner parties. Then she had been anticipating the Hindlesham Ball, where she had met Harry Cussons. She remembered him slipping her shoe back on, and smiled indulgently at her younger self. It was only three years ago, yet how much she had seen and learnt since then! And what other changes had there been? Lord Hindlesham was alone in his splendid house, while beautiful Della languished in the country, still not re-married, though Harry Cussons was about Town again – typical of a man, they always get the best of a bargain, May thought. Emily was still in India, but her new daughter was a sturdy baby, and though not forgetting her son, she had come to terms with her loss, and seemed to be enjoying the compensations of life in the East. Louise Dumer was Lady Canfield now, and Bertie, so rumour had it, had packed her mother off back to America on an extended visit. May suspected this was Louise's doing – Bertie was too easygoing to be bothered. Still, Archie remained footloose and fancy free, and would be at the dinner tonight, so May would be able to enjoy his goodhumoured banter, and try to cap his teasing jokes.

Three years! Did she look three years older? May pushed herself up out of the bath and surveyed herself in the full-length mirror. She gazed critically at her body, pink from the heat of the water. Her legs were long and supple, her waist as narrow as ever, her breasts firm and shapely. She bent closer and peered at her face. There were tiny lines of laughter and care around her eyes, but they were too fine to be noticed except on close inspection; her irises were as blue as ever, and her lashes long and thick. The glass steamed up, but May was satisfied. She stepped out onto the thick rug and wrapped herself in a host of fluffy towels, clean and warm.

Collins was waiting for her in the bedroom.

'This corset is very light for evening wear, Miss May.'

May laughed. 'I know, I had them specially made – I hate feeling trussed up like a chicken.'

Collins sniffed, but soon forgot her disapproval in the pleasure of dressing May's tall figure. 'Your grandmother is a wonderful woman for her age, Miss May, but it's nice to turn a young lady out for the evening.'

May was startled when she saw herself, dressed, in the mirror. She had chosen the gown almost on impulse, drawn by the glowing apricot which had been described as 'one of the colours of the Season', and the elegant lines so different from those dresses designated as suitable for a débutante. But now she was slightly shaken by the effect. The heavy crêpe mastic silk fell by its own weight into folds which draped themselves round her body and clung sinuously to the curve of her hips. The line of the bodice was simple yet perfect, accentuating the fullness of her breasts with soft draped chiffon of the exact matching shade. A narrow lace tucker emphasised the depth of her neckline rather than veiling it. The wide corselet band was almost barbaric, with its dull gold and silver bullion studded with stones, but it showed off dramatically May's slender waist.

Collins gave a soft 'Ah' of satisfaction and pride, then said briskly, 'Sit down, please, Miss May, so I can attend to your hair.'

In the mirror May watched the swift, sure fingers twisting and shaping, until the flowing waves and soft curls had appeared. Ada had been right – the shade of the dress subtly altered and changed the colour of her hair, so that it glowed almost pink, like a ripe peach, in the light of the dressing table lamp. Collins pushed home the last invisible pin, and she was ready. Lady Andover had offered her the run of her own jewel box, but May had decided this dress would need no adornment; now she knew she was right.

As she came down the wide staircase Archie was crossing the hall. She called down to him; he looked up and stood frozen, watching her descend. Then he came across, took her hand and raised it to his lips. May laughed, but Archie said, seriously, 'May, you look magnificent, you really do – you'll knock their eyeballs out tonight!'

'Well, tell me who's taking me in. Have I made all this effort for Sir Robert, or old Lord Oulton?'

Archie clapped his hand to his head in an exaggerated gesture of despair.

'No, worse than that!'

'Worse than Sir Robert – I don't believe it!'

'In a way, yes, because he's young and good-looking, but

242

he is rather a prig. I've got to admit that, even though he's a friend of mine. And he altogether disapproves of wealthy young ladies of fashion.'

May protested, 'But I'm not a fashionable young lady.'

'You're certainly rich, though. I saw him at the Club earlier today and told him I'd done my best for him, and that he'd be escorting in the Frears heiress. He just looked down his nose and said, "Really?" – and he's got an awfully long nose,' Archie added thoughtfully.

'Come on, Archie, now you've told me the worst, perhaps there's still time to do a swap.'

Archie shook his head. 'Not a hope. He's old Pennington's son, and you know how Grandmamma's still trying to marry you off – plenty of money there, too, on his mother's side. You must have heard me mention Tate, May, we were at Oxford together. Decent chap, old Tate, straight as a die, not that we had much in common – he used to read books, you know – still, no one's perfect, and I don't suppose he meant to get a First.'

'You're just jealous, because you only scraped a Pass degree, and everybody gets one of those.'

'That's right, May, everyone does – so why did Tate have to be different? A good rider, though – you should see him follow the hounds.'

May had decided by now that the rich, studious, priggish son of the Earl of Pennington was not going to provide the high spot of the evening's entertainment – after all, he could hardly demonstrate his prowess in the hunting field by vaulting over the epergne halfway through the meal.

She turned to Archie and asked briskly. 'What is Chef preparing for us tonight?'

By the time Archie had reached the confiture of nectarines May had decided that Archie's friend Tate could look down his elongated nose as much as he liked, as long as he left her free to enjoy her dinner.

'Chef is wonderful,' she said fervently to Archie. 'I don't know how he thinks of his dishes – I can't understand why no woman has ever snapped him up.'

243

Archie rolled his eyes in mock excitement. 'That's it May, that's the man for you, right on the premises. Why ever hasn't Grandmamma thought of that?'

May reached up and pinched his earlobe. 'I could do worse – you, for example!' Archie went into mock squeals of pain until Lady Andover appeared.

'Children! Will you never grow up?' But May saw her eyes were smiling, and she complimented May on her appearance. 'How right you are to leave those fussy frills behind.'

The guests began to arrive and the drawing room became a mass of vivid colours, intermingled with black and white.

'Good evening, Miss Winton.'

May spun round and there was Lord Hindlesham, his brown eyes alight with affection and pleasure. As she took his hand she noticed the new dusting of silver in the sleek dark hair at his temples, but otherwise he seemed unchanged by his ordeal. He had always looked older than his years, May suspected, and now others had caught up with him while he stood still.

'You look very well, May – nursing obviously suits you. We missed you last Season.'

May smiled at him. 'I was on nights, and just starting work when you idle denizens of the West End began to play.'

His eyes crinkled up. 'You sound very like your friend, Miss Carter. And how is Miss Carter? I saw her last winter, you know.'

May said, 'Yes, she told me. She claims you restore her faith in the aristocracy!'

He gave a smile, but there was sadness in it. He spoke softly, 'I think she restores my faith, too – you know she has the happy knack of being both serious and light-hearted.' Then his voice rose back to its normal level. 'But May, she seems so frail – can she really cope with the heavy work I know you do?'

May laughed outright. 'Don't be misled by Ellen's fragile appearance – she's as strong as a little Shetland pony. She's only had two weeks' sick leave in all the time we've been at St Katharine's, and that was just a poisoned finger, which everyone gets. As soon as they'd opened it up she was as right as rain.'

Lord Hindlesham winced and May remembered where she was. She must watch her choice of words – people were squeamish outside of hospital.

He asked, 'So she is set on making a career of nursing?'

May hesitated, then spoke slowly. 'I don't know. Ellen is so good with the patients, they think the world of her, especially the children.' May was conscious of Lord Hindlesham listening intently – what a kind man he was, so concerned about everybody, even a chance acquaintance like Ellen. She continued, 'But in nursing you get to a stage where you have to tell other people what they should do – order them about – and Ellen doesn't like doing that: she believes too much in people's freedom, or perhaps she's just too gentle. She was engaged once, you know, before she came to St Katharine's. Her fiancé died very suddenly of pneumonia. Sometimes, for all she seems to enjoy nursing, I wonder if she wouldn't have been happier married, and with children – though I would have missed her had she never come.' May ended confusedly.

Lord Hindlesham said in an odd tone, 'I'm sure you would, May, I'm sure you would.' His face had become withdrawn and distant, and May berated herself for talking of marriage and children to a man in his position.

She said quickly, 'But have you heard what Chef has in store for us tonight? Archie has told me all.'

At once Lord Hindlesham shed his introspective mood. 'No, tell me. I have heard that Chef's contributions to the diet at St Katharine's have been discussed in Very High Places!'

May began to laugh, and to tell him about the Royal Visit.

She was still chatting to Lord Hindlesham when she saw her grandmother begin to move amongst her guests, discreetly sorting them into pairs. Wherever had this dull Tate of Archie's got to? Then she caught a glimpse of her cousin edging through the throng towards her, before she turned back to her companion.

Then Archie was beside her. 'Ah, run you to earth at last.

245

May, may I present my friend Tate?' May turned with her hand extended, and found herself looking straight into the dark eyes of Walter Lisle. Archie's friend Tate was the young vicar of St Barnabas'.

Chapter Twenty-Nine

They both stood absolutely still. The noise and bustle of the crowded room faded, so that May could hear only the drumming of her heartbeats in her ears. Then a large, satin-clad bosom came to claim Lord Hindlesham, and at his murmured farewells May unfroze, and managed a smile in his direction, before turning back to the tall, immaculately-tailored figure before her.

She held out her hand. 'How do you do, Mr Lisle?'

Archie's voice was surprised. 'You don't know each other already, do you?'

May said, 'We have never been formally introduced – is that not correct, Mr Lisle?'

Walter Lisle finally found his voice. 'No, no we haven't, Miss Winton.' At last he took her hand, grasping it firmly as he shook it.

May felt a wave of acute embarrassment wash over her. She remembered that parting scene in the vicarage hall, and Mrs Tranter's words seemed to echo round the elegant drawing room. It was clear from her companion's expression that his thoughts were very similar. His face, which had drained of colour when he first saw her was now a fiery red, and May felt a matching tide rise into her cheeks. Archie, obviously totally bemused by their extreme reactions to each other, and realising there was a problem, moved in helpfully.

' 'Fraid you'll not get much social chit-chat from May tonight, Tate old boy, she's only come for the food, you know. My grandmother had to bait the trap with quenelles and soufflés and well-hung game, otherwise we'd never get her west of Aldgate pump.'

Walter Lisle picked up the cue gratefully. 'I must admit, Miss Winton, that the memory of Chef's luncheons has been a powerful inducement to me – I didn't know you would be here.' He realised what he had said, and stopped abruptly.

May saw Archie raise his eyebrows behind Mr Lisle's shoulder, and jerk his head towards the door. The procession for dinner was forming, and Lady Andover was trying to catch their eye. She began to move. Walter Lisle remembered himself and extended his arm to May and she placed the silken fingertips of her gloved left hand on the fine black cloth of his sleeve. They walked slowly towards the dining room. One by one the escorting gentlemen pulled back their partners' chairs, and, all too soon for May's peace of mind, she was sitting at the white damask with its gleaming expanse of silver and glassware; with Walter Lisle beside her and not one single conversational gambit in her head. What did you say to a young man whom you scarcely knew but whom on your previous meeting you had been loudly accused of seducing – and by a Bishop's relict, no less? Mrs Tranter's 'shameless hussy' rang in the air between them, and settled like lead on Chef's fragrant consommé. May picked up her spoon and with the first mouthful transferred the lead weight to her stomach. This couldn't go on; she must say something. She put down the spoon, turned to her companion and spoke.

'Mr Lisle, I am deeply sorry for what took place at our last meeting,' she faltered, then gathered her courage again. 'For seizing hold of you, and shaking you like that – and putting your visitor under such a terrible misapprehension.' The final words came out in a rush.

It was obvious that Walter Lisle wasn't enjoying his soup either. He said, in a tone that was almost desperate, 'Miss Winton, I feel responsible for the appalling manners of that dreadful woman.' His voice shook. 'She had no right to make those comments, and besides, it was all my fault. You had every justification for giving me a good shaking. I fully deserved it – however could I have let myself make such an indelicate remark to a young lady!' He gave an involuntary glance at the swelling chiffon folds of May's décolleté, then said loudly, 'I was totally mistaken.'

May, whose confidence had been rising at the undoubted sincerity of Walter Lisle's words, blinked at his final statement, and must have looked slightly hurt, because he suddenly dropped his spoon with a splash and said, 'Dammit, I mean it was a mistake to say it!'

May turned and looked directly at him. His face expressed such bafflement and confusion that she felt the beginnings of a schoolgirl giggle well up inside her. He looked back desperately, seeming to sense her amusement. May controlled herself, put her hand on his arm and said, smiling up at him, 'Mr Lisle, if you were indelicate, then I was immodest – I should never have seized hold of you in the way I did. Let's forget all about it.'

Walter Lisle slowly relaxed. He looked at her searchingly for a moment, then smiled back. He put down his napkin and held out his right hand to May.

'Is it "pax", then, Miss Winton?'

May nodded, and they shook hands solemnly.

When May looked round she saw that they had managed to miss the whole of the first course with their peace negotiations: the footmen were deftly removing the plates. She gazed in horror at her untouched soup, then leant towards Walter and under cover of his shoulder whispered to Robert behind her.

'Oh, don't tell Chef, please.'

A flicker of acknowledgement passed across Robert's well-trained face and May breathed a sigh of relief. She looked into Walter's amused eyes and explained.

'He takes such a pride in his creations – whatever will I say? We usually discuss the entire meal, course by course, before I leave: he has an exaggerated respect for my palate.'

Walter smiled, then nodded across the table. 'You'll have to ask George Hindlesham, he's the expert.'

'Of course, you're right, I will. I couldn't bear to upset Chef, not after all the food hampers he's sent us at St Katharine's.'

Walter Lisle grinned. 'I envy you. Mrs Lewis is a good plain cook, but plain is the operative word, I'm afraid.' He

249

leant towards her. 'I went to see Hetty again, but she said you'd been transferred.'

'Yes,' May replied lightly. 'I'm on Elizabeth, the children's ward. Temporary Acting Staff Nurse, no less – but only until Jameson's recovered from the measles.'

'I'm so pleased.' Walter's approval was warm and so obviously genuine that she blushed with pleasure. He went on, earnestly, 'Tell me, with your experience in the hospital you must be in a position to make a judgment: what are your views on the Drink Question? Are you a supporter of Prohibition, or do you believe in more liberal methods of persuasion?'

Unfortunately, at this interesting point in the conversation the Society Beauty on the other side of Walter, who had been eyeing his elegant profile in a predatory manner since the dinner began, finally pounced, and his attention was diverted. May in her turn found herself the object of the determined advances of the middle-aged bon viveur on her left, whose tactical manoeuvres she had been carefully ignoring up to this time. Still, at least she could give her full attention to the entrées now, since her neighbour only really wanted a pretty audience. What had the fish course been? She did hope Lord Hindlesham had been concentrating, or she would never be able to look Chef in the face the next morning.

The iced asparagus arrived while May's righthand neighbour was in full bore. However Walter had detached himself and he nudged May's elbow – deliberately? – so that her plate slipped slightly and in the ensuing apologies she was able to make her escape in turn.

Over the game course they thrashed out the Drink Question to their mutual satisfaction – they were in general agreement against Prohibition, but there were enough points of difference between them to add spice to their discussion.

Their respective neighbours claimed their attentions for most of the sweet course, but this time May cut her bore short with a swift, 'I think Lady Canning wishes to speak to you, Sir,' and turned back and smartly rapped Walter's wine glass so that it rocked dangerously and he had to steady it. The

Society Beauty retreated, rebuffed. May had a quick glimpse of Lord Hindlesham's simian face creased up in amusement across the table as he watched the little pantomime, and she felt herself blushing. He winked at her as he raised his spoon to the ramekins, and she began to feel it might be rather embarrassing to have to ask him for details of the finer points of the dishes she'd failed to savour. Still, it had to be done: she could never let Chef down – with his Latin temperament he was easily upset. As these thoughts were flashing through her mind she was smiling into Walter Lisle's dark eyes.

He said, 'You know, I can't get over the amazing coincidence of meeting you here tonight.'

'Well, Archie and I do share a surname.'

'But I still had no idea. The wretch quite deceived me – he kept burbling on about "my cousin May",' he looked self-conscious as he spoke her Christian name, but repeated it firmly, '"My cousin May, the Frears' heiress" – and talking about the shipyards. Why on earth did he call you that?'

May looked down at her plate. She said in a small voice, 'My mother was Mary Frears.' She felt Walter Lisle's eyes on the back of her neck.

He said slowly, 'And you still went to do the work of a general servant in the East End – because that's what it is, certainly for the first year, they work you like drudges. I admire you, Miss Winton.' His voice was warm and respectful, and May felt she had to put him right. She spoke quickly.

'Nursing is much more than mere drudgery, even at the beginning – there are the patients, you see. Besides, I was no Florence Nightingale. I was bored, totally bored – I'm not a good dancer, and my father won't let me hunt. There was nothing heroic about it: I went on an impulse.'

Walter said softly, 'But you stayed, didn't you?'

May, embarrassed, hit back. 'What of you, then? There are plenty of delightful country livings I'm sure you could have been introduced to.'

Walter looked back at her, and suddenly grinned. 'I'd be bored, Miss Winton, totally bored.' They both began to laugh.

251

They had to do their duty to their neighbours over the ices; then, all too soon it seemed to May, Lady Andover caught the ladies' eyes. At their anticipatory rustle the gentlemen sprang to their feet and drew back the chairs. As he did so Walter Lisle said, quite clearly, 'I'll see you later, Miss Winton,' and out of the corner of her eye May saw the Society Beauty direct at her a glare of pure envy. It struck May that Mr Lisle was undoubtedly the best looking man in the room. Feeling pleasantly smug she followed the Beauty's gleaming white shoulders from the dining table. Unfortunately she found herself standing beside her at the coffee cups, where her grandmother presided. The Beauty, gesturing towards May said with an adder's tongue to Lady Andover, 'I see your granddaughter has still not made some lucky fellow happy, Melicent?'

Melicent Andover handed the cup in a manner which subtly suggested its contents were pure cyanide. Her smile was brilliant.

'Why no, Mrs Farquhar. Darling May has risen above the fashionable world, she has a vocation; she nurses the sick and suffering poor of the East End.' Then, with a deft twist of the knife, 'That's why I was so anxious for her to meet young Mr Lisle; I knew they'd have so much in common.'

Mrs Farquhar retreated, and went to sharpen her talons on poor Louise Canfield.

May asked suspiciously, 'Did you really bring Mr Lisle here tonight just to meet me?'

'Goodness me no, my dear.' Lady Andover's face was surprised and ingenuous. 'It was Archie's idea; you know they've been friends since Oxford. And I knew his father well at one time – such an attractive man.' Her lips curved in a reminiscent smile. 'Unfortunately his son is just a little too high-minded – but I knew you could cope with him, dear.'

May began to suspect that her grandmother had intended to display her to Walter Lisle as a frivolous Society butterfly, let him indulge in his prejudices, and then spring her profession on him unawares. How typical of Grandmamma! May felt quite indignant on Mr Lisle's behalf; then it struck

252

her that, unintentionally, that was exactly what she herself had done. She repressed a smile.

Her grandmother murmured, 'George looks very well, doesn't he, dear, but I would be much happier if Della were safely remarried. I wonder sometimes if he pines for her, you know.'

May was horrified. 'Surely he wouldn't be so stupid!'

'My dear May, men are stupid, and they were married for a long time. So quixotical of him to acknowledge Harry's bastard as his own.' Melicent Andover moved away, leaving May gasping – really, the outspokenness of the older generation!

May was at the far end of the drawing room when Walter arrived in the first wave of the gentlemen. He paused in the doorway and looked round, but before he could move, a flutter of befrilled débutantes settled on him and drew him off to their sofa. May, deciding it was time she changed her position, rose from the sofa where she had been talking to Louise, and was immediately waylaid by a beaming Jonny Yoxford. He was such an old friend that it was impossible to evade him, and May was pleased to see him. It was a full fifteen minutes before she could pass him on to a limpid-eyed nymph in a mass of cream and pink rosebuds. Then suddenly James Carson, an old admirer, was in front of her, and she found herself edged into the window embrasure almost before she had had time to see that Walter had broken cover from the frills, only to be ambushed by Mrs Farquhar, who had brought up reinforcements in the shape of the malicious Lady Canning. May noticed, as James Carson shifted slightly, that Walter was indeed looking down his nose, as Archie had predicted, and she smiled to herself.

Mrs Farquhar bequeathed Walter to old Lady Benham, and May found herself sitting on the sofa where Walter had first started, under siege to a couple of young guardsmen who had never met May before, but seemed determined to remedy this omission as rapidly as possible.

'I say, Miss Winton, where has Archie been hiding you all this time? Chained up in a tower, what?'

The other interspersed, with ready wit, 'No, no, Ames old boy, Miss Winton would never be kept prisoner – she'd just let down her long golden tresses and Rumplestiltskin would climb up and rescue her!'

May laughed politely, though pretty certain they'd confused their fairy tales. She said firmly, 'I live and work in Poplar: the slum, you know.'

'Do you, by Jove – what fascinating things you young women get up to!' But it was all too clear that what they really wanted to discuss was the fascinating things young guardsmen got up to; she listened to their tales of Ascot, Henley and Hurlingham with the best patience she could muster.

She was beginning to think that she never would be able to finish the debate on the finer points of the teetotal movement when a *deus ex machina* appeared in the shape of Lord Hindlesham, with Walter Lisle in tow. Lord Hindlesham dispatched the two guardsmen in double quick time. May was not sure how he did it, but was very grateful – she felt if she heard one more tale of the horse that was just pipped at the post she would scream. The two men sat down on either side of her.

Lord Hindlesham said, 'Walter here tells me you need a résumé of tonight's menu – really, May, I don't know what you were thinking of, it's not like you to be so careless of your food.' His eyes twinkled and May found herself blushing, but he took pity on her and actually did give her a résumé, succinct and comprehensive. May asked a few pertinent questions which were quickly answered and then stored the information away in her memory for the following day. When he had finished Lord Hindlesham jumped up, made his farewells, murmured, 'Please give my best wishes to Miss Carter, May,' and then deftly intercepted a hovering Mrs Farquhar as she was about to swoop down on Walter.

'He's got a first class brain,' said Walter as May carefully shook out her skirts to conceal the vacant seat – this heavy silk was much less effective than débutante muslin, but it would have to do – 'But I do wonder whether he's in the wrong party.'

254

May felt she'd had this conversation before; perhaps Walter and Ellen should start a 'Friends of George Hindlesham Society', to steer him into different political channels. Thinking of Ellen she said abruptly, 'That wasn't my maid with me in Chrisp Street, it was a friend of mine, a fellow nurse.'

'Yes, I'd worked that out. But Miss Winton, I've been so puzzled – you must have had a reason – why were you cheering on that wretched woman with the knife?'

May was indignant. 'She wasn't a wretched woman, she's Mrs Jones.' Then she proceeded to spill out the whole sorry tale: Dolly Hills' unfortunate scalping; Billy's obsession with her hair; Big Liza on the ward – 'Honestly I was terrified'; the gin bottle; and Mrs Jones' plucky attempt to exact revenge.

Walter listened in silence. Then he said, 'I see, well, I think I do.'

May burst out, 'It was all that wretched Billy's fault – getting into such a state about her hair.'

Walter said slowly, 'I agree, he behaved unpardonably to his wife.' May thought wildly – did I mention Big Liza in Billy's bed? I think I did – and he's a clergyman. But Walter Lisle was continuing. 'Yet I think I can understand his being so upset by the loss of her hair – even if it were only one tenth as lovely as yours.' He leant forward, raised his hand and very gently touched May's hair with his fingertips. They both sat quite still.

'Have you two been exchanging stories of the good old days in the filthy slum, then?' Archie's voice broke the spell.

May turned round, startled, then they burst out together: 'It's not a filthy slum!' Walter stopped, May went on, 'Well, it is, but it's a very nice slum, too.' The men laughed. May was firm. 'Poplar has a park, and a pier, and a Town Hall – and there's the Docks. Docks can't be slums – the masts look so beautiful above the walls.'

Walter said quickly, 'Have you never been inside the East India Dock, Miss Winton?'

'No, I haven't, there's always a policeman on the gate. I suppose I could have asked my father, he's bound to know

255

someone. It is silly, when St Katharine's looks straight over it, and so many of our patients are dock injuries.'

'Would you like to go inside?' Walter's voice was eager. 'My father has connections with the East and West India Dock Company; I can soon get a pass. He often took me round as a child, I used to find it very exciting.'

'Yes, yes, I would very much like to.' Then May glanced at him, and hesitated – would Ellen or Ada be free to come as well? Archie, knowing Lady Clarence, understood her uncertainty. He said reassuringly, 'Don't worry, May, I'll come too, and chaperone you for the afternoon. I'd like to see some yachts.'

'Oh would you, Archie?' May was delighted.

Walter Lisle looked pleased. 'That's settled then. We'll have to let Miss Winton fix the day, since her time off is so limited. But Archie, old man, I don't think you'll see any yachts in the East India Dock!'

Archie made a face of comical dismay. 'Never mind, for the sake of dear cousin May, and in view of our ancient friendship, Tate, I shall be there.'

May turned back to Walter Lisle, and asked without thinking, 'Why does Archie call you Tate? I had no idea he meant you.'

Walter grinned. 'They all do.' He reached across to the tea tray, picked up a silver teaspoon and tapped it against the sugar bowl with a tiny 'ping'.

May said, 'Of course, I didn't think.' She laughed.

Walter said, 'It's not even spelt the same way, but once a nickname gets around it sticks.'

Archie leant over the back of the sofa and whispered in May's ear, 'And you know the syrup tins? "Out of the strong came forth sweetness"? He's very biblical, our Tate.'

May was conscious of Walter's simultaneous blush.

The party broke up soon after. Lady Andover had wanted to take May on to Lady Towcester's Ball, but May had been adamant. 'I haven't the energy, Grandmamma – we youngsters just don't have your stamina!' Lady Andover, aware of the long hours May worked, had let her off. May knew she

256

could easily have coped, but she still wasn't over-fond of dancing. Now, however, she wondered if Walter Lisle were going to move on with the rest of the party. But he shook his head to Archie's question.

'No, early service in the morning. I've indulged myself enough for one day. Miss Winton, may I escort you back to Poplar?'

'Thank you, but I'd have been locked out already, Mr Lisle. It's my day off tomorrow, so I'm spending the night in Arlington Street. I shall have a lazy day.'

Archie interrupted. 'May's idea of a lazy day, Tate, is to go and turn double somersaults at the Bath Club – still, each to his own. At least she'll be able to fish you out of the Dock if you fall in, she's like a salmon in the water.'

May was not sure she liked this comparison, but Walter Lisle was taking his leave, so she promised him she would communicate with Archie as soon as she had a free half-day in the week. He shook her hand vigorously and left.

May said goodnight to her grandmother and went upstairs, where Collins was waiting for her. She almost regretted the ball – she felt full of energy, and not at all ready for bed.

Chapter Thirty

To May's distress, on the Monday following the dinner party and long before she was due for a half-day off, she was summoned to Matron, who told her that Jameson would be returning from convalescence on Saturday, so May would be starting nights on Abraham Ward at 9 pm that Friday. Even Matron's unusual condescension in telling her that Sister Elizabeth was 'really quite pleased with your work, Nurse Winton,' failed to comfort May. She thought of the possibility of asking for a prearranged two-till-five one afternoon – but knew it was scarcely possible. The Consultants on Elizabeth Ward did afternoon operations and ward rounds, and as Acting Staff Nurse she was needed then; besides there was always the likelihood of being delayed in coming off duty.

May returned to Elizabeth feeling very downcast. As she reported back Sister said, 'Matron told me this morning, Nurse. Now don't let me forget to release you at midday on Friday, so you can get some sleep before your first night.'

May's head jerked up. 'No, I won't Sister – thank you so much.'

Sister Elizabeth looked rather surprised, but was too busy to waste time speculating about May's abrupt change of mood. May went off cheerfully to attend to Louie.

'You look pleased, Nurse – just got yer Sunday dress back from the pawnshop?' Louie screeched with glee at her own joke, while a laughing May tickled her toes until she squealed for mercy.

May wrote a hurried letter to Archie and waited on tenterhooks until a telegram arrived: 'Dock gates. One-thirty. Knock twice and ask for sugar.' May crumpled it up and threw it into the wastepaper basket – then retrieved it hastily and hid it in her Bible, in case one of Home Sister's spies should find it and report back that Winton, M.M.C., was planning to break bounds instead of going obediently to bed for the afternoon – one couldn't be too careful.

May was up before the rising bell on Friday morning, looking over her wardrobe. What did one wear for an afternoon at the Docks? Lady Clarence's careful training was useless here. It must be a trotteuse skirt; but she had several of those. She gazed longingly at a fine linen costume of the palest blue, but she didn't want to have to spend the whole afternoon trying to avoid dirty marks, so she pushed it back and settled on a well-cut but serviceable navy serge, and put it ready at the front.

Sister Elizabeth was as good as her word. She dismissed May at midday with a brief word of praise which brought the colour to May's cheeks. Louie said a rather tearful farewell, then May rushed down to first dinner.

She took her time dressing, taking great pains from her stockings up – these were black silk, rather extravagant for afternoon wear; but she might be climbing ladders, no point in risking the exposure of everyday cotton, May thought. At last she was satisfied with her reflection in the mirror. She looked trim in the tailored navy, but the effect was not too severe because of the red and white cross stitch panels on her fine linen shirt. Shoes and gloves were another problem – nothing looked worse than soiled white gloves, May knew, so she opted for heavier street ones of red leather, despite the warm weather. She had to wear walking boots, but she could not resist her most elegant pair, close-fitting at the ankle with toecaps of patent leather. She glanced at the time, then wielded her button hook briskly. A white sailor hat with a matching ribbon of red satin completed the outfit, and with a flurry of skirts she was off.

Minnie Emms, vivid in a tight-fitting scarlet outfit and with an improbably glossy bird perched on her hat, overtook May on the stairs.

'Just off to Fulham for my half-day, to see the old folks at home. Where are you going, then, May? Thought you were on nights tonight.'

'I am,' May admitted. 'Be a dear and see if the coast is clear for me, Minnie. I don't want Home Sister to spot me.'

'Okey Doke.' After a quick reconnoitre Minnie gave the signal and May scampered past the office.

'What are you doing, then, May?'

May assumed a Cockney accent and gave the well-worn Poplar explanation, 'I'm meeting a feller at the Dock Gate.'

Minnie laughed. 'That'll be the day, when you get up to tricks like that.'

As she spoke they came through the Hospital entrance and there, standing alongside the high stone archways and looking in their direction were the two tall, immaculately turned out figures of Archie and Walter Lisle.

Minnie gasped. 'An' I thought you were joking!'

Walter Lisle shot rapidly across the Dock Road, expertly side-stepping an ice cream tricycle. Archie followed a fraction behind him, but as they reached the pavement Walter fell back slightly and left Archie to speak.

'Hello, May. So they did give you a remission for good conduct after all.' He turned to Minnie, who was eyeing him with undisguised admiration. 'Is your friend coming too?'

May said hastily, 'No she isn't, she's on her way to Fulham.'

There was a squeal from Minnie. 'You spoilsport, May!' She nudged her in the ribs. 'Now don't do anything I wouldn't do.' With a provocative flick of her bright red skirts she was off down the Dock Road.

May muttered under her breath, 'That should give me plenty of scope,' and then glanced guiltily at Walter Lisle; he raised his eyebrows in a comic parody of outraged modesty, and she knew she was going to enjoy the afternoon.

Archie was gazing regretfully after Minnie's swaying hips. 'She looks a good sport – is that the girl old George met?'

'Certainly not,' May replied indignantly. 'Ellen is quite different.' Then remembering Minnie Emms' ready connivance over Home Sister she added hastily, 'But Minnie is very good-hearted.' She swung round to their silent companion, 'Good afternoon, Mr Lisle. I'm afraid Archie makes me forget my manners.'

260

Walter seized her proffered hand and shook it vigorously. 'Good afternoon, Miss Winton, I'm so glad we were able to arrange our outing. Come along Archie, it's too fine a day to spend on useless repinings on the main road.'

He took May's elbow and piloted her skilfully across the busy street. May quite enjoyed the sensation of being taken care of on this very familiar thoroughfare, and it was a pleasure to let someone else be the recipient of the carter's curses – hastily converted to an apology as he spied Walter's badge of office.

Walter Lisle was unperturbed. 'The dog collar has its uses you see, Miss Winton.'

The warmth of the sun on her back and the flutter of the ribbon on her light straw hat gave May a delightful sensation of being on holiday and she sprang onto the pavement with a swirl of her pleats.

Walter smiled down at her. 'You look as if you've just escaped from the schoolroom – you should have tied your hair in plaits with big red bows. Where has that wretched cousin of yours got to?'

Archie finished his altercation with the driver of the loaded wagon trying to turn into the Dock Gates, and bounded up to them.

'I must say, May, your slum citizens have got a fine command of language. I begin to see the attractions of this place – people are a lot livelier down here.'

Walter produced his pass, which the policeman did not look at. 'Back again so soon, Vicar?'

May looked questioningly at her companion, who replied rather self-consciously, 'I came down this morning to find out what ships were in dock, to show you.'

May was touched by his thoughtfulness.

As they came out of the archway she stopped suddenly, and Archie bumped into her from behind. She had caught glimpses of the scene before her in the past, but being inside the magic gateway was very different. The tracery of rigging on the slender masts visible over the high dock wall had always seemed so still and graceful, and somehow silent; but inside all was noise and activity. Her ears were assaulted with the shriek of steam whistles, the baying of horns and the confused shouting of voices; there was the intermittent rattling of chains. And there was constant movement: figures scurrying purposefully hither and thither, and a great crane moving along on stilts beside the high, blank, warehouses. Her eyes travelled on to the ships, their hulls looming sheer above the quays, overpowering at close quarters. Walter stood quite still and let her stare.

Archie's voice sounded in her ear, 'Come on, May, I want to see the rest even if you don't, get a move on.'

May shook herself, glanced at Walter's understanding face and walked on towards the action.

Walter warned, 'Watch out for the cranes and the trucks,' in a voice of such assurance that May asked whether he often came to the Docks.

'Not so much now, Miss Winton. I've only been in this area since the New Year – I was a curate in the Borough before – but my father often brought me as a child. My mother's family had East India connections. I remember the first time, we came on the train from Fenchurch Street. You run above endless narrow streets, with just glimpses of the river in the distance; then there's a viaduct and suddenly you look into a deep cavern below, full of water – and there was a white schooner, like a giant bird at rest. At least, that's how it seemed to me at the time.' He was a little self-conscious now. 'I was only eight, and very impressionable. I thought it was going to be the gateway to the Orient!'

'But it is, isn't it?' May looked up at him.

He smiled down. 'Yes, I suppose it is, but the journey ended amongst iron sheds, with freezing Lascars huddled against the wind – and it was raining.' He laughed. 'It was January, and over twenty years ago, Miss Winton.'

'So was it a terrible disappointment?' May felt sorry for the starry-eyed eight year old, cold in the wind and rain on a bleak quayside.

He recognised her concern, and said reassuringly, 'Indeed it wasn't. How could any normal small boy be disappointed

262

at all this?' He gestured to encompass the lively scene in front of them. 'But my most dramatic memory is from later: we came here once – I was at Eton by then – and they were unloading animals for London Zoo. It was an incredible sight, Miss Winton, the moving of those exotic creatures. There were lions and leopards, and a puma, I think, all snarling and growling with rage at being swung high over the side of the ship and onto the quay.'

'My goodness,' May exclaimed. 'Weren't you awfully frightened?'

Walter grinned at her. 'They were in cages, of course, Miss Winton.'

Archie burst out into loud guffaws at her confusion. 'That's typical of you, May – she's got a vivid imagination, my cousin, Tate. She'll have been thinking that the sailors played catch and chase round the decks, dodging wild beasts all the way from India.'

Walter said softly, 'Fortunately no one threatened to throw me to the lions, then.' He laughed at her blushes. May pinched the arm she was holding in revenge until he said, 'It was "pax", Miss Winton, remember? Come along, we've got lots more to see.'

They threaded through the men wheeling trucks along the side of the dock. One of them called, 'Afternoon, Nurse,' and May recognised a former patient and cried a quick greeting back.

Archie was insistent. 'Can't we go on board?'

Walter nodded. 'But not this one, down here – I arranged it this morning.'

The ship of Walter's choice seemed no different from the ones on either side, but he led them purposefully to it – 'The captain's expecting us.' A man in a peaked cap came forward to meet them. He shook them by the hand, looking searchingly at May as they were introduced; she supposed lady visitors were less usual.

'I'll take you round my ship – mind your hats, gentlemen, it's low in places.'

They began their tour below, in the hot, sulphurous-

263

smelling engine room. May insisted that she was quite capable of climbing down the narrow iron ladder. She glanced down as she made her descent and derived a naughty pleasure from seeing the dilemma of Walter Lisle, waiting at the bottom to help her off the last high rung. He was obviously anxious to watch that she was finding her footholds safely, yet trying at the same time to look as if he were not also catching glimpses of her shapely calves in their sheer black silk. May was glad she had given some thought to her stockings. But of course Archie had to put his foot in it by calling, just as Walter lifted up his arms to her at the bottom, 'I hope you remembered your best red flannel petticoat today, May.' Walter's face was a picture as he caught her neatly and deposited her very quickly on the iron plates of the deck.

They met the engineer and admired the massive, highly-polished machinery, obviously his pride and joy, then they climbed up the ladder again, Walter insisting on following the captain, so that Archie had to help May from the rear. Not that May needed much help: she was thoroughly relaxed now and moved about the ship as confidently as though it were Elizabeth Ward.

Before mounting to the bridge the captain glanced at Walter, and when he nodded said, 'I've something to show you, especially, Miss Winton. Look on the bulkhead.' He pointed to a brass plate. Obediently May looked up and read it, then started in surprise.

'The young gentleman told me you were Joseph Frears' granddaughter – this is a Frears ship, you see. It's nice and tight; your granddad built some bonny vessels.'

Walter's face was aglow with pleasure at May's delight.

Archie said, 'You've arranged a neat little surprise there, Tate. Lucky there was one in today.'

The captain laughed. 'It's likely enough, it's the biggest Tyneside yard. Now I must show you the bridge, then perhaps the young lady would like a cup of tea?'

The tea, when it came, was very hot and a dark teak colour. The captain was apologetic.

264

'I told the lad to make it weaker for a lady, but you know what these boys are like – cook's ashore.'

May smiled at him and sipped the bitter brew. 'It's exactly what I'm used to: hospital tea is notorious for its strength.'

The captain's face was puzzled. Walter said, in explanation, 'Miss Winton is a nurse at St Katharine's, just opposite the main Dock Gate.'

The captain dropped his cup with a splash and said, 'Well, I'll be danged – if you'll pardon the expression Miss – but I . . .' Then he recovered himself with an effort and said, 'I know St Katharine's well enough, I was in there only yesterday visiting one of my lads who'd ruptured himself, if you'll excuse me, Miss, – but of course, you'll know what I'm talking about. Screaming in agony he was, strangled something, they said.'

'Strangulated hernia,' May said. 'We get a lot of cases round here, because of the heavy work. Which ward is he in?'

'Simeon, with a big Sister, very bossy she was, ordering all the nurses around.'

May exclaimed, 'That was my first ward! But all Sisters are like that, you know, it's their job.'

Archie said, 'And May's been practising all her life – I feel sorry for your patients, May, I really do.'

The captain and Walter Lisle rounded on him simultaneously. 'The jobs these young ladies do, I couldn't stomach 'em myself – I take my hat off to 'em,' while Walter cried indignantly, 'May's patients are very lucky, I envy them, Archie!' Then he went pink with embarrassment and asked quickly, 'Have you finished your tea yet, Miss Winton? Captain Soames is a busy man.'

'Never too busy to entertain a nurse,' Captain Soames said heartily, 'And Joseph Frears' granddaughter, of course,' he added hastily.

But Walter was impatient to show May and Archie the other wonders of the Docks, so they thanked the captain for his hospitality and went ashore.

Chapter Thirty-One

As Archie handed May off the gangway he noticed her leather gloves.

'For goodness' sake, May, the day's sweltering, take your gloves off! We ditched ours ages ago, and Aunt Ju isn't here to scold you.'

May hesitated, but it was hot, so she obediently slipped them off – then wished she hadn't when she saw the men's eyes on her short, stubby fingernails and red, work-hardened hands. She curled them up and said defensively, 'It's the carbolic – we use so much.'

'Oh come on, May, we know you spent all morning scrubbing bedpans and other unmentionables.' Archie was amused. 'Don't worry, we won't tell Aunt Julia you removed your gloves in the presence of gentlemen.'

'Just one gentleman, Archie.'

Walter said smoothly, 'I'm sorry your opinion of me is still so low, Miss Winton! Here, give me those, I'll put them in my pocket. I thought Archie would be interested in the dry dock, but it's some distance – are you well shod, Miss Winton?'

'Yes, certainly.'

Archie murmured in May's ear, 'Best boots and silk stockings!'

May stepped back squarely onto her cousin's toe. 'You are a beast, Archie!'

Walter Lisle's agreement was heartfelt. 'Your remarks can be singularly ill-timed, Winton.'

Archie protested. 'I say, Tate, that's a bit steep, when I'm doing you a favour!'

Walter Lisle hurriedly began to tell them about the

proposed establishment of a Port of London Authority to administer all the Docks.

Their route took them over the dock entrance, and Walter looked suddenly worried at the narrowness of the footway above the sheer drop.

'Would you rather we stayed on this side, Miss Winton?'

'Of course not,' May retorted, 'I can swim, you know.' She stepped lightly and sure-footedly over the gates, gazing down at the brown water so far below without a qualm.

There was a large ship in the dry dock, and men were working on it at the far end. The descent to the depths was by a flight of slimy stone steps; May, determined to miss no experience on this adventurous afternoon climbed steadily down. Archie was amazed at the size of the exposed hull; he moved forward eagerly.

'I'll ask those fellows what they're doing.' He was off along the concrete bottom. May, following, walked into the damp shadows by the chocks. She stopped, and, head tipped back, stared up at the sheer blank sides soaring to the far-off sky. As she gazed up at the massive hull above her it seemed to start shimmering, it began to quiver – it was moving, poised to topple over and fall, and crush them utterly! She gasped and stepped jerkily back; she stood shaking, desperately fighting the urge to turn on her heel and flee and throw herself at the treacherous stone steps to scramble frantically up to the warm blue sky above.

Then, as she stood trembling, she felt firm hands grip her arms, holding her still, and Walter Lisle's voice, low and calming, murmured, 'Steady, May, steady. It's all right now.' And he held her until the fear passed, and her body sagged with relief.

She felt weak, and shaken, and foolish. 'I am sorry – I was being stupid.'

His voice, close to her ear, was gentle. 'Don't be silly, it can be very frightening. I was terrified the first time I came down here – I should have remembered.'

May didn't believe him, but was grateful. He said, 'If

you're ready, I'll take you up again. We'll leave Archie to explore.'

May looked, and saw her cousin's slim back in earnest conversation with the workmen at the far end, where the hull was being painted. She nodded.

'Yes please, I'm all right now.' But she was grateful for Walter's presence behind her, and his firm hold on her elbow as they went up the slippery steps. They reached the top and stepped on to the stone dock side. Her legs were trembling from the effort of making her muscles obey her. She gave a small sigh and leant against her companion's shoulder for a brief, comforting moment.

Then she moved away, saying, 'Pride goes before a fall – it serves me right for boasting at the lock gates. I do feel an idiot.'

'Well, nobody noticed.' His voice was comforting, and they stood in companionable silence, waiting for Archie, together in the warm sun.

Archie arrived panting and almost dishevelled, his hands smeared reddish brown.

'I say, May, it's fascinating. I never knew ships' hulls needed so much attention.'

'Whatever have you got on your hands, Archie?'

'Compo, May – anti-fouling composition,they put it on. Smell it, it beats carbolic hollow! Where are we going now, Tate?'

'We'll go to Brunswick Wharf.' Walter's voice was decided. 'It's one of the finest views on the Thames.'

They picked their way over the quayside to the wharf. Walter pointed down river.

'That's Bugsby's Reach.'

May gazed spellbound at the glittering, sparkling, swelling water, as they stood on the very brink of the river with the damp cool smell of mud in their nostrils and the soft soothing sound of the small waves against the wharf in their ears. The river was busy, and Walter began to pick out those craft he could name, and guess at where they had come from and where they were bound, but it was soon clear

268

that his favourites were the big Thames barges.

'Look at them, at rest they're almost ugly with their great flat hulls, but on the water they're so graceful – they dance to the tune of the breeze.'

May looked at his face, young and entranced in the sunlight, as he gazed at the sails. Suddenly, he seized her hand.

'Look, look at that one, beyond the tug, there, see how it's using the wind to turn against the tide. The helmsmen are so skilful, they work *with* the wind and the water, instead of fighting it, like those greasy, noisy tugs.'

Then he came back to Brunswick Wharf again and realised where he was, and released her hand as suddenly as he had taken it. May felt her fingers tingling with the force of his grip.

The afternoon seemed timeless to May as they stood watching the shining river with its myriad craft – swooping, gliding, chugging to and fro in front of them. Even Archie was silent. Then Walter took out his watch and said, 'We'll have to go back soon. I have a meeting with my churchwardens tonight.'

The spell was broken. May turned reluctantly away from the swift river and back towards the city behind them.

'I wondered whether you would both care to be my guests for tea. Mrs Lewis has baked a special cake for you, Miss Winton, to thank you for looking after Hetty – she'll be very disappointed if you don't come. You will, won't you?'

May remembered the last time she'd had tea at the vicarage, and hesitated, but Walter's face was pleading, and she didn't want the afternoon to end, so she smiled her agreement and Archie said, 'Come on, May, I'm hungry and don't pretend you're not – I'll never believe it.'

They made their way back to the Dock entrance, May still gazing interestedly about her. The men competed to summon the first cab, but as they tumbled in May noticed her bare hands.

'My gloves, please, Mr Lisle.' He retrieved them from his pocket and handed them over.

Archie expostulated. 'For goodness' sake, May, as if it matters. Tate's place isn't Buck House, you know.' But his tone was indulgent and he explained to Walter Lisle, 'If you knew my aunt you'd understand why May is so proper. Her step-mother fed her pages of etiquette books for breakfast every morning, toasted, and spread with butter and marmalade.' After a moment May joined in the laughter of the men.

As they alighted from the cab May surveyed the vicarage with interest – after all, she'd scarcely had time to get a good look at it on the previous occasion. It really was a rather unprepossessing house, but quite large – Walter Lisle must rattle around in it on his own. Then she looked even more intently at the tall, yellow brick building beside it. So this was Walter's church; she wondered what it was like inside.

The maid opened the door with a warm smile, but as they stepped inside May couldn't help feeling that a good session with a scrubbing brush and a bucket of soapy water would have improved the paintwork in the hall: the house bore the unmistakable signs of a bachelor occupant. She cringed slightly before entering the drawing room again but Shadrak, torn ear waving, leapt up from the sofa and purred round Walter's legs. May bent down to stroke him, glad of the distraction. As she straightened up her attention was caught by a big bowl of peonies on the table. Walter saw the direction of her gaze and looked gratified; May had already guessed from the geometrical arrangement of the flowers that he had been responsible. She walked over and delicately touched the pink petals.

'How beautiful!' Walter smiled at her pleasure.

'I say, May, that animal seems to know you!' May cursed Archie's sharp eye as she bent over to pick up the traitorous tom cat, and hide her blushes in his fur.

Walter, rather pink, hastily took Archie off to show him some object at the other end of the room, and gave May time to recover herself. After all, whatever had passed between her and Mrs Tranter, it was she whom Walter was now entertaining to tea, not the rabbit-nosed Agnes.

270

Archie ranged around the room, examining the ornaments, seeming unaware of the dusty smudges left on his hands as a result. He put a model of a sailing barge back on the mantelpiece, saying, 'Not at all bad, Tate. So you're still whittling away?'

'Oh, did you make that, Mr Lisle?' May jumped up and went to inspect the small craft. 'Why, it's very good!'

Walter Lisle looked self-conscious. 'It's just a hobby. I find it difficult to sleep in this hot weather, and I don't fancy reading theology books *all* the time,' he finished with a smile.

May looked at him, and realised that in some ways his life must be a very lonely one, cut off as he was from his own clan by living in the East End. After all, she had her friends in the same building, and a host of colleagues to work with, but Walter Lisle could scarcely spend his evenings chatting to Mrs Lewis.

'Do you have curates, Mr Lisle?'

He smiled. 'Yes indeed, three. I don't know what I'd do without them.' She felt oddly relieved by his reply.

The tea tray arrived and May poured. The crockery and cutlery were very clean, she was glad to notice; they saw enough cases of food poisoning in the East End without the young vicar of St Barnabas' being carried in with it. Not that he'd ever be a patient in St Katharine's – a private nurse would be the order of the day, and then, no doubt, his fond Mamma would whisk him off to Shropshire, pale and weak. Walter was looking at her in a rather puzzled way, and May realised that her scenario was really rather premature – he looked in excellent health. Indeed, when she looked at him with a professional eye she could see he was a superb specimen of the young, healthy male.

'More tea, Mr Lisle?'

'Thank you, Miss Winton.' He held out his cup to her.

Archie rattled on as usual, and May and Walter Lisle were content to listen, with only brief interjections. Then May glanced at the green marble clock on the mantelpiece.

271

Walter, watching her, asked, 'I thought this was your half-day off, Miss Winton. You're not on duty again today, are you?'

May could not tell a direct lie. She said lightly, 'The sick staff nurse on Elizabeth has recovered, so I've been transferred.'

He raised enquiring eyebrows and she had to continue. 'I'm starting on Abraham and Sarah Wards – tonight.'

His head jerked up. 'Tonight! You mean you're on night duty?' May nodded. 'Miss Winton, you should be in bed; or were you able to sleep this morning?'

May shook her head. 'Oh no, I worked this morning, until midday – it's quite usual, you know. We are supposed to go to bed then, but I have difficulty in sleeping when I'm on nights, and I never can beforehand, especially as I'm still on the day nurses' corridor until tomorrow. I'd have just lain there in this sweltering heat, getting more and more depressed – all the lovely fresh air from the river and the exercise has been the best thing possible.' Her voice was decided, and Walter Lisle ceased to argue; but she could see he was still concerned, so she exerted herself to make it quite clear that she was full of energy, and longing to go back on the wards tonight. She almost convinced herself.

At six o'clock Archie said he must be making tracks shortly, so May left the two men together while she ran downstairs to have a word with Mrs Lewis.

Back in the hallway, she turned to Walter Lisle and asked, rather shyly, 'I wonder, would you mind showing us round your church before we leave? I'd like to see it, and Archie's not in a hurry: he never is.'

Walter Lisle was clearly pleased. He took them through the small garden, past the dehydrated shrubs and into the shadows of the church porch. Inside it was cool and dim, but as her eyes became accustomed to the change in light May realised that it was very different from the churches she was used to. Even the hospital chapel had a sense of age about it, but this was obviously very new and raw. The pews were a sickly yellow pitch pine, and the tiles on the floor a jarring

272

red. Yet it had a sense of purpose, for all its newness: it felt like a church which was used, as if the cheerful, Sunday-morning-best-clothes-from-the-pawnshop throng of East End worshippers had only just left, and would be in again soon.

May walked down the aisle and studied the ornate metal screen, then turned to the pulpit, and tried to visualise Walter there, in his cassock, preaching to a Cockney congregation.

He misunderstood her interest and said, 'Yes, it is rather well-carved, isn't it?' She saw that it was: simple, but with firm, bold lines.

She lowered her gaze to the lectern. 'What a splendid eagle!' The bird's eye was commanding, the beak savagely curved and the talons of the great claws looked completely lifelike as they gripped the brass sphere.

Walter laughed. 'He's rather fat, though, isn't he? I'm not sure he'll ever be able to fly.'

'Of course he will, you wait – one Sunday morning in the middle of matins he'll suddenly flap his great wings and soar away up to the roof, and perch screaming on the rafters!'

Walter laughed and patted the arched neck. 'I can't allow that, old boy – you'll have to stay on your perch, where you're needed.'

Archie's voice was indignant. 'What are you two going on about? The thing's made of brass!'

Walter looked at May and gave the ghost of a wink. Then he said soothingly, 'Don't worry, Archie, I'll keep it securely chained up.'

Walter was going to set out to summon a cab from South Bromley station but May said firmly, 'Archie and I can perfectly well walk to the cab rank, Mr Lisle, if you'll just point us in the right direction.'

'Then I'll come with you, to see you safely installed – I don't want you getting lost. Archie doesn't know the East End.'

'But I do, Mr Lisle.' Then May remembered her experiences of several months back, and stopped protesting.

As Archie secured the cab May turned to their host. 'I have

enjoyed myself this afternoon. Thank you so much, Mr Lisle.'

'The pleasure has been mine, Miss Winton.' He paused, then asked, 'When you are on night duty, do you work every night?'

'Until we finish, then we get three nights off, but I usually sleep through the first twenty-four hours.'

'So there won't be any more dinner parties at Arlington Street?'

'No, the Season will be over by the time I'm on days again.'

He seemed to be searching for words, when Archie thumped him on the shoulder.

'It's been a most interesting experience, Tate old man. Can't get over that dry dock, it made quite an impression on me.' Walter Lisle flicked a glance in May's direction; she shivered. Archie continued unheeding, 'I'll have to look into this shipping business, perhaps it's the career I've been looking for. Can you fix me up with a job, May?'

Walter Lisle said, 'Frears are shipbuilders, Archie, not ship-owners. You've got a lot to learn.'

Archie was as irrepressible as ever. 'There's time, I'm only a youngster. Come on May, I want a quick canter in the Park before dinner.'

May looked back at Walter as her cousin hauled her into the cab. 'Goodbye, Mr Lisle, and thank you again.'

Walter hung on to the door as the driver started to close it. 'Thank you, for the pleasure of your company.' He paused, then as the driver looked impatient he slowly drew back, saying, 'If there is ever anything else I can do for you, Miss Winton, do please ask me.'

The door shut with a little click. Walter drew back and lifted his hand in salute. May raised hers in reply. Archie said, 'There you are, May, there's your chance. Ask him to put up a quick prayer that Chef will decide to do what that chap Soyer did – you know, in the Crimea – and dedicate his life to feeding the starving nurses of St Katharine's. Tate's a powerful prayer, you know.'

May said sharply, 'Oh shut up, Archie.' She threw herself back on her seat. Archie looked at her closely. Then he patted her hand. 'Not looking forward to nights, are you old thing? I know, it always knocks you sideways, I've seen it before.'

'Yes, yes you're right Archie. I don't want to go on night duty tonight.'

Chapter Thirty-Two

May's two previous spells of night duty had been in the cooler weather, when there had at least been the compensation of snuggling up in bed on a cold morning with a hot water bottle. Now she found it difficult to go to bed on a hot summer day; even when, in desperation she took off her nightdress and lay naked under the sheet with the window wide open, she still felt suffocated by the muffling heat. On the other hand, she was spared the sweating daytime toil on the wards, with the high collar gripping her neck and her black stockings clinging stickily to her legs. Then, even the special light-weight hunting corsets of silk elastic seemed to drag on her hips like chainmail.

At night there was a freshness in the air, never found by day in the East End. Also, Abraham Ward had a balcony, where the dirty linen basket was kept, so there were brief, reviving moments to be snatched there in the course of the night – but only brief, since the medical wards of Abraham and the smaller Sarah were both very heavy. Many of the patients were struggling for breath, or lying still, not making even the smallest of movements, staring at the nurses with wide, fever-bright eyes. And always there were men muttering strings of meaningless words, voices rising and falling in the far-off wanderings of delirium. They could be eerie wards at night, and May was often grateful for the never-ceasing summer hum of the city around her.

Yet as she walked through the big ward doors at nine o'clock each night, basket of provisions on one arm and swinging the bag containing her soft shoes in her hand, she felt a surge of satisfaction and pride: in fifteen minutes the wards would be hers. Sister Abraham and the two Staff Nurses would give their reports and depart, and she would be left in total control of sixty lives, and deaths, for ten long hours.

May knew by now that Matron's choices were not, as they had at first seemed, made in a random and unpredictable fashion. She had been chosen for this position because she was deemed capable of filling it: only a few third year nurses supervised double wards. Wright, the pro deputed to Sarah was a competent second year – without her May's nights would have been frantic indeed. Fitton, a first year, who was her own pro on Abraham was far less satisfactory.

Fitton was a late entrant to nursing. May guessed she was well over thirty, and knew she had spent some years as a school teacher. But her motives for making the change remained a mystery, since Fitton said little over their evening meals together, other than the occasional reluctant admission of tiredness. This May could recognise for herself, since the woman's aching feet and swollen ankles were revealed in her shuffling walk. May, remembering her own time of trial on nights in the hell of Isaiah, did her best to hearten Fitton, and gave such advice as she could; but the junior nurse was so much older than May herself, and was so reserved, that she felt self-conscious about instructing her, and so confined herself to practical demonstrations and supervision. These were certainly needed, since Fitton was slow and awkward with the patients. May often had to conceal her irritation at her subordinate's clumsiness, and remind herself that at least she was not careless and slapdash like some new pros.

If Fitton was silent and humourless then Wright, whenever May dashed through the connecting corridor to help and to supervise, had a ready smile and a quick response. Night duty seemed to leave Wright unmarked, and she often bubbled over with some small incident which had tickled her imagination. May suspected that her colleague's light-heartedness owed something to the preference which one of the house physicians showed for drinking his cocoa on Sarah Ward. However, May did not see herself as one of Matron's spies: on the contrary, she made a point of escorting Night Sister through the connecting corridor with an over-loud swing of the door. This brought Wright pink-cheeked from the ward, where often a cadaverous figure could be seen earnestly studying a temperature chart at the far end. May could afford to be tolerant: she knew Wright was too good a nurse to neglect her patients – indeed, May thought to herself, it would appear that her personal attractions were enhancing their medical care, since Charles Wilson spent so much time on Sarah Ward.

The spell of hot weather finally broke, and a cooling breeze blew in from the river, followed by rain, so that May felt fresher than she had done for weeks as she pushed open the doors of Abraham that night. Sister was grave.

'I'm afraid three of the pneumonias are near their crises, Nurse Winton. They will need constant watching, and we have a new admission, the patient at the far end on the right. The police brought him in this morning; they found him in a collapsed state under the railway arches. I don't know what to make of him, and nor does Dr Wilson. He may be a case of DTs, but he seems quiet enough at the moment. Sometimes these big men have no resistance.'

'Do we know his name, Sister?'

'No, not yet. No one has enquired of him, and his clothes suggested a casual labourer – perhaps he should have gone to the workhouse infirmary.' Sister gave the rest of her report and left.

May was kept busy with her pneumonias, grouped together in the middle of the ward near the night table; she was only able to make quick dashes to inspect the other patients. On one of these she noticed that Connor, a nephritis, was becoming distressed, and she had to call out Charles Wilson and set up a bronchitis tent around the bed. As the long spouted kettle hissed gently she was thankful for the cooler weather.

The regular ward routine was left largely to Fitton, who dragged herself uncomplainingly to sluice and linen room and then to the kitchen, to cook their midnight meal. Fitton was quite a good cook, whatever her other short-comings, and May sat down at the central table with anticipation, but there was no time to savour her food tonight. Within minutes she was up again, and while on her feet she decided to make a

278

quick dash to Sarah. Fortunately things were quieter there, and Wright cheerfully offered to cut and butter Abraham's breakfast bread as well as her own.

Fitton started to get up when May returned, but May, noting the dark circles round the older woman's eyes, signalled her back to her chair, and told her she must take the full half-hour.

'There's no need for both of us to be up – I'll ask you to relieve me later, thanks.'

May knew she wouldn't, but she didn't want to hurt Fitton's pride, since that seemed to be all that was keeping the other nurse going. Fitton slumped back without a word, and sat hunched over the table, chewing very slowly, as though the meal were sawdust instead of nicely scrambled eggs.

By five to five, two of the pneumonias were clearly holding their own, and May was bending over the third, her finger on his thready pulse, when she heard a choking cry from the far end of the ward. She glanced up sharply and at that moment the anonymous patient in the last bed reared up. May began moving swiftly forward, but Fitton, coming through the balcony door with the soiled linen bucket was there before her. She put a restraining hand on the man's shoulder and in an instant he lunged forward, flung himself out of the bed and sank his fingers straight into Fitton's throat. In front of May's horrified gaze he swept her off the floor and began shaking her from side to side like a rag doll. Fitton's mouth opened wide in a soundless scream and May was running – running as she had never run before. She swept a lotion trolley to one side with a crash, and was aware of several pairs of startled eyes staring from the beds – but she knew the men were too ill to give any help. Then she was there, and had flung herself on the man, dragging his arms back by brute force. Fitton fell against the bed and now May, in her turn, was fighting. He went for her throat – she felt the balls of his thumbs pressing – and for one dizzying instant she thought she had lost. But May was bigger and stronger than Fitton, and more determined. She wrenched with all the strength of her arms and managed to pull his hands away for a moment. And in that moment, out of the corner of her eye, May saw Fitton bend forward and sink her teeth into the man's calf. He squealed, a loud angry note, then suddenly shook May off and began to lurch down the ward. For one insane second May wanted to laugh at the sheer burlesque of the episode, but deadly seriousness returned as the man began to gather speed and May remembered the madness in his eyes and the helpless patients all around her. She forced her shaking limbs into activity and began to run again. The man was ignoring the patients, most of them incredibly still asleep, and was heading for the door – but it was the door in the side of the ward, the door which led to Sarah. May's mind screamed as she thought of that ward full of bedridden women, with only Wright's small form to protect them. She threw herself after him and reached the corridor only feet behind him. Then, suddenly, tiny Wright was there, her mouth a round 'oh' of surprise as she stared at the intruder; she was clasping a loaf to her bosom, but in the other hand glinted the sharp steel of the bread knife. The man saw it, skidded to a halt, turned on his heel, cannoned into May behind him, threw her against the passage wall and began to run back to Abraham. May pulled herself up again, turned to Wright and cried, 'The bell, *press the bell!*'

She just had time to see Wright's nod of comprehension before she was off again, gasping, bruised and panting, but still running. Below Abraham was Elizabeth Ward, and this thought lent wings to her feet. But the man did not pause; nightshirt flapping in the wind he was outside, and heading for the main entrance. Now May began to have fears for his safety: he seemed blind and deaf, and impervious to the sharp gravel under his bare feet. Had Wright reached the emergency bell in time, the bell which rang in the porter's lodge? Only seconds had passed, but it seemed to May as if she had been running in this mad flight for an eternity. Then he was past the porter's lodge, with the porter only just behind him – but behind him. May slowed down, her heart thudding against her ribs – at least he was away from the hospital, with its burden of vulnerable patients.

Then she heard a high-pitched, keening scream, the clanking hiss of a tram abruptly stopping, and the screech of iron-shod wheels and hooves striking cobbles. The shouts which followed told her the rest of the story, and as she walked out onto the Dock Road she felt the bitter taste of failure rise into her mouth.

Matron came to the ward half an hour later. Her face, beneath its immaculate headdress was set and grim.

'Your patient was killed, Nurse Winton.' Her voice was stern.

May bent her head. 'I'm sorry, Matron.'

'Why did you not ring the emergency bell at once? You know that is the correct procedure.'

May looked at the bell, winking malevolently at her from the first of the centre pillars. Her brain was dull and her arms and legs leaden with shock and fatigue. Should she have gone to the bell first? But if she had done, what of Fitton, who was even now attending to a patient down the ward, shaken and bruised, but undeniably alive? Yet she should have rung the bell. She felt too exhausted to even try and defend herself. Her throat was on fire where the man had gripped her neck and the right side of her body ached where he had flung her against the corridor wall.

Matron waited, but May only repeated, 'I'm sorry, Matron.'

The older woman's voice was icy. 'There will have to be an inquest. I will call in the House Governor this morning, and we shall have to consider your position, Nurse Winton.' Her skirts rustled as she swept through the door May held open for her.

Fitton came up for instructions. 'What did Matron say?' Her voice was hoarse and barely audible.

'She is sending for the House Governor. I should have rung the bell, first.'

Fitton swallowed painfully. 'But you didn't have time!'

May shook her head. 'I should have made time. It was my fault. A patient was killed, and it was my fault.' She felt utterly defeated.

Fitton gripped her arm and pointed to the bell. 'Where

were you standing when he attacked me?' Her rasping voice was urgent, but May was beyond rational thought.

She gestured to the middle bed. 'I was beside Harris.'

Fitton was reduced to a croak by now. 'But Winton, if you'd gone to . . .'

There was a stifled cry from the other side of the ward and May shook off Fitton's restraining hand and walked mechanically to the patient.

'Are you in pain, Mr Eli?' Her own voice, she noticed without surprise, sounded almost as strained and odd as Fitton's.

The morning round of washings and temperatures passed in a daze. Fat, jolly Sister Abraham came on early, with the day nurses, her face unusually serious. Matron had obviously spoken to her and she made no comment as May faltered over her report when she reached the far bed. May hoped she saw a gleam of sympathy in her eyes. Wright was pale and subdued; as they left the ward she put her arm round May's waist and gave her a quick hug, but neither she nor Fitton spoke as they went down the stairs together. Fitton walked painfully, as usual, but May noticed that her face was not collapsed, as it generally was in the mornings; her mouth was set in a determined line, though May knew that underneath the concealing collar her neck must be even more bruised and painful than May's own.

As they neared the dining room May turned away from the other two.

'I'm not going to breakfast.' Wright made a quick protest but May ignored it. She had broken such a major rule this morning that a minor infringement seemed immaterial. Had Ellen been there she might have gone, but Ellen was on days and so already on duty, and Ada too. There was no one else in the hospital May felt able to face this morning.

She fetched her cloak and bonnet from her room and left the Nurses's Home. But in the courtyard she turned away from the main entrance. She could not bear to see again the place where the body, tossed aside by the tram and broken by the dray, had lain amidst the inevitable small crowd of

282

sightseers. She slipped out through the side entrance, used by the tradesmen's vans, and into the quiet street of small, dark terraces. On the pavement outside the walls she hesitated, then drew a difficult breath into her parched throat and began to walk northwards. There was only one place she could go to this morning, and only one person she could talk to.

The church spire came in sight first and May fixed her eye on it as though it were a talisman. What if he were not there? But she thrust the thought from her – he had to be there. She pushed open the vicarage gate and aimed for the front door like a hunter making for its stable after too long a day in the field. It was the maid who came to the door. She looked startled when she saw May, but May was past caring.

'Yes, Miss?'

May's lips moved, but no sound came out. She stood in the doorway, swaying with exhaustion – she had got here, but now her mind was a blank. She stared at the maid, who spoke again, louder, and looked more and more puzzled. Then a voice called from inside, 'Who is it, Bessie? What's the matter?'

May's frozen limbs unlocked and she pushed past the bewildered maid and headed for the voice. Walter Lisle stood at the top of the stairs, with a shaving brush in his hand and his face half-covered with lather. May grasped the newel post and gazed up at him, wordlessly. He looked down at her for a moment, then was galvanised into action and sprang down the stairs two at a time. As he arrived in the hall May collapsed into his arms and sobbed and sobbed against his neck. She had a confused sensation of the soap on his chin damp on her forehead, then she heard him say: 'Open the study door, Bessie – and take this damn brush off me.'

She felt one of his arms tighten around her shoulders and the other reach behind her knees and he had swung her up and was carrying her through a nearby doorway. He put her down gently and she was half-sitting, half-lying on a leather covered sofa. He stood over her in his shirt sleeves.

'What's the matter, May? What's happened?'

283

But May could only shudder and gulp convulsively. As she moved, her stiff collar chafed unbearably and she wrenched it off. He stared at her neck.

'Who did that to you?' His voice was furious.

May shook her head. 'No one, he's dead – it was a patient, a delirious patient – I tried to catch him, and he's dead. He died in the Dock Road because I didn't ring the bell. It's my fault, Walter – I killed a patient.' She gazed despairingly up at him.

He said grimly, 'It looks to me as if he pretty nearly killed you first, May.'

May shook her head painfully and said, 'You should have seen Fitton, hers are worse.' Then she began to weep again, hopelessly.

She heard Walter go to the door and speak to the hovering maid. The maid went away and he came back and looked down at her again. Then suddenly he bent over her, picked her up again and sat down on the sofa with May on his lap. He held her tightly, cradling her head against his shoulder. May continued to sob. The maid came back; her voice was low and concerned.

'Here are the handkerchiefs, Sir, and the arnica. Shall I put it on?'

'No thank you, Bessie, I can manage. Would you ask Cook to put back breakfast? That will be all.'

The door closed and May sobbed on. Walter untied her bonnet and pulled it off, then he began to pat her on the back while he spoke to her gently. May felt her shudders become weaker and finally stop under the influence of his soothing voice, though she had no idea what he was saying. Eventually she pulled her head away from his shoulder, took a deep breath and sniffed. He pushed a large handkerchief into her hand and she blew her nose, then he wiped her face with another. She noticed the damp patch on his shoulder and said, low-voiced, 'I'm afraid I've made your shirt wet.'

'It doesn't matter, May.' He reached for a small bottle beside him. 'I'm going to put something on those bruises.' She sat obediently still while he dabbed the cold lotion on her neck. 'Are those the only ones?'

May managed a watery smile. 'I'm afraid the others are where you can't put anything on them, Mr Lisle.' Then she remembered the thud as she hit the wall and the squeal of the tram, and began to cry again, but more softly this time. And as she cried she felt her head droop and her lids close; so she surrendered to sleep.

Chapter Thirty-Three

May's return to consciousness was so gradual that at first she hardly knew whether she was awake or still dreaming. She looked drowsily at the blues and greens and ruby reds of the stained glass in the topmost panes of the unfamiliar windows. They sparkled and glowed in the sunlight. Then she lowered her gaze and there was a pair of grey-suited shoulders bent over a desk, with thick black hair curving into the nape of the neck above the stiff clerical collar. She felt as though she were floating, warm and safe and secure, waiting for Nanny's plump face to appear round the door with its warming smile and the familiar, 'Wakey wakey, dear.'

Then she moved and winced from the pain in her side, and suddenly reality came flooding back and she cried out. The shoulders turned instantly and it was Walter Lisle's face which looked at her, anxious and concerned.

May felt a flood of embarrassment wash over her, as she remembered her abandoned weeping in his arms. He reddened, too, but got up and came towards her as she struggled to sit up; he pulled forward a straight-backed chair and sat down beside the sofa. She smoothed down her skirts and pulled her cuffs into line, then raised her hands to her head and felt the great weight of her hair sliding down over her shoulders.

He noticed her look of consternation and said quickly, 'I'll call Bessie, she'll take you upstairs so you can wash your face and tidy up.' He went to the bell and pulled it, then added, 'We'll have breakfast as soon as you're ready. In here, I think – the dining room is rather gloomy in the mornings.'

He smiled at her, and she managed to smile back. Then she rose with as much dignity as she could muster, murmured, 'Thank you,' and followed Bessie upstairs.

In the bathroom the shaving brush was neatly placed on its

shelf and May blushed again for her untimely arrival. She peered at herself in the small mirror, fixed a little too high for her comfort, and saw that her face was pallid and drawn. Her eyes were puffy and red with weeping, and encircled with dark smudges. The bruises on her neck were greenish now, and she hid them under her collar; but there was little she could do to improve her ravaged face, though she felt better after splashing her eyes with cold water. She hesitated over using the obviously masculine comb, but then shrugged and picked it up – after wiping off his shaving soap with her hair it seemed silly to quibble at using his comb. She was soon ready, and smelt the appetising aroma of bacon as she came down the stairs. Shadrak met her at the bottom, and led her yowling into the study.

A small table was set in front of the fireplace and there was the smell of good coffee. Walter pulled back her chair and she sat down. Shadrak positioned himself expectantly at Walter's feet and May raised her eyebrows at her host and gave a small smile. Walter grinned. 'I'm afraid I get into bad habits on my own – he likes bacon almost as much as kippers.' He picked up the jug. 'Coffee?'

May sipped the fragrant brew. 'Wherever do you get this in the East End?'

He smiled. 'I don't. I'm afraid I make a raid on Pratt's every so often, and smuggle a hamper of delicacies past the customs barrier at Aldgate Pump.'

May laughed aloud, then remembered the events of the night and felt her face stiffen. Walter Lisle talked hurriedly on about his favourite foods, and May responded, hesitantly at first, then with more animation.

The breakfast was well-cooked, and despite the soreness of her neck and throat May managed to round off her scrambled eggs and bacon with three slices of toast. Then she put down her napkin and said wryly, 'The condemned man ate a hearty breakfast. Matron is calling in the House Governor this morning. Not that it makes any difference, even he can't bring a patient back to life. We have no Lazarus Ward at St Katharine's.' Her voice was heavy with self-reproach.

287

Walter leant forward and spoke seriously. 'May, now you're somewhat recovered, I want you to tell me exactly what happened.'

'It's no use, I should have rung the bell.'

'Stop reciting that like some sinister incantation and think, May.' His voice was commanding; so, haltingly at first, then with growing speed, May described the events of the night. Walter only stopped her once, to fetch a sheet of paper and make her draw a rough plan of Abraham and Sarah Wards, and the central pillars. He looked wonderingly at it and muttered, to himself, 'How on earth can they expect one woman to supervise all those beds?' Then he told her to continue.

When she had finished he sat frowning a moment, then said, 'I don't think there was any correct way out of this one for you, May, – no, don't start on about that bell again. If you had run back to press it I think there would have been a strong possibility that he might actually have strangled this other nurse, Fitton, judging by the state you're in – and you say she's smaller than you.'

'Then I should have rung it on the way back down the ward.'

'But again, May . . .'

May broke in. 'It's the rule, Mr Lisle. The emergency button is there for us to press in an emergency – and the man did die, you know.'

Walter sighed. 'Yes, you've got to live with that. But still . . .'

As he spoke May had noticed the clock. She hastily jumped to her feet.

'I must go now, the doors of the Night Nurses' corridor are closed at midday. Even if they ask me to leave I'll still have to go on duty tonight somewhere, we're so short-staffed.'

Walter Lisle looked horrified. 'Surely not – you're in no fit state to work tonight!'

May shook her head. 'I'll be needed. I must go now. Thank you for a delicious breakfast – and for being so kind.' She lowered her eyes, blushing.

'I'll fetch a cab from the station. I won't be a minute.'

'No, please don't trouble – I'll walk back.'

'You are not walking anywhere.' Walter Lisle's tone brooked no argument, and May sat meekly down again and tied on her crumpled bonnet as she waited.

He was back in a few minutes and helped May into the hansom, then jumped in beside her. They said little on the journey, and all too soon May felt her depression deepening as they reached the familiar streets near the hospital. The cab lurched left into the Dock Road. May turned to her companion.

'I'm sorry I called so early, Mr Lisle. I'm afraid it was very far from being convenient.' Her voice was prim.

'Not at all, Miss Winton.' His tone was formal, but his eyes smiled at her. 'I had actually been up for some time – the early service, you know; but as I'd overslept a trifle I decided to take a chance on not shaving first thing. I should have remembered your habit of catching me offguard.' His smile was so warm that May could not help responding; she forgot her worries for a moment. Then the cab jerked to a halt outside the main hospital entrance and she felt the colour drain from her face. He jumped out and helped her down. As soon as she reached the pavement she held out her hand.

'Good morning, Mr Lisle.'

He grasped it firmly, and stood there holding it, as if he did not quite know how to let go. Then he squeezed her hand gently again, said, 'Take care of yourself, May,' turned abruptly and was gone.

As May walked under the archway the tortoise came right out of his cubbyhole.

'Nurse Winton, Matron wants to see you – soon as you come in.' Her heart dropped and her feelings must have shown on her face because the old man peered at her from his small rheumy eyes and patted her arm awkwardly.

'There's worse things 'appen at sea, duck.' Then he shot back into his lair.

May felt tears rising at the unexpected sympathy, but she fought them down, squared her shoulders, and set off in the direction of Matron's office.

289

As she entered the outer office she saw Wright and Fitton sitting against the wall. Wright looked unusually serious, but it was Fitton's expression which surprised May: her undistinguished features bore a look of fierce determination. Both junior probationers were still in uniform, though Fitton's throat was swathed in a silk scarf. May had no time to do more than nod in their direction before she was ushered into Matron's sanctum. Matron was not alone: she had with her both the House Governor and the Hospital Secretary. She rounded on May at once.

'Where have you been, Nurse Winton? We've been looking for you this past half-hour.'

May felt a small spurt of anger. 'I was not aware that you wished to see me, Matron. I went to see a friend – a clergyman.'

Mr Henderson, the Hospital Secretary, said kindly, 'That was very understandable, Matron. I'm sure that after the distressing events of last night Nurse felt in need of some spiritual comfort.'

May doubted whether sitting weeping on Walter Lisle's lap could quite be construed as spiritual comfort, but she smiled gratefully at Mr Henderson as she concentrated on Matron's next words.

'Nurse Fitton went to see Colonel Gerrard this morning, and insisted on speaking to both of us, together.' Matron seemed somewhat baffled as to why she'd agreed to this. She continued, 'Nurse claims that you had no choice but to act as you did, and when I begged to differ she actually suggested a reconstruction of the sequence of events!' Matron's well-corseted bosom quivered; clearly she had not been in favour. 'Colonel Gerrard considered that, in fairness to you, Nurse Winton, we should adopt this plan. I have agreed, but only in view of your previous excellent record.'

May replied, 'I understand, Matron.' But she didn't understand at all. What was the point? She hadn't rung the wretched bell, and that was that.

'We will go now.' Matron rose majestically. In the outer office she beckoned to Fitton and Wright; they obediently got to their feet and brought up the rear of the procession.

When they reached Abraham Ward they found Charles Wilson there, talking to Sister. He jumped to his feet.

'Mr Wilson has kindly offered to play the part of the patient,' Matron announced regally. 'I gather his height is appropriate.'

Colonel Gerrard stepped forward, his military bearing very noticeable.

'Now, we must ensure that this operation goes like clockwork – we don't want any slip-ups. Nurses Wright and Fitton, please explain to Dr Wilson exactly what he must do. You, Nurse Winton, must act precisely as you did last night.'

The other three went into a little huddle; Fitton's voice was croakingly forceful. Sister Abraham smiled encouragingly at May, and patted her hand as they waited. As soon as Fitton gave the word Colonel Gerrard positioned himself by the crucial pillar and took a large stop-watch out of his pocket. The patients were agog – even the illest were looking eagerly around and May heard Sam Baines hiss just behind her: 'I completely missed it last night, Bobs, thoughtful of 'em to give a re-run, ennit?' But May felt detached from the general current of excitement; she stood passively waiting for her instructions. Fitton came up to her.

'Get into position, Nurse Winton, and do exactly as you did last night.' Her hoarse voice bore the unmistakable stamp of the schoolmarm. May obediently moved up to the eighth bed and stood with her fingers on the pulse of the pneumonia, who, she noticed with clinical objectivity, seemed rather better this morning.

The door from the balcony swung open; Fitton came through and approached the bed at the far end of the ward. As she reached out her hand Charles Wilson sprang up and seized her by the neck. Fitton gasped, in real pain, and suddenly everything clicked into place. May leapt up the ward, she was onto Charles, he grabbed her throat and she thrust him off. As she did so Fitton, sitting on the floor, slapped him smartly on the leg and he set off down the ward, May in hot pursuit. She was nearly on him as he jumped for the Sarah Ward corridor, dodging the Hospital Secretary stationed there, then Wright came out clutching loaf and breadknife, Charles turned, pushing May to one side, May screamed: 'The bell, press the bell!' and threw herself after Charles. She was already through the main ward door when Sister called her back. Charles had stopped, panting, and May skidded to a halt beside him, feeling suddenly dazed and shaken, her side throbbing painfully and her throat on fire as she gasped for breath. Charles took her arm and led her back into the ward. There was a tentative burst of clapping from the men as she reappeared, but Staff Nurse shushed them fiercely.

Colonel Gerrard clicked shut his watch, and walked forward. He spoke directly to Matron.

'We are going to have to alter the position of that bell, it's useless where it is.'

May realised the significance of his words and began to sag at the knees. Charles Wilson tightened his grip and whispered, 'Brace up, it's nearly over.'

Matron was still not appeased. She turned to May. 'I see that your position was difficult, Nurse Winton, but please remember that, as a result of your actions, a patient died.' Her tone was frigid and May lowered her eyes. But at that moment Sister Abraham stepped forward. She pushed Fitton in front of her and quickly whisked the scarf from round her neck to expose the livid bruises. She spoke directly to Matron.

'But as a result of Nurse Winton's actions, one of my nurses is still alive.' She turned to May. 'I hope I would have had the courage and speed to act as you did, Nurse Winton.' May gazed at the mountainous rolls of Sister Abraham's wide body, but she felt no desire to laugh. She said simply, 'Thank you, Sister.' Then she went up to the House Governor and held out her hand. 'I am grateful for your time and patience, Colonel Gerrard.' The Colonel looked surprised, then he seized her hand and shook it heartily.

'Sometimes a spot's so tight you can only trust God and do your best, I learnt that in the army. There's no easy way out.' His voice was gruff, but kindly.

Matron, as always, had the last word.

'Come along, Nurses, what are you waiting for? You're on duty tonight, remember. You should all have been in bed half an hour ago.'

May whispered a quick word of thanks to Charles Wilson before they all trailed meekly out behind Matron. When the latter left them at the foot of the stairs May turned to the other two nurses and thanked them. They were all quiet and subdued, but Fitton's exhausted face bore a look of satisfaction, and May was grateful for the older woman's determination; it would have been so easy for her to have let matters take their course.

Upstairs in her room May sat heavily down on the chair. She felt relief, but she was also aware that Matron was right: a man had died as a result of the actions she had chosen to follow, and she would have to live with that knowledge.

Tired though she was she wrote a short note to Walter Lisle before she undressed, telling him of what had happened. Then she risked Home Sister's anger by walking down the stairs to the post box, and dragged herself up again by the banister. She was sore and aching as she climbed into bed, but she fell asleep at once.

Chapter Thirty-Four

Stiff and bruised, with neck swollen, May went on duty as usual that evening, together with an exhausted Fitton. The pneumonias were better, but the nephritis took a turn for the worse, so the bronchitis kettle hissed steadily in the background throughout the long night. After breakfast May could only manage the briefest of walks; then she sat crouched in a chair in the Nurses' Sitting Room until allowed to go to bed. On her way upstairs she glanced in the letter rack and found one waiting for her, addressed in an unfamiliar but obviously masculine handwriting. It had been delivered by hand, and was a short note from Walter Lisle, expressing his relief at the House Governor's decision, and continuing concern for her in the distress she must still feel. She was grateful for his solicitude.

The inquest was held several days later: it was brief and formal. Evidence of the dead man's state of health and mental condition was given. The events of the night were related in flat, level tones, only the tram driver displaying any emotion: 'Gawd's truth, Yer 'Onour, 'e threw 'isself straight in front er me – nasty thing to 'appen on the Dock Road.'

A verdict of Accidental Death was returned, and Colonel Gerrard immediately escorted his three nurses straight back to the hospital. May thought she caught a glimpse of black hair and a clerical collar among the small crowd at the inquest, but she was not sure.

Before he left them she questioned Colonel Gerrard as to relatives of the dead man. He told her that the sister who had given evidence of identification had not seen her brother for some months. He had lived an itinerant life, picking up labouring work where and when he could, and, as far as anyone knew he had had no wife or other dependants. For that, at least, May was thankful; but in unguarded moments the scene flashed through her mind again and she agonised anew over the decisions she had made.

She confided this to Wright one evening, on their way to the ward, and later that night Charles Wilson came and sat down with her on Abraham, and told her kindly but firmly that she must now put the matter out of her mind.

'I constantly have to make decisions – sometimes they're right, sometimes I can never be sure, and sometimes, God help me, they've definitely been wrong. But it wouldn't do the patients any good if I gave up and did nothing for fear of the consequences. In any case, I honestly believe delay could have cost Fitton her life, and you didn't know Mary was going to appear like Lady Macbeth, knife in hand – without that your being at his heels might have been the only thing. . .' He shuddered, then smiled at May. 'So I have no doubts about the correctness of your decision, and I, for one, am damned grateful to you.' He pushed his chair back and left, with a quick wave of the hand. May knew he was right, and made herself stop wincing as she passed the far bed.

A week later there was a summons from Matron, who grudgingly informed May that her holiday would start in the second week of September. Then she added, almost as an afterthought, 'On your return, Nurse Winton, you will report to Matthias Ward, as Staff Nurse.'

May had never worked on Matthias, but she knew of it from Ellen, who had. Staffing on Matthias was a plum job – it was a large men's surgical, dealing only with serious cases. The work was interesting and rewarding and Sister Matthias, though strict, was fair, and the possessor of a keen sense of humour. The treble bonus of an end to nights, a holiday at Allingham to be looked forward to, and a return to a coveted position put the spring back into May's step as she left the office.

She needed the prospect of peace and fresh country air to keep her spirits up over the next few weeks. Even in the early morning the East End stank. The normal smells of the city in summer – ammonia and horse dung – were overlaid by the

295

reek of industry: rotting horseflesh, the chemicals of the paintworks and the sulphurous stench of the large gasworks on the Lea Marshes. On the streets, hot, unwashed bodies gave off their own pungent odour, so May occasionally took a tram to Victoria Park – it was a relief to see an expanse of green, however dried up and dusty. But often she lacked the energy and merely sought out the quieter side streets to the north for her morning walks.

One hot day in early September she was dawdling, peering idly into the doorways of small shops and watching the antics of the almost naked urchins in the gutter when a voice hailed her. She looked up, and there, pedalling towards her on an ancient bicycle, was Walter Lisle. He swerved dangerously across the road and juddered to a halt just as he seemed about to mount the pavement in front of her. The surprise of his appearance made her heart jump against her ribs, and it was a moment or two before she was able to return his smile.

He dismounted and came forward, hand outstretched, and they touched sweaty palms, and stood for an instant looking at each other. Then he said, 'I'm so glad I've met you, Miss Winton – I was about to write to you. I wonder if by any chance you will be free next Saturday? You told me once you spent three months on night duty, and then had some free time – isn't this due soon?'

His expression was so anxiously hopeful that May did not have the heart to tell him that her three nights off were being added to the start of her holiday – instead she heard herself saying that yes, she was free on Saturday, knowing full well that she had notified Lady Clarence of her arrival the previous evening.

He smiled warmly at her, then hesitated. 'Perhaps I should have explained first – I'm not offering you a very restful day. It's our annual Sunday School outing to Southend. Extra adults are a great help, and the youngsters often fall and hurt themselves – but it really is tremendous fun, and one of my lady church workers will be accompanying us, so you would have congenial company.'

May laughed. 'I shall look forward to it. I've never been to

296

Southend, but I've heard a lot about it from patients – they talk of it as a paradise on earth, a veritable Garden of Eden!'

Walter Lisle burst out laughing. 'That's not quite how I'd describe it, Miss Winton – but it's certainly an experience. Mrs Lewis will be preparing a picnic hamper for the helpers, so you don't need to supply anything. I'm afraid I must bid you goodbye now – I have an appointment with a colleague – but I'm so glad you can come.' He turned back to his bicycle.

May said quickly, 'I'll bring some first aid equipment, Mr Lisle, and perhaps some fruit; it's always pleasant in this weather.'

'Splendid!' Then as he put his foot on the pedal, he leant forward and said, softly, 'But, perhaps, no apples?' He winked at her and wobbled as he waved goodbye.

It took a moment for May, her brain dulled by night duty, to understand the allusion. Then her cheeks burned in the hot air – but after a moment she began to laugh.

That evening May wrote to her parents, explaining that she would be coming down on the Sunday, after all. She knew her step-mother had scruples about travelling on the Sabbath, but she would assume that May's duties made this inevitable. May felt rather guilty, but then told herself that she had been invited to Southend as a nurse – in any case, it was a Sunday School outing.

The next morning brought a note from Walter Lisle, giving details of the rendezvous, and in the evening May had to confess to Ellen and Ada, both off from six, what she had agreed to do. Ada told May she was a fool to delay her annual holiday for a trip to Southend of all places, saying bluntly, 'Tell me honestly, May, would you be so ready to go if that clergyman was short, fat, and fifty?'

But Ellen jumped in with a red-hot piece of gossip about eccentric Sister Timothy: 'On a motor-bicycle – truly – bouncing all over the Commercial Road, Adams said, and hanging on for dear life!'

May's blushes subsided under cover of Ada's exclamations of disbelief. She did not want to have to answer Ada's question, even to herself.

Saturday morning was warm and fine and it looked as though the sky would be clear beyond the industrial haze of the East End. May had slept most of the previous day, and all through the night, and when she woke, early, she felt surprisingly refreshed. She was excited, but firmly ascribed this to the nearness of her holiday – although, curiously, the charms of Allingham seemed to have receded somewhat from her mind. She almost regretted leaving Poplar tomorrow – almost, but not quite; the rotten eggs smell of the gas works had definitely gained the ascendancy this morning.

The good weather decided her choice of outfit. The lightweight costume of pale blue linen had hung unworn in her wardrobe all summer – she had scarcely changed out of uniform since her night duty had begun. She hesitated over her choice of blouse, then settled for a fine spotted muslin, with narrow frills at neck, yoke and wrist. Her straw sailor had been re-trimmed with blue ribbon the evening before, so she was soon ready. She had packed her handbag with lint and strapping; now she slipped in a small bottle of weak disinfectant, wrapped in some old cloths begged off Sister Abraham. The latter had proved very knowledgeable on the subject of Sunday School trips, though claiming that a wagon was much nicer than a train. May knew that Sister's father had been vicar of a country parish; she couldn't help feeling relieved that she was not riding through the streets of Poplar in a borrowed wagon – besides, it would take an awfully long while to reach Southend!

May was ready in good time, but in view of her pale-coloured suit and clean shoes she asked the tortoise to summon a cab, and rode northwards at her ease.

The wider area of road outside the church was overflowing when May arrived: there was a crowd of youngsters of all ages milling around. The driver reined in.

'Will this do, Miss? Nearest I can get.' He added cynically, 'Pawnshops round 'ere must be empty today.'

May, looking at the boys in their best suits and polished boots and with caps on their heads, and the girls, in Sunday dresses and clean pinafores, was inclined to agree.

As she jumped down she spotted Walter Lisle's dark head, in the middle of the throng, and felt suddenly shy. She paid the driver and then hung back. But as she stood, hesitating, there was a violent eruption in one corner of the crowd and a small figure pushed and pummelled its way through. There was a piercing cry of, 'Nurse, Nurse Winton – are you coming with us?'

It was Louie Brown, her left cheek and neck still showing only too clearly the scars of her accident, but her exuberance was undimmed. She jabbed the toe of her boot smartly into an obstructing shin, burst through and launched herself into May's arms. May dropped her bag and swung the girl round and round, laughing as Louie squealed ecstatically. As she set the excited child down she saw Walter Lisle moving through the crowd towards her, smiling.

Louie jumped up and down. 'I come wiv me cousins – I don't go ter this Sunday School, but me cousins asked Mr Lisle, and 'e says I could come – on account o' bein' so ill. Our 'Arry's an altar boy – 'e's the posh one o' the family!'

Walter Lisle held out his hand. 'So you know one of our party already – good.' He grinned down at Louie and gently tweaked her one stubby plait. 'I'm going to take Miss Winton to meet the curates and Miss Parkes – all right, Louie?'

Louie nodded, but hung back a moment against May's skirts. She touched her ravaged face gently. 'It's lookin' better, ain't it, Nurse?' Her voice was studiedly casual, her eyes shadowed.

May knew the girl was too bright to be fooled by a lie. 'It is less noticeable, Louie, and I think I could show you a way of arranging your hair, now it's grown a bit, so it fluffs out at the sides. I've got a comb and some pins in my bag – I could do it today, if you wish.'

Louie said seriously, 'Yes please. You can do it on the beach.' She raised her voice. 'You go wiv the Vicar now, Nurse.' She dismissed them both with a lordly wave. As they began to skirt round the crowd May heard her saying to another girl who'd just come up. ''Andsome feller, yer vicar, ain't 'e?' May smiled as Walter Lisle's ears went pink, but

299

then blushed in turn as the girl replied, 'An' your nurse is a smasher, ain't she Louie?' Walter turned and laughed at her.

The three curates were at the Church gate: one tall and broad, one short and broad, and a long, thin, bearded figure who looked much older than Walter – but May supposed there were late recruits to the Church, just as there were to nursing. May shook each hand in turn and there were murmured greetings, then Walter Lisle looked up with a pleased expression.

'Ah, there's Miss Parkes, punctual as always.'

May looked in the direction of his gaze and blinked in surprise. She had vaguely imagined Miss Parkes to be an elderly, spinsterish church worker, but the woman coming towards her was no older than herself and, despite her plain grey costume and unadorned hat, she was very good looking. Her hair was a dark glossy brown, parted in the middle and drawn back into a neat bun which suited her classically regular features set in a pale, almost translucent, skin. She clearly intended her complexion to remain at its best since in one hand she carried the least frivolous parasol that May had ever seen.

Walter Lisle smiled. 'Good morning, Miss Parkes, may I introduce you both? Miss May Winton, Miss Edith Parkes.'

The girl extended grey-gloved fingertips to May, who was immediately conscious of her bare hand – she had thrust her gloves into her bag on Louie's approach, and not yet retrieved them. There was no time to fumble with them now so she stepped forward to shake hands regardless. Miss Parkes barely touched May's fingers then moved back with a cool, appraising gaze. May smiled, the other woman moved her lips fractionally, then turned to Walter Lisle and said, in low, but very clear tones, 'Is it not time we left, Mr Lisle? It would not do to miss the train.'

'Er, no, no – of course not.' Walter Lisle seemed momentarily nonplussed, then he obediently jumped up on the porch steps and called the crowd to order in a stentorian voice.

Silence descended rapidly, and May was very impressed as the jostle resolved itself into orderly columns, each with several older lads as escort, while a number of mothers, some with babies and toddlers, brought up the rear. Obviously some careful preliminary planning had been done.

Walter jumped down and prepared to lead the first column, while the curates took one apiece. Edith Parkes indicated that she and May were to bring up the rear with the mothers.

May said cheerfully, 'So we're to be the camp followers.' She was rewarded with a silent look of distaste. May spoke more formally. 'Mr Lisle has organised matters most efficiently, has he not, Miss Parkes?'

There was a slight thaw beside her. 'Mr Lisle is an excellent organiser. So important in a clergyman, don't you think, Miss Winton?'

May felt privately that, though no doubt useful in a clergyman, there were plenty of other professions where organising ability mattered more – for an army officer, for instance? – but she decided that diplomacy would have to be the order of the day, and agreed politely. She had noticed Walter Lisle's cook among the mothers, looking much more spry on her legs now, but although Mrs Lewis had beamed in her direction and waved, she had then glanced at May's grey-clad companion and stayed where she was. May decided she could hardly rush off and join her, since Walter Lisle had clearly seen the two girls as being congenial company for each other.

When they reached Bromley station Louie appeared again and flew up and down like a dervish. May placed a restraining hand over hers until the train was safely in, when the crowd surged forward and an older girl, obviously one of Louie's cousins, seized her and hauled her off, flashing a quick smile in May's direction as she went.

In the compartment, once the other women were chatting to each other and soothing excited babies, Edith Parkes turned to May and said in a low voice, 'What is wrong with that child's face?'

May explained, 'She was badly burned, down one side.'

Miss Parkes folded her lips. 'Some of these East End mothers are disgracefully careless.'

301

May remembered Louie's mother weeping on Elizabeth Ward, thin and pale except for the great swelling abdomen which bent her back and seemed to draw all the life out of her: 'I'll never fergive meself – I fell asleep, I were so tired,' and later, as she sagged on a chair, 'Doctor says it's likely twins, Nurse, I dunno 'ow I'll cope, with six already and now Louie like this.' Mrs Brown had wept silently, helplessly.

May felt anger well up now, but Edith Parkes noticed nothing and continued, 'She should wear something over her face – it is not pleasant to look at.'

May said coldly, 'You should have seen it at Easter. I assure you her present scars are a great improvement.' She turned her head and stared out of the compartment window.

But the day was fine and sunny, they were bound for the seaside; she was not going to let Edith Parkes spoil it for her so she spoke to the girl again, asking how often she came to the East End, and what she did there. Miss Parkes warmed to this subject and lectured May on the importance of well-educated women serving the poor. Though May was interested to hear that this service apparently involved living at home and attending a pleasant collegiate community in West London, and only visiting the East End parish on two or three days a week, in the day time, and not always even then. 'Of course it's very important that we should keep up with our normal social life as well – one has a responsibility to one's family, you know; my elder sisters are married, so Mamma likes me to go about with her.' May wondered why Miss Parkes herself was not married; her face, though lacking in animation, was certainly beautiful, and she moved with elegance – her only fault was a degree of flat-chestedness of which Lady Clarence would have wholeheartedly approved.

In no time it seemed they were at Barking, where Walter Lisle popped his head into their compartment window.

'All well, ladies?' Then he shot off to quell an incipient riot further down the train. The whistle blew and they rattled over the points towards the green expanses of Dagenham and Upminster. Canvey Island roused a storm of cheering as they

302

drew into Byfleet, and May felt excitement rising as she gazed out over the wide Thames estuary.

The cry: 'Southend-on-Sea, Southend-on-Sea, all change here!' was the signal for a concerted surge by the Sunday School scholars, and even Edith Parkes went slightly pink, while May looked about her with frank enjoyment. She sprang from the train and took deep breaths of sea air – tainted, it was true, with the smoke of the locomotives, but sea air nonetheless. Walter Lisle leaped onto a baggage trolley and addressed the assembled multitude, and, miraculously, the columns re-formed and they were off. As they left the shelter of the glazed porte-cochère at the station entrance May was dazzled by the sunlight.

'What a beautiful day – the sky is so blue and the sun so delightfully warm!'

Edith Parkes replied by putting up her parasol, and they set off for the front at a sedate pace.

Chapter Thirty-Five

May was enchanted by Southend. It seemed to her to have all the liveliest characteristics of the East End but without its obvious drawbacks. She abandoned Miss Parkes to a seat in the gardens – 'No, thank you, Miss Winton, I feel quite drained by the heat already' – and she and Louie and Louie's cousin and Louie's cousin's friend rushed up and down the stalls on the front. They sampled the winkles, the whelks and the cockles, washing them down with vivid yellow lemonade and purchasing violently-coloured rock for later. The children bought cheap gew-gaws to take home to their families and Louie agonised over the choice of an appropriate gift for the surviving twin. 'It's still so little, Nurse, Ma keeps it by the range, even in this weather.'

Then they all made a mad dash for the pier, joining the general stampede, and rode the tram to the end. There they hung over the railings, enjoying the sea breezes, while May gripped Louie by the back of her pinafore.

Walter Lisle appeared beside them and leant over in his turn, saying to May, 'I have no fears – I know if I topple over you will instantly dive in and rescue me!' Then he proceeded to hang over so far, inspecting the girders below, that Louie's cousin became quite alarmed, so May and the girls seized hold of his coat tails and hauled him, laughing and protesting, back to safety. He moved off to speak to another group of his Sunday scholars, with a murmured, 'Fall in at one o'clock, remember.'

May and her party returned back along the pier and made a quick foray into the town, before assembling at the promenade gardens at five to one. They found Walter Lisle already there, sitting comfortably relaxed beside a cool and elegant Miss Parkes. He sprang up and offered his seat to

May. As she sat down she was very aware of her tumbled hair and grubby gloves, while her pale linen skirt showed only too clearly the marks made by the eager tugging of small, sticky hands.

They devoted the afternoon to the beach. The children rushed back and forth, paddling, leaping and squealing in the sunshine, while May attended to several minor cuts and grazes. Edith Parkes sat beside her on the rug which Walter Lisle had thoughtfully provided, looking as neat and prim as she had done first thing that morning. When the first wave of casualties had been dealt with May sat back on her heels and looked longingly at the frisking children – how deliciously cool the waves looked. And how lucky men were! Walter and the curates had simply removed their shoes and socks, turned up their trouser legs and gone in paddling with the rest. Then May noticed that the mothers with Mrs Lewis had formed a massed circle, and by dint of rearranging their voluminous skirts and carefully manoeuvring an old piece of sheeting were discreetly removing their stockings.

May looked at Edith Parkes, upright under her parasol, feet neatly placed together. She asked wistfully, 'I suppose you wouldn't like to paddle?'

An expression of absolute horror passed over the fine features. 'Certainly not!'

May gazed again at the enticing waves, then back at her companion, and made her mind up. She jumped up, ran across to the group of women and said, 'May I join you?'

Mrs Lewis' face smiled a welcome. 'Course you can, ducks. We're taking it in turns, see.'

The water was blissfully cold. May gasped and squealed with the rest. Walter Lisle saw her and waved, but did not come near, and the women stayed modestly in a group. May went back to the beach with the others when they had had enough, but not before a giggling Louie had bounced up and down in front of her and splashed her skirt and petticoats. However, they soon dried in the hot sun while May was busy back-combing Louie's hair and bringing it forward in loops

305

to lie on her cheeks. Louie peered with set face into the small mirror; then her expression cleared, she nodded approvingly and was off to join her cousins.

Later Walter organised a game of cricket for the girls and smallest boys – the bigger lads, of course, had their own well under way. May thoroughly enjoyed watching the expression that came over Edith Parkes' face when he suggested she might like to join them. 'Some of the older girls are a little embarrassed about playing, but as they're members of your Bible class, Miss Parkes, I thought perhaps . . .?'

Her refusal was polite but implacable, so May discarded her jacket and Walter took her off, saying, 'You'll have to do instead, May – I knew I could rely on you not to be too ladylike.'

At this May hung back, suddenly uncertain. Walter Lisle turned and looked full into her troubled eyes and spoke firmly.

'I meant that as a compliment, May – a true lady knows when not to be one.'

May doubted whether Lady Clarence would agree with this sentiment, but she smiled back and as the younger girls were calling, 'Hurry up, Mr Lisle, we want to get started,' he seized her hand and rushed her across the muddy beach at full pelt.

Archie, Bertie and an assortment of stable lads had taught May the right way to hold a bat and hit; it was soon clear that the other team would have to put Walter on to bowl if they were to have any chance at all. May did not want to hog the bat, so when he lobbed her a ball she hit it up, up, into a soaring arc, so that it came down into Walter's cupped hands. 'Howzat?' The other side cheered and her girls groaned.

May ran backwards and forwards fielding – the rules were rather bent, since naturally no one wanted to waste time sitting out, even though it was their team batting. Her hair finally came tumbling down, to Walter's obvious amusement, and she had to stop and quickly plait it and tie on borrowed ribbons. As she ran after the tennis ball with her long pigtails bouncing against her back she felt as if she were transported

306

over the years to her schoolroom days, before the rules of polite society had summarily curbed her freedom.

It was almost tea-time when the game was abruptly finished by two of the younger boys cannoning into Walter, so that they all fell into a sprawling heap on the beach. They unluckily landed on some sharp pebbles, so Walter scooped up the youngsters and, with one under each arm, they all made off to where Edith Parkes sat, guarding May's handbag. May attended to the two snivelling infants – whose solicitous elder sisters had by now turned up – and they rapidly cheered up when she pushed a sweet into each mouth after applying the antiseptic. The second one demanded, 'Kiss it better', and May laughed and did so, and the first one then clamoured for his kiss too. May turned next to Walter Lisle, and knelt at his feet cleansing the graze on his shin – aware as she did so of the strength and shapeliness of his leg.

She applied the second piece of strapping, patted his leg and said, as she had done to the children, 'There, all better now!'

Walter looked down at her, his eyes dancing. He spoke softly.

'Haven't you forgotten something, Miss Winton?'

May felt the hot tide rise from her throat, then she suddenly grinned. 'Why, so I have, Mr Lisle!' And she sprang up and popped a boiled sweet into his surprised mouth. He began to laugh, so that the sweet choked him and made him splutter, until the tall broad curate, who'd arrived from the boys' cricket, thumped him vigorously on the back. May's sides ached with suppressed laughter.

Tea was trays of buns and bottles of lemonade, bought in Southend; these were soon dispatched. Then Walter began to round up his flock. As the columns were reassembling he came over to May and Edith Parkes, still sitting decorously on their rug.

'May I help you up, Miss Parkes?' He held out two strong hands and Edith Parkes, barely touching his fingers, rose gracefully from the ground. He turned to May, sitting warm and happy in the sun, and held out his hands again. 'I'm not

307

sure such an athletic young woman as you, Miss Winton, needs any help!'

In revenge May reached for his hands and grasped them, then went limp, leaving him to pull. He blinked, then she saw the muscles in his arms flex as he took her weight, and with a mighty tug she was off the ground. Then, all at once, he let go. The quick pull had unbalanced her, and she stumbled and fell forward, and her hands clung to his shoulders. As she caught hold of him May felt a wave of pure joy wash over her. Instinctively she relaxed and let her body melt against his. She was conscious of his heartbeats, very loud, in his chest, and of his arms sliding round her and tightening for a moment – but it was only for a moment. Suddenly he let go, gripped her arms and pushed her from him. As soon as she was steady on her feet his hands dropped as though they had been burnt. His face was grim and set as he wheeled around and marched off across the beach.

May stood, still swaying slightly, shaken and humiliated as she had never been before. She put her hand to her cheeks, which were burning now with more than the sun. Edith Parkes' voice, glacier cold, spoke beside her.

'Would you care to gather your belongings together now, Miss Winton?'

May turned, and saw a look of complete contempt on the other woman's face, mingled with something else – triumph, perhaps? She looked away, fell to her knees, and began to pack her bag with shaking fingers.

The sun was brassy, and unbearably hot on the back of her neck as she picked up the rug and shook it out before folding it. Then she stood with the bundle in her hands, helplessly.

'Perhaps *I* had better see that that is returned to Mr Lisle.' Edith Parkes' voice stressed the personal pronoun, and May handed it over silently. Then she got control of herself.

'I think, Miss Parkes, it would be better if I travel back with Louie – the child is rather excited; she may need calming.'

A small smile played round her companion's mouth. 'Certainly. No doubt Mr Lisle will be happy to escort me to my compartment.' She walked gracefully away.

May found Louie, who did indeed look rather green, and took her into the farthest carriage. She carefully positioned herself as far away from the platform as possible, and when Walter Lisle came round to check that his party were all aboard she did not look up. Just past Hornchurch Louie was suddenly sick. The child's eyes filled with tears.

'Oh, I'm ever so sorry, Nurse – all down yer lovely skirt.'

May said, 'It doesn't matter, it needed cleaning anyway.' She took a cloth from her bag and wiped the child's face and mopped up her skirt. One of the mothers put a newspaper on the floor; May sprinkled some antiseptic and the smell almost went.

Louie soon perked up again and began to chatter to her cousin, so May sat back and closed her eyes, listening idly to the gossip of the other women. It was with a jolt that she realised they were talking about Walter Lisle.

'Now, Mrs 'Arper, a vicar needs ter be married, 'specially a good-looking bloke like that – 's'only natural.'

'Well, she certainly 'angs round 'im enough – opportunity's the greater part o' courtin', as me old Mum used ter say. And Miss Parkes is quite a looker – lovely 'air and skin. An' real posh manners.'

'Yes,' the third woman sounded doubtful. 'She's perlite enough, but . . .'

The others nodded, they obviously knew what she meant. 'Still, be different with the vicar, she's the same sort and all – wouldn't look dahn 'er nose at 'im.'

'Not 'er, she fancies 'im too much.' Mrs Harper gave a raucous laugh. She lowered her voice, but it was still audible to the appalled May. 'Mind you, she allus strikes me as a bit – well, you know . . .'

'Aye, my Jim says for all 'er looks she's not one as 'ud warm the bed fer a man!' The voice was complacent. The other women laughed, and there was a whispered exchange, and more laughter. Then the first voice spoke again.

'Still, I daresay vicars don't want that sort 'er thing – I reckon we'll 'ave the banns called by Michaelmas.' There were sage nods and the conversation moved on.

309

May felt a shiver of horror at the implications of what she'd just overheard. If Walter Lisle was engaged, or nearly so, to Edith Parkes, no wonder he'd pushed her away from him in disgust. How could she have forgotten herself like that? He'd only suggested her coming today to keep Miss Parkes company – and she, May, had literally thrown herself at him. It had been bad enough before, to have done what she did; but to have acted like that in front of his betrothed! Walter Lisle's grim face as she had last seen it swam before her closed lids, and it was only with a great effort that she could stem the tears of shame. Her behaviour seemed more monstrous and un-forgivable with every mile that they came nearer to London.

At Bromley Louie made her farewells.

'I've 'ad a luvely day, Nurse Winton, ta fer everythin' – me Dad said 'e'd come fer me.' She was off. May longed to follow her, but she couldn't go without a word; yet she shrank from speaking to Walter Lisle. She looked round desperately and saw Mrs Lewis. Thankfully she had only been in the next compartment. She ran up to her.

'Mrs Lewis, would you be so kind – I have to get back quickly, please explain to Mr Lisle for me – and thank him for a most enjoyable outing.'

She turned to the exit and then, to her dismay, saw Walter Lisle at the barrier, counting his flock through. She backed away – could she hide in the waiting room? Then she glimpsed the open baggage gate and rushed towards it. A porter tried to bar her way but she thrust a florin into his astonished hand and murmured, 'Please, I'm in a great hurry,' and he let her through and pointed to the direction of the road.

There was a cab waiting. She jumped in with a quick, 'St Katharine's, please,' and fell back against the seat. All she could think of now was to put as many miles between herself and Walter Lisle as she could, as rapidly as possible. She studied her watch. If she really hurried there was still time to catch the evening train to Suffolk.

She rapped on the trapdoor in the roof and when the driver opened it, announced, 'Please wait at St Katharine's, then

310

take me on to Liverpool Street – I have a train to catch.' She knew she must look untidy and dishevelled but the driver nodded, responding to the tone and accent of her voice, as she had known he would. He signalled his agreement.

At the hospital she rushed up to her room, changed at top speed and tossed a few things into her grip – she had plenty of clothes at Allingham. As she ran downstairs again she met Ellen coming up.

'I can't stop – I'm catching the evening train.'

Ellen asked anxiously, 'Is anything wrong, May?'

'No, yes – I'm going home, I'll write.' She continued her headlong flight, Ellen staring after her in consternation.

All the way along the Dock Road she willed the horse to go faster, and tried to pretend that catching the train was the only thing that mattered in the world. They drove into the gloomy cavern of Liverpool Street; she was out of the cab in seconds. She paid the driver and hailed a porter simultaneously, then ran to the ticket office. Mercifully there was no queue, and with the porter galloping beside her she reached the barrier just as it was about to close. She sped through, an official opened the door of the 'Ladies Only' compartment and she jumped in. The porter threw her bag in after her and she pressed a coin into his hand as the train gave a hiss of steam and began to move.

The two other occupants of the compartment looked at May askance, then returned to their magazines. They both got off at Chelmsford, where May summoned a porter and sent him with a telegram notifying Allingham of her arrival at Ipswich later that evening. Then, in the solitude of the compartment she finally gave way to her feelings, and let the tears stream unchecked down her cheeks.

311

Chapter Thirty-Six

The gardens of Allingham Place looked particularly beautiful in the bright summer sun: the green of the lawns, the glowing colours in the massed beds, and the scent of the roses wafting in through the open windows, all were conducive to calm and tranquillity. May sat with her step-mother in the morning room and wept inwardly.

She had arrived late on Saturday, tired and wretched. Sunday had dragged interminably, yet her parents had been so kind and thoughtful, so anxious that she should do just as she pleased after her long hot summer working in the East End. In return she had smiled and talked, and forced herself to look interested in the small daily affairs of Allingham and its neighbourhood. But all the time she had longed to be alone – to crawl into a corner and give way to childish tears. She did not, because she had spent three long years now learning to be calm, controlled and sensible. So she told herself she was being irrational and silly, and at times she almost convinced herself. But on Sunday, as they sat in the high, vaulted church, with the dust motes dancing in the sunbeams as they slanted to the warm grey flags, she remembered, with piercing clarity, Walter Lisle's pride as he had shown her and Archie round his raw, new church, set amid endless slum terraces and noisy pubs. And she gripped her prayer book tightly, and deliberately bit her lower lip until the pain of it brought her back to some kind of sense.

Again and again she recalled the force of his hands as he'd pushed her away on the beach, then let her go, suddenly, as if he could not bear to touch her – and the look on his face: it had been so stern, so forbidding. But of course, if what she had heard on the train coming back was true, then no wonder he had thrust her to one side. In May's mind his gesture became more and more forceful, until, though knowing it had not really been like that, she saw herself rejected contemptuously, and burned anew with the shame of it.

Monday had dawned clear and cloudless. For the first time in her life May could not eat her breakfast – even the small piece of toast which she made herself chew under the anxious eyes of her father seemed to stick in her throat. Now she sat with her step-mother, mechanically sewing a dainty jacket for Emily's daughter, thankful that Lady Clarence's sense of restraint was so inbred that it would never allow her to enquire, even obliquely, as to the cause of May's despondency. Instead Lady Clarence looked up and suggested that they both take a little stroll in the garden; May listlessly agreed. She was about to put away her work when the door opened and Haines himself stood in the doorway, his usual composure very slightly ruffled.

'M'lady, a gentleman has called. I informed him his Lordship was out, and that you were not at home to visitors, but he insisted on seeing you.'

Lady Clarence raised her eyebrows. 'He *is* a gentleman . . .?' Her voice was inquiring.

'Oh yes, Your Ladyship, he is a gentleman – though rather emphatic.' Haines looked down his nose. 'He gave his name as Mr Walter Lisle.'

May gasped, and her hand flew to her throat. Her step-mother glanced briefly in her direction, then spoke calmly to the butler.

'Show Mr Lisle in, please, Haines.'

May felt her heart thudding like a drum-beat in her ears. She stared down at her needlework, meaning to keep her eyes fixed on it, but as the door opened again she glanced up, involuntarily. Walter looked hot, and his thick dark hair was tousled. He was not wearing his dog collar, and without it he looked somehow younger and more vulnerable. He flicked a glance in May's direction, then advanced firmly on Lady Clarence.

'Please excuse this intrusion at such an early hour, Lady Clarence, but I have only just arrived from London.' He came to a sudden halt.

313

Lady Clarence, totally composed, murmured a greeting.

Walter seemed to be at a loss as to how to go on, so May, hot and embarrassed, said, 'Mr Lisle is a friend of Archie's, Step-mamma – they were up at Oxford together. He has a parish in the East End.' Then she in her turn stopped. She drew another breath and added desperately, 'Mr Lisle is the son of Lord Pennington.' Her inspiration was exhausted; she fell as silent as Walter.

Lady Clarence, however, had found her bearings now. 'Why, I remember your mother well, she and I were presented at the same Drawing Room – but I believe she does not go into Society much today?'

'No, no – she prefers to stay in the country.' Walter spoke abruptly, then lapsed into silence again. Lady Clarence showed no signs of flagging in this conversational impasse. She smiled and offered Walter his cue.

'I expect you are visiting in the neighbourhood, and so decided to look up my nephew's relatives.'

Walter blurted out, 'No – no, I came down to see May – Miss Winton.'

May bowed her head, her cheeks on fire. She could sense Walter's eyes fixed on her – pleadingly? – but she felt as though her tongue were attached to a lead weight. There was another pause, then Lady Clarence spoke with decision.

'May, my dear, go and put on your hat. I think Mr Lisle would like you to show him the grounds.'

May rose obediently, putting down her work with hands which trembled. 'Shall I call Fenton for you, Step-mamma?'

'No thank you, my dear, I shall not be accompanying you. The weather is a little hot for me today.' May stared at her step-mother.

'Hurry along, May. Mr Lisle is waiting.'

May felt very odd, like an actress in a play, as she walked through the door which Walter had sprung to open for her. Exit heroine, Stage Right – but she did wish someone would tell her what the next Act was about.

Walter Lisle was waiting in the hall as she came down. As soon as she reached the bottom of the stairs he seized her firmly by the elbow and steered her out of the open garden door. He walked so quickly across the terrace that May had to run to keep up with him, and he suddenly realised and slowed down, but soon speeded up again and May managed to lengthen her pace to match his.

As they strode over the lawn May asked, breathlessly, 'Where are we going?'

He pointed to a cluster of trees beyond the small lake. 'We'll go over there – I want to look at those trees.'

May could think of no reply to this. At last she ventured, 'Was it very hot in London, when you left?'

'It was yesterday, but I left very early this morning, on the five-ten; it was still cool then.' He fell silent again and May gave up her attempts at polite conversation, though she was longing to ask why ever he had left so early, and what had he been doing since? The train must have arrived soon after seven.

As if in answer to her thoughts he said, 'I walked from Ipswich – I thought your step-mother might be annoyed if I arrived too early.'

May was more and more bewildered. In that case, why had he not caught a later train? And why, oh why, had he come at all? Had he come to break the news of his engagement to Edith Parkes? Did he think, after her behaviour at Southend, that . . .? May cringed at the thought and concentrated on keeping up with her silent companion.

They marched on in the morning sun oblivious to their surroundings: they might have been pounding the streets of Poplar for all the notice Walter took of the grounds May was supposed to be showing him. When they reached the small copse he plunged in between the tree trunks; May followed, until they arrived at the landscaped glade in the centre, with its ornately fashioned iron seat. Here Walter suddenly stopped, and turned and faced her. By now his hair was on end and his face glistened with sweat; he looked very hot.

May said, 'Why don't you take your jacket off?'

'Good idea.' He smiled for a moment, and May felt her heart jump. He shrugged his jacket off, folded it neatly and

315

then looked round for somewhere to put it. May, with three years of service behind her, instinctively took it from him, then, looking around her, realised she was in a wood, and simply held it in her arms.

Walter took a deep breath and said, 'Why did you run away like that?'

May gaped at him. 'I didn't run away – it's my annual holiday, it started on Saturday.'

'But why didn't you *tell* me you were leaving London?'

May felt herself flushing – then she remembered the beach at Southend and hardened her heart. 'I didn't think you'd be interested.'

'Of course I was interested!' He was almost shouting. With an obvious effort he regained his self-control and lowered his voice. 'That wretched hospital – I went round to ask to see you on Saturday evening, and some woman with a face like a hatchet said you'd gone away! I thought you'd left for good, May – then she condescended to inform me you were on holiday, so I asked her where you'd gone and she looked at me as though . . .,' he paused, then cried indignantly, 'And I had my clerical collar on!'

'Oh dear.' May started to giggle, weakly.

He went on, 'Then that Matron!'

May stopped giggling at once. 'You didn't go and see Matron?' Her voice was shocked.

'Of course I did – Hatchet Face said I might care to do that.'

'I don't think she really meant you to, Walter.'

'Well, I did. And the Matron said: "I am not at liberty to disclose the whereabouts of my nurses to casual enquirers!"' He mimicked Matron's precise tones. 'I told her I wasn't a casual enquirer, but she still said no.'

'So what did you do then?' May was entranced at the thought of Walter storming this bastion of female power where neither his Byronic good looks nor his dog collar would open the magic door.

He looked rather shamefaced. 'I bribed the porter – that small shrivelled man at the gate.'

316

'Typical of a man to give me away! But he didn't know where I was going!'

'No, but he told me to ask for Nurse Farrar, and she'd know. So I did, and I waited hours in that courtyard – they wouldn't let me inside again – and when she came she said how did she know you wanted me to tell her where you were?' His voice was exasperated.

May was soothing. 'Well, Ada's a suffragette, you see.'

'What's that got to do with it? I've always supported women's suffrage – you know that, May.'

'Perhaps you didn't make your views clear.'

'I couldn't have cared less about the suffrage question on Saturday evening: I just wanted to find out where you'd gone.' He moved a step towards her.

May retreated a pace and he stopped. She asked, 'Did Ada tell you in the end?'

'No, another friend of yours turned up – the girl you were with in Chrisp Street market – she didn't even ask me what I wanted, she just came up to me and said: "May's at her parents' house, Mr Lisle, in Suffolk. I'll write the address down for you." And she did, straight away – she even offered to look up the times of the trains for me, but I told her I had a Bradshaw.'

'So you came.'

'So I came. But May,' his voice was suddenly young and pleading, 'I couldn't come yesterday, you do realise that – I wanted to, but I had to take the services and the schools. I'm sorry.'

May, who had not expected him at all, murmured sedately that she quite understood.

He regained his confidence. 'But there wouldn't have been all this bother if you hadn't run off on Saturday like that, without telling me where you were going. Why did you do that, May?' He was determined, yet anxious, and May knew she had to reply, however difficult it was.

She fixed her gaze on a small birch tree beyond his left shoulder and said, 'You pushed me away, on the beach – it was my fault, I know – I threw myself at you – but you pushed

317

me away.' She could not stop the break in her voice.

'I'm sorry, May.' He spoke very gently. 'I hoped you hadn't noticed.'

'Of course I noticed – and so did Edith Parkes,' she added with a touch of bitterness.

He sounded quite blank. 'What on earth has Miss Parkes got to do with us?'

May felt her heart give a little leap, then it settled down again. She gazed straight at him. 'Why did you push me away, Walter?'

She watched, fascinated, as the crimson rose in his throat and covered his face.

'We were in a public place.'

May spoke with difficulty. 'So you did think I behaved immodestly – I'm sorry. I understand.'

'No you don't!' Walter's voice was raised, he was almost shouting again. Then, more quietly, 'I'll have to try and explain.' May suddenly realised that he was acutely embarrassed. She watched him square his shoulders and begin to speak with an obvious effort. 'People think that because I'm a clergyman, that I shouldn't – well – that I should feel differently, but I don't.' May knew her bewilderment was showing on her face. He looked at her for a long moment, then said, 'Oh, May – when you leant against me, when I felt the softness of your body against mine – May, I wanted to take hold of you, and kiss you, and . . . Don't you see, I *had* to push you away, otherwise I couldn't have controlled myself at all – and it was a Sunday School outing!' As his voice rose in this last cry of frustration May felt the schoolgirl giggles welling up inside her – she fought them down, then he caught her eye, and she realised he saw the humour of his last outburst too, and they both began to laugh and laugh, leaning against the trunks of their respective trees. The tension of the last half-hour ebbed away, and left them weak and relaxed.

Then May, wiping her eyes, looked up at the flickering green mantle. 'Why did you want to look at these trees in particular, Walter?'

He smiled at her. 'Well, I thought this would be the opposite of a public beach.'

'Did you?' May's heart beat faster.

Walter's lips twitched; he spoke in a tone of assumed smugness. 'Yes, Miss Winton, I thought that as you had already thrown yourself into my arms three times, in public, it might be as well if we went somewhere more secluded so that when you did it for the fourth time I would be in a position to respond.'

May caught her breath, but her tone was light. 'You clergymen are so careful of your reputations, aren't you, Mr Lisle?'

'Yes indeed, we have to be, Miss Winton.' Then his voice changed. 'Come along May, what are you waiting for?' He moved a step towards her.

Still May hesitated. 'You seem very confident.' Her voice was uncertain.

He spoke softly. 'Yes, I am – your face is quite transparent, you know. Come to me, sweetheart.'

May looked into his loving eyes and all her scruples melted. She flung his jacket to the ground and launched herself into his waiting arms. He swept her off her feet and swung her round triumphantly, then when she was laughing and breathless he set her down and held her tightly, gazing into her face. She smiled, and raised her mouth to his, and their lips met in a long, satisfying kiss.

It was the stable clock striking midday which brought May back to reality. She sprang up from Walter's lap.

'The time – whatever will Step-mamma be thinking!'

Walter laughed. 'I think your step-mother is very shrewd, May – she's already asked me to lunch, you know, while you were fetching your hat. Where is your hat, by the way?' May looked round vaguely. Walter retrieved it from the grass and squashed it firmly on her head. 'There, you look quite respectable again now. Come along.'

May pulled him back, her other hand at the collar of her blouse. 'Walter, I can't go in like this – you undid these buttons, you can just do them up again!'

Obediently, with a frown of concentration, he struggled to fasten the tiny pearl buttons. May, standing still as he tugged clumsily at the little loops, suddenly remembered the long-ago scene in Harry Cussons' carriage, and the deft skill with which he had fastened her glove. She smiled up into Walter's serious face.

'You'll never make a lady's maid, my love.'

His reply was confident. 'Oh, I'll soon get the knack, May – practise makes perfect, you know.' He grinned, and May raised her hand in a make-believe slap, but found she could not hurt him, even in play; he laughed, and kissed the palm of her hand and held it. Then they were in each other's arms again, and it was only the thought of her step-mother which eventually made May pull herself reluctantly away. She stroked his hair with the tips of her fingers.

'We'll have to go in, sweetheart – or we'll be late for lunch.'

Walter smiled. 'And that would never do – I know how much you enjoy your food. Come on then.' He clasped her hand and they almost ran towards the house.

Lunch passed in a daze. May ate, but did not know what she was eating. Lady Clarence conversed, and Walter replied, but his mind was obviously elsewhere, and his eyes almost always on May. Lord Clarence's puzzled expression gradually began to clear, and, encouraged by his wife, he took over the main burden of the conversation from his guest.

As soon as the dessert had been served Walter, apparently oblivious of the fact that his host was reaching for an orange said, 'Lord Clarence, may I have a word with you, in your study?'

Lord Clarence cast a regretful look at the fruit bowl and stood up.

'Why, certainly, young man.' With a knowing look in his wife's direction he ushered Walter out.

May sat on with her step-mother, her cheeks glowing. Lady Clarence leant across the table and put her hand over May's.

'My dear – I am so pleased. He seems such an upright young

man. Have you discussed how soon you will give up nursing?' May looked at her blankly. 'In order to prepare for your marriage, May.'

May stammered, truthfully, 'We, we haven't discussed marriage, yet, Mamma.'

Lady Clarence's smile was radiant. 'Oh, May, I know I'm considered old-fashioned, but I am so pleased that you have both waited to speak to your father first.'

May, remembering how she had thrilled to the touch of Walter's hand on her breast, blushed scarlet.

In a very short time Haines was at the door. 'His Lordship wishes to speak to Miss May in the library.' His face was a picture of barely restrained pleasure.

May stood up and followed him. As she went into the library she saw only Walter, his face alight with welcome. Lord Clarence was jocular.

'Well, May, this young man seems to think you might be prevailed upon to accept his proposal.' Then he recalled his responsibilities. 'Would you like some time to think it over, my dear?'

May shook her head. 'I shall be delighted to accept Mr Lisle's proposal, Papa.' She looked across at Walter – he moved a pace towards her and she found herself almost running over the library floor, then she was in his arms again.

In the background Lord Clarence murmured, 'Hm, that seems pretty conclusive, I'll go and tell your Mamma.'

May managed to restrain herself until she heard the door click, then her lips found Walter's and they stood clinging to each other as one.

Epilogue – September, 1909

The ancient church was fragrant with the scent of massed banks of flowers. The gold of the bride's hair gleamed softly through her veil as she stood, so straight and slender, beside her tall, dark bridegroom.

'*And, forsaking all other, keep thee only unto him, so long as ye both shall live?*'

Lady Hindlesham gazed at the ivory satin back. How lovely May looked, and so slim! She looked ruefully down at her own thickening waistline. How strong-minded May had been, determined to finish her contract, and work her full year as a staff nurse; such constancy should, perhaps, make one feel rather ashamed – but then, everyone had to make their own decisions. She was so glad she'd been able to persuade George to let her come. He was the dearest of husbands, but he did fuss a little, sometimes – but she just couldn't have missed May's wedding. Strange to think that if it hadn't been for May rejecting Harry Cussons' proposal . . . It didn't bear thinking of – though George had had to endure the anguish of the divorce as a consequence.

Darling George, so kind, so generous, and always so understanding. She shifted slightly on the narrow wooden seat, then, catching her husband's glance of loving concern, turned to him and smiled her reassurance. He reached for her hand and gave it a gentle squeeze, and she entwined her fingers in his, warmed by his firm clasp. It was sweet of George to be so concerned, but she had been quite well, only a little tired, and her confinement wasn't due for another couple of months. Besides, how could she not have made the journey, however long, to May's wedding? After all, it was May who had first brought them together. And Ellen Hindlesham's thoughts went back to that blustery day outside the House of

Lords when she had cannoned so unceremoniously into the man at her side.

'For better for worse, for richer for poorer. . .'

Such a suitable match – breeding and wealth on both sides, and no doubt whatsoever of the good looks of this pair. Melicent Andover, her silvery hair soft and shining under one of Paquin's smartest new toques, gave a barely perceptible nod of approval. It had taken rather longer than she'd anticipated to marry her granddaughter off so satisfactorily, but she had finally achieved her goal. And one had to admit that although she would have found Harry Cussons a more entertaining grandson-in-law, Walter Lisle was probably a more appropriate choice for May – Julia's influence had bit deeper than anyone had realised. Besides, his eventual marriage to Della had dimmed some of Harry's old spirit – he was even getting a little paunchy these days, whereas Walter had such a beautiful figure – slim and lithe, yet so obviously well-muscled . . .

They did make a handsome couple. She'd nearly despaired of May at one point, the girl had seemed so engrossed in her nursing; but as soon as Archie had brought Walter Lisle back to tea that day and she'd heard him talk so intensely of the problems of his East End parish – then she'd known he was the one for May. Why, the very first evening, when they'd barely been introduced to each other, they'd got on so famously, she'd noticed it at once. Such a shame Walter would insist on staying in Poplar, and May was just as bad – completely determined. Not a healthy place for bringing up children – still, they would be re-opening the nurseries at Stemhalton this summer, for Bertie and Louise; May's babies could come and stay – she'd soon catch up with Louise, now this absurdly long engagement was over.

How much more sensible George's little Ellen had been. An unusual girl, not a patch on Della for looks, but George seemed quite besotted by her. Still, it must be quite a change for him to have a wife who refused to make even a pretence of using a separate bedroom – the servants had been quite shocked, Ursula said, but they always hated anything middle-class. And the girl was doing her duty fast enough. If any man deserved a son and heir after so long it was George Hindlesham, and it was so important to secure the continuance of these ancient titles.

Lady Andover's attention returned to the bride and groom. What beautiful children May and Walter would produce – perhaps a daughter with May's delicacy of feature allied to Walter's dark, dramatic colouring – but more docile than her mother, of course. Now whom could she marry? There was Elizabeth Chevron's son – one of the oldest dukedoms – but what of the young boys growing up at Marlborough House, grandsons of her old friend? And Melicent Andover's ambitions climbed steadily higher.

'*Those whom God hath joined together let no man put asunder.*'

Another good nurse lost to the profession, Matron sighed to herself. What an efficient Staff Nurse she'd made – really, it was a tragedy to see a young woman of such potential sacrificed on the altar of Hymen. Still a few faults to be ironed out, of course, but given a few years of running a busy ward . . . Nurse Carter lost as well – it was difficult to believe she would have married an Earl, even a divorced one, without the influence of Nurse Winton. One just had to be thankful that the final member of that trio was such a convinced suffragette – no romantic nonsense there, at least.

Weddings were so depressing – the only bright spot was the food, such a pleasant change from that served in the hospital. A reminiscent smile flickered for a moment over Matron's face. That naughty girl, Nurse Winton – speaking out to Sir James like that! But one had to admire her spirit, that's why she'd have gone far; obedience alone was never enough. And to think she'd nearly turned her down out of hand – if that other intending probationer hadn't backed out at the crucial moment. If any young woman had looked like a forlorn hope as a future nurse it was the fashionable Miss May Winton – far too good-looking, for a start. But she'd obviously had a healthy pair of lungs, always important, and beggars couldn't be choosers. Then, once she'd arrived she'd rolled up her sleeves and really put her back into it, and gone on from strength to strength. All that good work undone by one dark-eyed young clergyman – why, this young woman could have been one of the Great Matrons – what a terrible waste!

'Let the people praise Thee, O God: yea, let all the people praise Thee.'

Walter Lisle glanced sideways under his lashes at his beautiful bride. His gaze lingered – lovely, lovely May. So tall and strong and determined, and yet she could be so kind and gentle. How lucky he'd been to catch sight of her in the crude light of the Chrisp Street flares – even then he'd wanted to approach her. That was why he'd been so furious when he thought she was a silly Society girl, come thoughtlessly down to laugh at the poverty of Dockland. Poor May, how he'd ranted and raved at her – and she'd set her lovely mouth in an angry line and flashed her beautiful eyes with such scorn in his direction. What a disastrous beginning to their courtship!

One wouldn't wish pain on anybody, but how lucky it was that Hetty Barnes had been taken to St Katharine's when she went down with appendicitis, and to May's ward – suppose he'd never seen her again? The thought sent cold shivers down his spine even now. After all, it was pure chance that they'd both been at Lady Andover's dinner party – he'd known Archie for years, even heard him talk of his Cousin May, but he had had no idea of what she was.

May shifted slightly at his side; as she moved he felt her hand lightly brush his, and everything else was forgotten in an overwhelming surge of love and tenderness. Darling, darling, May.

Historical Note

The Royal Hospital of St Katherine was founded in 1147 by Queen Matilda, wife of King Stephen. It was built near the Tower of London. On 5 July 1273 Queen Eleanor, widow of Henry III, granted a new Charter, and from that time on the work of general nursing gradually ended, and the Hospital maintained the old and infirm, and a school. In 1825 the Hospital Church and Precinct were bought by the directors of the St Katharine's Dock Company, and the area cleared prior to the excavation of the Dock. The Foundation was moved to Regent's Park, near Gloucester Gate. For the purposes of this story I have assumed that St Katharine's remained a large hospital for the sick, and that on the building of the Dock it was simply moved eastwards, to Poplar. I have placed it on the site of the much smaller Poplar Hospital for Accidents, which was, of course, in existence in 1905.

Miss Lewin was the instructor at the Bath Club in 1905, but May's invitation to Lord Oulton might well have caused problems, since the Ladies' Display was only open to males who were relatives of members.

Mary Cholmondeley's *Red Pottage* was first published in 1899.

Lady Hermione Hamilton-Temple-Blackwood trained at The London Hospital, Whitechapel, 1899–1900. Her photo, with caption, was in 'The Lady's Realm' of June, 1904.

Will Crooks, the working class MP, was born in Poplar in 1852, elected to the London County Council in 1892, became Mayor of Poplar in 1901, and was elected as Labour Member of Parliament for Woolwich in 1903.